DAVID HOSP

THE BETRAYED

WARNER BOOKS

NEW YORK BOSTON

This book is a work of fiction. Names, characters, places, and incidents are the product of the author's imagination or are used fictitiously. Any resemblance to actual events, locales, or persons, living or dead, is coincidental.

Cover design by Diane Luger
Cover illustration by Tom Dietrich/Index Stock Imagery

Warner Books
Hachette Book Group USA
237 Park Avenue
New York, NY 10169
Visit our Web site at www.HachetteBookGroupUSA.com

Printed in the United States of America

Originally published in hardcover by Warner Books
First Paperback Printing: June 2007

10 9 8 7 6 5 4 3 2 1

For Mom and Dad,
who throughout my life have been
among my greatest sources
of love, understanding, support, and
inspiration.

Thank you . . . for everything.

"*Dark Harbor* is one jam-packed debut novel. Like any good thriller, its appeal lies in the literary action it provides, and the novel delivers, snaking through the neighborhoods of Boston like the Green Line and tying in the terrorist bombing with the rest of the novel just when you think Hosp may have forgotten how he opened the book."

—EDGEBoston.com

"David Hosp brings us an exciting debut thriller in *Dark Harbor*, with engaging leads and a solid plot. I look forward to his next novel."

—Bookloons.com

"This book grabs your attention right from the start and doesn't let go . . . Don't let this political thriller pass you by."

—MonstersAndCritics.com

"*Dark Harbor* is David Hosp's debut novel and what a novel it is! This book is a thriller filled with many twists and turns that will make it impossible for the reader to figure out who killed Natalie. With the subplots, David Hosp takes the reader on an exciting journey that they will not forget. You will not have a chance to get bored reading this one. David Hosp is a talented writer who will be on the bestseller list soon. Be sure to add this one to your reading list. It is highly recommended."

—BestSellersWorld.com

"Hosp pens a scarily believable tale of intrigue that will keep you riveted until the last page. And did I mention this is a first novel? A really good read."

—BookBitch.com

Also by David Hosp

INNOCENCE
DARK HARBOR

Acknowledgments

I would like to thank:

Those who have read, enjoyed, and supported my first book, *Dark Harbor.* Many of you have been kind enough to take the time to offer your praise, thoughts, comments, best wishes, and even constructive criticism. Writing is a somewhat solitary endeavor, and I greatly appreciate your encouragement and feedback;

My friends and family, who have been wonderful throughout the writing and publishing process, which has been a somewhat surreal experience for me so far;

Everyone at Goodwin Procter LLP, where I have practiced law for the past decade. No one could ask for more support from a group of partners and professionals at all levels than I have received from everyone at this great firm;

The "brain trust" of amateur editors who read and provided feedback on various portions of the manuscript for this book: Joanie Hosp, Richard Hosp, Martha Hosp, Joan McCormick, and Ted Hosp;

Maureen Egen, one of the greats in the publishing world. Thank you for being such a fantastic editor, friend, cheerleader, and person. This finished product owes a great deal to your help, thoughts, and advice;

Frances Jalet-Miller, who kept me honest, and made me sweat the details (big and small) to make this novel the best it could be;

Larry, Jamie, Jimmy, Emi, Paul, Michele, Tanisha, and everyone else at Warner Books for putting up with me;

Lisa Vance for being such a great agent/soundboard/ reality check;

Aaron Priest for giving me a chance; and

Joanie (my wife, my love, and my best friend), and Reid and Samantha, whom I love with all my heart: you give me purpose. Without you, nothing would make sense.

THE BETRAYED

Prologue

AMANDA KNEW SOMETHING was wrong as the Metro approached the stop at Eastern Market. The premonition swept through her like a chill on a summer night, unexpected and unwelcome, making her scalp tingle. Nancy noticed the change in her friend's demeanor and, eager to help, offered a salve. "Billy Slevan likes you," she said.

Amanda looked at Nancy and shook her head. "No he doesn't." She was a small, serious girl with dark brown hair and dimples when she smiled, which was far too infrequently.

Nancy pressed the issue. "Yes he does. I heard it. Rebecca told me he thinks you're pretty."

Amanda shook her head again. "He was talking about Amanda *Green*."

Nancy looked down at her shoes in momentary defeat as the train slowed into the station and the loudspeaker blared over the electrical whirring of the rails. "*This stop, Eastern Market. Eastern Market, this stop.*"

"You don't know that," Nancy persisted, though with less assurance.

The train stopped, and Amanda smiled in a way that

was meant to convince her friend everything was all right. "Yes I do," she said as the doors opened.

Amanda wished she could explain her mood to Nancy, but she would never understand. No one would. The last time Amanda had a feeling of dread like this was more than two years ago, and she still couldn't bring herself to think about that day. It seemed a lifetime ago.

The footfalls of the girls' stiff school shoes echoed through the cavernous station, far beneath the streets of southeast D.C. They walked without speaking, forcing their way through the crowds of adults that pushed past the two adolescents in bright blue plaid skirts and Bainbridge Academy sweaters. Bainbridge was the one part of Amanda's existence that had survived the upheaval, and she cherished every day there. Once, during that awful time two years ago, her mother had worried out loud whether she would be able to afford the tuition; Amanda had locked herself in her room for hours, sobbing into her pillow as her mother pleaded with her to open the door. The possibility of leaving Bainbridge had never been raised again. "We'll be fine," her mother reassured her; and they were.

In fact, things had gotten better in many ways. Amanda's mother, who had been a reporter briefly before she'd married, landed a job writing for the metro section of the *Washington Post.* Things had gone well for her, and there was talk of her being put on national coverage soon, which would mean more money and better hours. And yet when her mother told her of the promotion, an inexplicable shadow had darkened Amanda's face. It was as if experience had taught her that all good fortune was merely a prelude to tragedy.

Nancy and Amanda reached the foot of the escalator

that led up to the street, and Amanda's heart skipped. She paused as she looked up through the dizzying tube carved at a steep angle into the ground. Mildly claustrophobic, she closed her eyes and tried to think of something else. Nancy, who was aware of Amanda's phobia, prattled on in an attempt at distraction.

As the girls neared the top of the escalator, Amanda opened her eyes, breathing a little easier in spite of the foreboding that had nestled in her bones. She caught a glimpse of the long tunnel leading back down to the Metro, and vertigo gripped her briefly before she turned around and faced the gathering light of the subway entrance.

It was four o'clock on a beautiful Wednesday in early June when they walked out into the sunlight. Heading down Seventh Street, they passed Eastern Market, which was buzzing with activity as people bought fresh meat and fish for the evening meal, or browsed the stalls that sold everything from pots and pans to vintage clothing. Gentrification had come haltingly to the area in the 1990s, but its effects were unmistakable. BMWs now vied with late-model Chevys and low-end Toyotas for parking, and the prices at the shops in the market had risen dramatically.

The girls walked south along Seventh Street for a few blocks, leaving the BMWs behind, until they came to G Street. Amanda turned left and started heading east. Nancy grabbed her by the arm. "Where are you going?" she demanded.

Amanda looked at her. "Home," she replied simply.

Nancy looked down the street at the overgrown weeds that pitted many of the yards. As in the rest of the nation's capital, neighborhoods changed quickly from street to street in the area south of Eastern Market, and children learned early which routes were safe and which were not. "That's not a good block. We're supposed to walk around."

Amanda frowned and looked down the block herself. She knew that Nancy was right, and yet she wanted to get home quickly, as the feeling of dread continued to gnaw at her stomach. Besides, her grandmother was coming over that evening for an early supper, and Amanda, who was sensitive to the tension between her mother and her grandmother, wanted to be at the house to help her mother prepare. "This way's faster," she said stubbornly. "We'll be fine."

Nancy looked frightened. "I don't want to."

"Fine, then don't." Amanda knew that Nancy wouldn't let her go alone.

"Please," Nancy pleaded. "Can't we just go around?"

"No," Amanda said. "I'm tired of going around." With that, she turned and headed up the block. Nancy stood looking at her, biting her lip. Finally, she rolled her eyes and followed her friend down the street, running to catch up.

The two girls walked close together, their eyes straight ahead and turned down toward the pavement. They didn't see or hear a soul until they were halfway down the block.

The rustle came from up ahead of them, just off to the left from within a decrepit garden in front of a boarded-up house. Amanda glanced up quickly and saw the three men lounging on the front steps of the tumbledown building, each with a tall brown paper sack wrapped tightly around a bottle sitting between his legs. They leaned back on their elbows, sweat beading on their foreheads in the humid early evening air. There was a dangerous energy about them—a coiled tension in the way they regarded their surroundings.

"Yo, Jerome, check this shit out! Schoolgirls!"

Amanda redirected her eyes forward as she and Nancy quickened their pace. As unsettling as the young man's attention was, it didn't particularly frighten her. His voice betrayed a bravado that lacked intention, and living in the city had numbed her to such empty intimidation. The next voice she heard was different, though, and it sucked the wind out of her lungs.

"Hey, sugar," the voice said simply. It was low and measured, and full of a threat so plain that Amanda was instantly terrified. She continued to walk, but her legs felt dream-heavy, and her head spun with images too awful to acknowledge.

"I know you girls can hear me," the man said, a hint of impatience growing in his voice. "Don't be like that, all shy an' whatnot. You stop and talk to me, now, y'hear?"

Amanda could feel Nancy stiffen with fear as she kept her head down. *Keep walking*, Amanda urged silently. *Keep walking, and we'll be fine.*

"Stop!"

The man shouted the word with such fury that both girls froze. Amanda turned slowly. She looked at the man sitting at the top of the stoop, trying not to let her fear show, though she knew it was no use. His skin was almond brown, and his eyes burned out at her from under a broad forehead topped with a thin layer of hair cropped tightly to his scalp. He looked to be in his early twenties, and around his neck hung a thick gold chain with a ruby-studded pendant in the shape of a J at the center. The two other young men were looking at him now, and Amanda could see the trepidation on their faces, too, as if they feared that some unimaginable beast had been stirred. Their reaction deepened her terror. Then the man smiled, revealing the straightest, whitest teeth Amanda had ever seen. Under other circumstances, he might have looked handsome.

"You girls lost?" he asked.

Amanda shook her head back and forth slowly.

The man looked at her, shaking his head back and forth in time with hers. "No?" He scratched his head. "You lookin' for some candy, then?" He reached into his pocket and brought out a plastic bag thick with chunks of clear white that looked like rock candy, but weren't.

Amanda's head continued to shake back and forth. "No?" he repeated, but this time he seemed more doubtful. "You sure?" he pressed. At this Amanda nodded forcefully.

The man put the bag back in his pants but left his hand in his pocket. "What, then? Some lovin'?" Amanda noticed his hand moving in his jeans.

"No sir," Amanda finally managed to say.

The man took his hand out of his jeans and frowned, his smile disappearing like the sun ducking behind a bank of storm clouds. "Well let me ask you, then, what the *fuck* are you doin' here?" he asked, his eyes wide and his hands open as if in bewilderment.

"We're just going home." Amanda could hear the begging in her voice.

There was a long pause as the man with the gold chain rubbed his hands back and forth together slowly. "Just goin' home, huh?" he said quietly after a moment.

Amanda felt like crying, but she held back the tears. "Yes sir," she choked out.

"Yes *sir*," the man repeated. "I like that." He stood up, and Amanda felt the urge to run, but her feet seemed as if they had melted into the sidewalk in the heat and stress of the moment. She heard Nancy let out a gasp.

The man hovered at the bottom of the stoop as the tension crackled through the heavy air. He was close enough that Amanda could smell the booze mixing with the man's sweat. Then he pursed his lips and spoke again. "Well then, I guess you best be on your way, huh?"

Amanda was still frozen, wondering if she had heard the man correctly. But then something in his eyes betrayed his sincerity. It was an emptiness; a pain so thick it defied comprehension. At that moment, Amanda knew he was not going to hurt them.

"Yes sir," she said one last time.

The young man stuck out his bottom lip and nodded at them. "Yes *sir*," he repeated quietly again. Then he turned and walked up the stoop and through the open door of the decaying building.

Neither girl spoke to the other again that day, except to exchange a brief good-bye when their routes home diverged. Amanda didn't know how to feel. Her premonition, she assumed, had been a phantom. Having spent her first twelve years in a suburban cocoon, shielded from the threats of violence with which so many were forced to contend on a daily basis, she thought perhaps her intuition had suffered. It wasn't until she rounded the corner to her own street and saw her house that the dread returned.

She knew something was wrong when she saw that the curtains on the front windows were drawn. Her mother had chosen the little brownstone in large part because it faced south, and so received constant exposure to the sun. She made a production of opening the curtains every morning—"to let a little sunshine into our lives," she would say.

More ominous was that the front door was ajar. The two-story brick structure was on a pleasant block, but it was not the sort of neighborhood in which people left their doors unlocked, much less open to the world. When they had moved, her mother had been explicit with Amanda that the doors were to remain locked at all times, even when they were home; especially when they were home.

Amanda walked slowly up the street, her eyes never leaving the gap in the doorjamb through which she could see nothing but darkness. As she climbed the front steps, she was no longer breathing, at least not that she could tell. She hesitated on the top step, and a part of her was tempted to run in the opposite direction—to find a neighbor or a policeman to open the door and tell her what was behind it, so that the images wouldn't haunt her. But she knew she couldn't. Something was drawing her inside.

"Mom?" she called out quietly as she stood there, hand outstretched to the door, hoping against hope that she might hear an answer. When there was nothing but silence, she forced herself to take a deep breath as a tear ran down her cheek. Then she pushed the door open.

Chapter One

Jack Cassian leaned forward in the flimsy plastic chair, its aluminum frame creaking with every shift of his weight. His head hung low, his hair falling forward, obscuring an angular, attractive face that somehow retained its youthfulness in spite of all he had seen in his thirty-three years. "I'm not seeing Candy anymore," he said without emotion. "I never really thought it would work out, anyway, so I guess I shouldn't be surprised. She never understood anything about what makes me tick; one in a long list of things that she didn't understand. Like art. And literature. And childproof caps." He was looking down at the yellowing industrial tiles on the floor, and he could sense no movement from the figure sitting at his side. But then, he no longer expected a reaction.

"Guys at the station ask about you," he lied. "Couple of them say they might stop by: Hendrickson and Joe, maybe." He considered for a moment how far he should press the fabrication. "They probably won't, though, in the end. Things are pretty busy, and guys like them hate places like this, y'know?" Still no movement.

He cast his mind about for anything else worth

saying—anything that might make the charade seem more real. "Yeah, you know," he repeated just to fill the void.

Jack sat in silence for another moment or two before he was able to pry his eyes from the cracks in the dirty linoleum and look at the man sitting in the wheelchair beside him. The resemblance between them, which had been acute when they were both much younger, was still there, but atrophy had taken its toll. The cheeks were hollow now, and the shoulders—which had once been so broad and strong, thrown back in defiance of the world's injustices—were slumped forward, bony and frail under the lint-ridden bathrobe Jack had purchased a year ago. But the change was most evident in the eyes. They had once burned with joy and anger and mischief, a concentration of life that affected everyone and everything within their reach. Now they were empty sockets sucked back into a thin face, the whites turned yellow and lined, like the cracks in the floor of this godforsaken place. Whenever Jack Cassian found the courage to look there—into the eyes he had known his entire life—his pretense fell apart, and he understood that the man he once knew so well was gone. Above the eyes, the deep purple sickle-shaped scar rested in the divot that marred the man's forehead.

The buzzing of Jack's pager broke the silence. He let it vibrate a few times, still looking at the man next to him, whose blank stare remained unchanged. Finally, he unclipped the tiny device from his belt and looked at the number on the display. Then he returned the pager to its resting place.

He leaned forward, letting his head drop again as he brought his fingers together into a pyramid. "Listen, Jimmy, I'm sorry," he said. "That was the office. I gotta go out on a call." He sighed. "I'd planned to stay longer." He looked up again, and for just a moment the hope crept back into his heart; that lingering, illogical optimism that allows a person to believe, against all medical assurances, that maybe—just maybe—there might be some flicker of recognition. It was useless, though, and he knew it, in his head if not in his heart.

He stood up, straightening out his slacks and pulling on his sport coat. He took a step toward the door, then paused, standing behind the man in the wheelchair. The other man had still not moved since Jack's arrival, and had acknowledged neither Jack's presence nor his imminent departure. On his lap, resting askew between the arms of the wheelchair, was a new bathrobe, still sitting in the box with the wrapping paper flowering up from underneath. Jack leaned forward, his hand resting on the man's fragile shoulder, and kissed the top of his head.

"Happy birthday, bro," he said. Then he turned and left the room.

The trip down from the medical facility in Maryland took longer than expected, and by the time he reached D.C. it was after six-thirty. Cassian sped through the city, his thick brown hair whipped back as he slid his beat-up old motorcycle through the traffic.

He throttled back the engine and kicked the bike into a lower gear as he rounded the corner at Seventh Street. A police barrier had been set up outside the little townhouse, and a crowd had gathered at the perimeter marked out by the yellow police tape, like a swarm of flies along the edge of fresh roadkill. Cassian pulled up to the perimeter, where one of the officers waved him through.

"Wozniak," Cassian said, nodding in recognition at the young man in uniform. He took off his sunglasses and tucked them into the breast pocket of his sport coat.

"Cassian," the man replied, giving a halfhearted salute. He eyed the motorcycle as Jack put down the kickstand. "Still tempting fate on that thing, huh?"

Jack smiled. "Gotta tempt something, don't I?"

The patrolman smiled back. "I guess." He nodded up toward the townhouse. "Train's waiting on you," he said. "Been here for close to an hour. Seems like he's in a shitty mood."

"How can you tell?"

Wozniak shrugged noncommittally. "It's pretty grisly up there. Crime Scene got here about forty-five minutes ago, and they're working the place over."

"Jack!"

The shout startled them both, and they turned toward the house. There, on the landing just outside the front door, stood Darius Train. His huge lumpy figure looked tired, as always, and he rubbed a hand over his bald, dark brown scalp. "Jack!" he repeated. "Get up here!"

"Guess that's my cue," Cassian said to Wozniak. He looked over the officer's shoulder. The crowd was continuing to grow, and seemed to be getting more restless. "Keep these people back, okay? We're gonna have enough to deal with up there as it is."

"Sure thing."

As Cassian turned and headed toward the front door to the house, he heard Wozniak call after him. "Hey Jack!" Cassian turned around. "Thanks again for the Nationals tickets. It meant a lot to my kid," the officer said.

Jack waved him off. "I couldn't use 'em, and I didn't want them to go to waste."

"Yeah, well, still. I've never seen my kid so excited in his life. Washington even beat the Yankees. You imagine that? Made me look like a hero."

Jack smiled. "I'm guessing you already looked like a hero to your kid."

Wozniak nodded. "Thanks all the same."

Cassian squinted as he walked up the pathway toward the front door. The sun was beginning to set to the west, over toward the Capitol dome and the White House, but the temperature remained in the low nineties.

Detective Sergeant Train was watching him from the steps in front of the house, and he wore his usual look of annoyance. When Jack first made detective three years earlier and was told that he would be partnering with the giant, he'd had his reservations. Train, a veteran of more than twenty years on the force and a former all-District linebacker from one of the roughest areas of the city, seemed an unlikely fit for Jack, the product of a modest, pleasant suburb in Maryland. When they had first been introduced, Jack was sure he'd heard the man mutter the phrase "pencil-neck" under his breath, and there was no mistaking the look of disappointment on his face. In spite of their inauspicious beginning, however, the two had gelled quickly, their strengths and weaknesses complementing each other and making them a formidable team. In addition, they shared a sardonic sense of humor that seemed to grow naturally from the disillusionment of being a cop, and from dredging through the worst that human nature had to offer.

"Sarge," Cassian acknowledged Train when he reached the top step. He turned around so that they were both facing out toward the street.

"Detective," Train responded, and Cassian thought he sensed a hint of impatience in the tone. The older man cut a quick glance in Cassian's direction, taking note of Jack's casual slacks and the expensive shirt beneath Jack's sport coat. On the surface, no two men could seem more different. "What happened? You get the call in the middle of a manicure or something?"

"That's funny, Sarge," Cassian said. He looked at the rumpled gray suit his partner was wearing—one of five identical outfits he owned. "Really, I need to take more style tips from you." Cassian looked off into the distance, away from his partner. "I was visiting Jimmy," he said after a moment. "It's his birthday."

The look of annoyance disappeared from Train's face, replaced by one of concern. Jack wasn't sure which look bothered him more. "How's he doin'?"

Jack shook his head, ignoring the question. "What've we got here?" he asked.

Train stared at the younger man briefly before replying. "A fuckin' mess is what we've got here," he said at last. He took out his notebook and flipped it open. "Elizabeth Creay," he started. "Thirty-six years old. Reporter for the *Post.*"

"No shit?"

"No shit. We're gonna have a lot of people looking over our shoulder on this. Already got a call from her editor making demands for information."

"What'd you say to him?"

"I asked him where he was this afternoon between two and four."

Cassian nodded. "That must've gone over well. Did you ask him for a list of all the people she worked with, too?"

"Didn't have the chance." Train looked sideways at his younger partner. "It turned into a short conversation.

Hopefully it bought us some time, though, while he hollers at the captain."

"What else do we know?" Cassian asked, referring to the victim.

Train consulted his notes again. "Ms. Creay is—pardon me, *was*—divorced; one daughter, fourteen. According to relatives, the ex-husband lives out in Old Colony, Virginia."

"Old Colony? Nice town. How'd she get stuck in this neighborhood?"

"I guess we'll have to ask him that." The older detective shrugged. "She probably had a crappy divorce lawyer."

"As crappy as the guy you used?"

Train shook his head. "Nobody's that crappy." He looked down the street and frowned, the lines in his face deepening and his mouth drawing up tight. "She found her."

"Who?"

"The daughter. She was the first one here. Came home from school and walked in and found her. Neighbor heard her scream and called it in. The patrol car got here about ten minutes later and went inside—found the girl curled up in a ball." The silence stretched out between them.

"Where is she now?" Cassian asked finally.

"EMTs took her to the hospital. She still wasn't speaking. She's with her grandmother now." Train let the information sink in for a moment. Then he looked at Cassian. "You wanna go inside?"

Jack put his hands in his pockets. The crowd had doubled in strength since his arrival, and the onlookers were milling around excitedly. *Ants at a picnic*, he thought. Additional officers had been called in to keep the more aggressively curious back from the house so the Crime Scene technicians could do their work. "Not really," he replied.

Train nodded. "Tough shit," he said.

Cassian sighed. "Yeah, I know," he agreed. "Tough shit."

Chapter Two

"PLACE IS A MESS," Cassian commented, noting the obvious. Inside the house, the furniture had been upended and lay strewn about like debris in the wake of a tsunami.

"Wait 'til you see the upstairs," Train said. He pointed toward the back of the house, where a small area had been used as a study. "That's where we think it began." He swung his arm toward the rear window. "There's a parking space out back in the alley, and a door that leads from the backyard into the kitchen. It looks like a B&E gone wrong. Perp's in here—rifling through the drawers, looking for cash, silver, valuables, whatever—when the unfortunate Ms. Creay walks through the back door." He pointed to a large reddish brown stain on the carpet near the archway leading into the kitchen. "He got her at least once down here, then dragged her upstairs."

Cassian bent down and looked closely at the stain. It was thick with blood, and trailed off in the direction of the stairway. "Dragged her? We sure? Any chance she was still moving under her own power?" he asked.

"Possibly, but then why wouldn't she run outside where someone might have helped her? Upstairs there's no way out." Train shook his head. "It seems more likely she was dragged."

"Why would he drag her upstairs, though?"

"It looks like he was trying to get her to tell him where more valuables were—maybe get the code to her ATM card or something; that's becoming more common. The place was picked pretty clean; her purse, wallet, credit cards, all gone. Looks like some jewelry cases upstairs were looted, and if there was any silver, that's gone, too." Train pointed around the room to the smears of blood leading back out to the stairway. "The first wound must have been pretty bad to bleed this much"—he paused and shot Jack a serious look—"but he did a lot more damage upstairs."

Cassian looked around the room. It was nicely decorated, but not opulent. A few expensive-looking pieces—the desk and a heavy oak coffee table—had been skillfully complemented with traditional-style replicas and nicely framed prints. Two of the lamps on the floor looked as though they might have been worth something, but it was difficult to tell, smashed as they were. Cassian walked over to the desk and looked at the drawers, which had been left open, their contents scattered on the floor. "Anything interesting in these?" he asked.

"We haven't had a chance to inventory them yet," Train responded. "Don't touch—Crime Scene's still working upstairs, then they'll start down here." He pointed to the back of the desktop. "Computer's gone, though."

Cassian looked down and saw that, sure enough, a computer was missing. Standing empty on the desk was a docking station for a laptop—the kind that allows the owner to plug in and use a normal-sized keyboard and screen. "Nice catch, Sarge," Cassian said. "When did you become such a technology expert?"

"Fuck you," Train said. "Deter pointed it out."

Cassian bent down to look closer. "Top of the line," he said, noting the brand name. "Should fetch our boy a pretty penny."

"Hope it was worth killing for," Train muttered.

Cassian took a deep breath as he scanned the room. Then he exhaled loudly. "Main event's upstairs, huh?"

Train nodded.

"Okay, then," Cassian said without enthusiasm, "let's have a look."

They followed the trail of blood back toward the stairway near the front of the house, around the banister, and up the stairs, careful not to disturb any of the splotches so that the technicians could get good samples and photos. Train pointed out a few smears along the wall, near the floor. "That's the other reason we're pretty sure she was dragged," he explained. "Her initial wounds were above the waist, so in order to get that much blood so low to the floor she had to have either been dragged or been crawling."

As they rounded the corner at the top of the stairs, Jack took in the floor's layout. It was smaller than he expected. Straight ahead off the stairs was a small bathroom—the only one in the house—and to the left, he could see into a neat little bedroom that looked undisturbed. The bloodstains traced a path around the banister back toward the front of the house. "Master bedroom?" he asked with a tilt of the head.

"Yeah," Train responded. "That's the daughter's room." He pointed to the smaller bedroom on the left.

Jack poked his head into the room and looked around. It was pink and bright, with soft white carpeting on the floor. On the walls were hung colorful pastel prints and a map of the world in a gold ornamental frame. All in all, it was exactly what one would expect in the room of a well-adjusted fourteen-year-old girl. And yet something seemed forced, as if someone had tried to plaster normalcy over depression. Jack nodded to Train, indicating he was ready to proceed to the master bedroom. Train extended his arm in invitation. "After you."

As he stepped into the room the sickly sweet smell of burnt flesh pierced his nostrils and he choked back his lunch. He looked at Train, who nodded solemnly. Cassian took a few deep breaths to acclimate himself to the smell, and then briefly canvassed the scene. Several police technicians were working their way around silently, but Jack ignored them. He took note of the location of the woman's body, stretched out on the bed, covered in blood, but avoided focusing on the corpse—that would come later. Too often, he found, even seasoned professionals could become distracted when they began their investigation by examining the body and then working their way out into the rest of the crime scene. It obscured the larger picture, and caused them to overlook crucial details that seemed inconsequential in comparison to the enormity of the corporeal evidence. Cassian's practice was to focus on the crime scene at its widest possible point, working his way inward in concentric circles toward the epicenter of violence, only examining the body after he felt he had a full impression of the overall picture.

He started along the wall closest to the door, farthest from the bed where the body lay. He noticed immediately that the room was the most cheaply decorated in the house. Against the wall across from the bed stood a set of white lacquer bookcases, the kind that could be bought at Wal-Mart for twenty dollars. The shelves were lined with books, most of them big, heavily bound volumes of history, or biographical works dealing with prominent political figures. In front of the books stood a parade of pictures, mostly of a shy-looking girl progressing in age from birth to early teens, although Jack also noticed a few candids of a young woman who looked to be in her early twenties. She was relatively attractive, Jack noted, as he continued to pan around the room.

The wall farthest from the door looked out onto the street, although the shades were drawn. Again, Jack noticed that the window dressings were cheap, and failed to keep even the waning light from penetrating the room.

As he swung his line of sight around past the windows, he saw that the bedside table had been overturned. On the floor he could see a small lamp and a jewelry box that lay open and empty of all its contents.

He looked up at the wall above the bed. Two prints from the Metropolitan Museum of Art in New York, both of impressionist works—Monet, if Jack was remembering his art history correctly—hung in nondescript frames in a feeble attempt at adding color to the room.

Finally, almost reluctantly, Jack looked at the woman on the bed.

She was strewn over the queen-size mattress, her arms akimbo, and her legs bent at the knees, crisscrossed at an impossible angle. Her throat had been cut—deeply—and her neck was twisted to the side. Her face, jaw frozen in a perpetual scream, was stuck to the sheets with blood that had pooled from her wounds. The damage was extensive, and Cassian forced himself to stay focused.

He walked around to the other side of the bed to take a closer look at the woman's body. From that angle, he could also see a deep wound in her abdomen. "How many wounds total?" he asked, without looking away.

Train was silent for a moment, and it was Deter, the lead technician, who answered. "There's at least one in her belly. There may be more in that area, but we haven't moved her yet, so we can't be sure," he said. "There's the obvious cut to her throat—damn near took her head off. It's through all the way to the spine. Then there are a couple cuts to her arms that look like defensive wounds. Some of those blend into one another, so it may be difficult to get an accurate count." He paused and looked over at Train. "It's the burns we can't figure out, though."

Cassian leaned in and examined the woman's body more closely. He started at the feet, which were blackened on the soles and toes, the skin having been largely burned off. "They're regular," he said of the wounds, directing the comment to no one in particular.

"Maybe where you come from," Deter replied.

"No, I mean there's a pattern to them. It's like they're made up of lines and dots."

"We're pretty sure they were made with either a butane lighter or maybe an acetylene torch," Train posited. "They're popular with the crack crowd. Great for sparking rock. Our perp spent some time on the woman's hands and feet. By the time he got to her face, there's a chance she wasn't even conscious."

"Jesus Christ," Cassian whispered as he moved up to examine the woman's face.

"Yeah, I know," the technician said. "Effective torture, though. I'm guessing the guy got what he was looking for."

Cassian leaned in and took an even closer look at the facial wounds. "The magic question is: what was he looking for?" he said after a moment, looking up at Train.

"Money." Deter voiced his opinion. "You get a guy whacked out on crack or meth for a couple days, and they'll do anything to get what they need to buy their next fix."

"Maybe." Cassian mulled it over. "Let's walk through the chronology. It looks like the first wound was to her abdomen, that's probably the one inflicted downstairs. It was serious, but not serious enough to cause death; it just incapacitated her. Then, when the perp brings her up here, he takes out the torch and gets whatever information he's looking for. Finally, when he was done"—he pointed to her throat—"he kills her."

"Sounds right to me," Deter agreed. Train kept quiet and let Cassian continue.

"So how does he keep her still while he burns her?" Cassian asked. He ran his hand down along the woman's leg, toward her ankle. "There we are," he said at last, pointing to a light pink striation above the heel. Then he moved up to her arms. "And I'm guessing, if we look close enough . . ." He started examining the woman's wrists and forearms. "Here it is," he said, pointing at a spot just above her right wrist.

"Ligature marks," Train assumed.

"Yeah. They're faint, but they're there."

"She was tied up?" Deter asked.

"She had to have been," Train pointed out. "Otherwise, it would have been too difficult to inflict this kind of damage while she thrashed around."

"I wonder whether our boy was smart enough to take whatever it was he used to tie her up. Have your people looked under the bed?" Cassian asked Deter.

"I don't think anyone's been there yet," Deter replied. "We started with the rest of the room first."

Cassian looked around the room and located a cardboard box filled with latex gloves that had been brought in by the technicians. He pulled on a pair and then bent down at the side of the bed. He pulled up the bed skirt and looked underneath, careful not to disturb anything. Scanning the area near the wall behind the headboard, he hoped to find the rope that had been used to bind Elizabeth Creay, but there was nothing there. He was about to stand up when he noticed something else lying near the bottom of the bed.

"Sweet Jesus, tell me I'm this blessed. You got a camera, Deter?" he asked.

"Joe does," Deter replied, motioning toward one of the other officers.

"You wanna get a shot of this for me, Joe?" Cassian asked, still bent. The officer with the camera walked over to the side of the bed and bent down next to Jack. He put his eye up to the camera and snapped two shots in quick succession. Then he withdrew and Cassian reached under the bed to retrieve the object. He held it up so Train could see that it was an ornate silver lighter with a skull and crossbones on it. With a gloved hand, Cassian flipped open the cover and pressed down on the igniter. An angry, sharp blue flame hissed up, compact and controlled.

"I'm guessing Ms. Creay wasn't a crack smoker?" Jack asked.

Train shook his head wearily. "No indications like that. Christmas must've come early this year. What are the chances the perp is stupid enough to leave that behind? We'll know whether we've been naughty or nice when we see if we can pull a print off that."

"It'll suck if we get nothing but coal," Cassian agreed. He handed the lighter to Deter. "Tag that and put a rush on it to check for fingerprints."

"You got it. I'll have the prints run overnight."

"We found anything else interesting?" Cassian asked.

"Nothing yet, but we've still got some work to do before we get out of here," Deter replied.

Train nodded. "Let's make sure we're thorough. I've got a bad feeling about this one."

"Like always, Sarge," Deter confirmed. "Like always."

It was another hour before Cassian and Train emerged from the house, pausing on the stoop to catch their breath. The crowd had dispersed, and only a few onlookers remained, packed in tight groups, whispering to one another as the police detail started to break down the scene. The last rays of sunshine were filtering through the trees that lined the quiet little street in southeast D.C. Train raised his face to them and closed his eyes, letting the sun soak into his skin. It was almost as if he hoped the sunlight would wash away the reality of the horror he'd seen inside.

"You thinking about the daughter?" Cassian asked.

Train nodded. "How do you come back from that? From finding your mother like that?"

Cassian had nothing to say. There *was* nothing to say, and both of them knew it. Some things were out of their control, and to pretend otherwise was folly. There was always the slim hope that if they did their job well, they might provide some closure; perhaps conjure a face for the young girl to look at and say, *That's the one—that's the man who took my mother from me.* But even that was cold comfort. The damage was always permanent before they were called to the scene, and Cassian and Train knew that better than most.

"I'd like to get this guy," the sergeant said after a moment.

Jack squinted up into the sky. "I know."

"I mean I'd really like to fuckin' get this guy."

Jack looked over at his partner. Officer Wozniak had been right; this one had gotten to the old man. His face was deadly serious, and the lines around his eyes had grown deeper over the course of the day. It was the first time he had ever really looked his age. Cassian took out his sunglasses and put them on. He reached over and slapped his partner on the shoulder in a gesture of understanding. "All right, then," he said. "Let's get to work."

Chapter Three

SYDNEY CHAPIN SAT hugging her knees on the couch in her mother's living room—the living room in which she had grown up, in the house she had fled for college nine years before, vowing never to return. She played idly with the fraying cuffs of her jeans, unconsciously pulling and twisting on the loose threads. A white button-down oxford shirt hung haphazardly on her frame, the shirttails falling untucked over the denim. She was used to adversity, and considered herself a person who relished a challenge, but right now she felt numb.

She had been back in D.C. for three weeks, living in a basement apartment as she got settled in at her job as a research assistant for a law professor at Georgetown. It was a summer job; she had one year left in law school at Stanford, and she had originally planned to work for the summer at a large San Francisco law firm, but things had changed.

She'd begun talking to her sister, Elizabeth, more and more over the previous winter, which was unusual. They were nine years apart in age, and had never been particularly close. Yet that winter the bonds of sisterhood seemed enough to overcome nearly a decade's age difference and three thousand miles' separation. They had found, over the phone, that they had much in common, and Sydney came quickly to realize that she missed the connection she had once felt to her family. After much deliberation, she had decided to come back home to face her demons. She thought that together she and Liz might reunite the family. Now all of that was gone.

She'd been at the law school's library when one of her mother's assistants reached her to tell her about her sister's murder, and she'd gone immediately to the hospital to be with Amanda. Her first breakdown had come in the waiting room, unexpectedly, the tears streaming down her face as she sobbed silently, leaving ragged tracks on her cheeks. The second had come shortly thereafter as she was allowed into the hospital room to visit Amanda—the enormity of her niece's situation gripping her as she caught herself at the door, trying to stem the flow of her tears before she entered the room.

Since then, she'd felt nothing. It was as though she'd turned her emotions off to prevent them from overwhelming her completely. It was an unusual reaction for Sydney, who prided herself on her strength and compassion.

She barely heard her mother enter the room from the marble foyer, where the grand staircase to the second floor swept around in a regal ellipse, its carved oak banister smelling of rich wood polish. Lydia Chapin walked over to the bar at the far end of the room and began fixing herself a stiff drink.

"Do you want one?" she asked her daughter after a moment.

Sydney looked up. Everything seemed muted to her, as if she were underwater. "No." She shook her head.

"Do you not drink?" Lydia asked. "Or is it just that you won't drink with me?"

Sydney rubbed her forehead. "I just don't think my system could handle it right now. I don't know how to feel."

Lydia stared off into space. "Yes, I think there's a lot of that going around."

"How's Amanda?" Sydney asked.

Lydia's shoulders dipped as she set her drink down on the marble bar. "Who knows? She's sleeping now, thank God. The doctors think she will be all right, eventually. They gave her some sedatives, and they think after a long rest she'll be ready to talk." She picked up her drink again and took a long sip.

"Should we have kept her at the hospital?"

"Certainly not." Of this, at least, Sydney's mother seemed sure. "I'm not going to allow her to wake up in a sterile environment surrounded by strangers and doctors and nurses. Dr. Phelps will stop by early in the morning, and he said I should call him if she wakes before then—although he said that was unlikely to happen. Right now Amanda needs to be with her family."

"Her family," Sydney repeated in a hollow voice. So odd, she thought, that she and her mother should be all the family left for the fourteen-year-old upstairs.

"Yes," Lydia said firmly, as if reading her daughter's thoughts. "Her family." She locked her daughter in a hard stare. "Like it or not, we are the only family that girl has in the world." She brought her drink over to the sitting area and settled stiffly into one of the high-backed Queen Anne chairs, taking a deep breath before she continued. "You need to think about that. I know that we have had our . . . *disagreements* . . . in the past. But we need to put all of that behind us now. Whatever you think of me, Amanda needs you—needs us—and Lord help you if you shirk that responsibility." *As you have in the past*, was left unspoken, but hung in the air between them.

Sydney held her mother's gaze, searching her eyes—for what, she didn't know. Her mother still had a leathery disposition, but with it came a strength that Sydney had always admired in spite of herself. Only hours after learning of Elizabeth's murder, Lydia had already regrouped and composed herself sufficiently to think of the future. Sydney still couldn't even grasp the reality of the present. "She has you," Sydney said after a moment. "I've no doubt you'll get her through this, no matter what."

Lydia shook her head. "Not good enough." She set her drink down on the coffee table, moving a coaster over so she wouldn't leave a ring on the expensive mahogany. "I'm old, Sydney," she said. "I have no illusions about the way you and your sister viewed my skills as a mother; neither of you made any effort to hide your disdain. But I did the best I could. I *tried*. I may not have succeeded always—or even often—but I made the effort; and everything I did, I did because I thought it was in my children's best interest." She looked down at her hands, clasped tightly in her lap, and for just a moment Sydney thought she saw a crack in the veneer her mother displayed to the world at all times. Then she straightened her back and looked up at Sydney again. "But that was a long time ago, and I was younger then. I'm sixty-five years old now, and I'm too old and tired to raise another child—certainly too old and tired to do it by myself." She looked down at her hands again. "I'm asking for your help."

Sydney's eyes never left her mother's face. Before the summer, she'd been back to D.C. only once in the prior nine years—for her father's funeral five years before. Even then, she had stayed with a friend rather than at home. She spoke to her mother once a month, if that. Her mother had flown out to her graduation, and they had seen each other on a few rare occasions, but they were strangers now. Nine years out from under her mother's controlling fist had turned Sydney into a different person, independent and self-reliant. And yet now, here again, she felt insecure and tentative once more.

The years had changed her mother, too, she could see. The strength was still there, but there was defensiveness to it now—as though in the solitude imposed by her children's estrangement and her husband's death she had begun to question some of her most firmly held beliefs. Perhaps there was more complexity to her than Sydney had ever suspected.

"I'll think about it," Sydney said. She could see the disappointment in her mother's face—or was it anger? "I'll stay the night, at least," she added quickly.

"Good," Lydia said. "I'll have your room made up." She nodded, almost more to herself than to her daughter, and in her eyes Sydney thought she saw a brief look of triumph that brought back a rush of unhappy memories from her younger days, when her mother was able to manipulate her at will. Had this been what her mother had wanted all along—to bring her back under her control?

At the same time, once she agreed to help with Amanda, there was probably no going back. Even by staying for the night, she was sticking her toe in a tar pit from which she might never extricate herself, and as much as she instinctively cared for her niece, taking on the responsibility of raising her would require sacrifices she couldn't fully comprehend. Yet, did she have any choice? Could she ever leave her mother alone to deal with her niece—and more to the point, could she ever leave her niece alone to deal with her mother? The decision, she realized, had already been made.

She looked over at her mother once more, and noticed that an unusual calmness had settled over her. For just a moment, Sydney wondered if she might regret her decision.

Chapter Four

JACK STOOD NEXT TO his partner on the covered portico at the front door of the Chapin mansion. It was a towering Federal on three acres fronting Wisconsin Avenue, in the heart of Washington, D.C.'s most prestigious neighborhood. "Jesus," Train said to him. "I always thought this was an embassy."

"Easy mistake," Jack responded. "Most of the houses in this area *are* embassies."

Train took another look at his notebook to make sure they had the address. "I take it Chapin was Elizabeth Creay's maiden name?" he asked Jack, who had worked up the preliminary background on the murdered woman.

"Yeah," Jack replied.

Train looked up from the notebook, his expression prodding for more. "We get any additional info from the searches you did? Any idea what we're dealing with on the other side of the door?"

Cassian took out his notebook. "Lydia Chapin is the lady of the manor, as it were. She's Elizabeth Creay's mother. Also has another daughter who lives in California. Father and husband—"

"She married her father?"

Cassian made a face. "—father to Elizabeth, husband to Lydia—was none other than Aloysius Chapin—"

"Quite a mouthful."

"—the well-known industrialist."

Train's eyes grew wide. "You mean of Chapin Industries?"

"The same."

Train let out a low whistle. "I guess that explains the house, then, doesn't it?"

"Yeah, I guess it does. I wasn't able to get any real research done on the company yet—I'm planning on spending tonight doing that—but I did enough poking around to know it's one of the biggest, most powerful conglomerates in the United States. Aloysius was the third generation, until he died five years ago of liver cancer at the age of sixty-five."

Train shook his head. "Damn, too young."

"How old are you, Sarge?" Cassian asked his partner.

"Fuck off."

"Thought so. You've still got a few years, but you better start watching what you eat. The kind of crap you consume is likely to take its revenge."

Train glared at Jack. "Lots of ways to die young—food ain't the only thing that can take revenge. You hearing me?"

"Loud and clear." Cassian held up his hands in surrender, but allowed a sly smile to tug at the corner of his mouth.

"You ready?" Train growled.

"As ever," Jack replied, reaching out toward the door.

The doorbell startled Sydney, and she turned to look at her mother. Lydia didn't move, though, and a moment later the doorbell rang again. It was clear that Lydia had no intention of getting up to answer the door, and Sydney rose and walked out into the foyer.

She peered out through the expensive lace curtains that covered the glasswork at the sides of the ornate front door. Two men stood quietly on the other side, with a patience that unnerved her. They didn't pace, or fidget, or shuffle their feet; they stood perfectly still, as if they were accustomed to long stretches of waiting and watching.

She opened the door a crack, keeping the chain in place. "Yes?" she asked.

"Good evening," said the older one. He was a tall, barrel-chested black man who looked to be in his fifties. "We're looking for Lydia Chapin. Is she in?"

"Who are you?" Sydney demanded.

"Detective Sergeant Train, miss, D.C. police." He nodded toward the younger man, who was also tall, but thin and attractive, and looked like he couldn't be much older than thirty. "This is my partner, Detective Cassian." When Sydney didn't respond, the older officer continued. "I called earlier and left a message that I'd be stopping by to talk to Mrs. Chapin. We're investigating the murder of her daughter."

The murder of her daughter. In the tumult of the afternoon and evening, Sydney hadn't even thought about the reality in such stark terms. The notion shook her for a moment. "Yes," she said at last. "Can I see some identification?" She put some mettle into her voice as she said it, almost a habit now after two years of law school, where she was taught by liberal-minded professors never to relinquish control to those wielding government authority.

The older man looked at his partner, and the two simultaneously dug into their pockets like annoyed college students asked for their IDs by a suspicious tavern bouncer. They pulled out their police identification cards and held them up so she could examine them. After a moment, Sydney shut the door and unhooked the chain. Then she reopened it and waved them in.

"It's been such a hard day," she said. "I don't trust anyone or anything anymore."

Train remained noncommittal. "I don't think we've been introduced," he said.

"Oh, right," Sydney replied. "My name's Sydney. I'm Liz's sister." She paused. "Was her sister." Then she thought again. "Liz was my sister," she finally spat out, feeling exhausted by the effort. "Like I said, it's been a hard day."

The older cop looked sympathetic. "I understand," he said. "I'm very sorry for your loss." She liked him. He reminded her of a kindly uncle, or at least what she envisioned a kindly uncle might seem like. "I know how difficult this must be."

"Do you?" Sydney asked. She looked back and forth between the two detectives, wondering what they were thinking. She supposed it was an impertinent question, but she didn't mean it to be. She wasn't trying to challenge them, but was desperate to hear that there were others who did, in fact, understand what she was going through.

"I do," the younger cop said, and she turned and settled her gaze on him, probing his eyes, trying to determine if he was being sincere. After a moment, she concluded that he was, and she decided that she liked him as well.

"Thank you," she said.

The three of them stood there in the grand foyer of the enormous house in silence for a moment or two, until it became awkward. Sydney felt like there should be more that someone should say, but nothing came. At last she nodded to them. "My mother's in here," she said, pointing the way into the living room. The two detectives looked at each other, and the older one finally took a step in that direction. The younger detective—Cassian, she thought she remembered his name—fell into step behind his partner, and Sydney followed both of them into the room to introduce her mother.

Chapter Five

CASSIAN SIPPED HIS COFFEE leaning forward on the chair at the corner of the low-slung coffee table in the living room. Train, who had refused the offer of a beverage, was in a chair next to him, and the two women sat at opposite ends of the couch across the table.

Lydia Chapin was an enigma to Jack. She looked like she was in her late fifties or early sixties, but struck him as very well preserved, with a tightness around her eyes and chin that told him that she had had numerous "procedures," as they were known among the wealthy. Upon the detectives' arrival, she had summoned a maid from somewhere deep within the house and had cookies and coffee served, as if they were there to debate literature, rather than discuss her daughter's murder. In fact, everything about Mrs. Chapin seemed too put together—from her clothes, to her hair, to her makeup. It was only when Cassian looked into her eyes that he could see the stress of the day's events, and a hint of the loss she no doubt felt, but tried to hide.

"So you think it was a burglary?" she said, summarizing the preliminary analysis Train had just conveyed.

"Well, we're not leaping to any hard-and-fast conclusions at this point, Mrs. Chapin," Train said. "There are some indications in that direction, and your daughter lived very near to some dangerous areas, so it's a very good possibility."

"I told her not to move into that neighborhood," Lydia said angrily. "I told her no good could come of it, but my daughters rarely listen to me on such matters." She didn't look at Sydney, but her surviving daughter shifted uncomfortably in her seat.

"I guess the younger generation is that way with all of us," Train said. "My own daughter thinks I still belong in the 1950s." Lydia Chapin nodded icily, clearly offended at the notion that a lowly police detective—black at that—could place himself on her plane. Train cleared his throat. "Mrs. Chapin, I know this is hard, but was your daughter having any problems we should know about?"

"Not that I'm aware of."

"No gambling or anything like that?"

"Certainly not."

"Do you know whether your daughter used drugs?"

"Drugs?" Mrs. Chapin made it sound as if she had never heard the word before. "I know she decided to live in an area unsuitable for her and my granddaughter, but believe me, her sense of dignity would never have fallen so low as to allow her to take up those kinds of habits." She paused for a moment. "Not to mention the fact that she had a daughter to take care of."

"So you're sure? No evidence of drug use?"

"Not just *no evidence*, Detective; no drug use."

"Not even a possibility?"

"None."

Train nodded. "Did your daughter have any enemies? Was there anyone who had ever made any threats toward her?"

"I can't think of anyone who might have wanted to hurt my daughter," she replied. "She was always the loveliest young woman."

"No enemies?" Train pressed.

Sydney's head turned toward her mother as the question was asked. The movement was subtle, and although Mrs. Chapin did not return the look, there was something in the way her body stiffened that made clear she'd seen her daughter's reaction to the question.

"Certainly none that I was aware of," Mrs. Chapin said. The silence persisted as both detectives continued to stare at her, trying to draw her out. After a pause, her hand went to her chin, and then to her hair in a nervous gesture. "I suppose you would have to ask at her place of employment to be sure; there might be something there that I wouldn't know about." She spat out the phrase "place of employment" as if it was the vilest utterance she could bring herself to pronounce.

Cassian looked across the coffee table at Sydney. He recognized her from the photographs on the bookshelf in Elizabeth Creay's apartment. She was more attractive in person than she had appeared in the pictures, though it was an understated, effortless beauty. She had the preppie-gone-to-seed look that so many children of the wealthy affect in their twenties. She was still looking at her mother as if trying to catch her attention.

"How about you, Ms. Chapin?" Cassian asked her.

Sydney seemed startled when she realized that he was talking to her, as if she believed her mother's involvement in the conversation absolved her of any responsibility to participate.

"Me?" she asked, sounding foolish, as she turned to Cassian.

"Yes, you," Jack replied. "Can you think of anyone who might have wanted to hurt your sister?"

She shook her head tentatively, looking at her mother as she did. "I've been out on the West Coast for the past nine years," she said, as though it answered the question. "I'm in law school out at Stanford."

Jack nodded. "Good school," he said. "Great basketball team."

"Tiger Woods went there, too, didn't he?" Train added.

"That's right, he did," Jack agreed. "I can't remember if he graduated, though." The two officers nodded at each other like they had hit upon some matter of importance with respect to Stanford's athletic programs. Then Jack turned back to Sydney. "Can you think of anyone who might have wanted to hurt your sister?" He asked it as if it was the first time he'd raised the subject.

"Well," Sydney began. She cast a furtive glance over toward her mother at the other end of the sofa, but Lydia Chapin continued to look straight in front of her. "There's Leighton," Sydney said.

"Oh, please!" Lydia objected. "Leighton would never do something like this."

Jack looked back and forth between Lydia and Sydney; neither of them would meet his eyes. Then he looked over at Train, who shrugged his shoulders to indicate that he, too, was in the dark. "Who's Leighton?" Cassian asked, directing the question to Sydney.

She took a deep breath. "Leighton Creay. Liz's ex-husband."

Cassian flipped through his notes. "I have her ex-husband listed as a John Creay."

"Leighton's his middle name; that's what he goes by. It's a family thing: J. Leighton Creay."

Both detectives looked expectantly at Sydney, waiting for more. When no further explanation was forthcoming, Jack pursued the issue. "Is he violent?"

Sydney looked at her mother again. "When their marriage ended a couple of years ago, things got . . . unpleasant." It sounded to Jack like "unpleasant" was a euphemism Sydney had learned from her mother.

Again silence overwhelmed the room, and this time it was Train who pressed the issue. "Could you define 'unpleasant' for us a little? Did they stop exchanging Christmas cards, or are we dealing with something a little more serious?"

"We will not define anything for you, Detective," Lydia interjected firmly. She gave her daughter a stern look before turning back to Train. "Really, I can't imagine anything more offensive. Drugs . . . private marital issues . . . it would almost seem as though my daughter were the suspect in this inquiry, rather than the victim."

"I'm sorry you feel that way, ma'am," Train replied in a steady voice. "But we're conducting a murder investigation, and we need to know who we should be talking to."

"Well, I would think you should be talking to the people in that dreadful neighborhood where my daughter chose to live. As you said, this appears to be an unfortunate burglary." She took a deep breath and shook her head. "There would seem to be no reason, then, to dredge up old, painful memories, or to besmirch my daughter's good name—and the name of her family. Particularly when it looks like those issues have nothing to do with my daughter's death."

"Looks can be deceiving," Jack pointed out.

"You have no idea, Detective," Lydia Chapin replied. Jack thought he caught the hint of a threat in her tone.

"Are we missing something here?" Train asked. "I'd think you'd want to do anything you could to find whoever killed your daughter."

"Obviously we will provide whatever information we can to help with the investigation, but my daughter's marriage is not relevant here. Neither is Leighton; he didn't do this."

"Why are you protecting him?" Train pressed.

"I'm not protecting him; I'm protecting my family."

"But Mom, if there's any chance that Leighton is involved, shouldn't we—" Sydney began, but her mother cut her off.

"Hush, child, before you do damage!"

Lydia Chapin's outburst startled everyone in the room. She had been so calm and self-assured throughout the interview—right down to her cookies and coffee and polite evasions—that the eruption seemed out of character. Even Sydney seemed shocked, Jack noticed, and she immediately shut her mouth. The room was still for a moment as Lydia collected herself. Then she turned back to her visitors.

"I apologize," she said, although no apology seemed to be intended. "It has been a long day and I'm tired. I'd like you both to leave now, please; I don't want my granddaughter disturbed. If there is anything else we need to discuss, we can do it at a later time."

Jack and Train looked at each other. Train, who had been leaning over with his elbows resting on his knees, sat up straight in his chair. "Ma'am, I know how terrible this day has been, but we've got to do our job. If we go back to the station without getting the basic information"—he gave an apologetic shrug—"well, let's just say that our boss won't be too happy with us."

Lydia Chapin seemed to consider this for a moment. "Your boss reports to the chief of police, I assume?" she asked at last.

Train hesitated. "Yes," he said after a moment.

"Who, in turn, reports to the mayor, presumably?"

Train frowned as he nodded.

"Then you needn't worry, Detective," she said. "I'm having dinner with the mayor later this week, and I will be sure to tell him what an excellent job you two are doing." She stood up, flattening her skirt against her thighs. "You can face your superiors without fear," she concluded, gesturing toward the foyer in a clear attempt to usher the detectives out of the house.

"I don't think you understand," Jack objected.

"No, Detective, it's you who doesn't understand." She looked directly at Cassian, and he could see the steel in her eyes. It was set hard and firm within her core, and Jack could tell that she would be a formidable adversary in any setting. But as he looked into her eyes, underneath the determination he could see something else. Agony. He could see the anguish under the woman's resolve trying to fight its way out to the surface. Any more pressure, Jack thought, and she might just lose her control.

And then it was gone; the pain and sadness had disappeared from her eyes. Jack opened his mouth to say something—to see if he could draw the anguish back toward the surface—but she cut him off with a wave of her arm. "Please, Detective. Don't make me call my lawyer. That won't help any of us."

Chapter Six

"THAT WAS WEIRD," Jack said once they were outside.

"You could say that," Train agreed. "Rich people," he scoffed. "I'll never understand 'em, as long as I live." He looked over at his partner. "You grew up rich, right? Ivy League, silver spoon, and all that crap?"

"William and Mary. Not actually Ivy League. And I didn't grow up rich—not by those people's standards, anyway. That's a whole different ball game in there."

"You think the mother's really just protecting the family's reputation?" Train shook his head. "It's hard for me to believe. I mean, her daughter was murdered, for Christ's sake. Doesn't there come a point where some things are more important than your reputation at the country club?"

"You'd think so, wouldn't you?" Jack agreed. "Then again, when you're talking about this kind of money, the family's reputation takes on a whole different level of significance."

"Whatever."

"In any case, we need to add the ex-husband to our list of possibles to check out."

"Leighton," Train scoffed. "Nice fuckin' names you white folks are partial to."

"Oh, okay, Darius."

Train scowled. "Don't even start with me."

Cassian sighed as he looked down at his watch. It was nine-thirty, and his day had begun before six. *I'm underpaid*, he thought as he felt the stress pulling at his shoulders, twisting his neck into knots. He thought about his brother and the empty stare that was all that was left of him.

"You wanna grab a beer?" Train asked.

Cassian shook his head. "Not tonight."

"Okay." Train nodded. "Get at it early in the morning tomorrow, then?"

"Do we have a choice?"

Sydney sat at the edge of the bed in her childhood room. It looked nothing like it had nine years before, when she still lived in her parents' house. Gone were the models and posters of her youth; gone were the ribbons and trophies she had earned in various different sports; gone was any hint that the room had once been her sanctuary.

She couldn't bring herself to feel hurt, or even surprised anymore, though. Her mother had never been sentimental. Within a week after Sydney's father died, her mother had cleared the closets of all of his clothes, shipping them out to Goodwill even before her husband had been laid to rest. "No point in wasting closet space," she had explained coldly. "Besides, it isn't as though we ever had a son who might like to keep some of his things." The comment had wounded Sydney at the time, who had always sensed a hint of disappointment from her parents that she had not been born male.

As she sat in her old room, her emotions shifted back

and forth between anguish and fear: anguish at her sister's death, and fear over what it might mean for her own future. She also found herself feeling angry: angry at her sister for leaving the world; angry at God for letting her sister be murdered; angry at her mother for her inability to show any semblance of maternal sensitivity and warmth; but most of all, angry at herself for letting herself be so manipulated by her mother.

She got up from the bed and began to disrobe, slipping out of her jeans and shirt, leaving them crumpled on the floor as she stood in her underwear. Her mother had had the maid lay out an old nightgown on the bed, and Sydney picked it up to examine it. It was an ungainly thing with long sleeves and a high collar. She tossed it on the chair in the corner of the room and went to the drawer, pulling out a well-worn T-shirt. She took off her bra and slipped the T-shirt over her head, then climbed into bed.

She turned out the light and lay back on the pillows, staring up at the ceiling. Why had she let her mother bully her in front of the two police officers as she had? She was no longer a scared little child, and she was beholden to her mother for very little anymore. And yet she had let it happen.

Then, as she lay there in the quiet, another question came to her—one that suddenly seemed more pressing: why had her mother so adamantly defended Leighton? Certainly Leighton had originally been her mother's choice for Elizabeth, and as had always seemed the case, she had gotten her way. When the marriage ended, Sydney knew there had been recriminations between Elizabeth and her mother. Still, even for all her mother's prior support of Leighton, it was hard to imagine that she would still protect him. Things had gone too far for that, hadn't they?

And yet Sydney had allowed herself to be silenced by her mother, and she was angry with herself for that. Never again, she vowed.

Chapter Seven

LESS THAN A MILE from the Chapin home, Peter King walked up Twenty-eighth Street, Northwest, at a neutral pace. He kept his head still, seemingly indifferent to the world around him, but his eyes darted from side to side, taking everything in. Physically, he was the kind of man who drew no attention. He was neither tall nor short; neither fat nor thin; and his hair was the sort of middling brown that stood out to no one. As he walked, he unconsciously clutched his right hand into a fist, rubbing his thumb compulsively over the stub of a little finger that had been blown off during a particularly trying mission in the first Gulf War.

At R Street he turned left, crossing Twenty-eighth. As he walked, he turned his head, ostensibly to look for traffic, and his trained eyes assessed the entire street, noticing every detail. He'd chosen the time and place well. Washington was a sleepy town after midnight, and the area was deserted. He swung his head in both directions and saw no one; within an instant he'd ducked into Rock Creek Park unnoticed.

So far, so good, he thought as he entered the park and turned right, to the north, up the chosen path. He kept alert, though he knew there was no danger now. His planning had been perfect, and his execution . . . well, if not perfect, at least exceptional. Besides, this wasn't like the old days, living in a world where any slip could have cost him his life. Here in the civilian world, there was room for error, even if no one in his profession would acknowledge as much out loud.

He followed the narrow path along the ravine that had been carved over centuries by the waters of Rock Creek as they flowed through the area that now served as a central artery of the nation's capital. The park was thick with vegetation and the heavy scent of lilac and rotting wood; trees overhung the narrow paved paths that runners used every day, and the underbrush looked impenetrable.

As King walked, he kept alert for anything that might seem out of place, more out of habit than caution. It was a practice born of more than a decade's worth of mercenary work. He noticed nothing.

A few hundred yards into the park, he came to a fork in the path and followed it left, deeper down toward the center of the ravine. After another fifty yards, he came to a cul-de-sac in the path, where his client was waiting for him.

"You do nice work," his client said as he approached. Standing as he was in the dark, only his silhouette was visible, though King could make out the wisps of short blond hair around the edge of his head.

King had met the man only once before, though he'd checked his references carefully. Lee Salvage was one of the most "connected" private investigators in the District, and not necessarily in the good way. The word on the street was that he had a healthy disrespect for the finer points of the law, and an unhealthy taste for cheap booze that had become exacerbated in middle age. King was used to working only with former military personnel, and the idea of working with a man like Salvage disturbed him. But, largely because of his moral flexibility, Salvage still had access to the wealthiest clients, and farmed out much of his dirty work. As a result, King was pleased to have been contacted by the man.

King nodded and reached into his pocket, drawing out a small stack of computer disks. He handed them over. "Is this all of them?" Salvage asked, and King nodded again. "What about the computer?"

King put his hands in his pockets. "She said she lost it a week ago. Said she left it on the Metro, maybe, but she wasn't sure."

"A reporter? Losing her computer? Seems unlikely, doesn't it?" Salvage seemed perturbed. "You believe her?"

King nodded. "I was very persuasive in my interrogation. If there had been anything she could have told me to make me stop, she would have." He let a slight sneer show on his face. "You told me she would be difficult, but she folded quickly."

"I may have overestimated her," Salvage admitted. "I could only go by what my client told me." He leaned over and picked a suitcase out of the bushes to his right, handing it over.

"Fifty thousand?" King took the suitcase in his gloved hands.

"You want to count it?"

For a moment, King worried that he'd offended the man, and he quietly shook his head. "Let me know if you have any other jobs in the future," he said.

"I will. You should disappear for a while, though. Just to be sure."

King gave a thin smile. "If you insist. Just keep me in mind in the future. And next time, see if you can make it a little bit more of a challenge." He hoped the other man appreciated a hint of bravado.

Salvage nodded. "As I said, I may have overestimated her."

As King turned and started heading back up the path in the direction he had come, Salvage pulled a small nine-millimeter pistol out of his pocket; a silencer was already attached to the barrel. He pulled the trigger three times in rapid succession, hitting King twice in the back and once in the base of the skull. He pitched forward and fell face-down at the edge of the path.

"Then again," Salvage said to King's corpse, "I may also have overestimated you."

He put the pistol in his pocket and moved forward, rifling through the dead man's clothing, removing his wallet and checking to see if there was anything else that might be used to identify the body. Then he rolled King's body off the edge of the path, over a small ledge and into the thick bushes, making sure it couldn't be seen by a casual observer wandering down the path. With luck, it might be weeks before the remains were discovered. Indeed, he wasn't too far from the spot where a young intern's body had evaded hundreds of police and National Guardsmen following her affair with a prominent congressman. And even once the body was found, there was nothing to tie King to Salvage—or his client—and there was little need for worry.

Satisfied with his evening's work, he took a quick look around. "No loose ends," he said to himself. Then he picked up the suitcase and headed out of the park.

Chapter Eight

THE PHONE STARTLED CASSIAN out of a deep sleep, and he reached over to grab the receiver off the bedside table. "What?" he grunted.

"Rise and shine, partner, we got work to do." Jack recognized Train's voice, and he rubbed his eyes, glancing over toward the clock. Seven-thirty. He'd overslept.

"Yeah, yeah," he grumbled. "Gimme twenty minutes."

"I'll be there in ten." The line went dead and Cassian let his arm fall over his eyes, stretching against the fatigue. He took a deep breath, feeling his chest expand, bringing him to life. He rolled his legs off the bed and sat up, looking around his bedroom. He lived in a two-bedroom off Dupont Circle—nicer than the places most cops could afford, but then Cassian was still single, and the revenue from a modest trust fund his parents had established for him and his brother augmented his salary. He was lucky in that respect; while his family had never been wealthy in the manner of the Chapins, he'd been left with enough money to choose a career based more on his interests than his income. He'd wandered for a few years after college, working at a random series of jobs that included everything from carpenter to assistant curator at an art museum. He hadn't joined the force until his mid-twenties, but in spite of the difficulties, he'd never second-guessed his decision. It was the least he could do for Jimmy.

Thinking about his brother wouldn't help him through the day, though, and he stood up and headed to the shower. Train wouldn't be happy to be kept waiting.

Eleven minutes later, Cassian walked out the front door of his apartment. Train sat in the obese unmarked Crown Victoria, double-parked on the narrow street, leaving just enough room for other cars to get around him. He turned his wrist and tapped his watch, looking back up and shaking his head at his younger partner. Jack shrugged and walked around the car, climbing into the passenger seat.

"Just getting up, are we?"

"That's right," Jack admitted. "Some of us worked into the early morning."

"On?"

"Research," Jack said. "I thought it might be interesting to know a little bit more about the Chapins. They're even bigger than I thought."

"Yeah, well, I'm sorry to say that you probably could have gone to bed early and gotten a good night's sleep, for all your poking around is likely to get us in the end."

"How so?"

"I talked to Deter first thing this morning. We got a clean print off the pocket torch we found in Elizabeth Creay's apartment, and it came up cherries on the computer."

"Really?" Jack thought of the hours he'd spent the night before doing research. He almost felt disappointed. "Anyone we know?" he asked.

"Yep," Train answered. He raised his eyebrows as he looked over at his partner. "Jerome Washington."

"Jerome Washington?" Jack groaned. "Our Jerome Washington?"

"That's the one."

"Shit, I thought he was still locked up. When did he get out?"

"He served two years and got early parole nearly a year ago. Word is that he went right back to the streets."

"Big shocker. Where else were you expecting him to go?" Cassian asked sarcastically.

"I don't know," Train said, a simmering anger in his tone. "Don't they teach these people anything in lockup? Don't they give them some sort of job training or something?"

Cassian frowned. "You serious?" He wagged his head. "What do you think, a few lessons in woodshop and an ex-con can walk out to live the American dream? We don't have enough computers in the schools in the District, but you think the government is going to spend any money educating a bunch of degenerates and killers? And remember, this is Jerome we're talking about. You really think he'd be interested in studying to be a mechanic or a refrigerator repairman?"

"You never know."

"Yeah, you do. You remember what he did to that kid who crossed him? Ugly shit, partner."

"He was never convicted of that. We only proved up the B&E."

"Right. Never convicted. Musta' been innocent, then, huh?"

Train was pulling his car through traffic on Pennsylvania Avenue, around the endless detour at the 1600 block that had been in place since the attacks of September 11, 2001. "Yeah, I know," he admitted. "But I knew

Jerome before he was a killer. I grew up around his family—good people for the most part. He just got sucked into the life when his father left. Started dealing some drugs on the corner and breaking into houses; it was downhill from there and he got meaner and meaner. Family was helpless."

Cassian looked out of the window at all the suits hurrying on their way to work. They all looked the same in their dark blue pinstriped uniforms with their power ties and their expensive leather briefcases. Washington was a city where image was everything, and the minions that turned the great gears of democracy protected their administrative turf from any perceived attack, guarding their images carefully. They cast a polished veneer on the city during the daytime, projecting cleanliness and efficiency. But at night, when they had all headed off to their suburban homes in Virginia and Maryland, the real city came to life, its heart beating out a less even, more human rhythm. "A year and a half in lockup's a long time," Cassian pointed out. "You think he was mean before, I bet he was a pussycat compared to where he's at now."

"I know," Train replied. "I just keep thinkin' that maybe there's hope. He was a good kid once."

Jack scratched his chin. "I don't think you change from the kind of mean he became, bro. Once it's in you it eats everything good left."

Train was focused on the road, and wouldn't look over at Cassian. Finally, he gave a heavy sigh. "I guess we'll find out soon enough."

The trip from Dupont Circle to the southern reaches of the District was a journey filled with contradictions, much like the city itself. Expensive apartment buildings nestled close to decaying brick houses, and excavators and chain-link fences promising shiny new glass-and-steel office towers seemed to creep perilously close to lonely free-standing structures, the great trenches dug to accommodate future parking lots undermining the integrity and stability of their neighbors both figuratively and literally. At one traffic light, a young man in an expensive silk suit and polished thick-soled shoes crossed in front of Train's car, followed closely by an old man in rumpled, threadbare clothes. *Beggars and thieves of all walks of life*, Train thought. The old man pulled out a greasy squeegee from under his stained jacket and advanced on Train's car. Cassian pulled out his badge and tapped it on the windshield in warning, drawing an angry, if resigned, frown from the man, who simply moved on to attack the next car. Once out toward the southern part of the city, though, the neighborhoods settled into a more regular pattern of decreasing affluence as the officers headed toward one of the most dangerous areas of Washington.

Train pulled the car up to the cracked sidewalk at the corner of First and P streets, Southwest. It was the neighborhood where he'd grown up; where he'd been a hero as a football star at Anacostia High, setting city records in nearly every defensive category—records that stood to this day. He could still remember the celebration on a long-ago Thanksgiving weekend when they'd won the city championship. The entire street was lit up, with people out on their front porches, sipping beers and homemade peach wine, and smiling. *Smiling!* He had never seen his neighborhood smile with pride the way it had that night, and for a brief moment they'd had reason to hope. In that awful fall of 1968, after the city had been torn apart by riots and protest and war, and just when it seemed to many black Americans that all hope had been stolen by assassins' bullets, Darius Train had given this tiny, run-down, desolate neighborhood something to believe in again. It was still a moment that inspired great pride for Train—and great pain.

As he and Cassian got out of the car, Darius paused, looking up at the ramshackle little townhouse. A battered plastic pink flamingo stood in the tiny garden in front of the structure, giving the two detectives a wary eye, as though it had already seen too much.

"This isn't gonna be pleasant," Train said. He'd known Jerome Washington's mother, Shantal, and her family growing up. Their mothers had been friends, and when Shantal was a little girl, more than ten years his junior, she, like everyone in the area, had worshipped D-Train—the local hero. Three years ago, when Cassian and Train had arrested her son for dealing drugs, it had devastated Shantal; not just because her son was going to jail, but also because her family had been disgraced in front of the great Darius Train.

Cassian nodded. "You want me to take care of it, and you can wait in the car?"

Train couldn't tell whether his partner was kidding, and there was part of him that was tempted to take him up on his offer, but he knew he couldn't. He shook his head. "Let's get this over with."

They ambled up the front walkway, only to be drawn up short by a high-pitched call from the front porch of the house next door. "Darius Train!" came the voice, startling them both.

Train looked over and smiled as he recognized the face. He made a motion for Cassian to relax for a moment, and he strode across the burnt-out grass to the little house, its yellow paint chipping away. "Is that Miss Thelma Thornton?" he called out in a deep, resonant voice.

"Oh, you know it is, child." The woman on the porch laughed. Darius could barely see her over the solid wood railing. She was a frail slip of a woman, her hair thinning a bit on top, her shoulders bent forward with age. "Lord, it has been too long since we've seen you 'round here, son. A body might begin to think that you'd forgot where you came from."

Train leaned his huge frame over the railing and took the woman's tiny hand in his, kissing it as though meeting a queen. "No, no, Miss Thelma," he said, letting a slight drawl slip into his voice. "You know there ain't no chance of that. I live over closer to center of town since I transferred to the station on Capitol Hill." He gave her a huge smile. "I don't get down around here quite as often as I like, but you know I could never stay away from you for too long."

Thelma Thornton chuckled lightly at that. "Oh, you always were the smooth child, but you shouldn't be wastin' it on an old hag like me." She smiled brightly, revealing a gap where her two front teeth had once been. Then she noticed Cassian behind Train and her smile dimmed slightly. "Have you lost your manners, Darius?" she scolded Train. "Who's your friend?"

Train looked over his shoulder and flushed. "That's my partner, Jack Cassian," he said, looking guilty.

"Nice to see you, ma'am," Jack offered.

"Humph," the old woman grunted, turning her attention back to Train. "You boys here on official business, then?" she asked, raising an eyebrow.

"Well . . ." Darius sputtered, caught off guard by the question.

"Never mind," Thelma said. "I don't want to know. My business is my business, and yours is yours." She cast a quick glance over toward the Washington house, where the detectives had clearly been headed before she stopped them. "The same goes for everyone else in this neighborhood." She bowed her head a moment, as if in mourning. Then she raised it again and her smile had returned, though Darius thought he saw a tinge of sorrow in the corner of her mouth. "I'm just glad to see you, son," she said. "It's people like you that have given a lot of us hope." She looked over his shoulder again, toward Cassian. "You know you're riding with a legend here, right, mister?" she called out.

"He's mentioned it," Cassian replied, smiling, enjoying Train's embarrassment at the attention.

"Best damned athlete this city's ever produced in any sport—least this corner of it. An' one of the finest people, too."

"Yes ma'am," Cassian said. "We're still debating where to put the statue down at the station."

She looked at Train again and nodded toward Cassian. "Smart mouth on that one, huh?" she said quietly.

Train looked over at his partner. "Yeah," he admitted. "You'd like him."

She nodded slowly. "Probably would, at that." She looked down at her hands. "I won't keep you anymore, son," she said, "but I sure am glad to see you."

"Thank you." Train took her hand and kissed it again. "Me too."

"Now you git," she ordered, and Train turned and walked with Cassian back toward the house where Shantal and Jerome Washington lived.

Chapter Nine

THE DOOR SWUNG OPEN on the second knock, and Train wondered whether the woman standing at the threshold had been watching the exchange at the house next door. Shantal Washington had aged significantly since Train had seen her at Jerome's sentencing. Although he'd been the arresting officer, his testimony at the hearing had been muted, and he'd argued for leniency, telling the judge that he'd known both Jerome and his family for most of his life, and that he believed there was still something worth saving in the young man. Shantal Washington's attitude toward Train hadn't softened, though, and she still blamed him for the two years her son had lost in prison.

"Shantal," Train said, nodding at the woman in the door. "How you doin'?"

"What're you doin' here, *D-Train*?" Shantal's voice was full of anger as she spat out his high school nickname.

Train sighed, realizing that there was no way to ease his way into the encounter. "We need to talk to Jerome," he said.

"What fo'?" Shantal Washington demanded. "Ain't you done enough to him yet?"

"I think it'd be better if we left that between him and us," Darius answered. "He here?"

"No." She shook her head. "He ain't."

Train frowned at Cassian, then turned back to Jerome's mother. "This is the address he listed with his parole officer. If he moves, he's supposed to let them know down there. If he doesn't, it's a violation of his parole."

Jerome's mother looked nervous. "He still lives here, he just ain't here right now."

"Is he at work?" Train pressed.

Shantal Washington bit her lip. "He got fired," she finally admitted, shaking her head. "His boss said you couldn't trust no convict." She shot a glare at Train. "That's what you did to him."

The muscles in Train's jaw clenched as he fought back the urge to defend himself. It wouldn't do any good, and it would only make things more difficult. "We need to talk to him, Shantal. It's important."

"Yeah, well then I guess you gotta come back later, 'cause he ain't here now." She shook her head and looked like she was going to cry. "Why don't you just leave him alone, Darius?" she said after a moment, her voice pleading. "You ain't taken enough of his life?"

Train considered their position. They had no warrant, and couldn't force their way in to check the place out without facing charges later. Besides, looking at Shantal he could tell she wasn't lying; her son wasn't there. "All right, Shantal, we'll come back later. You tell him we're lookin' for him, though, okay?"

"Yeah, I will," Shantal said. She glared at the two officers as they turned and walked away. "He's a good boy!" she called after them. "You leave him alone now, you hear?"

Train heard, but he was already down off the porch and headed back toward the car.

"What now, boss?" Cassian asked as they climbed back into the car.

Train flipped open his notebook. "I've got the address of the place where Jerome's parole officer got him a job. We could head over there, but I've got a feeling that'll be a dead end. Shantal's got no reason to lie about him getting fired."

"Might be worth a shot anyway," Cassian said. "Sure beats the hell out of sitting here waiting for him to come home, sweating our balls off in this goddamned car." He looked over at Train. "Too bad we don't have a neighborhood watch program set up out here," he joked. "Somebody might have seen the man recently."

Train thought for a moment, and then suddenly opened the door to the car again. "We do," he said as he got out. He walked up the lawn toward Thelma Thornton's house, right toward the old woman, who was still sitting on her porch.

She saw him coming and started shaking her head. "Don't you do this to me, Darius Train," she said as he neared the porch.

"Do what to you, Miss Thelma?" He tried to force a smile.

"You can gimme that fool's grin all you like, but I can see the look in your eyes. You want me to say something that's gonna get somebody in trouble." She shook her head again. "Good Lord, son, don't you know I still gotta live here?"

Train held up his hands. "Okay, okay," he said. "I won't ask you to say anything that'll get anybody into trouble. We're just looking for Jerome, next door, and his mother doesn't know where he is. I just thought, maybe, y'know, because you always seem to know everything going on in the neighborhood, you might have an idea where we might find him."

Thelma Thornton shook her head once more, though less forcefully this time. "Just like the police to use an old lady for information." She looked at him. "I'd have hoped you'd be better," she said.

Train returned her look, his own eyes deadly serious. "It's important, Miss Thelma," he said. "A young mother was murdered yesterday. I'm not lookin' to jam Jerome up for something he didn't do, but we gotta talk to him. And the longer it takes for us to find him, the worse it's gonna be for him."

She sighed and let her needlepoint fall onto her lap. She leaned in and spoke quietly. "Now I don't know for sure, you understan'," she said reluctantly. "A lot of what I hear is nothin' more than rumor."

"We'll take anything we can get, Miss Thelma. Even rumors." Train knew that Thelma's rumors were generally more accurate than anything printed in the daily papers.

"I heard he's running a shack down on G Street—you know, the one near Eighth? My guess is that you'd find him there," she said. Then she added quickly, "You know him, though, Darius. He was a good boy once. It's just the damned drugs that changed him." She looked him in the eyes again. "And prison."

Train felt as though he'd been slapped, but it was worth it. He'd gotten the information he needed. "Thanks, Miss Thelma, I appreciate it."

"If you really appreciate it, you'll go easy on that boy, Darius. An' you'll remember who you are an' where you come from."

Chapter Ten

CASSIAN KNEW THE "SHACK" Thelma had referred to. It was a run-down, boarded-up townhouse on G Street between Seventh and Eighth—only blocks from Elizabeth Creay's house—that harbored, at any given moment, between five and twenty lost souls who used the shelter to indulge whatever particular demons plagued them. It was mainly crack cocaine, but crystal meth and heroin were not unusual either.

The prospect of raiding this particular type of spot was never appealing; by nature it was a dangerous, unpredictable task, made all the more so by the reality that any number of the residents could be armed—and high. As a result, Cassian and Train called in two squad cars for backup so they could mount a full-scale assault on the dwelling.

They met up with the squad cars a few blocks from the house and parked in back of a gas station off Pennsylvania. Train quickly mapped out their strategy. "Kiper and Halston," he said, pointing at two of the officers. "You go through the alley and block any escape out the back. Minnelli and Jackson, you'll go in through the front with me and Cassian." All four of the cops nodded. "Remember, we're looking for one guy in particular—Jerome Washington—we're not looking to clean the place out as a matter of policy. Detain all those inside until we know whether we've got our guy. If you see anything obvious—weapons or drugs actually in the possession of anyone you pat down—we'll take them in, too, but that's purely a secondary issue. Hold your fire unless you face an affirmative threat. I want to get out of this without anyone getting hurt."

The four officers nodded again.

"Okay, Kiper and Halston, you two take off. We go in exactly five minutes."

The two officers headed out, and Jack took a moment to check his weapons. Like most police officers, he carried two, one in a shoulder holster and one strapped to his ankle. He looked over at his partner, who had unlocked the shotgun from underneath the front seat of the car. "That may be a little overkill, don't you think?" Cassian asked. "Remember what Miss Thelma said: 'You gotta take it easy on the boy.'" He mimicked Thelma Thornton's high-pitched voice.

"If you knew what was good for you, you wouldn't disrespect a woman like that. She's seen more shit than you'll ever hear about, and she still keeps her life wired tight." He nodded toward the shotgun in his hand. "As for this, it'll let the people inside know we're serious. If they get the idea we're being tentative, this thing could get out of control pretty fast."

"Speak softly and carry a twelve-gauge?" Cassian asked.

"Something like that."

Cassian shrugged and walked around to the back of the car. He popped open the trunk and took out two

Kevlar vests with POLICE stenciled across both the front and the back. He took off his sport coat and threw it in the backseat. Then he slipped his arms through the straps in one of the vests. After he'd buckled himself in, he took the second vest and tossed it on the hood of the car in front of Train. "You forgetting something?" Cassian asked, nodding at the vest.

"Nope," Train said, shaking his head.

"Come on, Sarge, the city shelled out millions of dollars so we could each have one of these. The least we can do is wear 'em."

Train scowled as he picked up the vest, holding it up in front of his huge torso. "This thing doesn't even cover me," he pointed out. "It only works for skinny little white boys." He tossed the vest back on the hood.

"Let's not make this a racial thing," Cassian cracked. "I don't want any of our people mistaking you for one of the bad guys and taking you out by accident." He pointed to the yellow lettering on his own vest. "See? This makes clear which team you're on. And like you said, we're better off going in with a strong message." Cassian picked up the other vest and held it out to his partner. Train could be stubborn, he knew, but he generally gave in to reason.

The huge man rolled his eyes as he slipped off his suit jacket. It was a struggle for him to get the vest around his frame, and once it was on it looked comical, the protective padding covering only a small portion of his chest. It was all Cassian could do to suppress a smile.

"Don't fuckin' start with me," Train warned his partner, sensing the younger man's amusement without even looking up.

"What? You look great," Cassian deadpanned. "I'm sure it covers part of your heart, at least." He caught

Train's glare, but looked down at his watch to avoid eye contact. His face became serious. He looked over at the two remaining officers, who were similarly clad in protective gear. "It's time," he said. "You boys ready?" He could feel the tension in all of them. As a cop, there were few things more dangerous than walking into a crack house. There was always the very real possibility that one of them might not walk back out alive. It was one of the things about the job that had taken Cassian a while to get used to, and as he snapped his spare gun into his ankle holster, his mind went to his brother. Then he looked up at Train. "You good to go?" he asked.

Train picked up the shotgun, which he'd rested on the hood of the car as he pulled on his vest. He pumped a round into the chamber. "Let's get this over with," he said.

Chapter Eleven

TRAIN COULD FEEL HIS HEART beating as he and Cassian came up the street from the east. Minnelli and Jackson simultaneously hurried in from the west, the two cars converging directly in front of the derelict house. The approach allowed them to get a good look at the entire block to scope out any hidden dangers. The street was quiet, though, and they exited their cars quickly.

All four of them ran silently up the front steps and fanned out on either side of the door. Train held up his hand, counting to three with his fingers, and on signal Jackson stepped in front of the door and kicked in the decaying portal.

"Police!" Train shouted. "Everyone down on the ground!"

The interior of the house was dark, and it reeked of sweat and sex and despair. There were five people in the main room, lounging in various states of drug-induced stupor. Two of them—a young man and an older-looking woman—were fully unconscious, splayed out on the floor in a corner of the room on top of each other, bare from the waist down. The other three—two teenage girls and a man who looked to be in his early twenties—were reclining on a torn, stained sofa in the middle of the room. They looked up in confusion. One of the girls cracked a nervous smile and covered her face bashfully.

"Down!" Cassian shouted at the three on the couch, pointing his gun at them. "Get down on the floor!"

The three addicts continued to stare at the officers. The young man's mouth worked back and forth involuntarily.

"Down!" Minnelli, the youngest of the officers, shouted again, getting frustrated. "On the ground!" He reached out and grabbed the man by the back of the neck, pulling him forward and forcing him down on the ground. The physical contact seemed to break the spell.

"Hey!" the young man protested. "Fuck! Get off!"

"What are you doing!" one of the girls shouted. "Lay off him!"

"You too, girls, down on the ground," Train said loudly. His voice was more controlled, but he held the shotgun at attention. Both girls on the sofa looked at each other and moved slowly onto the floor.

"Fuckin' cops," one of them muttered.

Once they had the three addicts on the floor, Train looked up at the other officers, who had done a quick tour of the first floor of the townhouse. "No one else down here," Minnelli said. Just then, they heard footsteps from upstairs, and they all swung their guns over toward the staircase. Then it turned silent again.

Train looked at Jackson. "You got these guys?" he asked, pointing to the five people lying on the ground.

"Yeah, I got 'em, Sarge," Jackson replied.

Train nodded to Cassian and Minnelli. "Okay, let's go," he said, moving toward the staircase.

"I've got point," Cassian said, stepping in front of Train and heading up the stairs. He moved with fluid grace as he panned his gun up, tensed for anything that might move or jump out at him. It took only a few seconds for him to climb the stairway and round the corner at the top, with Train and Minnelli right behind him.

The second floor was in better condition than the first. The entire area was open space except for a door at the far corner. A fraying rug covered the weathered floor, but a few of the boards that had covered the windows had been removed, letting some light in. A good-looking black man with close-cropped hair in jeans and a T-shirt sat on a large overstuffed chair near one of the windows. A thick gold chain hung around his neck with a large ruby-studded "J" weighing it down.

"Freeze!" Cassian shouted at the man.

He held his hands up. "I'm frozen, man," he said calmly.

Train and Minnelli rounded the corner at the top of the stairs behind Cassian, guns drawn. The man on the chair seemed to recognize Train instantly. "D-Train," he said, shaking his head. "I shoulda guessed."

"How's it goin', Jerome?" Train responded, still swinging the shotgun in every direction, checking to make sure there was no one else on the second floor. "You alone up here?" he asked.

Jerome Washington shrugged. "Far as I know."

"And how far would that be?" Train asked. He moved over toward the door at the end of the room as Cassian and Minnelli kept their weapons pointed toward Jerome.

"You know," Jerome replied. "Far as I can know. I been sleeping."

"What's behind the door, Jerome?" Cassian asked as his partner tried the knob. It was locked.

"Bathroom," Jerome answered. "You probably don't

want to go in there, though." He waved his hand in front of his face. "I had some Mexican fo' breakfast, you know what I'm sayin'?"

"I thought you said you were sleeping, Jerome," Train said, stepping back from the door and considering his options.

"Yeah, well, you know. I been sleeping for a while, but I was in there earlier."

Train looked at Jerome and then turned back toward the door. After another moment's thought, he stepped back and reared up on one foot. He shifted his significant weight as he lunged forward and kicked open the door with a deafening crash.

The gunshots rang out instantly, two of them exploding the wood by the doorjamb, and the third hitting Train squarely in the chest. The huge man went down, rocking the entire house as he hit the floor.

"Sarge!" Cassian yelled, moving quickly to the side of the door. He grabbed his partner and tugged at him with all the strength he had, dragging him out of the doorway. Train winced as he rolled over, grabbing at his chest. He coughed and sputtered as he felt for a hole in the Kevlar. As helpful as the vests could be, the prevalence of armor-piercing "cop-killer" bullets on the street made them far from a guarantee. After a moment, he was sure that he was all right. His ribs would ache for days, he knew, but he'd survive.

Cassian was also running his hands over Train's vest, searching for any sign of penetration. "You okay?" he was yelling. "Are you hit anywhere?"

Train shook his head. "I'm fine," he managed to say at last.

Cassian nodded at him, and then turned to Minnelli,

who was still pointing his gun at Jerome Washington. "Stay with him!" Cassian ordered. Then he got to his feet and slid across the wall toward the edge of the bathroom door. Train watched as his partner set himself and then swung into the room, pointing his gun into each corner. It was empty.

Train got to his knees, still shaky from the impact of the round in his chest. It felt like someone had hit him with a baseball bat. He looked over at Minnelli, whose eyes were wide, but who seemed well in control of Washington. He nodded at him. "Stay here," he said, confirming Cassian's orders. Then he got to his feet and followed Cassian into the bathroom.

Cassian was already over by an open window in the corner of the room, but was plastered up against the wall. "You all right?" he asked again as he inched closer to the edge of the window.

"Yeah. You?" Train kept low, in part to avoid any shots coming through the window, and in part because the pain in his ribs made it difficult to stand straight.

"Oh, just fuckin' great." With that, Cassian gave a smile and thrust his gun through the window.

The shooter was moving quickly, crab-walking down the shallow-sloped roof at the back of the house a short jump down from the bathroom window. Train came up behind Cassian so he could see what was happening. The suspect looked young—Train was guessing only fifteen or sixteen—and he flew down the structure, disappearing over the edge of the roof just as Cassian seemed to get him within his sights.

"He's going down, out the back!" Cassian yelled. Train wondered where Kiper and Halston were. They were supposed to be covering the back alley to prevent anyone from escaping in that direction. He felt his chest tighten at the notion that the little punk might get away, but then he saw the officers. They were partially concealed behind some overgrown bushes toward the end of the backyard. Just then, the shooter emerged on the ground from behind the roof. He was limping, now, and he looked up at the window, raising his gun and firing off two shots that went wild, missing Cassian and Train by several feet.

Cassian drew a bead on the young man, and appeared ready to shoot, but Train tapped his shoulder and nodded toward the other officers. "Let them get him," he said.

The young man was moving below again, sprinting toward the gate at the back of the lot that led into the alley. As he ran, he looked back over his shoulder twice, to be sure that no one was shooting at him. That was his mistake.

The first blow caught him completely by surprise, landing on his wrist, just above the hand that held his gun. It made a sickening sound that Train could hear from all the way up in the window as the bones in the boy's forearm snapped. Train watched as the young man looked up just in time to see Halston raising his police baton again. He tried to duck, but the second blow caught him behind the ear and he went down hard, unable to make a sound.

The two officers in the yard pounced on the boy, labeling him with kicks and punches to the head and torso.

"Stop!" Cassian yelled from the window. The two officers looked up with expressions of shock. Train couldn't tell whether it was shock at their own brutality, or at the fact that Cassian was calling them off. There was a momentary standoff, as Halston and Kiper seemed inclined to pick up where they'd left off. As the senior detective, Train knew they would take their cue from him. He felt his ribs, and recognized that there was a part of him that wanted the beating to continue. Shooting at a police officer should come with drastic repercussions, and too often the judicial system allowed suspects—particularly young suspects—to walk too freely. There was a part of Train that wanted revenge.

At the same time, he knew that it would be an empty revenge, and it would leave him unsatisfied. "Call it in," he said to Cassian quietly, pulling away from the window, signaling an end to the retribution.

Chapter Twelve

MINNELLI HAD CUFFED Jerome Washington by the time Train and Cassian returned from the bathroom, but he still had his gun pointed at the restrained man, just in case. Train still felt awful, but better than he had a right to expect, given the circumstances.

"What happened?" Minnelli asked.

"Halston and Kiper got him going out the back," Cassian said.

"Alive?" Minnelli looked hopeful that the answer would be no.

"More or less," Cassian replied. He looked over at Train, who was still holding his ribs. "You sure you're all right, Sarge? Even with the vest, a direct hit like that can do some damage."

Train nodded. "I've had worse," he said. "Couple of Advil and a scotch, and I'll be fine." He looked at his partner, and the two exchanged a nod of understanding. They were both fully aware that Train would be dead if Cassian hadn't forced him to wear the vest.

Cassian turned to Washington. "Anyone else up here we should know about, Jerome?" he asked.

"I don't have nothin' to say, man. I just stopped in here

for a rest, y'know? I don't even know who that was in the bathroom. Damn, I thought the place was empty."

"Yeah, I can see how that might happen." Cassian looked at Minnelli. "You search him?"

Minnelli nodded. "He's clean." He pointed to the chair where Washington was sitting. "There's a stash underneath him, though. I didn't touch it yet. I didn't want to mess up the evidence."

Train looked over at Cassian. He was in too much pain to get down on his knees to take a look, so Cassian took the hint and pulled a handkerchief out of his pocket, walking over toward Washington. He went to the side of the chair and knelt down, lifting up the fabric of the chair. "Oh, my!" he exclaimed in mock surprise. He reached under the chair and pulled out a plastic bag filled with crack cocaine. "Got a good little business working here, huh, Jerome?"

"Shit's not mine," Jerome said sullenly.

Cassian looked around the room. "Really? Well, you're the only one here, aren't you? That's a pretty unfortunate coincidence for you."

"You got a warrant?" Washington challenged.

Cassian laughed, looking at Train. "Look who's turned into a jailhouse lawyer."

"We don't need a warrant, Jerome," Train said. "You see, you're a trespasser here." He raised his eyebrows. "I'm assuming you don't own this place, right?" Jerome said nothing. "I'll take that as a no. So you don't have what they call an 'expectation of privacy' here. You can look that up in the prison law library when you get back there. Plus, I'm also guessing that was one of your runners who went out the window after he took a shot at us, so we have the right to search any area you—the suspect—might be able to reach to grab a weapon. I'd say under the chair qualifies. Any way you look at it, you're in a whole heap of shit."

Washington glared at Train. "You got a hard-on for me, D-Train? You got nothin' better to do? I thought you were workin' homicide these days, anyway. You come back after me just for kicks?"

"Actually, I'm the one having fun, Jerome," Cassian said. "Sarge over there looks at this kind of thing like a job. I see it as a cheap entertainment."

"We came here just to talk to you, Jerome. We weren't lookin' to jam you up, but now that we've found the rocks, we may be in a different position. Unless you talk to us."

"Fuck you, D-Train. I want a lawyer."

Train shook his head. "That's your right—and your call, Jerome, if you want to make it. But you may do better if you just talk to us first."

Cassian pulled Washington up out of the chair roughly, elbowing him in the stomach and leaning in close as he doubled over. "I think you should take the man's advice."

Washington glared up at Cassian and then turned back to Train. "Bullshit, Train," he spat out. "You can call off your boy, here, 'cause I ain't buyin' it. You ain't never looked out for me. Not when I was growin' up, not when you busted me the first time, and sure as shit not now."

"You're wrong, Jerome," Train said.

"Save it, D-Train. Mr. high school hero. Mr. college star. What you say don't mean shit to me. Look where all your 'success' got you—bustin' your own people in your own neighborhood. Save your sympathy and your self-righteousness—it's all a bunch of bullshit to me anyhow."

Train looked at Jerome Washington for a moment, and he could feel his shoulders tighten. There was a part of him that wanted to take a swing at the young man: to feel the satisfaction of knocking him senseless. He'd get away with it, too. A bruise or two on a suspect brought into the station house was almost expected, and if Washington complained, it would be his word against the word of two detectives and a patrolman. Neither Cassian nor Minnelli would take sides against Train.

But Train knew he wouldn't do it. As much as he might have enjoyed pummeling the young man, to do so would only prove him right, and Train was better than that. At least, he thought he was.

"Let's put this piece of shit in the car and get him down to the station," Train said, rubbing his chest. Then he turned and headed down the stairs.

Chapter Thirteen

SYDNEY CHAPIN SAT in the library of her mother's house, staring out the back window into the generous yard that was ringed with tall trees and a wall of bushes that surrounded the property. With all the coverage provided by the greenery, you'd never know that the house stood in the middle of one of the nation's largest cities.

The house was quiet. Her mother had disappeared a little after noon; she'd said that she had to make some "arrangements," and although she hadn't elaborated, Sydney assumed she was attending to the details of Liz's funeral.

Amanda had slept through the night, which was a blessing. She'd awakened briefly while the doctor was there in the morning, and although she still hadn't spoken, she seemed more aware and responsive than she'd been the prior day after her gruesome discovery. She'd fallen back to sleep quickly, aided by the pills coaxed down her throat, and the doctor didn't expect her to wake again before the evening. "A shock like this exhausts the system," he'd explained. "If she's still not speaking in a day or two, we'll take her in to a neurologist, just to be sure, but I don't expect that to be necessary." That left Sydney alone in the house, for all intents and purposes.

She walked over to the small marble table near the library door; the day's newspapers had been fanned out there on the table as always. The *New York Times*, the *Wall Street Journal*, the *Washington Post*, and the *Washington Times* were all laid out in order of national renown, crisp and neat and imposing.

She picked up the *Washington Post* and unfolded it so she could see the entire front page. The story was there; below the fold, but on the front page nonetheless. "Post Reporter Knifed to Death." That was the headline; not very dignified, Sydney thought. The article itself seemed to take pains to describe in the fullest possible detail the physical violations visited on her sister, even teasingly pointing out that the police "would not comment on whether Ms. Creay had been sexually assaulted." Of course, the police had told the family that there didn't appear to be any sign of rape, but as long as the newspapers could work sex into the article, even in its vilest form, it would seem more sensational. It was, Sydney believed, proof that the media were willing to devour even their own in the pursuit of any story that would sell.

And yet the story wasn't all bad. It contained a glowing account of Liz's life; a life with which, as she read, Sydney became acutely aware she was unfamiliar. The article described Liz's involvement with various charities and civic organizations. It detailed interviews with several of the people whose lives her sister had touched: a lonely old woman who had lost her son to gang violence whom Liz made time to visit every week; a young girl to whom Liz had been a tutor and a mentor; a fellow volunteer at the Special Olympics. Each of them told stories of boundless kindness and energy, and these made Sydney feel angry again at the loss of her sister.

The article also mentioned many of the news stories Liz had written in the past two years since joining the *Post*, describing most of them as powerful and controversial. She had been responsible, the paper said, for leading an investigation into the former mayor's office that had proved politically devastating, and had been credited with costing him any chance at reelection. She had investigated irregularities in the trading of the city workers' pension fund, which had led to the indictment of several prominent fund managers. She had shined a light onto the practices of several city hospitals that were accused of gouging people without medical insurance, violating numerous federal laws in the process.

In all, other than the unnecessarily detailed description of the circumstances of Liz's death, the article was complimentary and well written, and Sydney found herself again wishing she'd known her sister better. She felt a thirst to understand her only sibling in a way she knew she would never have the opportunity to do.

It took a moment before she realized she was crying, and the tears brought to her a recognition of the strange cocktail of anger and sadness that was flowing through her body. She wiped her face and cleared her throat; there was no point in wallowing. That wasn't what Liz would want her to do.

Sydney got off the leather chair and turned toward the door. She took a step in that direction before she froze, a feeling of absolute emotional panic ripping through her.

Amanda stood in the doorway. Her hair was a mess, and she was wearing sweatpants and a dirty T-shirt—the same T-shirt they had put on her when they'd put her to bed the prior evening. But it wasn't the disheveled appearance that so startled Sydney; it was the expression on her face. She looked calm—poised, even—as though nothing out of the ordinary had happened to her in weeks.

Sydney stood as still as she could, afraid to make any move lest she unsettle her niece. The fear that raced through her heart was the worst she'd ever experienced—the terror of her own inadequacy. Faced with the pain and need that was so plain in Amanda, Sydney worried that she wouldn't be strong enough to help her in any way that would make a difference.

"Amanda—" she began, and then stopped. She had no idea what to say. What do you say to a fourteen-year-old girl who's just found her mother brutally murdered in her apartment? "Good morning," she managed at last.

"Is it morning?" Amanda asked, her voice even but stilted, as if emotions couldn't make it past her vocal cords.

Sydney looked at her watch. "No, I guess it's not." The two of them stood silently for a long moment, neither of them moving. "How do you feel?" Sydney ventured tentatively.

Amanda's eyes went down and focused inward, as if taking genuine stock of her well-being in response to the question. After a moment, she gave a look that seemed to fall somewhere between a nod and a shrug. "Where's my mom?" she asked.

Sydney gave no visible reaction, even as her heart rate doubled. *How am I supposed to handle this?* She looked closely at her niece, wondering whether she'd lost the memory of having found her mother. It was possible; after all, who could imagine a more traumatic experience?

"Amanda, your mother had an accident," Sydney said softly, with as much tenderness as she could.

"My mother's dead," Amanda said, rolling her eyes slightly. "She was murdered—I haven't forgotten." Sydney felt like her niece had been able to read her face. "I want to know where her body is."

Sydney was rocked by the matter-of-fact tone of Amanda's voice. In many ways, it reminded her of her own mother. She recovered quickly and took a deep breath. "She's down at the hospital," she said, answering Amanda's question. "At the morgue." Her own words sounded harsh to Sydney, but they seemed to satisfy Amanda.

"Where's Grandmother?"

"She had to"—*make your mother's funeral arrangements*, Sydney thought—"run some errands."

Amanda nodded, and the two of them stood in silence again, looking at each other almost as strangers, both petrified of each other. And then something happened. Amanda glanced away for a brief second, and then looked Sydney in the eyes. "Sydney?" she started.

Sydney focused hard on her niece, and for the first time she noticed that the teenager's lower lip was quivering ever so slightly, the tears beginning to gather in the corners of her eyes, like puddles in the rain, welling until they spilled over, running down her cheeks. "Yes?" Sydney answered.

"What happens now?"

Sydney could feel her own tears falling again now, dribbling down over her lips and off her chin freely. She moved forward, opening her arms to Amanda, who took two quick steps and nearly fell against her, sobbing. Sydney closed her arms around the girl and held her tightly, rubbing her back, trying to find the words to comfort her.

"Now," she said at last, her own voice sounding foreign to her, "we work together—you and me and your grandmother. We put our lives back together and we move forward—because that's what your mother would have wanted us to do."

Amanda buried her face deeply into Sydney's shoulder, holding on to her as if for dear life, sobbing harder now. And yet, somehow, Sydney sensed that some of the emotion spilling out of the young girl, mixing with the grief and fear that was inevitable, was relief.

Chapter Fourteen

TRAIN WAS STILL HOLDING his ribs when he walked into the First District station house on Capitol Hill. He let Cassian deal with Jerome Washington to avoid any residual temptation to exact some retribution, and he held back a few yards as he watched his partner manhandle the drug dealer through the booking process.

"We got a real scumbag here, Fritzy," Cassian said to the desk sergeant, pushing Washington hard into the front edge of the high counter.

"What's on the menu for him?" the graying, deliberate officer on the other side of the counter asked.

"Let's start with possession with intent to distribute." Cassian held up the bag of drugs in the evidence pouch. "Toss in a little trespassing, a touch of parole violation, a dash of conspiracy, and top it all off with a heaping helping of attempted murder of a police officer."

The desk sergeant raised his eyebrows at Washington. "You got a lot on your plate, son," he said.

"That's bullshit!" Washington protested.

Cassian smacked him in the back of the head. "We'll figure out what's for dessert once we've had a chance to chat."

"Sounds like a swell date to me," Fritz replied. "Before you settle in for the duration, though, Reynolds wants to see both you and Train in his office."

Cassian nodded. "That's fine. Just have Minnelli and Johnson process him and stick him in one of the interrogation rooms, okay?"

"Will do."

When Train and Cassian entered Reynolds's office, they were disappointed, though not surprised, to see Chief Harold Torbert seated in one of the chairs in front of the captain's desk.

"Train, Cassian," Reynolds began, "I believe you know Chief Torbert." He raised his eyebrows to warn the detectives that the meeting might not be pleasant. Reynolds had a manner of communicating nonverbally that way. He was popular with his men, who recognized that he'd risen to his position as a result of his police skills, rather than political prowess. He was a pragmatist, but his loyalties remained with his men, and they returned that loyalty in kind.

"Not well," Train said. "I think we've met only once." He offered his hand reluctantly.

Torbert was short and heavy, with an oily complexion and a toupee that looked as though it had been a decade at least since it had fit his scalp. He was an adept pencil pusher with little street experience, and he'd always made it clear to those beneath him that the chief's office was nothing more than a brief stopover on his way to political office. "Sergeant," he said in a voice that came more from his nasal passages than from his chest or throat. His hand felt boneless and slick to Train, who had to work to keep from wiping his own hand on his trousers when he took it back.

"The chief stopped by to get an update on the Creay murder," Reynolds said. He rolled his eyes again.

"That's right," Torbert agreed, settling his flab back into his chair. "I understand we got a fingerprint at the scene." Train noted the man's use of the word "we," as though he'd actually had some role in the investigatory process.

"We did," Train said.

"And?" Torbert pressed.

"We just picked up a suspect. Jerome Washington; a small-time dealer with a history of B&Es."

"Excellent, excellent," Torbert said excitedly, rubbing his hands together. Train thought he heard them squish. "It's good to see that we're working this so quickly. I'm sure you're aware of the importance of this matter; she's from a very prominent family—and a reporter to boot."

"Yes," Train said. "I can see how her murder would be more important than others."

Torbert nodded his wattle up and down, missing Train's sarcasm. "Exactly, exactly! We have to make it seem as though we're making progress."

"Or," Cassian interjected, "we could actually make progress." Torbert glared at him. "It's just another way we could go." Cassian shrugged.

Torbert stared at Jack for another moment, but clearly felt no need to introduce himself to the junior detective. "Of course, of course," he said. "Real progress. But you can see how important perception is in this particular case, as well. This Washington person, he's in custody?"

"He is."

"Good, good. I'll have our PR people draft a statement for immediate release."

"Hold on, Chief." Reynolds held up his hand to quell the outbursts about to fly from Train and Cassian. "If I may suggest it, we haven't even interviewed Washington yet. A release is probably premature, and it could cause us problems down the road if we're wrong."

"Yes, yes, of course." Torbert waved a dismissive hand at the captain. "We'll keep it very general and noncommittal for the moment, and of course we'll wait for the detectives' input once they've had a chance to work the young man over a bit." He smiled, revealing sharp little teeth.

"We may also want to look into other leads," Cassian pointed out.

The smile disappeared from Torbert's face. "What other leads?"

"Well, for example," Train began, "we're gonna want to talk to the victim's ex. And we'll want to rule out anyone else in the family as well."

The chief shook his head back and forth, an agonized expression on his face. "Out of the question, out of the question. You clearly don't know who we're dealing with, here."

Reynolds cleared his throat. "Chief, we can't soft-pedal this thing just because of who the victim is."

Torbert pressed his hand against his chest, as though wounded. "Soft-pedal? Who said anything about soft-pedaling? I just want us to focus on the most promising lead so we can move the investigation along as quickly as possible. That's clearly this Washington person. And if that also means that for the moment we can avoid upsetting one of the most powerful women in the District—a woman who is shattered by the loss of her daughter, by the way—well then, I suppose that's just our good fortune, isn't it?"

The three police officers in the room looked at one another in silence. "She got to you, didn't she?" Train said at last.

Torbert spun on him. "Pardon me, Sergeant?" His beady little eyes narrowed angrily.

"Mrs. Chapin. She said that she'd use her contacts to spare her family any inconvenience or embarrassment. She got to you."

Torbert stood up and turned to Reynolds. "Captain, I trust this matter will be handled in the most complete and efficient manner possible. Please have the detectives give you their input for the press release as soon as they're through with Mr. Washington." With that he left the room, not even pausing to acknowledge Train and Cassian on his way out.

"I feel dirty," Cassian said after the door closed.

"Just make sure you wash your hands before you eat," Reynolds agreed. "I wouldn't want you two catching the virus that turned him into whatever he is." He sighed heavily. "Unfortunately, one of the things he is is my boss. It'd certainly save me a pretty big fuckin' headache if you could close this one out quickly."

Cassian looked at Train. "You hear that, Sarge? We wouldn't want a little thing like a murder to cause the captain any headaches, would we?"

"Heaven forbid."

"You boys know what I mean. Get it right. Just get it right quickly, if possible. And let's run out the Washington lead first to see where it goes."

"Don't worry, Captain," Cassian said in a nasal impression of Torbert. "We'll handle this in the most complete and efficient manner possible."

Chapter Fifteen

JEROME WASHINGTON SAT in the dingy interrogation room, eyes straight ahead, hands clasped together, silently waiting. He didn't look into the one-way mirror behind which he knew the police were sitting, watching him—measuring him. He'd played this game before. It seemed a game he'd been born playing.

As outwardly calm as he was, his mind was racing, running through the various scenarios he faced at the moment. He was still on probation, and just by being at the crack house, he suspected he could be violated—sent back to finish out another eight months of his original sentence. That would be bad, but he could handle it.

The bigger issue involved the drugs that had been found under the chair when Train and Cassian had burst into the house. They were his. The cops knew it—hell, everyone knew it. The only question was: could they prove it? He'd taken the drugs out of his pocket and tossed them under the chair when he'd heard the police come through the front door. Anyone with any sense knew that drugs lying under a chair would last all of five seconds in a crack house. Still, with all of the traffic the place got, it might be difficult for the police to prove they were his beyond a reasonable doubt. The only danger was that they might be able to pull a fingerprint off one of the bags, but Jerome thought that was unlikely.

If they could tie the drugs to him, Jerome knew he was done. The rocks were well over the amount needed for a conviction under the federal "drug kingpin" laws. That meant he could be sent away for good—and that was simply unacceptable. As much as he'd learned to handle prison, he had no intention of being there for the rest of his life. He'd rather take the whole world down than spend his days rotting on the inside. He had to play the game, and he had to find out what the police had.

The door swung open and Train and Cassian walked into the room. Jerome focused on Train. He was the more senior of the two, and he'd been a legend in Jerome's old neighborhood. *D-Train*: the greatest high school football player to ever stalk the fields at Kennedy Park; the standout at Virginia, who'd been predicted to be a top draft choice to the pros before his knees gave out; the young man who'd dealt with the adversity and, unlike so many other college athletes banking on a lucrative pro career, had gotten his degree; the cop who'd returned to the city to fight a losing battle on the streets in and around his old neighborhood; the man who'd arrested Jerome three years earlier on a bullshit B&E charge. At least they hadn't been able to tie Jerome to anything else at the time.

Train pulled a chair out from the table across from Jerome; Cassian hung back against the wall on the other side of the room. "Got some bad news for you, Jerome," Train said.

"What's that?" Jerome scoffed.

"Public defender's office is a little backed up. Looks

like it's gonna be another five or six hours before they can get someone here to talk to you."

Jerome shrugged. "I did two years, Train. Think I can handle six hours." He folded his arms. "Besides, where else would I rather be?"

Train smiled. "Then I suppose you won't mind if we keep you company for a little while, huh? Maybe talk a little?"

Jerome knew he had to be careful. He'd been in the system long enough to know that, having asked for a lawyer, the police couldn't ask him any questions directly—unless he agreed to talk. But he also needed to get whatever information he could from the cops in order to figure out where he stood, and he knew the public defenders that were assigned by the courts were often useless—aging hacks who were looking to collect as many fees from the state as possible by funneling as many clients as they could through the system, or wide-eyed idealists right out of law school who knew little about the law, and less about the realities of the criminal justice system. Jerome decided to try walking the tightrope.

"You can talk about whatever you want, Train." It was ambiguous, and might tempt the cops into disclosing what they had, without waiving Jerome's rights.

Train and Cassian shared a look before Train continued. "Looks like you got some problems, here, Jerome."

Jerome laughed. "Problems? Man, you don't know from problems. You wanna talk problems? You've come to the expert." Washington broadened his smile into a big goofy grin. *The Man always likes to see the Sambo shit. No matter what color the Man happens to be, it shows I know my place.*

"You think this is some kind of a fuckin' joke,

Jerome?" Train looked pissed, and Washington wiped the smile off his face.

"No sir, Sergeant Train, I surely don't." He had to play this carefully.

"You know why we brought you in, Jerome?" Train's face was serious.

"Yeah," Jerome said. "Somebody put they' rock under my chair, an' now you think it's mine. I'm tellin' you, I don't know whose shit that is. You think I'm gonna be dumb enough to carry when I'm on probation?" He tried his best to look sincere. "I mean, I ain't no saint, but I ain't no idiot neither, right?"

"The name Elizabeth Creay mean anything to you, Jerome?" Train asked directly.

Washington racked his brain. What the fuck was going on? "No."

"How about the address 114½ G Street, Southeast? That ring any bells?"

Washington shrugged. "I know where it is, if that's what you're askin'."

"Ever been there?"

"Not that I remember. What the fuck you lookin' for, Train? You wanna gimme a hint, and maybe this'll go a little faster?"

Train nodded at Cassian, and without a word his partner reached into his pocket and pulled out something wrapped in a plastic bag. He handed the bag to Train, and Train placed it on the table between him and Jerome.

Jerome looked down and saw the distinctive skull and crossbones on the lighter in the bag. He frowned before he caught himself and evened out his expression. Train had already noticed his reaction, though.

"It's yours, isn't it?" Train asked.

Jerome thought for a moment before he spoke. "That wasn't with the shit that was in the house," he said finally.

"Then what's the harm in admitting it's yours, Jerome?" Train encouraged him.

Washington looked back and forth between Train and Cassian, wondering what was going on. He smelled a trap. "You think I'm fuckin' stupid?" he asked.

"Yeah, we do, Jerome," Cassian shot at him from his perch against the wall on the other side of the room.

"That's funny," Washington replied. He turned back to Train. "Your little white boy there's funny. You teach him to be so fuckin' funny, D-Train?"

Cassian tensed visibly, but Train held up his hand to prevent a disruption. "You don't want to be making enemies right now, Jerome. You're in a world of shit, and you can only make things worse."

"You're scarin' me, Train," Washington scoffed. He wasn't about to lose his bravado. The truth of the matter, though, was that Train *was* scaring him. "Look, you an' the DA wanna waste your time tryin' to make possession stick in front of a jury, you go ahead, but the fact is the shit under the chair wasn't mine, an' you can't prove it was. You can lie an' say that torch was with the shit, but you an' I both know it wasn't."

"This isn't about the drugs, Jerome. You've got much bigger problems than that."

"You wanna tell me what other problems I got?"

"Let's try murder. How's that work for you?"

Jerome thought Train was joking for a moment, but as he stared into the huge man's eyes, he could tell he was serious.

"What the fuck're you talkin' about, Train?" he asked cautiously. This was a development he hadn't anticipated.

"That's right, Jerome," Cassian confirmed, tossing a manila folder down on the table. "Oh yeah, you've hit the big time, scumbag."

Washington looked from the folder lying on the table to Train and then back again, unsure what to do.

"Open it, Jerome," Train said. "It's nothing you haven't seen before."

Washington reached out his hand hesitantly. He looked one more time at Train, who nodded his head. Then he flipped over the cover to the folder, looking down at the images inside. "Goddamn!" he exclaimed, making a face that hovered between revulsion and fascination. "Some white bitch had a bad day, fo' sure."

The pictures were in color, and the image of Elizabeth Creay screamed out from the glossy eight-by-tens, her face barely recognizable from the burns, and the wounds to her neck and abdomen having pooled blood onto the mattress.

Train sat back in his chair. "Look at her, Jerome," he said quietly.

"I'm lookin'," Jerome said, though his eyes were focused on Train.

Train leaned back in his chair, and he spoke slowly. "Her name was Elizabeth Creay, Jerome. She had a daughter, you know that? Fourteen years old. Did you know that it was her daughter who found her like this? That'll fuck a person up, but I guess you never really cared about that, did you? As long as you got the money for your fix, right? How much did you take off her, maybe a few hundred dollars? Maybe another thousand for the computer and whatever else you could carry away? What's that, Jerome, enough to get high for a week or so?"

"I don't know what the fuck you're talkin' 'bout, man!" Jerome insisted.

"Bullshit, Jerome," Cassian barked. "This girl lived at 114½ G Street—less than two blocks from the shithole where you've been hanging out for months, where we picked you up today, and where your boy in the other lockup tried to put a hole through Sergeant Train's chest. That's your shack; you run it, from what we hear on the street, and nothing happens in that neighborhood without your say-so. The murder looks like a burglary gone wrong—the kind you made your name with. And then there's this." Cassian picked up the plastic bag with the lighter in it.

Washington rubbed the back of his neck, looking venomously at Cassian, who was holding the bag in his face. "What about it?" he demanded.

"We found it right next to Elizabeth Creay's body, and do you know what? It's got your fingerprints all over it." Jerome Washington's eyes widened and he muttered something under his breath. "That's right, shithead," Cassian continued. "How hard do you think it's going to be to get one of your homies to confirm that this lighter is yours? Nice little skull face on it and all—it's pretty distinctive." The room was silent for a moment or two as everyone looked at the pocket torch, still resting between Train and Washington.

It was Train who finally spoke. "I'd like to help you here, Jerome. I really would. This is a serious mess you're in. D.C.'s federal jurisdiction, and between the rock under your chair and the way you burned the woman, the feds will probably want to take over and go all the way with you. You're not just looking at jail time—you're looking at the needle." Train rubbed his hand over his bald head. "I don't want to see that. I don't want that for your mother. We knew each other growing up. We're from the same neighborhood. I want to see if we can save your family the pain of going through an execution, but the only way to be sure is for you to come clean on all this now." He leaned forward and looked Washington in the eyes. "If we're gonna save your ass, you've got to start talking to us. Tell us what happened."

Washington looked away. He was tempted to keep quiet. He had some idea what the cops were after, and he knew he was probably screwed, but the gambler in him wanted to take a chance. "You'd never believe me," he said after a minute.

"Try us," Cassian shot back.

Washington looked at Train. "It wasn't me," he said.

Train sat back in his chair. "Okay," he said slowly. "Who was it?"

"I don't know the man's name or anything like that, but I can describe him," Washington said. "He bought a rock off me yesterday morning." He nodded toward the plastic bag on the table. "Bought that torch, too."

"Is that the best you can give us?" Cassian jeered.

Washington ignored him and focused on Train. "It's true, I swear. Yesterday morning, I was sitting on the stoop at G Street, and this car pulls up to the curb, and a guy waves me over."

"What kind of a car was it?" Train asked.

"I don't know," Washington said. He saw Train's eyes roll. "A sedan," he ventured. "It was a sedan. Nothin' fancy, at least nothin' I noticed. It was dark, though, maybe blue." Train was paying attention again, but Washington could tell he was making little headway. "So the car stops and the guy waves me over. I walk up to the car, and the guy tells me he's lookin' for some rock. I tell him how much, and he says fine. I thought it was weird because he didn't look like any kind of doper. But then, I know some people—the rich white kind of people—that have their chauffeurs or whatever buy for them. So he and I make the deal, and I start walkin' back to the stoop, but he calls me back and asks me if I got anything to spark it with. I tell him no, but he says he'll pay a C spot for any butane I got lyin' around." Washington's eyes were focused on Train as he spun out the story, trying to gauge whether the detective was buying it. "Well, y'know, I liked that torch there, but a hundred's a hundred, so I give it to him. He gives me the money and drives off." He paused, breathing heavily. "That's the last I saw him."

Washington finished speaking, but kept his eyes on Train.

"You got anything else?" Train asked, his face unable to conceal his skepticism.

"Like what, man?" Washington asked. "What more can I tell you? That's the God's truth."

Train rubbed his forehead in exasperation. "Well, what did this guy look like, for instance?"

Cassian shifted his stance against the wall, grunting slightly. "We really going to listen to this crap, Sarge?"

Train ignored his partner. "Go on, Jerome. Tell us what he looked like."

Washington fidgeted in his seat. "I don't know," he said hesitantly. "He looked like a white guy."

"Oh, okay," Cassian snorted. "And we all look alike to you, right?"

"An' he had brown hair, I think, and a regular kind of face. He was in his car, so I don't know how tall he was, but I didn't get the feeling he was too big."

"So you're giving us 'brown hair, not too big, and a regular face'?" Train stared at Washington, shaking his head. "That's gonna make your story a little difficult to verify, don't you think, Jerome?"

"He was down a digit," Washington spoke up quickly.

"Down a digit?" Train asked, not understanding.

"That's right, down a digit. A finger—the man was missing one of his pinky fingers. I noticed it when he was paying me."

"Oh, for the love of God," Cassian growled. "What is this, a rerun of *The Fugitive*? What next? You gonna tell us the one-armed man helped him out?"

"Which hand?" Train asked.

"The right one."

"Brown hair, regular face, normal height, missing a finger," Train repeated slowly. "That about it, Jerome?"

Washington opened his hands. "That's all I got."

"We should be able to find this guy by nightfall, right, Sarge?" Cassian quipped.

Washington looked up at Cassian, and then turned to Train. He gave a dismissive shake of his head, leaning back in his chair. "You think I give a fuck anyhow? Shit, lawyer'll carve this case to fuckin' pieces. I'll roll the fuckin' dice, an' if you spend your time goin' after me, the man who did this gets away. Who gives a fuck, though, right, Train? Bitch probably deserved it an' all."

"You could get the needle, Jerome. You really want that for your mother?"

"Fuck my mother," he said quietly. "Not sure she ever gave a shit about me anyhow. I get the needle, then I get the needle. Who gives a shit about one more dead nigger in this city, right, Train? But the fucked-up thing is I didn't do this, so you chew on that." He laughed bitterly.

"You think about whether you can live with that, you self-righteous motherfucker!"

"What do you think?" Train asked Cassian once they were outside the room.

Cassian scratched the stubble on his chin. After a moment, he said, "I don't know. It's his lighter and his fingerprints, and this story about the nine-fingered man's a little too far-fetched for me to buy."

"But . . ."

"But something just doesn't feel right. Maybe he deserves an Oscar, but something about his eyes and his voice made me believe him—at least just a little."

Train nodded. "I had the same reaction."

"So what do we do?"

"First thing we do is make sure the chief isn't overcommitting on the press release." Train nodded his head toward the captain's office and the two of them began moving in that direction. As they passed the front desk, though, Cassian stopped and tapped Train in the chest to get his attention.

"What?"

Cassian pointed to the front desk where a couple of reporters were pulling sheets off a stack of paper, poring over their contents. Cassian walked over and pulled a sheet off for himself. He shook his head in disgust as he handed it to Train.

Train read the headline out loud. "*Police make arrest in murder of* Post *reporter,*" it blared. He read the two-paragraph report, amazed at the degree to which it implied that the crime had been solved. When he finished it, he balled it into his fist and tossed it into the trash can. "So much for getting our input."

Chapter Sixteen

SYDNEY SAT ON THE FUTON COUCH in the apartment she'd rented in the Adams Morgan section of town. She'd stopped by to gather a few things to take back to her mother's house. She was still ambivalent about moving in with her mother, but it seemed as though that bridge had already been crossed.

She sighed as she reached into the leather case and pulled out her sister's laptop computer. It was a large, powerful model, and it held all the research Sydney had done to date for Professor Fuller at the law school. Liz had loaned the computer to her a couple of weeks earlier when Sydney told her that she had arrived in D.C. without many of her belongings, which were being shipped cross-country. Sydney hadn't returned the computer to Liz before she was murdered, in part because it was a much better model than the desktop that had finally arrived from California, and in part because she knew her sister did most of her work on the desktop the paper provided her at the office.

She flipped open the laptop, and it came on automatically, the rhythmic, whimsical tones letting her know that the machine was warming up and would be ready for her in a moment. As the electrical pings and clicks reached a crescendo, the screen lit up with the ubiquitous Microsoft logo, holding in place for a moment as if to confirm Bill Gates's control over the world, and then fading to the standard main screen. After another brief pause, the Outlook program automatically opened and Sydney was greeted with a message: *Good morning, Elizabeth. Today is Friday, June 9th. Would you like to confirm your schedule?*

Sydney felt like she'd been kicked in the stomach. Death seemed to have its greatest impact in the seemingly insignificant details of incurable absence. The silly little computer greeting drove home the reality of her sister's death with surprising force, serving as a painful, terrible reminder of all the meetings and soccer practices and music recitals and dates her sister would miss.

She hung her head, and then on impulse, driven by her profound sense of loss, she clicked on the icon that read, *Yes, confirm schedule, please.* Another window popped open, and Sydney scanned the events of the day her sister had planned. There was an editorial meeting at ten in the morning with Chris Plumber, her boss, presumably to discuss the stories she was working on. Liz was supposed to have lunch with a friend at one o'clock—Sydney wondered whether she should get in touch with the woman to cancel, but decided against it—and there was a notation that Amanda was due home from school by four-thirty. Other than that, the schedule was empty.

Suddenly, without even realizing she was doing it, Sydney began scrolling forward and backward through her sister's Outlook schedule. Monday, Tuesday, Wednesday, back to Tuesday, Friday, Saturday; Sydney flipped aimlessly through the catalog of her sister's days, looking for everything and nothing in particular. And then she stopped, staring at the screen in shock.

Wednesday, June 18th. Two days before—the day Elizabeth was killed. For some reason, Sydney had the sick thought that there should have been some sort of notation around three-thirty marking her sister's death. Perhaps *Meeting with Maker* would be appropriate, she thought, and then immediately felt guilty for allowing such sick, inappropriate humor to creep into her head. But there was nothing noted in the computer, just an entry that she and Amanda were having dinner with Lydia at around six o'clock. The only entries before that were for another editorial meeting at ten o'clock, which Sydney suspected was a daily meeting, and a conference scheduled with someone named James Barneton at twelve-thirty.

Sydney lingered over the fateful day's schedule for a moment before focusing on the twelve-thirty conference. *James Barneton.* She knew that name, she was sure, but she was having trouble remembering from where. She racked her brain until it finally came to her. It was from Georgetown Law School, where she worked. He was a professor of law and political history. Her boss, Professor Fuller, was friendly with Professor Barneton, and had introduced her to him a couple weeks earlier when she had walked in on a conversation between them in Fuller's office. Barneton was, as Fuller described it, a star in the academic world. He had published two successful texts within the past few years, one in political history and one in constitutional law, and his lectures were always the best attended at the university.

She looked back at the computer screen. *Twelve-thirty.* That was only a couple of hours before Liz was killed. Scrolling down the schedule, she noted that there was nothing else on her sister's plate that day before the dinner with her mother. That meant that Barneton was likely the last person Liz talked to before her death—except, of course, for her killer. It was strange, she thought, that Liz had been in the same building where Sydney worked so soon before she was killed. For some inexplicable reason, it made her feel cheated. Obviously, Liz had no idea what lay in store for her later in the afternoon, and yet Sydney felt that somehow, had she had the chance to see her sister that afternoon, perhaps something might have been different. She knew how illogical that was, and yet she couldn't shake the feeling. She wondered what had led her sister to the Georgetown campus to talk to Barneton, and she felt a growing need to know more about her sister's final hours. She had to visit her office at the law school later that day anyway, just to check in. Perhaps, she thought, she would stop by and talk to Barneton.

James Barneton strode through the crowded halls of the Georgetown University Law School with the confidence of a Hollywood movie idol. That's what he was, after all, he thought. At least within the confines of the ivy-perimetered academic arena, few had earned the same respect and attention he commanded. In his mind, as he walked, he could hear the whispers of the students, particularly the female students—*There goes Professor Barneton! God, he's handsome!*

He was handsome, too, he knew. Or at least he had been once. He'd passed fifty several years before, and some might now more readily describe him as distinguished than handsome, but he was sure he still had the ability to capture the imagination of a fair number of women, even those in their mid-twenties.

He rounded the corner and pushed his way through the doors that led to the faculty suites on the fourth floor. His office was in the corner of the building—prestigious real estate in the perk-conscious world of academia. As he neared the turn in the hallway, he noticed a young woman hovering just outside his door. She was attractive, he noted, and he smiled to himself, a feeling of warmth and power spreading through him as he felt the confirmation that, even approaching sixty, he could still turn women to jelly.

"Dr. Barneton?" the woman asked him as he approached.

"Yes," he confirmed. He smiled his most confident smile.

"I'm Sydney Chapin," she said, as though that should mean something to him.

He looked at her, keeping up the smile. Did he know her? He searched his memory. He found it hard to believe that he would have forgotten her, though she did seem vaguely familiar.

His face clearly betrayed his uncertainty, because she stumbled into what seemed to be an explanation. "We met briefly once before; I'm working this summer as a research assistant for Professor Fuller."

"Yes, of course." Barneton nodded enthusiastically. "You must be here to pick up the new chapter on the Warren Court—I know Martin has been dying to review it." He waved her into the office. "Come in, come in. I know I've got it lying around in here somewhere."

"No, no," the young woman stammered, losing her

composure. "I'm not here for Professor Fuller. I'm here about something else." She hesitated. "My sister's Elizabeth Creay—she came to see you the other day; at least I think she was scheduled to come see you."

Barneton frowned. "Oh, yes," he said after a moment. "She did." The woman just stood there looking a little lost and confused. "Did she have additional questions?" he said at last, no longer comfortable with the silence.

The young woman shook her head. "No," she said. "Well, actually I don't know, maybe she did." She seemed to lose her train of thought, and he continued to look at her; she smiled apologetically. "I'm sorry, this is hard." She rubbed her forehead nervously, and then looked him straight in the eyes. "She was murdered later that day."

It was odd how she said it; without any emotion whatsoever, as though she was relating a fact of little or no consequence. It wasn't the news of her sister's death that startled Barneton, but the manner in which the news was delivered.

He looked at her for a long moment until he saw it—a tremble in her eye that somehow conveyed more sadness and emotion than any spoken words ever could have. He reached out and beckoned her over to one of the chairs in his office. "Sit down, and let's talk."

Chapter Seventeen

SYDNEY SAT IN A SOFT overstuffed leather chair in the corner of the office. It was a huge space, and bespoke both Barneton's importance and his ego. He was over near the opposite wall from her, working the electric coffeemaker on the credenza.

"Coffee?" he offered.

"No thank you," she shook her head. She already felt pathetic intruding on the well-known professor's life. What had she really hoped to learn? "I'm sorry," she said after a moment's silence. "I know how strange this must seem, my being here. I don't even know why I came."

"How did it happen?"

"She was stabbed to death. In her home. It was in the papers."

He frowned. "Now that you say that, I remember seeing a headline about a reporter being murdered, but I didn't read the article. I never put it together with your sister's visit."

"It looks like it was just a random burglary."

"Drugs?" Barneton asked.

Sydney nodded. "Probably. That's what the police

seem to be assuming—just someone looking for money to buy drugs."

"I'm very sorry." Barneton shook his head sadly. "She seemed like an extremely intelligent, engaging individual. It must be a great loss for you."

"It is," Sydney said. "More so for my niece—her daughter." She thought for a moment, and then added in a fit of honesty, "Liz and I hadn't been close." She looked up at Barneton. "We were trying to become close, though."

The professor finished preparing his coffee, then walked back and took a seat across from her. "So what brings you here?"

She looked at her hands, which worked nervously back and forth in her lap. "I wanted to know why she came to see you the other day."

Barneton set his coffee down and leaned back in his chair. "Why does that interest you?"

It felt to Sydney as if she was being tested. She shook her head. "Like I said, I don't even really know. You were the last person to talk to her before . . ." Her voice trailed off, and then she started again. "You work right here—right down the hall from where I'm working. It seems strange that she didn't tell me she was going to be here." Was that it? Was she jealous or angry that Liz had actually been in the building and hadn't stopped by to say hello? Sydney didn't think it was that simple. "I guess I'm just curious about the last few hours before Liz died," she concluded weakly.

Barneton nodded. "I think I understand. You're still in shock, of course, and you've been confronted with a tragic, completely foreign situation. I suspect you're treating her death as something to be solved—something to be fixed. I'm sure it's normal to gather all the information you can, so you can sit down and analyze it—try to make sense of it." He spoke like a professor, with a tone that was at once paternal and condescending.

"I thought your specialty was the law. Do you teach psychology, too?"

Barneton smiled. "Strictly amateur in this field," he admitted. "Though I'd wager I'm one of the better amateurs. Most people don't realize that law relies on an innate understanding of psychology to choose its direction. After all, the goal of the law is to get individuals to conform to collective goals and norms. In order to accomplish that, you have to understand what makes people tick." She shifted in her chair, and he seemed to notice that she was uncomfortable being psychoanalyzed. "It's not a bad thing, what you're doing," he tried to reassure her. "Just remember that, no matter what you find, death is something that ultimately can't be solved—and certainly can't be fixed." He looked at her in earnest, leaning forward and staring straight into her eyes.

"I understand that," she said.

He leaned back in his chair again. "Good. Now, what is it that you wanted to ask me?"

"I wanted to know what she came to see you about."

He took a deep breath and held it for a moment before letting it escape his lungs in a massive sigh. "Eugenics," he said.

"Eugenics?" she prodded.

He nodded. "Yes, eugenics. Or, I suppose, to be more accurate, not eugenics generally, but the legal history of eugenics in this country."

"I don't understand."

"Neither did I, but it was a fascinating conversation. We talked for over an hour."

"Eugenics?" Sydney repeated, still baffled. "Hitler, right?"

"Well, yes, Hitler is the most extreme and well-known proponent of eugenics. But eugenics extends well beyond its use in the Third Reich. Eugenics is the science of controlling the gene pool—improving it, in theory—through selective breeding. It was a theory of social science based on Darwinism that was dominant throughout almost the entire first half of the twentieth century."

"I don't think I've ever heard of eugenics except when someone was talking about the Nazis."

"That's not surprising. We all like to shift history to focus on the sins of others, rather than to examine our own failings. And, in all fairness, the Nazis were the most active proponents and followers of eugenics. Their notions of 'racial purity' and superiority gave rise to a massive eugenics program to 'cleanse' the gene pool. In pursuing his goal, Hitler implemented mass sterilization programs to weed out what he considered 'inferior' genes. Most of these programs were directed toward the handicapped, or mentally retarded, as well as gypsies, Jews, and foreigners. In a few short years, he had more than three hundred and fifty thousand people involuntarily sterilized. As I'm sure you know, he wasn't ultimately satisfied with sterilization as a long-term cure of what he considered 'bad genes,' and as a result instituted his Final Solution—the death camps."

"Why would my sister have been interested in Hitler's social science policies?"

"She wasn't. As I said, she was interested in the history of eugenics in America."

"American Nazis?"

"No, no." Barneton shook his head. "It was far too widespread in this country to simply be labeled a 'Nazi' issue. Eugenics has had a long history in the United States. In fact, this country was the first to try to apply the principles in government programs, and many of Hitler's own sterilization laws were taken directly from model laws in effect in the United States."

Sydney frowned. "I find that hard to believe. How could there be that many ignorant people controlling the country?"

"Well, what seems like ignorance to us now seemed like self-evident truths to many people a century ago. And I'm not talking about ignorant people; I'm talking about some of the most intelligent, progressive individuals of the times. People like Oliver Wendell Holmes, probably the most famous, brilliant, and well-respected judge we've ever had on the Supreme Court; Margaret Sanger, one of the leaders of the early feminist movement and a founder of Planned Parenthood; scientists from Yale, Harvard, Columbia, Stanford, the University of Michigan, and NYU."

"But wasn't the eugenics movement discredited after we found out what Hitler had been doing?"

"Certainly the term 'eugenics' fell out of favor in the second half of the twentieth century, but the notion of improving the gene pool has never died. Most of the states in the nation have had forced sterilization laws at one time or another, and in several instances the laws survived into the late 1970s. These laws allowed states to sterilize criminals, prostitutes, the mentally retarded—all without their permission. Most government studies estimate that between sixty and two hundred thousand people were involuntarily sterilized in the United States between the 1920s and the 1970s, but some experts believe that the numbers could be far higher."

"But couldn't the courts stop this kind of thing from taking place?"

Barneton raised his eyebrows. "Of course they could have. But they chose not to. In fact, they supported it." He got up and plucked a text off one of the many shelves. He flipped through the heavy volume. "The question of whether states could involuntarily sterilize an individual based on the principles of eugenics actually made it all the way up to the Supreme Court in 1927, when Virginia wanted to sterilize a prostitute named Carrie Buck who had been diagnosed as an 'imbecile.' Her mother and daughter had also been diagnosed as imbeciles. It took the high court fewer than four pages to conclude that the state of Virginia was well within its rights, and Justice Oliver Wendell Holmes delivered the decision of the Court. In the ruling, Holmes concluded that, 'It is better for all the world, if instead of waiting to execute degenerate offspring for crime, or to let them starve for their imbecility, society can prevent those who are manifestly unfit from continuing their kind. . . . Three generations of imbeciles are enough.' "

"That's awful," Sydney gasped, recoiling.

"Yes, it is," Barneton agreed. Then he took a sip of his coffee. "But remember, many of those who believed in eugenics thought they were doing the right thing—that which was best for mankind. And many of the general principles of eugenics survive today in progressive, modern medical practices. In recent years, scientists, none of whom would consider themselves eugenicists, have developed ways to 'improve' the genetic code. With the mapping of the human genome, the hereditary architecture of the human race, in the 1990s, scientists have been able to isolate certain genes that are responsible for various diseases and conditions. 'Gene therapy,' or the medical application of 'fixing' these genes, is likely to be one of the next great leaps in the history of modern medicine—on a par with the development of sterile surgical procedures, or the development of antibiotics."

The professor in Barneton had fully taken over, and Sydney felt like she was in a lecture now. He was growing more and more animated, and she could see why his classes were so well attended. "Think about it," he continued. "In a few short years, we'll not only be able to 'fix' defective genes—genes that cause disease—we will also be able to enhance our genetic makeup. We'll be able to make sure that our children are intelligent, or tall, or athletic."

"That's far different from a eugenics program that weeds out weak genes through sterilization, or murder," Sydney protested.

Barneton smiled. "That's exactly what your sister said." He sipped his coffee. "And of course you're right, arguably, from a traditional moral perspective. But you're really talking about trying to achieve the same goals through different methods. It's the difference between what might be called 'positive eugenics' and 'negative eugenics.' With gene therapy—'positive eugenics'—the goal is to correct defective genes and allow people to procreate freely. With 'negative' eugenics, the goal is to prevent those with defective genes from reproducing at all." He paused and looked at Sydney in earnest. "At the macro level, however, the direction in which we are heading is arguably every bit as dangerous as the eugenics programs that tried to weed out 'inferior genes' through sterilization and murder. In both cases you're talking about limiting the gene pool. No matter how you set out to accomplish that, it still has serious biological consequences."

"But if all that's being done is to weed out bad genes, how can that be anything but a positive thing?"

Barneton shook his head. "Nature doesn't make judgments about 'good' and 'bad' with respect to the gene pool. Nature only cares about what helps the species survive in every possible situation. The most important genetic principle for the survival of the human race is diversity." Sydney felt lost, and Barneton explained. "Take, for example, sickle-cell anemia," he began. "It's a genetic disease that results in the production of misshaped blood cells that are less effective at carrying oxygen. In some cases, the disease can be fatal. As a result, it could reasonably be viewed as a 'bad gene' disease that could potentially be cured through gene therapy. However, what's interesting about this 'disease' is that it is a recessive genetic condition, meaning that a person must inherit it from both parents, both of whom must be carriers. Those who are carriers, though, are resistant to malaria, and, particularly before the widespread use of pesticides, were more likely to survive in malaria-infested areas of the world. In those situations, the 'disease' allowed people to survive in a broader range of environments. The same could potentially be said for all genetic 'defects.' "

Sydney still looked confused. "And this is what Elizabeth came to talk to you about? Gene therapy?" she asked.

"No, not exactly," Barneton admitted. "We've strayed a little bit from the conversation that I had with your sister. She asked me for any information I might have about some of the eugenics programs from the 1950s and '60s, and how they were implemented in mental institutions."

"Why?"

"I assume it was because, a number of years back, I wrote a book on the changing interpretation of fundamental rights in the context of constitutional theory and the power of the states to regulate reproductive and medical rights. The bulk of the book deals with issues like abortion and voluntary euthanasia—issues that are still at the forefront of the legal and political agendas of this country—but it also had a chapter on the origins of eugenics and the various programs that were deemed legal in the twentieth century."

"No, I don't mean 'why you,' I mean why was my sister interested in the topic at all?"

Barneton tipped his head to the side. "I don't know, really; she didn't say. She told me she was a reporter, and I guess I assumed it was for some sort of story she was writing. The way mental institutions were run in the middle of the last century would shock most people today. The patients were often used for medical testing and generally received very little actual therapy. I had the impression that your sister was writing an article about it all. I have to say, I don't think I was very helpful to her."

"Why not?"

"She wanted to know specifically how sterilizations were actually carried out, and what kind of medical testing was performed. She seemed particularly focused on what went on at the Virginia Juvenile Institute for the Mentally Defective—one of the state-run facilities that sterilized thousands of people into the 1960s."

"There's really a place that's called that?"

Barneton chuckled softly. "Not anymore. It was renamed the Virginia Juvenile Institute for Mental Health in the 1970s. Most people just call it the Institute. In any case, I didn't have any of the information she wanted. I'm a bit of an expert on the development of political and legal theory in this area, but I'm afraid I've never done any real research into the nitty-gritty of what actually happened 'on the ground,' as it were. As a result, I didn't have much information to give her. She said that she'd been up to the Institute, and I think she was hoping to follow up on some of the things she'd seen there."

Sydney leaned back in her chair. She felt like there was something she was missing, some important information that she should be asking about but that was eluding her. "Was there anything else that she asked you about?" she asked finally.

Barneton thought for a moment. "No," he said, "nothing I can think of." He looked at her with an expression of sympathy. "How about you? Have I answered all your questions?"

Sydney nodded. "Yes, thank you for your time. You've been very kind."

"Not at all."

Sydney rose and walked to the door. Barneton followed and extended his hand in a warm gesture. "I know it's silly," she said, "but if you think of anything else you discussed with my sister, will you let me know?"

Barneton nodded and clasped both of his hands over hers. "Of course. I'm very sorry for your loss. As I said, your sister and I had a very pleasant conversation, and I'm distraught to hear of her death."

Sydney nodded to him in thanks and walked out the door.

Chapter Eighteen

Jack Cassian stood on the front steps of the Chapin mansion. Although it was evening, the temperature still loomed near eighty, and the air was heavy with the taste of honeysuckle and wisteria. He was off duty, technically, but still on the job. Chief Torbert had made it clear that although they were to intrude on the Chapin family as little as possible, he still wanted them to keep them up to date on the investigation. Train had personal business to attend to and was already offended at the special consideration granted the wealthy family, so Jack had offered to give that evening's update.

Sydney Chapin opened the door, dressed much as she'd been the last time he'd been there—worn jeans and a loose-fitting top—and her hair was down, falling in golden brown streams around her shoulders. It took a moment for him to realize how attractive he found her. Her beauty wasn't obvious in the way it was for many attractive women; she had the kind of looks that snuck up on you.

"Detective Cassian, right?" she asked, interrupting his musings.

"Yes. Hi, Sydney," he said, feeling oddly unsure of himself. "I'm sorry for disturbing you during the evening again."

"That's all right, Detective. My mother and niece went out to dinner—Amanda's been cooped up here all day, and my mother thought it would be a good idea for her to get out of the house, even if just for a little while. It's pretty much just me here."

"Oh," Cassian said stupidly. "Well, I have an update on the investigation, but maybe I should come back tomorrow when everyone's here."

"No, no," Sydney insisted. "Please, tell me what's happening, and I'll pass the information on to my mother and Amanda. I won't get to sleep without knowing."

Jack nodded. "Okay." He stood in the doorway for a moment before suggesting, "Should I come in?"

"Oh, yes, of course," Sydney said, looking flustered. She opened the door wider and ushered him in. "I'm sorry," she said. "It seems like I've been walking through the last couple of days or so in a haze."

"You seem better tonight than the other evening," Jack commented. It was true, too. The color had returned to her face, and there was a certain determination to her carriage that had been absent the first time they met. She led him into a huge kitchen and offered him a seat at a polished granite island the size of Nantucket.

"Well, yeah, I hope so," she said matter-of-factly. "I was a mess. I'm still a bit of a mess now, but I think the shock has worn off, at least."

"It'll take some time," Jack said. "Don't rush it."

She nodded. "So, what have you found out about Liz's murder?"

"We've got a possible suspect."

She nodded. "I read that in the newspaper. I think the police chief also called my mother."

"I'm not surprised."

"My mother was thrilled with how quickly you all are moving on this. We're very happy you caught the man."

"I'm glad, although I should warn you that we haven't charged him yet. We still have to complete our investigation."

"Still, it's good that you found him so quickly, isn't it?"

Jack nodded. "That's the way it usually works. Most murders are either solved in the first day or two, or they're never solved. In this case, we got lucky with a fingerprint."

"Have you learned anything about the man who you've arrested?"

"Nothing surprising. He's a lowlife and a drug dealer who hangs out in your sister's neighborhood. We've run into him before, but never for something like this."

"But you're pretty sure he did it?" Her voice sounded hopeful.

"He's our best suspect right now," Cassian said. "We checked his alibi; not surprisingly, a couple of his homies swear he was with them, although we think their stories will probably break down in the end. We're also looking to connect him to your sister's credit cards or any of the other things stolen from the apartment."

"What happens if you can't?"

"That's up to the prosecutor. I'm not convinced we'd have enough to convict on the fingerprint alone, but you never know."

Sydney walked over to one of the two huge refrigerators that took up almost the entire space along one wall of the kitchen. She opened the door and pulled out a bottle of beer, turning to look over her shoulder at Jack. "Can I offer you anything—beer or something?"

Jack was tempted. He was technically off duty, after all, and sharing a drink with this attractive young woman would be nice. On the other hand, he knew he'd catch hell if it ever got back to the chief, or even to Train, for that matter. "Just a water would be great, thanks."

She pulled out a Heineken for herself, and an Evian for him. She handed him his water and reached into a drawer for an opener. Picking up her beer in one hand, she flicked her wrist and the bottle top flipped off and landed in the garbage bin next to the enormous island.

"Impressive," Jack commented.

"Thanks," she said. "I bartended my way through college."

"Really?" Jack looked around the kitchen at all of the top-of-the-line appliances and expensive custom-carved cabinetry. "I wouldn't have pegged you as someone who would have had to work their way through much of anything."

Sydney frowned. "If I'd wanted to be under my family's control, I'm sure I could have avoided getting my hands dirty," she agreed. "But as long as I'm making my own money and paying my own way through my life, nobody can tell me what to do. Besides, I thought it would be fun—and a great way to meet guys."

"And was it?"

"Fun? Yes." She took a sip of her beer. "I met a lot of guys, too—just never any of the right ones." She seemed to study him for a moment, and he found himself wondering what she was thinking. "It wasn't until I got interested in the law that I gave it up. Funny how sometimes in life a direction finds you, rather than the other way around, you know?"

"I do," he replied.

"How about you?" she asked.

"How about me what?"

She shrugged. "Is that how you ended up on the police force? Just drawn to it?" She was still looking a little too closely at him, and it unnerved him.

"Family business," he said after giving the question brief consideration.

"Father?" she pressed.

He shook his head. "Brother."

"He must be proud," she said. He didn't reply. "Well," she continued, letting the subject drop, "if there's anything we can appreciate in the Chapin household, it's the pressures of the family business."

"I got that impression the other night."

She nodded. "My mother's a handful, isn't she?"

"That's one word for it." Cassian remained noncommittal.

"When I was younger, my father ran the family business and my mother ran the household. When I say she ran the household, I mean she *ran* the household." She pulled the label off her beer as she spoke. "When my father got sick, my mom took over the running of the company, and you know what?" She looked up at Cassian.

"What?"

"She turned out to be a better CEO than my dad."

Cassian looked at her closely. Her head was down again, and her fingers worked at the label. "Must have been hard when you were growing up, having someone that demanding running the house."

She shook her head. "There were a lot of people she was tougher on than me." She turned her head on a swivel, as if to check and see whether anyone was eavesdropping on them alone in the kitchen. Then she cupped her hand and whispered, "Like *The Help*." Cassian recognized the imitation of her mother's voice. She smiled conspiratorially at him, and he couldn't help smiling back. Then her face turned serious. "And my sister," she added.

"How so?"

She sipped her beer again before she answered. "She was much older than me, so there was a lot more that was expected of her. She was the one who was supposed to help with the business, which means she was expected to be perfect. You know, when I was growing up, I never saw her lose—at anything." She put her beer down. "Can you imagine living with that kind of pressure?"

"Can't be easy," Cassian agreed, trying not to get in the way of her thoughts.

"No, it can't be easy," she echoed him. "And then, add to that the pressure to produce a grandchild—preferably a grand*son*." Cassian raised his eyebrows at her and she held up her hand. "Don't worry, Detective, I'm fine with being a woman—always have been. I just always got the feeling that my parents were hoping to have at least one son." She looked off into space for a moment. "I suppose that's only natural, but it always seemed to add extra pressure. I think once it was clear that Liz and I were going to be their only children, they put their hopes into having a grandson."

"Is that why your sister got married?" Cassian asked quietly.

Sydney nodded. "She never really loved Leighton."

She rolled her eyes. "My parents loved Leighton, though. At least, they loved the package that Leighton presented. He was tall and good-looking and funny, and he came from a family that could trace its roots back to the *Mayflower*—even if the money the family once had was long gone." She raised her beer in a mock toast. "What more could you want in a husband?"

Jack raised his bottle of water, meeting her toast. "You tell me," he said.

"You could want a man with a brain," she said. "Or maybe one with a conscience, or a heart, or some self-control." She seemed to realize she was letting her anger show, and she cut herself off.

"What happened?" Jack pressed.

She sighed. "Things seemed good for a while, at least on the outside. Amanda was born within a year of the wedding, and even though she was a girl, my parents were thrilled to have a grandchild. Leighton had been working at one of my father's companies before they got married, in a minor executive's position, but after the wedding he started to work his way up the corporate ladder in spite of his obvious shortcomings. Everyone seemed happy."

"But it didn't last?"

She shook her head. "Maybe a few years. I don't really know what happened first—who lost interest in who. At some point it became clear to my father that Leighton wasn't smart enough to be tapped as a real successor, and the rapid promotions came to a halt. Leighton and Liz drifted apart; he started drinking heavily; there were rumors about him sleeping around. Then Liz started feeling resentful and trapped. Unfortunately, Amanda got trapped in the middle of all of it. At some point, Liz felt like she'd had enough, and she confronted Leighton; that's when things got really ugly."

"What happened?"

"Leighton was out with one of his girlfriends—he wasn't even really trying to hide them anymore. Amanda was over at a friend's house across the street, so Liz had the house to herself. She packed a couple of bags for herself and Amanda and waited for Leighton to get home. When he got home, he was drunk. She told him it was over, and he hit the roof. He told her she wasn't going to leave; that she belonged to him. She asked him why he cared, when he had the other women in his life, and when they hadn't had any physical relationship to speak of in years. I guess that sent him over the edge, and he started beating her. Badly."

Cassian sat still in his chair. He wanted to say something, but it felt somehow like interrupting her would cut short the wellspring of information.

"He started tearing her clothes off as he beat her; first with his fists, but then at some point he switched to using the handle of a broken golf club that must have been lying around. Liz never really talked to me about it until this winter, when we started to get closer for the first time. She said that when he was beating her and tearing at her clothes, he kept screaming, 'You wanna get fucked? There, now you're fucked!' And then he raped her." Cassian's eyes widened, and she nodded. "Yeah, I guess all the beating turned him on," she said.

"That's sick," Cassian noted with a quiet, seething anger in his voice.

"You haven't heard the worst part," Sydney said. "At some point during all of this, Amanda came home."

"And saw all this happen?"

Sydney nodded. "She'd forgotten her sleeping bag or something like that, and she'd walked back across the street from her friend's house to get it. Apparently she came in and saw what was happening. She started screaming and picked up a metal poker from the fireplace and attacked Leighton while he was still on top of Liz. They left that night, and I don't think Amanda has seen or spoken to her father since."

Cassian shook his head. "Jesus, this girl's gone through hell a couple of times, huh?"

"She's had it rough," Sydney agreed. "But she's tough. She's got a lot of both Liz and my mother in her—for good or bad."

"Why didn't your mother want you to tell us all this the other night?"

Sydney shrugged. "I don't know. I'm pretty sure my mother tried to convince Liz to work things out with Leighton—'for the good of the family'—and she and Liz got into a huge fight. I think Liz blamed my mother for pushing her into the marriage in the first place." She looked at Cassian as she tried to explain her mother's behavior. "I also think it's just still difficult for my mother to admit that everything in Liz's life wasn't perfect."

Cassian shook his head. "It's still information that we should have been given at the outset of the investigation."

"I know. That's why I'm telling you now." She hesitated, looking at him with trepidation. "Do you think Leighton could have done this?"

"From the sounds of things, he could be capable of something like this. It's not a significant leap from beating and rape to murder." He shook his head. "We'll have to have a talk with him, obviously, but it looks far more likely right now that Jerome Washington's our man. The whole MO fits his pattern, and, like I said, we've got his fingerprint at the scene."

Sydney picked up her empty beer bottle and threw it into the trash. For a moment, she seemed lost, as if there was something she wanted to do, but she couldn't figure out what it was—like when you walk into a room and realize that you've forgotten what you were looking for. "God, it's frustrating. It just seems so . . . I don't know, random. If it had been Leighton—or maybe someone she'd written an article about—I think I'd have an easier time with that. At least then there would be someone to hate, and as angry as I'd be, at least her murder would make sense to me. But this feels almost more like she was just at the wrong place at the wrong time. That probably sounds crazy."

Cassian set his water on the endless polished granite in front of him and regarded her in earnest. "You and your family—and especially your niece—are going to go through a wide, bizarre range of emotions over the next few weeks and months. None of it's crazy. It's all a part of dealing with this type of extreme trauma."

She was studying his face, and it made him self-conscious again. "You don't talk the way I'd expect a cop to talk."

He smiled unsteadily. "I'm not sure how to interpret that."

She tilted her head. "Neither am I."

The moment stretched on and his self-consciousness deepened. At last, he cleared his throat. "I should be going," he said. "I just wanted you and your family to know where we were on all this."

The words seemed to snap Sydney out of the trance she'd fallen into. "I appreciate that," she said. "And I'm sure my mother will, too." Again there was silence between them, though briefer. Then she continued. "I'll walk you out."

He followed her to the front door. "Thank you for the water," he said as she opened the door.

"No problem," she replied.

He stepped out onto the front porch and began heading down the steps. Then he stopped and reached into his jacket pocket. He pulled out a business card and handed it to her. "That's my phone number at the station house," he said. "My cell number is on the back. If you or Amanda or even your mother find that you're having trouble dealing with all this, give me a call and I can hook you up with some great people to talk to at various victims' services outfits." He looked at her. "They can really help."

He wanted to say more, but nothing came to him. After a moment of standing there on the steps in silence, she nodded at him and he nodded back. Then he turned and headed back down the stairs without another word.

Chapter Nineteen

LEE SALVAGE SAT in his dingy office on Eleventh and Q, eyeing the bottle of bourbon on his desk. The window to the first-floor office was crusted over, which was fine with him, given the crappy neighborhood. He could have afforded better digs, but his current environs were more conducive to his line of business.

Besides, he thought, once he finished this job, he could retire to wherever he wanted. There was a time when he wouldn't have thought of giving up his gig, but time and booze had sucked much of the bloodlust from him. He was still in reasonably decent shape, and was one of the best in the business, but something had changed. He still felt no guilt at the things he was required to do, like killing Peter King, but he felt no excitement either.

He held the phone to his ear as he fought the siren song of the Old Crow only inches away. He moved his free hand from the bottle and ran it through his wispy blond hair, just to keep it occupied.

"What the hell was she doing at Barneton's office?" his client was demanding, as though Salvage had sent Sydney Chapin there himself.

"Not sure," he replied. "She works at the law school, so it's possible that it was work-related."

"Is that what you think is likely?"

Salvage picked at his ear. "No."

"Is it possible that the visit was personal in the more traditional sense of the word?" the client asked. "You're aware of Barneton's reputation with women, I assume."

"Of course," Salvage acknowledged. He toyed with the notion and dismissed it. "I don't think she's the type to fall for Barneton's shtick—particularly two days after her sister's murder."

"What was she doing there, then?" The client was growing more and more distressed, which annoyed Salvage. He deserved better than this shit. On the other hand, he was used to it. People only came to him when they were desperate; only those in panic mode were willing to spend the kind of money required to retain his services. He provided a buffer between them and whatever unpleasantness they needed taken care of.

"Again, I don't know. It's possible she found out that her sister met with Barneton on the day she died. It could be a simple matter of curiosity."

"Curiosity is exactly what we're looking to avoid."

"The police think they've got their guy in Jerome Washington," Salvage pointed out. "That's the important thing."

"For the moment, yes, that's true," the client agreed. "But we can't afford any further poking around into our affairs."

"Understood." Salvage hesitated. "Do you want me to have someone take care of the girl to be on the safe side?"

"No. It would look suspicious if she was killed right after her sister. That would only raise new questions."

"There are ways to make it look plausible. No one would question it."

The client considered this for a moment, but remained unmoved. "We'll revisit that as an option if it becomes necessary in the future, but for right now, I just want her watched. And Mr. Salvage?"

"Yeah?"

"I want you personally involved from now on. I had no idea you were going to farm out the Elizabeth Creay matter to Mr. King, and I'm not pleased. The fewer people involved, the better."

"You don't have to worry about Mr. King anymore. Besides, if I have to handle everything myself, it'll cost you more."

The client laughed bitterly. "Do you think I care about cost? This cannot be allowed to go any further. If it appears she's moving in a direction that would cause any significant risk, I give you complete discretion to handle the matter as you see fit."

Salvage reached out and ran his fingers down the bottle lovingly. "Understood," he replied. Then he hung up the phone and stretched out in his chair as shouting erupted outside, followed by gunshots. *Just get through this job*, he reminded himself, *and you're in the clear.*

Chapter Twenty

JACK CASSIAN AWOKE the following Monday feeling restless. The investigation into Elizabeth Creay's murder seemed stalled. Washington's alibi, though shaky, seemed to be holding, and they hadn't been able to tie him to anything stolen from Creay's apartment. If nothing moved the investigation any closer to a solid case against Washington they would probably have to start chasing down other angles, an option none of the higher-ups in the department seemed anxious to exercise.

Sydney Chapin's revelations about Liz's ex, Leighton Creay, had highlighted the most likely second suspect in their search for the killer, but they were still getting pressure from above to run out everything with Jerome Washington before turning to anyone else. If something didn't break soon, he and Train would have no choice but to confront Leighton with the information Jack had learned from Sydney.

Sydney was a remarkable woman in many ways, he reflected as he lay in bed contemplating the week ahead of him. She was attractive, to be sure, but there was something more to her than just her looks. Something besides her appearance that made her different—a depth and intelligence that accentuated her outward appearance and made her looks irrelevant. He stretched against the sheets and pillows. Well, not *irrelevant*, he thought as he smiled to himself.

He was sure that he'd felt something between them the previous Friday evening when he'd visited her mother's house. The way she'd looked at him went beyond the occasional transference those touched by tragedy experienced toward those who helped them cope through the trauma. He wondered whether he could invent an excuse to see her again. It would be transparent, he knew, and arguably inappropriate, but he was tempted nonetheless. He felt the sheets acutely on his body as he thought about her.

The phone rang, shaking him loose from his daydream. He reached over and grabbed the receiver. "What?" he said sharply.

"Have we abandoned all efforts at improving our phone manners?" Train's voice came through the phone.

"I was just lying here feeling good about myself for the first time in a while, and you had to go and interrupt it," Cassian grumbled.

"Is there a young lady there feeling good about you, too?"

"Unfortunately not," Cassian admitted. "But that doesn't make the moment any less special."

"It should," Train pointed out. "In any case, the moment's over."

"What's up?"

"We've got a cold one, lying off a path in Rock Creek Park up here near the Twenty-eighth Street entrance."

Cassian looked at his watch. *Six-thirty.* He wondered how it was that Train always seemed to get this type of information so early in the morning. "Okay," he said. "I'll meet you there in a couple of minutes."

Cassian pulled his battered motorcycle up onto the curb at Twenty-eighth Street between two squad cars that were parked in front of the entrance to the park. He nodded and flashed his badge to the officer who was standing sentry on the sidewalk, guarding the pathway that led down to the creek.

"Train here?" he asked the patrolman. Everyone knew who Train was; at his size, he was difficult to miss.

The cop nodded. "Got here a couple of minutes ago. He's down the path to the right," he said.

Cassian ducked under the police tape that had been strung across the park's entrance and started down the path. A few hundred yards along, he spotted Train talking to Deter. His partner beckoned him over. Cassian could see several technicians picking their way carefully through the bushes to the left of the path, toward the creek, where he assumed the body had been discovered.

"I'm just getting the rundown," Train said. "You wanna walk through what you've told me, to get our sleepy friend here up to speed?"

"Sure," Deter replied. He moved them over toward the bushes. "We've got a very deceased white male, probably in his early forties, shot at least three times from behind. Two shots hit just under the left clavicle, and one entered the back of his skull. Either very professional or very lucky. Any of them could have been fatal—we'll have to wait for the autopsy to be sure which one did the job."

"Any idea who our unfortunate friend might be?" Cassian asked.

Deter shook his head. "No wallet, no papers, no nothing. We're assuming for the moment that it's a basic robbery. Judging from the condition of the body, I'm guessing he's been here for three or four days. He's well dressed, so somebody's probably already missed him either at work or at home. I'm sure we'll pull something from the recent missing persons reports, and that will help identify him. Our best bet is that he was just taking a walk in the park one night last week and the local welcome wagon came up behind him." Deter made a gun with his fingers, his thumb pointing upward like a hammer. "Pop! Pop! Pop! The perp then takes his wallet and whatever else the guy might have had with him, and rolls him into the bushes."

"So what's the guy doing walking through the park at night?" Train asked skeptically.

Deter shrugged his shoulders. "People do some stupid things, Sarge."

"We don't need to hear about your love life, Deter," Cassian joked.

"Look at it this way," Deter continued, ignoring Cassian, "if no one ever did anything dumb, we'd probably be out of our jobs."

"I'd be happy to find something else to do for a living," Train offered.

"Right," quipped Cassian to Deter. "Sarge has always had an interest in pursuing a career in ballet." The huge man shot a warning glare at his partner, which Cassian ignored. "More to the point, does it fit the MO of any other recent killings?"

"I think the manner of killing is a little too crude to qualify as an MO," Deter said. "We've had a couple of quick-kills down in Anacostia that are a little similar, though. Maybe the pinheads down there decided to come up to the nicer end of town for a better class of victim."

"Do we have anything at all to help us identify the vic?" Cassian asked. "Anything that might generate a list of suspects?"

Deter shook his head. "Nothing. Guy could be anyone. Average height, average weight, brown hair."

Something about the way Deter described the victim seemed familiar to Cassian. He chuckled quietly after a moment's reflection. "Probably missing one of his pinky fingers, too, right?" he joked, winking at Train as he said it.

"News travels fast," Deter said. "You talk to one of the guys on the forensics team out on the street or something?"

Cassian's smile disappeared and he looked over at Train. He could already see the consternation showing on his partner's face. "What're you saying, Deter?" Train asked cautiously.

Deter looked confused by the detectives' sudden change in demeanor. "I'm not saying anything," he said. "You're saying it."

"Saying what?" Cassian demanded, the feeling of dread growing in his stomach.

"About the guy's finger," Deter said defensively. "He's missing one of his pinky fingers, like you said."

"Which one?" Train demanded.

"What's the difference?"

"Tell me," Train pressed.

Deter thought for a moment. "Right hand," he said finally.

Both detectives stared hard at Deter, then glanced at each other, exchanging a look of understanding. Finally

Train turned back to Deter. "Let's put the analysis of this scene at the top of our priority list, okay?"

"It could be a coincidence," Cassian pointed out.

Train looked at his partner over his coffee cup as he took a sip. They were grabbing a quick breakfast at a Dupont Circle coffee shop, having finished up at the crime scene. Train's head hurt. "I don't believe in coincidences anymore. Do you?"

"They do happen," Cassian argued halfheartedly. Train rolled his eyes. "They do," Cassian persisted. "And this one isn't even that big a coincidence, really. A missing finger? Lots of people lose fingers, probably. What does it mean, necessarily?"

Train frowned. "It means we've got to look into it a little more closely." He was torn. For days they'd been working under the primary assumption that Jerome Washington killed Elizabeth Creay. Even if he wasn't completely sold on the notion, he couldn't get beyond the fact that Jerome fit the crime, and Train loathed the idea that they were going to have to abandon him as a suspect. It would also mean going back over the case from square one, and precious time had been wasted that might prevent the murder from ever being solved. It would also mean digging deeper into Elizabeth Creay's personal life, and the lives of her family, a process that, given the prominence of the clan, posed serious political drawbacks.

All of these considerations rattled in Train's head, making clear the argument that they should just leave the whole thing alone. After all, Cassian could be right. It could just be a coincidence, and there was no question that the city would be better off with Jerome Washington locked away. He'd already been charged with the possession, and the DA's office had been pressing Train to make the murder rap stick. In some ways, the easiest thing to do would be to let the prosecutorial machinery grind Jerome to a pulp and be done with it. But then, Train thought, there was the Truth.

The Truth was what had drawn Train to the police department in the first place. During that turbulent time in the early seventies, when Train saw the system used to the disadvantage of blacks, the notion of investigating crimes free from any bias based on race or creed or color, in a true quest to find the Truth, had been what had inspired him to find a purpose when all of his athletic hopes and dreams had fallen apart. So often, he knew from bitter experience, the police treated crime as a statistical shell game, using the department's conviction rate to tout its success and convince a frightened public that they were getting their money's worth. That approach had often resulted in the conviction of people—usually black people—who, while not necessarily innocent in the grand scheme of things, had not committed the crimes for which they were convicted. He'd vowed to change all that, and as much as he hated to admit it to himself, Jerome's accusation that no one in the city cared about "just another dead nigger" had struck a nerve.

"What do you want to do?" Cassian asked.

Train knew what he had to do. "Go down to the morgue," he said to Cassian. "Get a head shot of the John Doe from the park this morning, and get nine other head shots of dead white guys with brown hair."

"We gonna give Jerome a lineup?"

Train shrugged. "Seems like the only way to be sure."

Cassian shook his head. "There's no way it's gonna make any difference," he pointed out. "Even if Jerome's telling the truth, the odds that he'd be able to recognize this guy from a head shot after he's been dead and lying in the bushes for a couple of days are still about a thousand to one."

Train nodded. "No argument," he conceded. "But it seems like we've got to give him that chance."

Chapter Twenty-one

LYDIA CHAPIN WALKED briskly through the lobby of the Hay-Adams Hotel across the street from the White House. Had she looked to her left, into the oak bar that had served as an informal negotiating room for three generations of power brokers in the nation's capital, she might have seen two or three people she would have recognized. The intimate little cubbyhole was frequented by congressmen and senators who depended on Chapin Industries' generous political contributions to fend off cyclical challenges every election. That dependence led to access and influence, and had always served Chapin Industries well.

But Lydia wasn't interested in talking shop. She needed only one thing at the moment—a pay phone. Certainly she couldn't make this call from her home or from any of the offices at the company's headquarters, and she'd been warned that her cell phone wasn't "secure," whatever that meant. She understood enough, though, to realize the technology was available to intercept cell calls over the airwaves, so that unwanted eavesdroppers might overhear something too dangerous to be made public. A pay phone made the most sense; one that couldn't be linked back to her, and which would provide adequate protections from intrusion. That was what made her think of the Hay-Adams. It had been catering to Washington's elite for more than a century. It was the favored spot for those seeking privacy, those who considered themselves "on the inside"—diplomats and foreign dignitaries and industrial tycoons. It was rumored that much of the world's fate during the second half of the twentieth century had been determined within the walls of the quaint hotel on Sixteenth Street. Wars had been planned, treaties negotiated, coups plotted, and because of its particular clientele, Lydia recalled, the pay phones offered more privacy than most.

She walked through the lobby and past the front desk. The desk clerk looked up and, not recognizing her as a guest, actually thought to ask if she needed help. But she carried herself with the self-assured air of the unquestionably wealthy, and he quickly decided that she properly belonged there—guest or not—and went back to the mundane administrative task demanding his attention at the moment.

She rounded the corner and came upon the pay phones. They were lined along the wall, each with its own booth and door that closed fully to provide privacy. There were five of them in all. She walked down the aisle, noting that the first three booths were taken, their occupants each talking animatedly into the receiver without a hint of sound escaping from the enclosures. Lydia was gratified at the privacy of the booths, but suddenly worried that she might have to wait for a phone. That wouldn't do; she was already late. Fortunately, as she continued to walk down the row, she saw that the last two booths were unoccupied. She slipped into the last one on the row.

A light came on automatically when she closed the door. She looked around, satisfied with the enclosure. The walls were lined in perforated leather, and a well-cushioned chair extended out from the wall, allowing her to sit.

She lowered herself onto the chair and took the receiver off the hook. Holding it away from her face for a moment, she examined it with disdain, as though it were too common for her. After a pause, she pulled a handkerchief out of her purse and wiped off the mouthpiece. Replacing the handkerchief into her bag, she reached in again and pulled out a slip of paper with a number written carefully on it. She squinted at the paper as she reached up and dialed the number.

"Hello?" The phone was answered before the first ring was completed.

"Hello," Lydia replied.

"You're late." Leighton Creay's voice was snippy. "I told you to call at twelve-thirty, and it's already quarter to one." Lydia held her tongue in spite of the petulance. It was all she could do to keep from screaming. "It seems our circumstances have changed," he continued after a brief pause.

"I don't see how," Lydia replied, but the break in her voice betrayed her.

"Yes you do," Creay replied, gaining more confidence. "You're a smart woman, Lydia. Always have been; so don't waste my time."

She hated that the man had dared to use her first name. "What do you want?" she asked slowly, trying to control the rage in her voice.

"More money, of course."

"We had a deal." She knew she sounded weak and plaintive, but there was little she could do about it.

"We had a deal before things changed. I kept that deal. Now the deal is over and it's time to renegotiate."

"Nothing in our deal made any mention of what would happen if the situation changed as it has. I don't see why—"

"Because I said so," Leighton said forcefully. "I know you never really cared about your daughter, so now the question is: do you care about your granddaughter?"

"You're scum," Lydia said through clenched teeth.

Creay laughed. "Oh, Lydia. I think that coming from you I may have to take that as a compliment." Then the laughter was gone. "Have the money for me by tomorrow, or don't plan on ever seeing Amanda again."

Lydia thought for a moment, trying to set aside the anger she felt and work rationally through all the issues with which she was confronted. "How much more?" she asked.

"I think, in light of all that has happened, double our original deal would be reasonable."

Her head spun. She couldn't allow herself to be played in this way, she knew, or it would never end. "I can't get the money by tomorrow," she lied.

"Then we'll just have to charge you some interest," Creay replied. "I think an extra hundred grand would be reasonable for an extra day."

"You'll have the money by the end of next week," Lydia said. "But you should be careful who you threaten like this."

A low, confident chuckle came over the line. "Lydia," Creay chided, "I have no interest in anything but the best of relationships with you. The end of next week is fine, but let's call it an extra two hundred thousand in interest. That shouldn't present a problem for someone in your position."

Lydia was seething. "You really are scum," she said.

"Now is not the time for you to play tough, Lydia. You know what I'm capable of." There was a long silence on the line, and then Leighton asked, "Friday, then?" Hearing no reply, he continued. "Have the money ready and I'll contact you." Then the line went dead.

Lydia was shaking with impotent rage when she hung up the receiver and left the luxurious phone booth in the lobby of the Hay-Adams. How could this happen? She knew that the phone calls would never stop. Not until her family and her company were bled dry. *After all that I've done, I will not let that come to pass.* By the time she reached the front door of the hotel the shaking had subsided. Resolve had settled into the core of Lydia Chapin, and a plan was beginning to take shape in her mind.

Five seconds. That's all it took.

Train and Cassian walked without explanation into the interrogation room at the District lockup, where Jerome Washington was sitting expressionless in a bright orange jumpsuit, courtesy of the corrections department, and shackles around his wrists and ankles. Jerome protested at first, demanding, "I want my lawyer," as they pulled two folding chairs up against the table.

"Shut up, Jerome," Cassian warned. "This is for your own good."

Washington gave a snort of disbelief, but was quiet.

Train sat down and put the stack of pictures facedown in front of him. "I'm going to lay out ten pictures here on the table, Jerome. And I want you to tell me what you see," he said.

"Why?"

"Because Sergeant Train told you to, asshole," Cassian told him.

"Trust me, Jerome," Train said. "This may be your only chance." Then he flipped the ten pictures over quickly so they were laid out in two neat rows of five. All of the men in the pictures were dead. Cassian had borrowed them from the District morgue's office. They were all Caucasians with brown hair, generally fitting the same description. Cassian had tried to choose pictures as closely resembling the John Doe from Rock Creek as possible; no reason to make this little farce any easier for Jerome. The man found that morning was in the bottom row, second from the left.

Jerome took five seconds, his eyes scanning over the images in the pictures, looking from one to the next until he came to the man from the park. When his eyes lit on that image, they widened, his mouth dropping open as he pointed. "That's the motherfucker!" he shouted.

Train shot a glance at Cassian, who rubbed his temples as if in pain. "That's what motherfucker, Jerome?" Train asked.

"Get the fuck outta here, Train," Jerome said, his voice filled with anger. "You know goddamned well what motherfucker that is!"

"I don't, Jerome. Tell me."

"This is bullshit!" Jerome looked back and forth between the detectives. Then, at last, he threw his hands up. "That's the motherfucker who bought the dime bag and the torch off me. That's the motherfucker in the blue sedan who was down a digit." He looked expectantly at Train. "This mean I get the fuck outta here now?"

Train shook his head. "No, Jerome. It doesn't."

"The fuck it don't!" Jerome shouted back. "You found

the man. He's the one who did the bitch on G Street, not me. I know it, and now you know it, too. So you go on and get me the fuck outta here!"

"We don't know shit, Jerome," Cassian shot back. "All we know is that you're looking at the needle, and so you're looking for any way out of this mess. You'd say anything to make that happen." He picked up the picture Jerome had identified. "We don't have any idea who this guy is. Besides, you're already being charged with possession, and as an accessory to attempted murder based on the shots your friend took at Sergeant Train."

"Those are bullshit charges, and you know it!"

"Now you're telling me what I know, Jerome?"

"Then why'd you bring me in here to show me these?" Washington demanded, his manacled hands slapping awkwardly at the pictures on the table. He stared down both officers, and this time it was Train and Cassian who looked away first. "Thought so," he proclaimed in triumph.

Train looked back at Washington. "We'll get back to you," he said, filling his voice with as much moral authority as it would hold. He got up out of his chair and Cassian followed him toward the door.

"Man, that's bullshit!" Washington called after them. "You'll get back to me? I didn't do the bitch, Train." He was pulling at his shackles, straining to still be heard. "You know I didn't do this, Train!"

The door closed behind the two detectives, and they could still hear Washington screaming in the room behind them. "What do you think now?" Train asked his partner.

Cassian shrugged. "I don't know what to think at this point. Seems like a pretty big coincidence." Train nodded. "Then again," Cassian suggested, "we really don't know what the hell's going on. I mean, for all we know, Jerome killed our stiff from the park, and he made up the story hoping we'd find the body and it'd look like he'd been set up."

"Interesting theory," Train said. "You think it washes?" Cassian shook his head slowly. "Me neither." Train rubbed his bald scalp. "The only thing I know at this point is that I don't like the feeling this case is giving me. I think we may need to dig a little deeper into Elizabeth Creay's life."

Chapter Twenty-two

THE SUN WAS OUT on the Wednesday Elizabeth Creay was interred in the cemetery behind Christ Church in Washington, beating down on the mourners relentlessly as they sweated in the early summer D.C. humidity. The programs, which Lydia Chapin had ordered from a posh stationer in Georgetown, and which were filled with inspirational passages from the New Testament, were appreciated more as makeshift fans than as guides to spiritual healing. Dressed in a simple dark gray suit, Sydney thought the weather was the final cosmic insult heaped upon her sister, who had always preferred the cool of late autumn and had suffered terribly through Washington's summers. She stood just behind her mother and Amanda, letting her eyes wander, taking in the somber menagerie that had gathered at the family plot.

She was amazed at the sheer number of people. The death of someone so young, brought about by such violent means, could, she supposed, bring out even the most casual acquaintance, but the mood of the crowd suggested a grief more genuine than mere curiosity could explain. Sydney found herself wondering how many people would show up at her own funeral were she to die so young. Fewer, certainly, she concluded. It was petty of her to feel the pangs of jealousy at seeing the outpouring of emotion at her sister's funeral. But there it was; the final, dying gasp of a sibling rivalry that had defined her relationship with Liz until only months before her death.

Sydney put those thoughts out of her mind. Her focus should be on Amanda, she resolved, for whom the day would be the hardest. The girl was directly in front of her at the casket, standing straight and brave next to her grandmother. She was shorter than Lydia, and less substantial through the shoulders, but something about her posture suggested a kinship between the two. Both had their chins high, and carried themselves with a regal defiance. Lydia was wearing a black satin jacket buttoned at the front to the neckline, where the high lace collar of her white blouse took over. Amanda had been unable to find anything to wear that her grandmother deemed suitable, so she wore a newly purchased charcoal dress with a hint of a floral pattern sewn into the shadows of the fabric. "It sends the right message," Lydia had explained when she picked out the dress, and while Sydney had been livid at her mother's insensitivity, she had to admit that the outfit had a remarkably appropriate feel.

Sydney turned her attention back to the crowd. Most of Liz's friends and coworkers from the *Post* were on hand; the editor in chief, the section heads, Liz's editor, as well as an army of reporters and columnists. Many of the people with whom Liz had worked on various charities and civic organizations were also there. And then there were Lydia's people, who included many of Washington's power brokers, from senators and congressmen to high-priced lawyers and lobbyists. There were even a couple of talking heads from the twenty-four-hour news stations, no doubt looking for an angle on the story of Liz's death.

As Sydney panned through the crowd, her eyes were drawn to an enormous, dark figure she recognized instantly on the outskirts of the gathering. *Detective Train*, she thought. He stood out in the crowd, as huge as he was, his head hovering several inches above the average attendee. Looking to the right of him, she saw Jack Cassian also. Her heart gave an involuntary start; not necessarily one of infatuation, she thought, but certainly one of curiosity—the seed of infatuation. She'd felt it before, the other night when he'd stopped by her mother's house. It was a feeling of discovery and excitement that delivered a slow drip of adrenaline in his presence and made her extremities tingle.

Both detectives noticed her looking in their direction, and they nodded respectfully. Their expressions conveyed a sincerity of condolence that she had no reason to question, and yet she wondered why they were there. It would not be unusual, she supposed, for the detectives who had investigated a murder to develop some personal posthumous attachment to the victim, and for that attachment to draw them to a memorial service. But as she looked at their faces, she suspected there was something more. As sincere as their acknowledgment seemed, there was also something else mixed with the sympathy. There was an alertness to their eyes as they examined the crowd, almost as if they were evaluating and cataloging suspects. Jack noticed that she was continuing to watch him as he observed the crowd, and he seemed uncomfortable, as though he'd been caught at something illicit.

She frowned as she turned back to the interment. The Anglican priest, who had clearly never actually known

Liz, was finishing his emotional and fictitious remembrance of her deceased sister. Others might find it comforting that one could be so fondly eulogized by a complete stranger, but it made Sydney feel sad. It was as though a person's life meant little in its specifics; that the standard platitudes could be applied equally to all.

The service concluded, and Sydney approached the casket with Amanda and Lydia, each of them placing a rose on the expensive polished maplewood coffin. Then Liz's remains were lowered hydraulically into the ground next to their father in the family plot that her parents had purchased over twenty years before. She noticed that the tract of land was large, pocked only by the two headstones marking the final resting spots for Liz and their father—plenty of room for generations to come and go, only to be corralled in death under the watchful eyes of her parents. The thought chilled Sydney.

After the priest finished the final benediction, and the light humming of the hydraulic winch ceased, signaling that Liz's body had reached the bottom of the pit, the crowd began to disperse. A number of brave souls approached the family to offer their personal regrets, only to be greeted by her mother's icy formality and her niece's painful reticence. Sydney tried to generate enough small talk to paper over the uncomfortable moments, but even she found it difficult. After the first few attempts, she abandoned the effort and fell back on empty nods and vapid, expressionless "thank you"s in response to the myriad condolences.

When the stream of well-wishers hit a lull, Sydney took the opportunity to drift over toward Cassian and Train. She'd expected them to be among the first to depart the cemetery, unlikely to be interested in prolonged expressions of emotion, but they hadn't left yet. They remained at the edge of the crowd, standing patiently as the mourners filed out past them.

She nodded at Train. "Detective," she said. And then to Cassian, "Detective Cassian." She held Cassian's eyes for several beats longer than she had Train's, and wondered whether Jack's partner would notice. Not that she would care.

"Miss Chapin," Train said politely, "once again, we'd like to express our deepest sympathies, and those of the entire department, at your sister's death."

"Thank you," she replied after a moment. "I appreciate both of you being here." She looked back over at her mother and Amanda. Lydia was shaking hands with one of Liz's colleagues from the newspaper, her smile so waxy and stiff that it was painful to look at. Amanda, standing next to her grandmother, seemed to have drifted off into her own mind. She was staring at the ground, expressionless and still.

Cassian followed Sydney's gaze and commented, "It looks like your niece could use your help."

Sydney agreed. "So could anyone foolish enough to talk to my mother."

"You should be over there with them," Cassian said. Train cleared his throat to make a point, and Cassian added, "We do need to talk to you about something, though."

Sydney frowned. "You want to talk now?"

Train seemed inclined to, but Cassian put his foot down. "No, you need to be with your family. We can handle it later."

Sydney was perplexed, but another glance over at Amanda was sufficient to convince her that she needed to get back to her. She was reluctant to leave without some idea about what the detectives wanted. She hesitated, and then she said, "We're having people back to the house for a light lunch following the funeral. Why don't you stop by, and we can handle it then?"

Cassian looked doubtful. "Are you sure you don't want the full day with your family? We can do it tomorrow."

"Does it have anything to do with the investigation into Liz's murder?"

Train nodded.

"Then I want to deal with it today," Sydney said. "So would my mother, I'm sure." Then, after a moment's thought, she added, "And that's what Liz would have wanted, too."

Cassian looked at Train and the older officer nodded.

"I'll see you there in a little while, then?" Sydney confirmed.

"Yeah," Cassian said. "I guess you'll see us there."

Chapter Twenty-three

TRAIN FELT SELF-CONSCIOUS as he looked around the huge dining room in the Chapins' house. It wasn't his skin color that set him apart so acutely, although there were very few black people there. No, what made him feel so out of place was far subtler than that; something in his stiff demeanor that seemed to flag the fact that he didn't fit in. In most circumstances of his life, his size was a significant asset. He was able to utilize his physical advantage to control situations, to intimidate when necessary, and to direct others as he deemed best. At this moment, however, his size seemed more a liability. He felt like a professional wrestler invited to tea at Buckingham Palace; as though with every turn of his enormous frame he was likely to smash into some priceless set of china. Worse still, there was no way to hide, and no way to blend in among those who had gathered to mourn at the Chapin mansion. He felt exposed as people cast curious, even concerned, glances his way when they passed him, and he started to wish he and Cassian could find a way to talk to Sydney Chapin quickly and get out of the house.

He slid his back against the wall in the dining room,

trying to make himself as small as possible as he attempted to get his partner's attention. Cassian was over at the dining room table, filling a plate with lobster salad, croissants, and a touch of caviar. "Might as well eat while we're here," he'd said. "After all, we're not likely to get a meal this good anytime soon." Cassian was right about that, thought Train. The spread on the dining room table was remarkable. Salads, meats, pastas, and soufflés were lined up alongside a number of dishes that Train couldn't even identify, but which looked expensive. He found himself wondering how many semesters of his daughter's college education he could pay for with the amount of money that had been expended on this meal.

"It's delicious," a voice interrupted his thoughts. Train turned to his left and faced a diminutive gentleman who appeared to be well into his eighties. His balding head held only a few wispy strands of gray hair, which were carefully matted down to his scalp and failed to cover the large liver spots and overgrown moles that crowded his skull. His shoulders were stooped, making him seem even smaller than he'd probably been as a younger man, and he craned his thin neck upward to look at Train. And yet for all of his obvious frailty there was a compelling twinkle in his eyes. He reminded Train of a kindly wizard from a child's fairy tale. He was nattily dressed with a courtly manner, and there was something strangely familiar about him. "I noticed you weren't eating," the man continued. "I can assure you the food is delicious." He smiled in a warm, friendly way that contained a hint of condolence and melancholy appropriate to the occasion.

Train nodded. "I'm sure it is." He couldn't fight off the impression that he knew him. "I'm not really hungry," he lied.

The man nodded, accepting the explanation. "Were you a friend of Elizabeth's?" he inquired.

"No, actually," Train replied. "I'm with the police department."

"Ah," the man said, brought up short. "Are you one of the detectives working on the investigation into Elizabeth's murder?"

"Yes, I am."

The man put his hand out. "I'm Irskin Elliot, one of the Chapin family's oldest friends."

Train looked at the man again, and he realized why the man had seemed so familiar. Irskin Elliot had once been one of the most powerful men in politics. A former governor of Virginia, a one-term senator, and once the United States attorney general, he had been a leading liberal politician throughout the 1970s and '80s. Train shook his hand. "I knew the Chapins had powerful friends," he said, "but it's a true privilege to meet you, sir," he commented.

Elliot smiled humbly. "Trust me, there's no privilege in meeting a politician in decline. There are others here far more deserving of adulation."

"I doubt that."

"You shouldn't," Elliot said. He pointed around the room. "The man in the corner over there is the principal of the largest pharmaceutical company in the world. Worth billions of dollars; and I'm sure you recognize the man he's talking to."

"The vice president."

"That's right. And over against that wall"—Elliot pointed to the far end of the room—"is the man who's likely to be the next president of the United States."

"He looks familiar."

"Abe Venable. He's the Senate majority leader for the Republicans. Very conservative. A senator from my own state of Virginia, no less."

"It certainly is an impressive crowd."

"Exactly. By comparison, I'm little more than an artifact." He smiled again, and Train smiled back.

"Well, if not a privilege, it's at least an honor. I remember when you marched with Martin Luther King. At the time it was a risky thing for a southern governor to do. It meant a lot to many of us, though."

"It cost me some political support at the time," Elliot said. "Ah well, sometimes the right thing to do isn't always the easy or political thing to do." His eyes evaluated Train. "And as far as whose honor this is, I suspect you've got that backwards," he said. "When I was governor of Virginia, there was a star football player at the University named Darius Train. Judging from your size and your age, I suspect I have the pleasure of meeting him."

Train's face turned grim. He hated discussing his football career. "That was me," he admitted reluctantly.

"You were an All-America your first two years there, if I recall."

"You have a remarkable memory."

"Not really. In a state like Virginia, if the governor doesn't know exactly what's going on with the University's football team, he's dead in the water. Many of the voters seem to think that the primary standard by which the state's chief executive should be judged is the University's record under his tenure." He smiled at the thought. "What happened after your second year?"

"Injuries," Train said simply.

"Too bad." Elliot shook his head. "You were one of the best. Still, from what I hear from the Chapins, you seem to have found your calling. They are very pleased with the way the investigation has proceeded. I'd like to convey my personal appreciation as well. It's such an awful time for everyone, and having confidence in the people handling the investigation is an enormous burden off everyone's shoulders. Perhaps in the end your injuries were all for the best."

Train shrugged. "I'm happy enough doing what I'm doing, although I missed out on a lot of football. And you?" he asked, changing the subject. "You're still in politics, aren't you?"

Elliot chuckled to himself. "Technically, I'm still in politics," he said, shaking his head. "Though the fact that you have to ask reinforces my point about politicians in decline."

"I'm sorry," Train stammered. "I don't follow politics very closely."

"It's fine, Detective. I'm Secretary of Health and Human Services; it's not a very glamorous position, and it rarely takes me into the public eye. It gives me the chance to be useful, though."

"You're serving in a Republican administration?" Train was surprised. "That's a little unusual for a lifelong Democrat, isn't it?"

Elliot shrugged. "It's unusual, but not unheard of. Particularly in today's world of rancorous partisanship, having one or two cabinet members from the opposing party can help lend an administration at least the appearance of bipartisanship. For good or bad, I've reached the unenviable age at which people seem to regard me more as a statesman than a politician. As a result, both sides of the aisle seem to think I can provide them with cover and credibility—as long as I stay reasonably in the background."

"Do you miss the spotlight?"

Elliot shook his head. "The spotlight often gets a little too hot for my tastes, and there are many compromises that must be made to keep it shining on you." He pointed over again toward Abe Venable. "Do you think he's enjoying this?" he asked. Venable stood stiff-backed and somber, his aquiline features judging everything around him with jealous disdain. He was surrounded by sharp-looking business types, each of them looking desperate to keep his attention. "People like Lydia Chapin are crucial to anyone making a run at the presidency, as are those in the oil industry, the pharmaceutical industry, and on down the line. As a result, he has to listen to them—what's the common parlance these days?—*suck up* to them. It requires a certain flexibility of personality I no longer possess. Besides, I've had my time in the sun; in my old age, I prefer the shade."

Train nodded.

Just then, Sydney Chapin approached them from across the room, her expression heavy with the weight of the occasion. When she reached them, she addressed Elliot. "Uncle Irskin," she said, her voice carrying equal measures of warmth, affection, and relief. She hugged the older man tightly, almost as if clinging to him for protection. "I'm so glad you're here."

Elliot hugged her back. "Please, don't thank me," he said. "I feel awful that I haven't been here more over the past few days. I've been swamped, and I couldn't get away. I haven't been able to forgive myself."

"We understand, Irskin. We're just glad to have you here now."

"And I am here now, child. I'm here for anything you need." He took her hands in his and looked her in the eyes. "How is the prodigal daughter doing?"

"I'm okay."

"Really?" He raised his eyebrows skeptically. "This isn't quite the homecoming I would have hoped for you."

"I'll be fine eventually," she said. "It's hard right now. I'm trying to focus on Amanda, though."

Elliot nodded in understanding. "Is she going to be all right, do you think?"

"I do," Sydney said, and there was the force of conviction in her voice. "She's got a lot of my mother in her."

"Ah yes, your mother." Elliot rolled his eyes slightly, but in an affectionate way. "I spoke with her briefly when I arrived, but I'm hoping to sit down with her for more time this afternoon. She seems in control."

"Any surprise?"

"No, none." Elliot tilted his head to the side. "Do you think she's really doing all right inside, though?"

"Mother?" Sydney sounded surprised at the question. "Have you ever known her not to be all right?"

Elliot frowned. "I don't know," he said. "I know that she's been under an enormous amount of pressure since your father died. Taking over the company has been very difficult for her, I think, and I'm not convinced she's really been herself lately."

Sydney patted his hand. "I haven't seen a change," she said confidently. "I think she's doing just fine."

He patted her hand back. "Good. But remember, I'm always here if you or anyone else in your family need anything." They hugged again, and Train, who had been ignored throughout the exchange, felt even more self-conscious. He cleared his throat and looked for a tactful way to excuse himself.

"I'm sorry," Sydney said, realizing that she had not even acknowledged Train's presence. "Uncle Irskin, have you met Detective Train yet? He's one of the detectives investigating Liz's murder."

"Yes, we were just reminiscing about both our times in the past in Virginia."

"I had no idea that you two were related, though." Train noted the reference to "Uncle Irskin."

"An honorary title only," Elliot said. "As I mentioned, I've been close to the family for a very long time."

"Irskin started his career working with my grandfather's company," Sydney explained. "That was a long time ago, though; before he got into politics."

"Seems like a lifetime." Irskin smiled. "But I was always grateful to your family for the opportunities they gave me." He looked at Train. "I was also Elizabeth's godfather, and I was extremely close to her, so I feel like I've lost a child myself."

"I'm very sorry," Train said.

An awkward silence set in until Sydney addressed Train. "Detective Train, you and your partner said you had something you wanted to discuss with me earlier. Now might be a good time. I'm a little tired of accepting condolences from people I've never met, and I could use a break."

"If now works, that's fine. We just need to grab Detective Cassian."

As if on cue, Cassian came around the dining room table, a full plate of hors d'oeuvres in his hand. He walked over to the group of three and nodded to Train, who looked back and forth between Cassian's face and the plate in his hand in disapproval. Cassian didn't seem to notice. "Hello, Sydney," he said.

"Detective Cassian," she replied. "I'd like you to meet Irskin Elliot, an old friend of the family." Cassian frowned, clearly trying to figure out how he knew the man.

"He was a senator and once the attorney general," Train said, supplying the information Jack was missing.

The light seemed to go on in Cassian's mind. "Yes, of course," he said. He extended his hand, and then, noticing that it was greasy from all the food he'd eaten, he looked around for something on which to wipe his hands. He saw a stack of linen napkins on the dining room table and put his plate down, picking up a napkin and rubbing his hands together on it. Then he turned back to the group and extended his hand again. "Sorry about that," he said. "It's a pleasure to meet you."

Elliot smiled. "Don't worry about it. And I'm sure the pleasure's mine."

Train nodded to Cassian. "Sydney was just saying that this would be a good time to talk, Jack."

"Are you sure?" Jack asked Sydney. "We could do it another time—a little later in the day, after everyone has left."

She shook her head. "I'll take any excuse to get a break from this. Amanda's with my mother, and I'm feeling a little claustrophobic. We can go sit out on the terrace if you'd like."

"That sounds fine," Train said, cutting off Cassian before he could raise any further concerns.

"I suppose that's my cue to excuse myself," Elliot said. "It was a pleasure meeting both of you, Detectives Train and Cassian." He turned to Sydney. "And you," he said, taking her hand. "Don't ever hesitate to call if you need anything." She nodded. "Take care of Amanda and your mother. They need you right now." She nodded again, and then reached out and they hugged once more.

After they'd broken their embrace, he smiled supportively and walked off toward the buffet table. She watched him hobble away, his thin frame looking as though it might be knocked over if anyone he passed sneezed. Then she took a deep breath and wiped her eyes with the back of her hand, bracing herself. "Let's go outside," she said.

Chapter Twenty-four

"YOU SAID YOU DIDN'T THINK Leighton did this," Sydney said. She felt as though the walls were closing in on her.

"He may not have," Cassian said. "But we want to be sure."

"The papers said you arrested the man who killed Liz—this Jerome Washington person." She couldn't believe this was happening. "Why would you have arrested him if you weren't sure?"

Train answered the question. "He's still in custody, Sydney. But we don't have enough to charge him with your sister's murder yet, so we need to rule out any other suspects. Jack told me some of what you told him about what happened when Liz and Leighton split up. Sounds pretty rough. We were wondering if you could fill in some more of the details."

She shook her head. "I don't know that there's anything more I can tell you," she said. "I was living in California at the time, and Liz and I weren't close back then. I knew she and Leighton were getting a divorce, but I had no idea what had really happened until I started talking to Liz more and more this winter." She shook her head in exasperation. "You may have noticed we're not the most open family on the face of the planet."

"Do you know whether Liz had seen or heard from Leighton since they split up?" Train pressed.

"I don't think so," she replied. "As far as I know, she never had any contact with him again after that night—except through their attorneys."

"Were charges ever filed against him?" Cassian asked.

She nodded. "Originally. I think there were charges that were filed originally, but they were dropped."

"Why?" Cassian asked.

She shook her head. "I don't know," she said.

"But you have your suspicions," Train said, picking up on her hesitation.

"You have to understand, Detective, this family exists in the public eye. I can't imagine what impact it would have had on my mother's world if a public trial had been held and the world learned that her daughter had been raped by her own husband—a Chapin Industries executive, no less. I always assumed that my mother found a way around that."

"You think she convinced your sister to drop the charges to buy his silence and save the family some embarrassment?" Train asked.

Sydney shrugged. "It wouldn't surprise me."

Train shook his head, and Sydney thought she sensed some disgust in his expression. She couldn't blame him.

"Does Leighton keep in touch with Amanda at all?" Cassian asked.

"No," Sydney said emphatically. "That was the one thing Liz was clear about. She said that Amanda would never have to see Leighton again."

"Hard to believe a court would allow her that peace of mind," Train said. "Even with violence between a husband and wife, judges usually bend over backwards to make sure that both parents can stay involved in some way with the children. And if Leighton was never convicted of a crime, I would think that he would at least have been allowed supervised visits."

"All I know is that Liz was certain that Amanda would never have to see her father again." She could see the skepticism on the detectives' faces. "Look, it's not like this was really ever an issue. Leighton wasn't exactly the most caring father in the first place and I don't think he's ever expressed any kind of an interest in staying in touch with Amanda. As for Amanda—well, after what she witnessed, could anyone really be surprised that she had no interest in seeing him?"

"Still," Cassian said, "if Liz had found a way to keep Leighton from seeing his daughter, it could provide a motive for murder."

Train nodded. "If someone tried to keep me from seeing my kid, I could see myself doing just about anything to make them pay."

Sydney shook her head. "I think you're wrong. From what I know about Leighton, I don't think he cares about anyone else enough to be driven to violence over a little thing like losing his daughter."

"Where is he now?" Cassian asked.

"I don't know. I think he's still out in Old Colony. He doesn't work for Chapin Industries anymore—no big surprise there—but he must be doing okay. Liz used to say he spent most of his time hanging out at the Old Colony Golf and Polo Club, so he must have some money." She let her head drop into her hands. "I just can't imagine how hard this will be for Amanda if Leighton really had something to do with Liz's murder."

"I wouldn't jump to that conclusion yet," Train said. "And I certainly wouldn't tell anyone that we're looking into this. Like I said before, at this point we just need to complete the full investigation and run down every lead."

"On that score," Cassian said, "is there anyone else we should be looking at? Anyone you're aware of who might have wanted to hurt your sister, or who had threatened her in the past?"

Sydney shook her head. "Not that I know of. She did a lot of the kind of investigative reporting that tends to make people angry, so I'm sure she had her share of enemies, but I don't know who she rubbed the wrong way in the past."

Jack nodded. "We're having one of the assistants at the department put together a quick list of possibilities based on your sister's published articles. I guess we were wondering whether she ever told you of anyone specifically who she was afraid of."

Sydney thought for a moment. "No one I can recall," she said at last.

"How about anything else that wouldn't be in her published articles—anything that didn't make the paper, or that she was still working on? We need to come up with as complete a list as possible."

"Did you check her computer at work?"

"We did, but we haven't come up with anything useful."

"She did most of her work on her office computer, but I can also check her laptop," Sydney suggested.

Train shook his head. "It was stolen."

"What?"

"It was stolen by whoever murdered your sister," Train explained.

"No it wasn't. I've got it."

Train and Cassian looked at each other. "What are you talking about, Sydney?" Jack said.

"Liz's laptop. I borrowed it a couple of weeks ago."

"Why didn't you tell anyone?"

"Nobody asked me."

Train rubbed his head. "We're going to need to see that computer," he said.

"That's fine. It's at my apartment. You can get it whenever you want, but she mainly used the desktop at work, I think, so there's probably nothing useful on it."

"We'll need to take a look at it anyway. We'll arrange to have it picked up. Now, is there anything else you can think of?"

Sydney thought about her conversation with Barneton. Liz had been looking into something having to do with eugenics, but Sydney had no specifics, and certainly no reason to suspect that it had anything to do with her death. "I can't think of anything," she replied after a moment. She was sure that they would merely scoff at the notion that Liz's visit with Barneton was relevant. Worse still, they could take her seriously and waste precious time in their investigation chasing down a rabbit hole that would only upset the professors at the law school—doing herself no favors.

She looked up and noticed that Cassian and Train were still looking at her, as if they expected her to say more. She pursed her lips and kept silent. Finally, after what seemed an eternity, Train stood up and looked at his partner. "Next stop, Leighton Creay's house?" he said.

"Looks that way," Cassian replied.

Lydia Chapin stood at the bay window looking out from her living room, past the manicured front lawn, out to the street and toward the city. It was dark out now, and the house was quiet save for the distant clatter of china as the caterers packed up from a long day. She brought her drink up to her lips and paused as she caught sight of her hand gripping the glass, the skin pulled transparent over white knuckles; the bones showing through with greater and greater determination each year as though eager for their inevitable freedom from confinement.

She closed her eyes and took a deep swallow.

"How are you holding up, Lydia?"

The voice came from behind her, but she didn't turn. It was familiar enough to require neither identification nor formality. "I'm fine. Thank you, Irskin."

A hand found her shoulder, its weight barely enough to register, and yet strong and comforting. "Honestly, Lydia?"

She turned halfway, sidestepping the diminutive older man, unable to meet his eyes, and walked over to the bar to refill her glass. She took half of it in one sip. "I told you, I'm fine."

Elliot shrugged; *as you wish.* Then he walked over to the bar himself and poured a drink. He sipped in solidarity with her. "She loved you, you know," he said after a moment.

"Please, don't."

"She did, though. You've always been too hard on yourself—a trait your children inherited—but Elizabeth loved you very much in spite of it."

Lydia moved away from the bar, still unable to look Elliot in the eyes. She knew she would flinch, and she was afraid of what he might see. "That's nice of you, Irskin. You've always been a wonderful friend."

"It's not friendship, it's the truth. Elizabeth loved you. Sydney loves you, too. You must try to stay focused on that. Hold on to that, and it will sustain you."

"I know." She didn't actually know, but she felt compelled to keep up appearances.

"I hope so. Sydney and Amanda need your strength, now more than ever."

Lydia put her drink down and brought her hands to her face. "I don't know how much strength I have left, Irskin."

He sat next to her and patted her knee. "Yes you do. You do, because you must. As long as you keep that in mind, you'll find all the strength you need."

"Do you believe in God, Irskin?" she asked impulsively.

He folded his hands together as he leaned back against the sofa. "They say there are no atheists in foxholes," he said. "Old age is a foxhole."

"Pascal's wager?"

He shook his head. "It's not nearly so self-serving or calculated as that; at least I like to think not. I'm just old enough to see the connections—the continuity—that escape the young. It's not that I like to think that our lives mean something, it's that I know they do. You can see that in Sydney and Amanda, can't you? Their very existence gives your life meaning."

She looked away from him. "I suppose you're right. I sometimes forget."

"You shouldn't. You're very lucky."

She stiffened as she kept her eyes averted. "Thank you for being here, Irskin. It's a great comfort, and if there's ever anything I can do for you, please let me know."

"There is," he replied. She looked at him. "Stay strong," he said after a moment. "Your family needs you right now."

Chapter Twenty-five

THE DETECTIVES' DRIVE OUT TO OLD COLONY was uneventful; there was even an air of leisure to the excursion. It was the day after Elizabeth Creay's funeral, and the humidity had eased temporarily, though the temperature still hovered in the low nineties.

Rolling out from the city, past the monuments and across the Arlington Memorial Bridge, Cassian was reminded, for the first time in ages, of the surface majesty of the city he called home. Spending most of his time scraping through the grit of the worst neighborhoods, he often lost sight of Washington's charms. Built to overwhelm foreign leaders, the District was imperious in its bearing. White marble domes and obelisks and columns shimmered from every corner of the city in the afternoon sun, proclaiming the dawning of a new age of governance and power unrivaled since the passing of the Roman Empire the neoclassical architecture was designed to evoke. As Train's car circled the Lincoln Memorial, with its scrubbed façade draping the massive watchful countenance of the nation's savior, Cassian recalled those better things that had called him both to his city and his profession.

Once across the river and into Virginia, the detectives

passed through Arlington and Tysons Corner. After that, the scenery turned green and lush quickly, and Cassian thought about his youth growing up in a clean, upper-middle class town in southern Maryland. For just a moment, he considered what might have been if he'd chosen a different path.

"Thinking you made the wrong choices?" Train asked, as if he'd read Cassian's thoughts.

"Never." Cassian laughed. "How could anyone be happy out here?"

"Sure," Train said skeptically. "Upstanding, good-looking white boy like you from the suburbs coulda had all this without even sweating. Nice home; two kids in the honor society; pretty little blonde wife with pretty little tits and an ass like a ten-year-old boy." Train belly-laughed at the notion.

"Fuck off."

Train laughed more loudly. "And a dog, right?" He looked over at Cassian, whose attention was focused out the passenger window, pretending to ignore his partner's comments. "Yeah, that's right, a dog. I see you with one of those big retrievers—what do they call them—Labradors or goldens? One of those big dogs, all slobbery and stupid that come up and lick your crotch when you get home." He smiled and his teeth lit up the car in the sunlight. "Life like that, you might even get laid once in a while."

"Look who's talking. From what I can tell, yelling at your ex is the closest thing to a physical relationship you've had since I met you."

Train's smile ebbed, but only slightly. "You talk more shit than any white man I've ever met, boy."

"Oh, what's the matter, Sarge? It's only fun when the crap's running downhill? Remember, you and I both chose the same life."

"Choosing had nothin' to do with it for me," Train

pointed out. "Once my knees gave out and the agents and pro scouts stopped calling, this was the best life I coulda hoped for. What's your excuse?"

Cassian was silent for a moment. "After everything that's happened, this is the best life I could have hoped for, too," he said at last.

Cassian's tone chased what was left of Train's smile away. "Your brother?"

"My brother." Cassian nodded.

Train tilted his head to the side, looking at the younger man in the passenger seat. "Gotta let go of the guilt," he said. "Shit'll eat you up and keep you from being happy."

"You happy?"

"Don't go by me, partner; you can do better."

They pulled into a circular driveway when they saw the number on the mailbox they were looking for—666 Cherry Blossom Lane. "Bad omen," Train commented solemnly.

The house was a graying old lady of a structure, in desperate need of attention. It was a three-story colonial that had been converted into a rooming house with six apartments, two on each floor. They checked the mailboxes and saw that Creay was in one of the ground-floor units. They looked up at the house, with its wide blue shutters that were peeling at the corners, and a porch that ambled its way unsteadily around from the front door, disappearing behind both sides of the house. There were no cars in the driveway, and no activity in the yard. Everything was eerily quiet.

Train and Cassian stepped out of the car and onto the white gravel driveway. Their feet crunched in the silence with every step toward the house. They walked up the steps and rang the doorbell to apartment number two, waiting patiently for someone to let them in. After a few moments, Train reached out and rang the doorbell again.

When it became clear that no one was coming, Cassian walked down the porch, peering into the windows. "Not exactly the Ritz, is it?" he said quietly. "I didn't know there were places this crappy in Old Colony."

Train walked over and shaded his hand against the glass so he could clear the reflection and get a good look into the house. The interior was dark and gray, with furniture that was more functional than fashionable. "Looks like Mr. Creay lost more than his wife in the divorce," Train commented.

"Been known to happen," Cassian said.

"Yeah, but few of us have so far to fall."

"What do you think?" Cassian asked.

Train shrugged. "I think there's a good chance that Leighton might feel a little pissed about his current living situation. Particularly after spending a decade or so getting used to the Chapins' money."

"You think pissed enough to kill his ex?"

"Could be. We've seen people kill with less motive, and this guy already has a record of violence with her. One thing's for sure, we definitely need to talk to him." He looked at his watch. "It's still early; where does he work?"

Cassian shook his head. "He doesn't, really. From what I've found out, he's been doing some 'consulting' since he left Chapin Industries. Word is, he essentially runs his 'office' out of the Old Colony Golf and Polo Club, waiting for clients to find him."

Train took one more look through the windows into the sad little apartment. "Even I wouldn't be happy living here," he grunted. Then he sighed. "Well, as long as we're already out here, we might as well head over to the club to see if we might get lucky. Could be interesting."

Chapter Twenty-six

THE DRIVEWAY UP to the Old Colony Golf and Polo Club wound endlessly around great centuries-old deciduous trees, up a steep incline to a plateau at the highest point in the area. All around the approach, carefully manicured hedges were punctuated by exquisitely crafted stone walls. Beyond them, Train could see an expanse of rolling green out through the fairways and toward the polo ground. *Golf and polo*, Train thought; two more things he would never understand about rich people.

Cassian was looking out the window to the right as they drove, toward a long, low-slung structure gleaming white and red near the polo grounds. "That must be where they keep the ponies," he said.

"What?"

"The polo ponies. That must be where they stable them."

Train's head swam. "I'm still having a hard time getting my mind around the fact that there are still places in the world where they play polo."

"You kidding?" Cassian said slyly. "In Caucasian circles, it's still one of the most popular sports around. I was quite a player myself when I was younger."

Train frowned. "You played polo? Please, Jesus, tell me you're kidding."

"I'm serious. All white kids play polo in the suburbs. It's required."

Train shot his partner a glare and caught the grin on his face. "You're fuckin' with me," he said. It was not a question.

"Yeah, Sarge, I'm fuckin' with you." Train turned back toward the widening driveway that was nearing its end. After a beat, Cassian added, "It's not just white kids; sometimes we let Asians play, too."

"Keep it up," Train challenged. "It's gonna be a long day."

"Ah yes." Cassian locked his jaw, mocking an upper-class drawl. "To be among the right sort of people again. Makes you feel right at home, doesn't it?"

"You do that so well," Train commented on the accent. "Practically a natural, I'd say. Careful your voice doesn't stay that way."

"Aw, c'mon. You could do it too with a little practice. Just imagine a stick wedged so far up your ass that it's pushing out your jaw," Cassian said, drawing a hearty laugh from Train. "Conquer the accent, and even you might be able to join a club like this someday."

"You think they've got an affirmative action program here?"

They pulled up to the front of the clubhouse and parked their car in a spot right in front of the entrance clearly marked "Members Only." They got out and looked around, taking in the scene. It was a beautiful place, there was no question. The clubhouse, which looked down on everything around it, seemed as though it had been painted that morning. It was a huge plantation-style structure with towering pillars flanking the front door. From there, it stretched out in every direction, running down from the peak of the hill on which it was situated.

"Subtle," Cassian commented on the impression the structure conveyed.

"As a pointy white hat," Train agreed. Glancing around he could see men—older white men—ferrying themselves around in neatly ordered groups of four, hanging out of tiny golf carts like circus clowns. Some of them failed to hide their shock upon seeing Train get out of the car, and he wondered whether it was obvious that he was a cop, or whether they simply couldn't get past the color of his skin. The latter, he suspected.

Train and Cassian walked up the front stairs, onto the wide front porch, through the doors, and into a grand foyer. Thick oriental carpets covered the floor of the entryway, swallowing the sound as they walked through the doors. On the walls, ancient faded watercolors, most of them of dogs and hunting scenes, clung to the false glory of a time long since past. To the left of the doorway, set back toward one of the walls, was a heavy dark wood secretary's desk, with a prim mousy man in a blazer and striped tie sitting in an uncomfortable-looking armchair. Seeing Train walk through the door, the prig leapt to his feet, clearly under the apprehension that something was dreadfully amiss.

"Can I help you, sir?" The officious little man clearly meant for his inquiry to sound impressive, perhaps even a little bit threatening, but to Train it merely confirmed his administrative impotence.

Train took note of the gold nametag on the man's lapel with the club logo on it in gold leaf and writing informing him that this was Tad Jennings, Club Manager. Jennings was half Train's size, and he reacted to the larger man's assessment of him as though he'd been slapped in the face. Train intensified his stare. "We're looking for Leighton Creay," he said slowly, in his deepest voice. "Is he here?"

Jennings wrung his hands involuntarily. "Who are you, please?" It sounded to Train like a plea for mercy.

"We're the police," Train responded, his eyes never leaving Jennings's as he took out his badge and flipped it open for the little man to inspect. He noticed that Jennings hardly even looked at it. Instead, his gaze broke from Train and moved to Cassian, who by that time was wandering around the room slowly, looking at the artwork on the walls. He reached up to straighten a picture that had slipped slightly and was hanging askew, drawing a squeal of agony from the nervous Mr. Jennings.

"Please don't touch that!" He hurried over and put himself between Cassian and the dim picture on the wall, as if protecting a threatened child. "That's eighteenth-century! It's very expensive!"

There was a long silence in the room as Cassian and Train exchanged bemused shrugs. "Right," Train said at last. "So, is Mr. Creay here?"

"We don't give out information about our members' comings and goings," Jennings said, regaining his composure somewhat. He straightened his back visibly and pointed his nose in the air to reach his full height in defense of what he clearly viewed as one of the guiding principles of his existence. "Ever," he added for emphasis.

"That sounds pretty firm," Train said.

"It is, sir. It is a rule that we view as central to our role in providing an escape for our members."

"That makes sense," Train admitted. "After all, you gotta have rules, don't you?"

"We believe so, sir, yes." Jennings clearly thought he was emerging victorious from the exchange.

"I can see why." Train turned to Cassian. "Looks like they got a rule against telling us if Mr. Creay's here, Detective Cassian. That means we made the trip out here for nothing."

"Damn shame," Cassian said. "Seems like a huge waste of our time—and of the money that the taxpayers are shelling out for our salaries."

"It does, doesn't it?" Train smiled at Jennings. "But rules are rules, I guess."

Jennings began to look queasy. "Yes. You can see why—"

Train cut him off. "You know what might make the taxpayers feel better?"

Cassian shook his head and pantomimed a look of ignorance. "I don't know, Sarge; what would make the taxpayers feel better?"

"If we could figure out something else we might be able to investigate out here." Train looked straight at Jennings, who had turned pale. "You think of anything else we might be able to investigate out here, Detective?"

Cassian struck a pensive pose. "Interesting thought, Sergeant Train. Let me mull it over for a moment." His expression changed, and he looked seriously at Jennings. "I saw some of your members smoking cigars out on the course, Mr. Jennings, isn't that right?"

"Some of our members enjoy a smoke, yes sir." Jennings was struggling to keep his back straight.

"I'm just betting you keep a humidor for those who

'enjoy a smoke,' don't you?" Cassian imitated Jennings's tone. "Rent out space in it to the members."

Jennings's expression soured in condescension. "We would never 'rent out space,' as you put it, Detective, but we do have a humidor. I don't see what you're driving at. This is Virginia—and a private club at that—we have the power to set our own smoking policy. There's nothing illicit about that."

"Not unless there are Cuban cigars in the humidor," Cassian pointed out. Jennings's eyes immediately dropped to the floor. Cassian continued. " 'Trading with the enemy' is still the technical charge, if I'm remembering it right. A few years back, there was a big scandal in New York at a couple of the athletic clubs. Turns out the managers were letting the members keep illegal Cuban cigars in the club humidors."

Train was nodding. "Yeah, I remember that. A bunch of the members had to pay huge fines and got into a lot of trouble." He paused. "It's not like any of them went to jail or anything like that, though."

"That's true," Cassian agreed. "They could all afford high-priced lawyers who got them off without any jail time." He walked over to another of the paintings on the wall that was tipped slightly to one side. He reached up and straightened it, all the while looking at Jennings. "As I remember, only the clubs' managers spent any time in jail."

In spite of the climate-control system, little beads of sweat were visible on Jennings's narrow forehead.

Train leaned in close to the man. "We really need to talk to Mr. Creay," he said, again in his deepest, most confidential tone.

To his credit, Jennings managed to keep his composure well enough to cause Train to wonder, if only briefly, whether he would crack. He even held off the temptation to wipe the sweat from his brow as his face turned in on itself and he considered his options. Finally, his expression collapsed completely, and his lips tightened into a tiny aperture, drawn in against his teeth in agony. "Members' bar," he said quietly in defeat, his mouth barely moving as he spoke.

Train raised a questioning eyebrow, and Jennings drew in a heavy, disgusted breath. He nodded over his shoulder. "Down the hallway, second doorway on your left."

Chapter Twenty-seven

SYDNEY DROVE SOUTHWEST along Interstate 81, the radio in her blue Honda Accord blaring out tunes by Alanis Morissette, Butterfly Boucher, and Mark Knopfler from a D.C. alternative rock station. It felt good to get away, even if only briefly. It had been such an awful, surreal week, and having a moment to herself just to clear her mind was a welcome respite.

She patted the dashboard of her aging car affectionately. She'd thought recently about trading in the vehicle, but hadn't been able to bring herself to do it. It had been the top-of-the-line model nine years earlier when she bought it, and it had taken her from coast to coast and back again—the chariot she'd used to escape the confines of her family's expectations. It still performed admirably most of the time, though it had recently begun to have trouble with the starter. Still, she felt an undeniable loyalty to the car, and was reluctant to give it up.

She hadn't told anyone where she was headed, not just because she didn't want to be disturbed, but because she knew that no one would understand her motivation. Better, she decided, to satisfy her own curiosity and leave everyone else in the dark for the moment. Her mother thought she was clearing up a few things at work, and her boss assumed that she was still dealing with family issues related to her sister's death. As a result, she had been able to slip away without anyone asking any questions.

She passed the junction with Interstate 64 toward Charlottesville at around noon and kept driving, down into the more rural portion of Virginia, where the suburban sprawl gave way to rambling fields, farmyards, and overgrown forests. Her radio no longer picked up the Washington stations, and even the Charlottesville radio fare began to fade. She flipped around the dial, searching for something to feed her alternative rock appetite, but found primarily an assortment of conservative talk and Christian rock radio stations. She finally settled on a country station and continued barreling down the highway to the sounds of Clint Black and Merle Haggard, being treated only occasionally to crossover artists like Shania Twain and Bonnie Raitt.

As she drove, she let her mind wander aimlessly through the events of the past week, eager to free her mind from the constraints of rational evaluation and find clarity in her unfocused emotions and impressions. As the mile markers flashed by in greater and greater numbers between exits, she began to feel fortunate in a perverse way. She'd spent years waiting for her life to begin, waiting for something of import to happen that would signal that her existence had purpose and meaning and direction. Sometimes, she thought, security and routine are fulfillment's greatest enemy, lulling us into a patterned stupor that obscures the reality that time slips away faster than we can fathom. It is often only the catastrophic events of our lives that rattle us from complacency and free us to take a good look around to see the importance of things so easily taken for granted: the connections of family; the strength that comes from being relied upon; the excitement of a new romance (even one only beginning to take root).

As she pulled up the long, tree-lined drive, she looked up at the bright blue sign that hung from the stone pillars guarding the entrance to the grounds. "The Virginia Juvenile Institute for Mental Health," it read. *The Institute*, Barneton had called it.

From the look of the buildings and surrounding fields, it could have been a second-rate boarding school, with its clusters of red-brick structures gapped by swaths of green common. All that seemed missing was a horde of students rushing across the campus to classes or activities or athletics. But here, it seemed, the residents had little for which to hurry.

As she pulled into a parking space in the lot near the main building, she wondered what could have happened in this place that had caused her sister to make the five-hour trek—and from here to Professor Barneton's office. Looking at the quiet, lonely campus, she was convinced now that she had wasted her own time as well, that there could be nothing important she could learn there.

She sighed as she actually considered throwing the car into reverse and heading back to the city. Still, she thought, she'd made the trip already, so she might as well satisfy her curiosity. But she couldn't imagine what had brought her sister all the way out here. After a moment's hesitation, she made up her mind, got out of her car, and walked up the front steps of the main building.

Chapter Twenty-eight

CASSIAN COULDN'T WAIT to confront Leighton Creay. Ever since Sydney had described how he'd raped his wife, Cassian had been itching for any excuse to get in the man's face. With any luck, he thought, Creay might be stupid enough to give them cause to arrest him—maybe even resist a little, so Cassian could give him a quick shot or two to punctuate his disgust.

He walked through the door marked "Members' Lounge" with Train directly on his heels. It was eleven-thirty on a Thursday morning, and the room was predictably quiet, with only two people there. One was the bartender, in his early twenties, leaning idly behind an enormous oak bar, wearing a stiff white collared shirt with a black bow tie. The second was a man who looked like he could be in his early fifties, with thick blond hair graying at the temples, leaning over a table at the far end of the room, reading a newspaper.

"Can I help you?" the bartender asked, looking away briefly from the *SportsCenter* that was looping on the plasma television above the bar. It was clear from his demeanor that he knew neither Cassian nor Train were members, and therefore spared them the obsequiousness demanded by some of those who belonged to the club. His voice was more curious than condescending, though, and carried none of the self-righteousness they had witnessed in the club manager's initial greeting.

Cassian walked over to the bar and took out his badge, flipping it open but shielding it from the view of the man at the far end of the room. The blond-gray man hadn't even looked up. "We're looking for Leighton Creay," Cassian told the bartender quietly. "Your boss told us we could find him in here." He flipped his head over in the direction of the man at the table. "That him?"

The bartender nodded and gave a half-smile that conveyed his amusement—though not necessarily his surprise—at the notion that Creay might have a problem with the law. Cassian nodded back at the bartender and took out a ten-dollar bill, sliding it across the bar. "Thanks," he said. "We may need to talk to you a little later, if that's all right."

The bartender pocketed the cash. "Always willing to do my civic duty."

Cassian looked at Train and motioned him over to the table at the far end of the room. The man sitting there didn't move as the two detectives approached him. "Leighton Creay?" Cassian asked.

"Yeah," the man said, still without altering his position or deigning to look at the two policemen.

"We'd like to talk to you about your ex-wife."

Creay's body stiffened, but he kept his nose buried in his newspaper. "So talk," he said, his voice betraying his defensiveness.

Cassian was silent for a moment, hovering over the table with Train close behind him, letting Creay feel the impact of his presence. "Did you know she was killed?"

Creay finally pulled his eyes off the newsprint in front of him and looked up at Cassian. His eyes were dull green and angry. "Of course," he said. "I read the paper." He waggled a corner of the section he was reading for emphasis. Cassian was tempted to punch him right then and there, but he knew it wouldn't be productive. Still, it took a moment for him to harness the hatred he'd already developed for the man. During that pause, Creay frowned. "You cops, or did Lydia send you?"

"Cops," Train replied sharply.

"Prove it." Creay's eyes never left Train's. Train's face broke into a broad, malevolent smile. He reached into his pocket and drew out his badge, which he carried in a leather billfold. He tossed it on the table, where it landed with a loud thud. Creay eyed it suspiciously, then leaned over, touching one corner of the worn leather as though it carried a pestilence and flipping it open on the table to reveal the badge and Train's identification. "Darius Train," Creay read aloud. "Catchy name. You Irish?"

The smile faded from Train's face, and Creay held his hands up as if he expected to be hit. Then he looked at Cassian. "I suppose you've got one of these, too?" he asked.

"Similar," Cassian replied. "Picture's not as pretty, and the name's different—Cassian." He took out his badge and held it up without showing it. "You wanna take a look?" There was a challenge in his voice.

Creay considered the offer, visibly evaluating Cassian's level of overt hostility. He shook his head. "That's all right, I'll take your word for it." The man's instinct for self-preservation wasn't totally lacking, Cassian noted.

"Mind if we sit down with you for a couple of minutes?" Cassian asked, swinging his leg over the back of one of the chairs and taking a seat. "You know, just to shoot the shit a little?"

"As long as you don't consider me the shit, I guess that's fine." He waved a hand toward one of the other chairs, inviting Train to sit down.

Cassian laughed in spite of himself. "Let's see how it goes," he said. "No promises." He waited for Train to sit down. The huge detective pulled a seat close to Creay, so that the two of them flanked him.

"You guys sure you don't want to just sit on my lap?" Creay asked.

"We didn't see you at your wife's funeral," Cassian said, ignoring Creay's quip.

"Ex-wife," Creay pointed out. "Elizabeth and I . . . weren't close. Not since the divorce, anyway."

"Don't you mean before your divorce?" Cassian asked. "You meant to say that you weren't close since before your divorce, right? I'm guessing at least not since the night you raped her."

Creay looked back and forth between the two detectives. "I see you've been talking to Lydia."

"Why do you say that?"

"Because you clearly have the wrong idea about me already." He sighed heavily, as though he'd spent his life oppressed. "Look, like it or not, my ex-wife was a lying bitch who tried to destroy my reputation by making up stories about me. If you think I should have gone to pay my last respects to a person like that, well then, we're just going to have to disagree. It's a pity she's dead, I suppose, but I don't really give a shit."

"Stories," Cassian said, considering the word. "Stories can certainly do a man's reputation some damage. Particularly when his daughter tells the same version of the stories."

"Kids are impressionable." Creay shrugged, although he looked wounded momentarily.

"You keep in touch with Amanda?" Cassian asked. It sounded rhetorical.

Creay shook his head. "My ex-wife—the woman you're so concerned about—turned her against me. She won't see me anymore."

Train let a low, slow whistle escape his lips. "That's no good. Can't imagine what I might do to my ex if she turned my daughter against me. And that on top of lying about me? Trying to ruin my reputation?" He raised his eyebrows. "You better believe that with all that, you just never know what even a reasonable man might do, do you?"

Creay glared at Train, his anger visible, though under control. "Yeah, well maybe you've just got a more volatile temperament than some men, Detective."

"Could be." Train nodded slowly. "What about you, Leighton? What's your temper like? You willing to let some—what did you call her? lying bitch?—do that kind of damage to you and get away with it without paying a price?"

Creay crossed his arms defiantly. "Listen, Detectives, I'm a little busy here," he said, nodding down at the newspaper spread out on the table. "If you've got anything you really want to ask me, you can go right ahead, but this psycho-cop-mindfuck you're getting into is just a little boring, okay?"

Cassian chuckled. He could feel his animosity toward Leighton Creay growing as he remembered the picture Sydney had painted of the man raping her sister. He looked closely at Creay, examining the lines on his face. He originally had estimated him to be in his early fifties, but up close he could tell he'd been wrong. Mid-forties seemed more likely, though it was clear that the mileage had taken its toll. "You're a pretty tough guy, aren't you, Leighton?" He didn't wait for a response. "Fine, let's start by finding out where you were last Wednesday afternoon."

"What time?" Leighton inquired.

"Thought you read the paper, Leighton. I'm surprised you didn't find that in the articles about your ex's murder."

"I focus primarily on the financial section."

Cassian stared right through the man. "Between two-thirty and four," he said at last.

"I was here," Creay said. "Well, not actually 'here' as in 'at this table,' but I was here at the club. I was playing golf."

"You got anyone who can corroborate that?"

"Yeah, I do. Three people—all the guys in my foursome, including Bill Whitledge, the club's pro. Three of us chipped in and got a playing lesson."

Cassian jotted down the name in his notebook. "Who were the other two?" he asked.

"Cy Badlichuk and Dan Klines." He flipped a page on the paper he'd been reading. "Is that all you need?" he asked. "Because I've really got to get back to work here."

Cassian looked over at the paper, and then peered under the table and around the empty room. "What is it that you do, Leighton?" he asked. "I mean, you're sitting here in a country club before noon on a Thursday reading a newspaper. I don't see a computer; I don't see a briefcase; I don't see a cell phone. So I'm wondering to myself, just what kind of 'work' it is that you've got to get back to."

"I'm a consultant," Creay said a little too defensively. "And my cell phone is in my locker. We're not allowed to use them inside the clubhouse."

"Ah, well, that explains a lot, I guess," Cassian said sarcastically. "What kind of consulting is it that you do?"

"Financial consulting."

"You wanna be a little more specific?" Train growled.

"Not really, no," Creay snapped back. He and Train squared off momentarily in a staring contest, but Creay clearly realized quickly that he would lose. He relented. "For some clients, I advise them on the stock market—specific issues, more general trends, the works. With some clients, I'm called in to do a financial evaluation of a company that they're looking into acquiring. It can be any number of things, really."

"Sounds impressive," Train said. "How's business these days?" He pointed toward the paper. "You don't look too busy."

"Looks can be deceiving, Detective," Creay cracked. "I have to follow the news very closely in order to do my job effectively. I'm doing fine, though your concern for my well-being is heartwarming."

"You really sure you're doing okay?" Cassian pressed.

Creay gave an exasperated sigh. "Yes, Detective Cassian, I'm doing fine. You needn't trouble yourself worrying about my financial future."

Cassian shrugged. "Okay, Leighton, if you say so. But here's the thing: we stopped by your place earlier, before we came out here to see if we could find you. We knocked on the door, rang the doorbell—even looked through the windows to see if you were there. And do you know what we saw, Leighton?"

"I'm all ears," shot Creay.

Cassian gave an angry grin. "How would you describe what we saw, Detective Train?"

"Oh, I don't know," Train said contemplatively. "A shithole? Yeah, that's probably the best way I could describe it. An absolute fucking shithole."

"Right," said Cassian. "Good description. I was having trouble coming up with the right words, but 'shithole' pretty much sums it up. So I'm wondering now, if things are going so well, why is it that you're living like you get your meals at a soup kitchen?"

Creay didn't flinch, but his face was two shades paler. He looked back and forth between the two detectives. Finally he said, "I'm in the market for something new at the moment, if you must know. Until I find the right housing opportunity, there's no point in wasting my money on rent—there's no equity in it."

"In the market for something new," Cassian repeated. "You hear that, Sarge, he's looking for a new place as we speak." He looked back at Creay. "You know, I'm glad we found you out here, 'cause I've been thinking about moving out to this area myself. I'd be looking for a smaller space, obviously—being used to the city and all—but I'm guessing we've got similar tastes. Why don't you give me the name of the real estate agent you're working with? That'd be a huge help to me."

Creay's face was stone. "I haven't chosen one yet, Detective. I thought I'd do some looking around on my own first and get a sense for what was out there."

Cassian stared straight at Creay, his eyes penetrating the man's façade. He knew he was lying. "Well, shit, yeah, I guess that makes sense. Gotta figure out what's out there, huh? That make sense to you, Sarge?"

"Makes perfect sense to me."

"Yeah, me too. But you be sure to tell me once you've decided who you're going to use, okay? I want to know the minute you make your choice."

"You'll be the first person I call, Detective," Creay said. "Are we done?"

"Almost. I have one last question," Cassian said. "When we first got here, you asked whether we were cops, or whether Lydia sent us. I'm assuming by 'Lydia' you were referring to Mrs. Chapin, right? So, I'm wondering why you think Lydia Chapin would have sent people like me and Detective Train here out to talk to you?"

Creay continued staring at Cassian. Then he folded his newspaper, gathering it up as he stood. "Gentlemen," he said. "It's been a pleasure. If you have any further questions, let me know, and I'll have my attorney get in touch with you." Then, without another word, he walked out of the room.

Chapter Twenty-nine

SYDNEY CHAPIN SAT in the comfortable office of Dr. Aldus Mayer, MD and PhD, superintendent at the Institute. It was pleasantly decorated in what cutting-edge interior designers would mockingly call the "traditional" style. The desk chair on which he perched was leather-backed and wood-framed, and complemented the sturdy oak desk that took up much of the room. Sydney sat in one of the wooden university chairs that faced the desk.

"I'm very sorry about your sister," Dr. Mayer was saying. "I must say, when I first contemplated the notion of moving to a facility in an area as rural as this, I was petrified at all I'd be missing compared to a more lively, metropolitan region. But then I hear stories like this, and I thank God that I escaped all the madness of urban life." He used the word "madness" without a trace of irony. "That said, I'm not sure exactly how we can help you."

Sydney took the measure of the man in front of her. He was small and thin, with narrow shoulders and a sharp, nervous face. He looked every bit the midlevel medical bureaucrat that he'd clearly become in his role as superintendent. And yet, in spite of his outward appearance, his manner and voice had a calming effect, and Sydney sensed that underneath his governmental façade there was a genuine and caring doctor. "I'm not sure how you can help me, either," she admitted. "I guess all I really want is to talk to whoever my sister met with when she was out here."

"Yes, I talked with her briefly, and I know she met with Drs. Zorn and Golden. I've sent for both of them, and you're welcome to chat with them, but I'm still not clear why this is so important. You can't really imagine that her visit here had anything to do with her murder in Washington, can you?"

Sydney frowned as she shook her head. "No, probably not."

"Then why come all the way out here?"

Sydney's frown deepened. "I'm not sure. I can't explain anything that I'm feeling right now. Initially, I was just curious—about anything and everything having to do with my sister and her life. And then, when the police suggested that maybe Liz wasn't killed by a random burglar, I guess I got caught up in trying to work through all the other possibilities. On some rational level, I know it makes no sense for me to have driven all the way out here, but I somehow felt like I had to do something—*anything*—to make myself feel like I was accomplishing something for my sister."

Mayer sighed in a sympathetic way. "Well, as I said, we'll be happy to answer any questions you may have, and we'll do whatever we can to put your mind at ease; but I wouldn't get my hopes up too high."

She smiled back at him. "Thank you." She took a notebook out of her shoulder bag and flipped it open on her knee, pulling a ballpoint pen out of her jacket and readying herself to take some notes. "So, do you have any idea why my sister came out here—what she was looking for or investigating?"

Mayer shook his head. "I know only that she was looking for information about the way in which this place, the Institute, was run back in the old days—in the 1940s, '50s, and '60s—before the state mandated a systematic reform. I've only been here for a few years, and I'm not much of a history buff, so there was very little I could tell her. As a result, my conversation with your sister was very short, and I merely referred her on to Drs. Zorn and Golden. They've been here longer than anyone else, so I was guessing they'd have the best chance of helping her."

"You don't have any idea what she was after?"

Mayer hesitated. "Well," he began, "I do know that she was looking for information about the treatment of the inmates prior to the reform. She seemed particularly interested in any experiments that were performed, and the practice of eugenics that was active at the time. But I don't know why."

"Inmates?" Sydney let some shock slip into her tone. "Don't you mean patients?"

"Today, yes, they're called patients—of course. Back in the middle of the twentieth century, though, they were called inmates, and, sadly, that's more or less how they were treated." Dr. Mayer could clearly see the horrified expression on Sydney's face. "You must understand that this facility was entirely reformed thirty-five years ago, and no longer follows any of the practices from the decades before." He sighed in admission. "It is true, though, that back when this hospital was known as the Virginia Juvenile Institute for the Mentally Defective, it took a vastly different approach to the 'treatment' of those who were sent here. Back then, any child with an IQ judged to be below 80 who didn't have anyone to take care of them was eligible to be committed here. Once they were here, there was little hope of release."

Sydney frowned. "My understanding is that an IQ of 80 may be a little low, but it's hardly a cause for institutionalization."

"Certainly that's true today, and many doctors have recognized that IQ tests are of limited value in measuring a person's overall intelligence. They are often a better test of what a person has learned than of what they may be capable of learning. That's particularly true in children. The tests also suffer from cultural and linguistic biases that tend to favor those people who have been raised with a particular kind of background. But back when this Institute was founded in 1922, there was a strong national movement afoot to cleanse the American society of inferior genes, so any child who was deemed 'inferior' for whatever reason might potentially find their way here. In many respects, that movement remained strong through the 1950s and into the 1960s."

"That's terrible."

"It is," Mayer agreed. "Worse still was that the testing that was done at the time made modern IQ tests look like paragons of scientific measurement. Very often they assumed a basic knowledge and skill level, even when testing children who'd had no education whatsoever. As a result, a great many children who most likely had average or above-average intelligence levels were probably condemned to grow up in this institute, and many others like it across the country at the time. Eventually, this place became nothing more than a dumping ground for society's unwanted children—orphans, abandoned children, offspring of convicted criminals. Sometimes even wealthy families sent their children here if they were embarrassed by them: if they were slow, or if they had clear abnormalities that might call the family's genetic suitability and strength into question." He shook his head. "I'd like to think that at least those parents thought that their children would get treatment here."

"But the children didn't, I take it?"

The buzzer rang on Dr. Mayer's phone and he flipped on the intercom. His secretary's voice could be heard both over the phone and through the closed door. "I'm sorry to interrupt, Dr. Mayer, but Drs. Golden and Zorn are here to see you."

"Thank you, Lisa," Mayer said. "Please send them in." He turned back to Sydney. "As I said before, I only arrived here a few years ago, so all I know is the lore. These two will be able to tell you much more."

The door opened and a man and a woman came in. They both had on white medical coats, and they both looked to be in their sixties. Sydney and Dr. Mayer rose for the introductions. "Sydney Chapin, these are Drs. Golden and Zorn; Doctors, this is Sydney Chapin." He paused for a moment, unsure what else to say. Then he added, hesitantly, "Ms. Chapin is the sister of Elizabeth Creay, the reporter from Washington who was here to visit us a few weeks ago."

A look of understanding broke on the older woman's face. "Oh, my word—the woman who was murdered!" She stepped forward and took Sydney's hand, holding it in her own in a manner that felt more like an embrace than a handshake. "I read about your sister's death in the paper. I was shocked. She seemed like such a kind, caring person. I'm so sorry."

"Thank you," Sydney responded.

"My name is Sandra Golden. But you can call me Sandy."

The other doctor who'd walked into the room with Dr. Golden extended his hand, though it was stiff and awkward in comparison to Golden's. "Mark Zorn, Ms. Chapin," he said. "It's nice to meet you, and you have my deepest sympathies as well."

"I appreciate that."

A moment passed during which no one seemed to know exactly what to say. Mayer finally stepped in to fill the void. "Sandy, Mark, Ms. Chapin is here to follow up on her sister's visit. She's trying to determine why her sister was here, and whether her visit might have had anything to do with her murder."

Sandra Golden let out an audible gasp and put her hand on her chest. "You don't really think that's possible, do you?" she asked.

Sydney shrugged, feeling foolish and awkward. "I don't know," she said. Then she corrected herself. "No, actually. I guess I really don't. The police thought they had the murder solved, but now they seem unsure, and I found out Liz had been up here asking questions, and then she was in Professor Barneton's office right before she was killed—" She was talking quickly, hardly taking a breath, and she realized her explanation wasn't making any sense, particularly to the three doctors who had no idea what she'd been through in the past few days. She could read the sympathy in the eyes of the psychiatrists evaluating her as she spoke, and recognized that it bordered on pity. *They think I've lost my mind*, she thought. *Then again, maybe I have.* "I don't know why I came, really. I feel silly now." She fought back tears of frustration as she stopped talking.

Dr. Golden stepped forward again and took her by the arm, guiding her back down into her chair. "Sit down, dear," she said. Then she turned to Mayer and directed him. "Aldus, have someone fetch Ms. Chapin a glass of water, please."

"Yes, of course," Mayer said sheepishly. He flipped the intercom on his phone and asked his secretary to bring a glass of water.

Golden sat in the chair next to Sydney, still holding her arm. "Don't worry, dear, this is all quite normal." The older woman smiled and Sydney felt remarkably comforted. "You're looking for a way to be close to your sister—to keep her with you as long as possible. You're also struggling with the guilt of being the sibling who didn't die, and that guilt naturally makes you want to do something to help your sister—to make things right and relieve yourself of the guilt. What better way than finding her killer?"

Golden smiled again. "Mark, sit down," she instructed Zorn. He took a seat against the wall without questioning her. "I think you'll find that your sister's visit here had nothing to do with her murder—in all candor, I don't see how it possibly could—but we will do whatever we can to help you."

"I already told her that her sister was asking questions about what went on at the Institute prior to the reforms in the 1960s, and that I directed her to you two because you've been here longer than anyone else," Mayer explained.

Zorn nodded. "That's true, although I didn't come here until several years after the reforms had been implemented, so I didn't have much information to give your sister either," he said. "I told her that Sandy was the only one still here who was involved in the reforms themselves, and that she would be a better person to talk to."

Golden looked from Mayer to Zorn, and then back to Sydney. "I talked to her for quite a while. I couldn't answer all of her questions, or even most of them, but it did seem that she found some of the background information I gave her helpful."

"What did you talk about?" asked Sydney, who had regained her composure.

Dr. Golden took a deep breath, as though steeling herself against a terrible force. Then she patted Sydney on the knee. "I talked to her about what we found when we were sent here to reform this place."

Outside in the parking lot, Lee Salvage ambled through the maze of cars toward the main building. He had donned a baseball cap and some sunglasses, both appropriate accoutrements for the hot weather and remarkably efficient at obscuring the way a person looks. Had anyone noticed him, they wouldn't have given him a second thought. He could have been a relative of one of the patients, or one of the many vendors who ventured far out into the woods to fulfill their lucrative government contracts with the Institute. The parking lot was empty, and those within the building were otherwise occupied with the business of looking after their charges.

Toward the front of the parking lot, he passed the blue Honda Accord with the California license plates he'd been following from a distance for the entire morning. As he came parallel with the rear tire, he bent down to tie his shoelace. After pulling the laces tight, he went to stand up, resting a hand on the rear wheel to steady himself.

One would have to have been watching him very carefully to notice the long, thin knife in his hand as he inserted it between the rim and the tire. The aperture barely made a sound as air began leaking very slowly from the tire. He withdrew the knife, and the hole healed itself, at least for the moment. The tire would hold, he knew, until the car started moving and the additional pressure from the motion forced the slit open. Then the leak would work its effects gradually, though with increasing speed as the tire sagged. It would take thirty miles, maybe forty, by his calculations before the tire would give out completely. *That should be just about right*, he thought.

He stood up and straightened his cap, keeping it low on his forehead to hide his blond hair. He took two steps toward the building, and then made a show of snapping his fingers as though he'd forgotten something in his car, and turned to head back to the far end of the lot. Once he was safely back to his car, he flipped open his cellular phone again to take a look, though he knew what he'd see. Still no service. He cursed. It would be better if he could check with his client to confirm his plans, but it looked as though that would be impossible. He could drive down to the nearest town to find a pay phone, but that was fifteen miles up the road, and not knowing how long the girl would be, he couldn't leave her for that long.

He rubbed his chin. Fate had made the decision for him, it seemed. His orders had been clear: *If it appears that she is moving in a direction that would cause any significant risk, I give you complete discretion to handle the matter as you see fit.* That was how his client had instructed him, and that left him little choice.

Chapter Thirty

"I WASN'T A PART of what went on here prior to 1968," Dr. Sandra Golden said firmly. They were still in Mayer's office, and Sydney's attention was completely focused on the older woman. "I made that clear to your sister, and I want to make it clear to you. I tell you that not in defense of myself, but so that you'll understand that much of my knowledge isn't really knowledge—it's reasonable assumption, calculated speculation, and logical conclusion. We'll probably never know the full extent of what happened here, but it is true that I probably know as much as almost anyone else."

"How?" Sydney asked breathlessly.

"I was one of the first people sent here to carry out the reforms. I was young and idealistic, with a brand-new medical degree and a specialty in psychiatry. I don't know if I would have chosen to come here under the best of circumstances, but it was still unusual for women to be doctors at the time, and jobs were hard to come by. I'd planned on getting some seasoning here by working with hard cases, and then moving into private practice." She sighed heavily. "But after we saw what had happened here, I was never able to drag myself away."

Golden leaned forward in her chair and addressed Sydney directly. "To give you some background, you must remember that the world was changing in 1968, and that meant the entire world was changing—including the medical establishment. In the real world, you had the idealists fighting for racial equality, sexual equality, nonviolence, and basic civil liberties. In the medical community, you had doctors fighting the same sorts of battles. The medical community in general, and the psychiatric community in particular, were still entrenched in a more traditionalist approach—treat the symptoms when possible, and isolate the patient or disease when not. Many of the younger doctors, however, were starting to approach medicine and psychiatry differently; taking a more patient-centric view, and working hard toward integrating those with problems into normal society, rather than isolating them."

She drew herself up in her chair and continued. "You have to realize how all of this impacted this place. As you've probably already learned, back then, this place was known as the Virginia Juvenile Institute for the Mentally Defective." Sydney nodded, and Golden shook her head in frustration at some unseen force. "I think people had some idea about the problems here for a long time," she said angrily. "It was a place that was still mired in the treatment schemes and medical philosophies of the 1930s. The driving principle was that people were born into their station in life—born smart or stupid, tall or short, sane or crazy—and that the most that could be done with those deemed 'defective' was to control their evil tendencies, usually through inhuman discipline. The ultimate goal, of course, was to keep them from infecting the greater population, and keep them from perpetuating whatever defect they had by preventing them from reproducing in the normal course.

"In 1968, however, a more progressive and proactive doctor was appointed to oversee all of the state's medical facilities—including this one. He fired everyone in this place, just about, and brought in a whole new team of young idealists to try to turn this place around. That was when I came." She shook her head as the memories came flooding back.

"That was a hard time," she continued. "The things that I saw when I arrived—I couldn't have imagined them in my worst nightmares. We found rooms with shackles attached to brick walls smeared with feces. We found leather straps and chains and bludgeons, and other instruments of torture we couldn't even identify. We found children who'd been beaten so badly that even radical surgery couldn't correct the mutilations. We found older boys—men, really—who were in their twenties and hadn't been released or transferred to another facility as required. Children as young as twelve had already undergone significant, and in some cases experimental, lobotomies; children had been sterilized; children had been used in experiments. And of course, as you'd expect in a place like that, sexual abuse was rampant. The inhumanities visited on the poor children who were unlucky enough to have found their way here were breathtaking." She paused. "And we found graves," she said in hushed tones. "We found so many graves, unmarked and uncared for, that we didn't know what to do." She looked at Sydney for a long moment. "There should never be that many graves in a facility for children."

Sydney shivered. "It must have been awful."

"It was more than awful."

"How did the children die?"

"We don't know," Golden said. "When the first team of us arrived, we found the Institute deserted by the former medical staff. Most of them had seen the writing on the wall and had resigned weeks earlier. The guards abandoned the place a day or two before we were scheduled to arrive, probably realizing that they might be held responsible for some of what we found. Only some of the maintenance crew remained, and they didn't even have keys to the parts of the facility where the patients—or inmates, as they were called then—were kept. When we got here, we found that most of the children hadn't been fed for days, and had only been left with enough water to get them through to our arrival. We lost four of the younger ones to complications from dehydration in our first week."

The room was silent for a moment, until Mayer interjected stiffly, "Of course, this was a long time ago, and the practices from back then have been entirely abandoned."

"It's true," Golden agreed. "After the shock wore off, those of us who were brought in to change this place made a promise to each other to make sure that nothing like what we saw would ever happen in this place again. We worked tirelessly to turn this facility into a model of what good juvenile psychiatric care should be. I'm happy to say that I think we've succeeded in large part. Obviously, no facility is perfect, but I believe that for the past quarter century we've done an exemplary job not only of housing or 'controlling' our charges, but also of providing them with the best therapy and education we can, to give them a fighting chance to live full, satisfying lives in the real world when they leave here." Her face grew dark.

"But there are still times when I wake up in the middle of the night in a cold sweat because some painful shard of memory from those first few weeks has been kicked loose in a dream, and I find myself right back here in 1968, reliving the horror."

Sydney looked for a long time at Golden. "And that's what my sister wanted to talk to you about?"

"Well, that's what we did, in fact, talk about. But your sister was also looking for much more specific information about what went on here before I arrived, about who was responsible, and who participated in what activities—information I wasn't able to provide." Sydney gave Golden a quizzical look, and the older woman continued. "You see, dear, we never really found out exactly what went on here. As I said, based on what we found, we can make some pretty educated guesses regarding the types of 'treatment' patients were subjected to, but we don't have any specific information about any of the activities."

"How is that possible?"

"When our predecessors abandoned the Institute, someone absconded with all of the records. Or destroyed them—we were never really able to find out. It took more than a month to determine who all our patients were, how long they'd been here, and what was really wrong with them."

Sydney was shocked. "Wasn't anyone ever prosecuted?"

"I'm afraid not, dear," Golden said. "Our priority at the time was to help the children who had been left here to rot. We left the investigation into any wrongdoing to the law enforcement people in the state, and as far as we ever found out, nothing ever came of the inquiries."

Sydney was indignant. "It's hard for me to believe that nothing was ever done about what went on here."

"I understand your feelings, but you really shouldn't be that surprised. Remember, these were society's unwanted children. No one cared to face our collective responsibility in leaving them here and turning a blind eye. In addition, without the records of what went on, it would have been difficult to prove anything, and none of the children here had any interest in facing their tormenters in court. You also need to remember that this was 1968. There were so many 'greater' injustices in the eyes of the country at large that were being fought over. The last thing anyone in the state wanted was to drag this issue out into the open."

"So my sister left here without getting any of the information she was looking for," Sydney concluded.

Golden looked hesitant for the first time of the afternoon. "I don't know about that," she said. She cast a glance at Mayer. "I decided that there was really only one person who might be able to give her some of the information she was looking for."

"Who was that?"

Golden hesitated again. "Willie Murphy," she said at last.

"Good heavens, Sandy!" Mayer exclaimed. "What on earth were you thinking?"

Golden squared her shoulders in her chair defiantly. "I was thinking that Willie might be able to help Ms. Creay," she said. "And maybe even that Ms. Creay might be able to help Willie."

"Who is Willie Murphy?" Sydney asked.

Mayer ignored the question. "You had no right," he said. He sounded more disappointed than angry.

"Who is Willie Murphy?" Sydney repeated her question.

Golden addressed Mayer. "Aldus, I've been trying to reach him—really reach him—for more than three decades. I thought if he wasn't able to talk to me, then maybe he'd be able to talk to her. He'll never really be well until he lets some of what happened out."

"You still should have talked to me first," Mayer said.

"Please!" Sydney said forcefully, and all eyes turned toward her with a look of surprise that suggested that they'd momentarily forgotten she was in the room. They looked back and forth among one another, clearly hesitant to speak. The silence in the room was oppressive, and made Sydney feel uneasy. "Who is Willie Murphy?" she demanded again.

"He's a class-A dickhead, isn't he?" Cassian commented. They were riding back into the city, without any firm answers. Nonetheless, Cassian had no doubt how he felt about Leighton Creay.

"Yeah," Train agreed. "He's not stupid, though. He's not going to give us anything easy on him, and he knows he doesn't have to talk to us unless we drag his ass in on a warrant. If we do that, you can be damn sure he'll lawyer up so fast that we won't find out what he's had for breakfast."

"He'd probably even enjoy the opportunity to rub it in our faces."

"No doubt," Train said. "On the other hand, no matter how big an asshole Creay is, it still doesn't mean that he killed his ex."

"No, it doesn't. But I'd really like it if he did. I'd love

to nail the smug little bastard." Cassian was fuming quietly. "Sitting up there in his country club with his smart-ass remarks. He's the kind of asshole who'd make a seriously satisfying bust."

Train looked at his young partner. "You want him, then you gotta find a way to go after him."

Cassian nodded. "I'll start digging through his finances—find out how much money he's got and where it's coming from. That'll give us a better idea of what he's up to. I'll also start asking some discreet questions about who he's been hanging out with recently. He's probably too smart to have done this himself, and I'm guessing his alibi will hold up, but it's still possible that he hired someone for the job."

"Sounds good."

"It's not going to be the easiest thing in the world to build this case, Sarge. You know that, right?"

"I know it," Train said. "That's why I'm so glad I'm working with such a fucking genius."

Chapter Thirty-one

THE MUSIC REACHED her while they were still on the stairs, working their way down through the intestines of the huge brick building that served as the Institute's central structure. Sydney could hear the humming of the overstressed electrical system struggling to feed the requirements of the medical facility, and it reminded her of every other public building she'd ever been in, where the needs of today are satisfied by pushing the technology of yesterday to the limit. She could hear the notes, though, through the constant buzz and the dark depression of the basement, cutting the air in a precise yet carefree fashion, echoing off the cement and steel. Bluegrass. Sydney recognized the tune as a variation on one of Dr. John's classics, and knew enough about music to appreciate the skill with which it was being played.

"He's quite gifted in many ways," Sandra Golden said with a sad smile. "It's tragic to think of what he might have done with his life under better circumstances."

"He was here when you arrived in 1968?"

Golden nodded. "He was. He was nineteen at the time, and as near as we could tell, he'd been kept alone in a dark cell for over a year. He was barely human when we found him—curled up in a ball, covered in his own excrement, babbling softly to himself. It took six months before we could get him to start speaking coherently, and even then, he seemed to have forgotten everything that happened to him before we got here. Either that or he's simply chosen never to talk about it. In any case, I've been working with him for a long time to try to chase the demons from his mind, but he doesn't seem to want to cooperate. When your sister got here, I thought maybe she'd be able to get him to remember more."

"I don't understand, if he was nineteen in 1968, then he must be in his fifties now."

"Fifty-seven last month," Golden confirmed.

"Then how can he be a patient here? I thought this was a juvenile facility."

"Oh, he's not a patient," Golden explained. "He's our maintenance man. You see, we treated him for over a year after we arrived, but after a while, because of his age, we had to transfer him to another facility where they tried to get him ready to enter the real world and have a productive life. When they ultimately released him, things didn't go well." She shook her head. "How do you prepare a person who's been locked up in his own private hell for most of his life to deal with the 'real world'? He drifted from job to job without any success, got taken advantage of, got used—got tired, I guess. Then he turned to drugs and disappeared for over a year. I remember feeling responsible—like there was something more I should have done." Sydney could hear the stress in Golden's voice.

"Then one day, about five years after he'd left our care, he showed up again. It was during the winter, and we were having one of those freak ice storms we sometimes get out here. It was cold and dark, and I was looking out my window, dreaming about better weather, when I saw him. He was standing in the field in front of the building, just looking up, still as a statue. He was in terrible shape; battered and drug addled. We rushed him inside, and took care to nurse him back to health. Then, while we were trying to figure out what to do with him, our generator broke. In a big-city hospital, that's not that significant a problem, because you've got the power company, and you've got backup power supplies. Out here it's just us, and no one could figure out what was wrong. He was just starting to move around a little better, and he asked if he could take a look at it. He said he'd worked briefly for an electrician, and thought he might be able to help. Sure enough, he had the place up and running in a matter of hours, and it occurred to us that this might be the best place for him. He's a natural with machines. And this way, we were able to keep trying to help him."

They rounded a bend in the narrow basement hallway, and the music grew stronger. Sydney could see a light drifting through a doorway at the end of the corridor. Golden stopped her at the threshold. "He prefers to be alone when he plays," she explained. "I think this song's almost done."

Standing at the doorway, half blocked by the doorjamb, Sydney could see a shriveled man with white-gray hair slumped over a guitar on a wooden chair behind a gray metal government-issue desk. His eyes were closed, and his fingers flew across the fretboard of his beaten old six-string. His ivory skin was so pale it was almost translucent, and his shoulders were pinched together, swimming under a heavy denim workshirt that looked at least two sizes too large. Sitting there in the wan light of the single bulb in the lamp on his desk, he looked to Sydney like an apparition—a middle-aged Boo Radley whose alabaster fingers danced nimbly upon the guitar without even seeming to touch it, producing a melody at once sad and hopeful.

When the music ended, Golden poked her head into the room. "Willie, it's Dr. Golden. I have a visitor with me. Can we come in?"

At first Sydney thought the man hadn't heard, because he sat eerily still, eyes closed, straining as if to hear something. "Ain't done yet," he said in a quiet, even voice.

Golden signaled for Sydney to keep quiet and still for another moment. After a brief pause, the man opened his eyes and placed the guitar carefully into a weathered case that lay open against the wall. "Wasn't dead yet," he said, seemingly to no one in particular. His head was still down and he was flicking the catches closed on the guitar case.

"Who wasn't dead yet?" Sydney asked Golden, still unsure whether to engage the strange man directly in conversation.

"The music," the man answered Sydney's question himself. He sat up and looked at the two women by the door. Something in his eyes gave Sydney a start. They were pale blue, flecked with white and pierced by pupils the size of pinpricks. But it was something behind the eyes that unsettled her. "The music wasn't dead yet," he explained. "It was still out there, hangin' on to the air, tryin' to get out. I had to wait till it was gone." Sydney had no idea how to respond, and wondered whether he was being serious or merely playing with her.

"Willie," Golden said, walking into the little office ahead of Sydney, "I'd like you to meet a friend of mine. This is Sydney Chapin."

Willie nodded, but did not extend a hand. "Hello, Miss Sydney," he said.

"Hello, Willie," Sydney replied.

"Sydney wants to talk to you about Elizabeth Creay, the woman who came to visit you a few weeks ago. You remember Ms. Creay, don't you?"

"I remember her." Willie nodded. He looked at Sydney again. "You got her eyes," he said.

"She was my sister."

"Willie," Golden said softly, "Sydney's sister Elizabeth was killed recently. She was murdered. You understand? Sydney wants to know what you talked about with her."

Willie shook his head. "I had me a bad feelin' for her," he said. "She carried death with her. She was nice, though. I'm sorry, ma'am."

All at once Sydney felt a rush of emotion over the loss of her sister. She choked it down. "Thank you, Willie," she said, her voice quavering.

Willie nodded. "I'll leave you two alone to talk," Golden said, withdrawing from the room.

As the door to the tiny office closed, Sydney felt lost once again, and a little uneasy in the presence of Willie Murphy. There seemed to be some power to him—a confidence born, perhaps, of the knowledge that he'd endured the worst inhumanity his fellow man could inflict and had survived. There were wounds, that much was clear from his posture and the drawn expression, but they had not overtaken him.

"Your sister seemed like a good woman," he said, breaking the silence between them. "Sometimes you can tell, just from bein' in a person's company, whether they good or bad. I got to feelin' she was good."

"I think so," Sydney agreed.

Willie looked down at his hands. They were the only part of him that conveyed any physical strength. They were disproportionately large, and the calluses and grime on them made them seem less vulnerable than the rest of him. "So what you wanna ask me?"

Sydney cleared her throat. "I wanted to know what you talked with her about."

Willie took in a deep breath, expelling it in a long sigh. "We talked 'bout a lot of things."

"Can you remember anything specifically?"

He nodded. "Reckon I could." He looked up from his hands and faced her, his eyes meeting hers and drawing her in. They were luminescent, and the light they gave off seemed to rival the illumination from the lamp on his desk. "I told her 'bout my job; what it is I do here, and how I take care of all the buildings. I told her how I know somethin' 'bout bein' a patient here, so I can sympathize with those poor souls here now."

"Did you talk to her about what it was like when you were a patient here?"

He nodded slowly. "I told her how I got here, first." He closed his eyes slowly as he cast his memory back to his conversation with Elizabeth Creay and beyond. "How I was shipped here from Richmond after my parents was killed in a car crash in nineteen an' fifty-seven. How they took me to a room in the state hospital the day my daddy—he held on longer than my ma—passed on, and how they put a test in front of me and told me to answer the questions. I told her how I screamed at them." A dark smile crept across his face. "Damn, but how I screamed at them."

He opened his eyes and looked at her again. Sydney

could see the anger behind them. "You imagine that? Eight years ol' and they want me to take a test less than an hour after I watch my daddy gone to heaven?" He shook his head in disgust. "They heard things outta my mouth I don't think they'd ever heard before. I was kickin' and screamin' and throwin' the papers at anyone who came near me till two big ol' security guards tackled me and held me down. I remember this doctor—some long-necked, evil-lookin' man—speakin' down at me and sayin', 'This one's ready for the Institute, eh boys?' " He laughed and a tear rolled down his cheek. "I don't think I'd remembered that day till your sister came here and started in on me with all her questions. I thought the docs here were somethin' with they questions, but your sister got 'em all licked."

"What happened when you got here?" Sydney asked.

He shook his head. "You too, huh?" He sat back in his chair and looked down at his hands again. "That's what your sister kept pushin' at." His eyebrows drew together, knitting a scowl. Sydney couldn't tell whether it was an expression of anger or sadness. "Some things are better left buried in the past," he said at last.

"But my sister made you remember?"

"Some." Willie moved his mouth like he was chewing on something distasteful. "I'd started remembering some on my own over the years, but I always buried it again. Your sister started pokin' just underneath the surface, and some of what was shallow came out."

"What was it?" Sydney was breathless.

"Beatin's mainly." He looked at his knuckles as though searching for a scar long covered over. "They could deliver a beatin' somethin' awful. Not like what you'd imagine it'd be, or what you see in the movies, or what you read about.

Worse. Much worse. So bad you piss blood for a month, prayin' that you'll piss your life away, 'cause you know if you heal it's gonna start all over again."

"Do you remember who beat you?"

Willie Murphy scoffed at the question. "It was all of 'em. Guards mainly, but sometimes the docs, too."

"Would you remember who they were if you saw them?" Sydney asked. "Would you be willing to testify against them if you had the chance?"

"We talkin' 'bout stuff that happened forty years ago, mainly. You think anyone's gonna listen to the words of a moron 'bout somethin' that long ago?" Sydney looked away in embarrassment. "Yeah, Miss Sydney, that's the official diagnosis I got when I came here: *moron.* They say they stopped using the word, but that's what's on my papers."

Sydney didn't return his smile. "If you could remember, though, would you testify against the people who did these things to you if you had the chance?" She asked the question pointedly.

His face turned inward, and then grew dark. "No, I wouldn't. I don't even know if I'd trust myself to figure out who it was if someone gave me the chance, an' I don't suppose it'd take the best lawyer in the world to make me look foolish—particularly after all these years of no memory. It wouldn't serve no one—least of all me." He relaxed again, or maybe it was just that his shoulders slumped even farther from the fatigue of talking about the past. "'Sides, I 'spect I lost any rights I had when I took the money a while back."

"The money?" Sydney asked. "What money?"

"Settlement money, they called it," he replied. "From one of them group lawsuits. What do they call them?"

"Class actions?" Sydney guessed.

"Yeah, that's it. Class action. That's what I was told. I was part of a class. I got some money 'cause I was part of a class." He chuckled. "Makes it all sound civilized, don't it?"

"And this was for the beatings you suffered?" Sydney asked.

Willie frowned. "No, not the beatings. It was for the testing."

"The testing?" Sydney felt lost.

"Medical testing," Willie explained. "They used us as guinea pigs for anything they felt like. Who'd care? Bunch of morons out in the woods, who'd complain? So when they wanted to figure something out, they'd get a group of us together and test things."

"What sort of things?"

"Who knows?" He laughed sadly again. "An' who really cares? It wasn't nearly as bad as the beatings. Lots of times, being tested just meant we got better food—cereal mainly, but in our position we couldn't complain. They say there was stuff in it, but you couldn't tell from the taste of it. And when you were in a test, none of the guards touched you. Those were the most bearable times I had here."

"Were you hurt as a result of the testing?" Sydney asked gently.

"Depends on what you mean by hurt," Willie said. Then, in response to her confused look, he blushed. "They say I can't have kids." She looked away to avoid his embarrassment. "Not that it ever mattered much to me, though," he went on. "I never learned how to love nobody, anyhow. You spend that much time bein' beat, bein' put down, and you'll never really learn how to act like a real person again." He looked off into space. "Everything normal in you just fades away, like the music. It clings to the air for a while—bounces off these stone walls and tries to keep itself goin', but after a while, the air is too thin, and the walls are too cold, and it dies out."

Sydney had no idea what to say. "Who gave you the money?" she asked after a moment.

"A lawyer," Willie spat. "He said it was comin' from the government an' some of the companies the government was usin' to carry out the tests. Said I was the 'named plaintiff,' whatever that means, and congratulated me for bein' a beacon of justice." He shook his head. "The people here—the people here before Dr. Golden an' them others came—they took everything from me. They took my childhood. They took my manhood. They took any chance I could ever have. An' the lawyers gave me twenty thousand dollars in return. Some beacon of justice, huh?" He looked away. "I don't even know how long ago it was. Ten years, maybe more. A sharp-dressed lawyer from D.C. walks down into this basement an' tells me he's made me a bunch of money. Even has a check cut already. Tells me all I have to do is sign a few papers, an' the money's mine. Twenty thousand dollars. For everything I'd lost. For everything I'd suffered through. Twenty thousand dollars."

"What did you do?"

Willie's eyes dropped. "I signed the papers and took the check," he said. For a moment, Sydney thought the man was going to cry. "And then I shook the man's hand, and I thanked him," he said with disgust. "Twenty thousand dollars for everything they'd done to me, and I *thanked* the man!" His body shook violently, and for a moment Sydney thought he was crying. It was only when he picked his head up that she saw the bitter smile on his face and recognized the spasms as laughter. "Maybe they was right all along," he said through gritted teeth. "Maybe I am a moron."

She wanted to reach out and touch him, to provide some warmth and comfort, but from his posture he seemed incapable of receiving it. "You're not a moron," was the best comfort she could offer. "Did you tell my sister anything else?"

Willie shook his head. "No ma'am. Nothin' else I can remember. I'm real sorry."

"Nothing at all?" she pressed.

He looked long and hard at her. "Nothin' at all," he said.

She could tell that their conversation was over, and she rose out of her seat. "Thank you very much for your time, Willie," she said.

"You're welcome, Miss Sydney," Willie replied.

She walked to the door and opened it. Just as she stepped through the doorway, Willie spoke again. "I meant what I said, Miss Sydney."

She turned and looked at him. He seemed even smaller than he had when she first walked in the room. "What's that, Willie?"

"Some things are better left buried in the past."

Chapter Thirty-two

IT WAS PAST SIX O'CLOCK in the evening by the time Sydney was on the road again, heading back toward Washington. She wouldn't make dinner at her mother's house—not with a five-hour drive ahead of her. She pulled out her cell phone to call and let her mother and Amanda know that she would be late, and not to worry; she flipped open the phone and had started dialing before she noticed that the service indicator was flashing. Not surprising, really, she thought. Most cellular coverage tended to center on populated areas around cities and suburbs, and it didn't take a sociologist to recognize that this mountainous region in southwestern Virginia clearly didn't qualify. She put her cell phone away and reminded herself to call from a pay phone once she was closer to civilization.

She was disappointed at how little her investigation had yielded. The Institute itself was eerie in its isolation, and its shadowy past seemed the stuff of horror movies, but she'd come across nothing that would suggest any connection to her sister's death. Even Willie Murphy's tale led nowhere in the end. He couldn't remember who was responsible for his horrific treatment all those years ago, and if he could, what would it matter? He was right; any decent attorney would be able to shred him on cross-examination, even if he were ever willing and able to identify any of the people responsible for his suffering. Moreover, the statute of limitations had most likely run out on anything other than a murder charge—and proving up a murder charge three or four decades old was a virtual impossibility. Nothing she or her sister had learned seemed to suggest a motive for murder on anyone's part.

And, of course, that made sense. Even Jack Cassian and his partner still thought Elizabeth had probably been killed during a random burglary. They were only looking for additional information to rule out any other possibility—prudent, she knew—to make sure that they had the right man. Perhaps Dr. Golden had been right, and Sydney's excursion had more to do with coming to grips with her sister's death, and with her own feelings of guilt and anger, than with any rationally held belief that Liz had been torn from her as a result of some larger conspiracy. She cursed her foolishness as she drove along the deserted rural highway back toward the real world.

She hadn't passed another car since she'd left the Institute, she realized, and the quiet of the road was disconcerting. The narrow dirt shoulder slipped precipitously into dense forest, and there were no houses, stores, or gas stations within sight. The feeling of isolation did nothing to brighten her spirits. She should have stayed back in D.C., she thought. Amanda needed her, and instead of being there for her niece when she could provide the most comfort, she'd wasted an entire day in a backwater state mental hospital. Perhaps she was the one who needed to be committed.

She had the radio turned up, and the crooned refrains of rednecks bemoaning their lost loves, lost dogs, and lost trucks (not necessarily in that order) helped to block out the heavy slapping noise from the rear of the car. It wasn't until the steady percussion started to throw off the handling of the Accord that she turned down the music and heard the steadily increasing grind of metal on asphalt.

She pulled off the road and onto the dirt shoulder, stopping the car and slamming her fist on the steering wheel in frustration. This was the last thing she needed.

She got out of the car and stood at the edge of the road. She was in the middle of nowhere, and there were no cars or structures in sight; the forest through which the lonely road had been carved looked nearly impenetrable. At times like this, she was amazed at the vast amount of land in America that remained untouched. The afternoon sun tossed shadows off the cloud of dust that her car had kicked up when she pulled off the road. She brushed the hair out of her eyes and groaned in frustration.

She walked to the rear of the car to evaluate the situation. It was the rear left tire that was flat, and from the looks of it, it was completely shot. The metal rim looked to have sunk into the dirt shoulder. She kicked at a rock and headed back to the front seat to pop the trunk release to get at the spare.

She was just opening the door when a flash of light on the highway caught her eye, and she squinted into the sun to the west to see a car coming toward her at a distance from the direction of the Institute. She straightened up and shaded her brow to get a better look at the vehicle. It looked like a dark blue American-made sedan: nondescript, probably a Buick or a Chevrolet.

Sydney walked back to the rear of her car, considering whether to flag down the approaching car and ask the driver for help. It seemed silly; after all, she was perfectly capable of changing her own tire. At the same time, she was exhausted from a long and emotionally draining day, and there was a part of her that was willing to play the damsel in distress. After a moment's thought, she decided against it. The feminist within her, passive though it most often was, couldn't justify such a blatant stereotype. Besides, she figured, any person whose help she would welcome would stop to lend assistance of his own volition. So she simply stood by the side of the highway, watching the car approach.

The sedan slid along the narrow sliver of road, down a long incline toward her. At first she was convinced that it would speed on by, leaving her to change her own tire. A hundred yards or so before it reached her, though, it decelerated rapidly and pulled to the shoulder behind Sydney's Accord.

Sydney felt a wave of relief sweep over her as the fresh cloud of dust stirred by the sedan began to settle. She would have help changing her tire, and she hadn't needed to compromise her principles. She waved the dust out of her face, straining to get a better look at her savior through the tinted windshield.

He emerged a moment later, stepping out of his car with a slow, tired air about him. He had wispy blond hair and ruddy, sagging features. He might have been attractive earlier in his life, but something about him seemed defeated, and even a little hostile. Sydney shivered, but she shrugged off her intuition, dismissing it as a by-product of the stressful day, and of the unsettling feeling of being stranded on a lonely country highway.

"Car trouble, ma'am?" the man asked as he approached the rear of the car. He was smiling, and his drawl made him seem friendlier than Sydney had first pegged him.

"Yeah," Sydney replied. "Looks like I've got a flat." She pointed ineffectually at the rear wheel.

The man bent down and took a look. "I'd say so. Did you hit something?"

"I don't think so. The car just started shimmying gradually and it took me a few minutes to figure out what was wrong."

"That makes sense. It looks like the rim is bent from running on asphalt."

Sydney frowned. "Is that a big problem?"

The man smiled. "Not really. It'll cost you a little more when you get it fixed, but as long as you've got a spare, I should be able to have you out of here in a jiffy." He stood up, still smiling, and extended his hand. "I'm Mike," he said.

Sydney hesitated. She was unaccustomed to giving out her name to complete strangers. "Sydney," she said at last, knowing it would be rude to say nothing. "Thanks for stopping, Mike. Not everyone would be so nice."

He laughed. "Yeah, well we're a friendly bunch out here. Nothing like the folks in D.C. People there'd let you rot by the side of the road."

"That's probably the truth." Sydney laughed as well.

"If you pop the trunk up there, I'll get the spare out and we can see how quickly we can have you on your way."

"Sure thing. I can't tell you how grateful I am." Sydney walked back up to the driver's side door, opening it and stepping inside so she could reach the trunk release.

She was truly grateful to this stranger for stopping to help her. She had no doubt that she would have been able to change the tire herself, but only after consulting the manual and taking the time to figure out what she was doing. Mike seemed competent, and would surely have her back on the road in a matter of minutes. That was good; the visit to the Institute had taken far more time than she had anticipated, and the sky was already fading to orange. Darkness would fall soon, and the last thing she needed was to be changing a tire on a dark, deserted, one-lane highway.

She reached over toward the center console and flipped the switch releasing the trunk latch. She looked into the rearview mirror and saw the trunk door rise, obscuring Mike, who was still standing behind the car, from her view. "There you go," she called. "Is there anything else I can do to help?"

"No thanks," came the reply. "If you just stay up there, I'll have you out of here in no time."

Exhausted, Sydney leaned back in the seat and closed her eyes for a moment. This was pretty good service, she thought; he wasn't even asking her to help. So why was it, she wondered, that she was bothered by such a nice man? He'd been a perfect gentleman, and had kept his distance. And yet something about him seemed off. It was something he'd said that she couldn't put her finger on. She replayed their brief exchange in her head, but could identify nothing specific.

She sighed. It had been such a long day that her mind was probably just playing tricks on her. She'd feel better when she got back to D.C.

As she sat in the driver's seat of her car, for some reason that phrase stuck in her mind. *Back to D.C.* She repeated it over and over again without understanding why. Then suddenly it hit her, and she knew what was bothering her about Mike.

She sifted through their exchange again, and focused on what he'd said. *We're a friendly bunch out here. Nothing like the folks in D.C. . . .*

How had he known she was from Washington? The license plates on her car were still from California, and this far out into the mountains there were several other cities she could be from—Richmond, Fredericksburg, Raleigh—and that was assuming she had to be from a city at all. So how had he assumed she was from D.C. with such certainty? Something felt dreadfully wrong, and her heart started pounding as she sat up quickly, her head spinning around toward the back of the car.

It was at that moment that the man's arm came through her window, grabbing her around the neck and squeezing her throat closed.

Chapter Thirty-three

THE THIN SMILE HUNG ON Lee Salvage's face like an icicle. It had been so easy, he reflected, that if he'd had a conscience, it might have bothered him. She was trusting and weak, and there was really no challenge. After she'd popped the trunk open, he'd wasted no time; as quickly and quietly as he could, he'd moved up along the side of the car and grabbed her before she perceived any danger.

Now, holding on to her throat with his left hand, he reached his right hand into the car to gain some leverage and apply greater force to her neck. As he worked, he hesitated for a moment, looking closely at her face as it turned red and her eyes wheeled in terror. She was attractive. It was unprofessional, he knew, to take note of such a thing at a moment like this, and to allow himself to become distracted. In this case there was little risk, though; a girl as pampered and unsuspecting as Sydney Chapin would hardly present any significant resistance. He wondered whether, had his life been different, he would have ever had a chance with a woman such as this. He liked to think so. He knew that some women had found him attractive once, but he'd never been able to form any emotional bonds with anyone. Silly to even think of it—this girl would be dead in a matter of seconds.

Even now she was leaning into his hand, cutting off her own oxygen more quickly, rather than pulling away. It was odd, he mused, how people so often reacted to an attack in the manner least likely to save their lives. He might not even need his right hand to apply additional pressure, though he knew it was best to be sure.

He leaned his head through the door to get better leverage, and all at once he knew something was wrong. Suddenly and without warning he was blind, and it felt as though his face was on fire. His eyes seemed as though they were melting, and his throat swelled and burned, preventing any air from reaching his lungs. He ripped himself back instinctively from the car door, and his hands flew to his face as he dropped to his knees. He coughed and choked and sputtered, writhing on the ground.

After a moment, he was able to catch his breath, and he realized he would survive. He felt fortunate, but just for a moment. It took only that long for him to realize he had greater problems than he'd realized, and the epiphany lasted for little more than a flash. As he struggled to open his eyes and assess his situation, he felt the sharp crack on the back of his skull and he pitched forward, the burning world around him dissolving into darkness.

Sydney saw the hand a split second before it closed around her throat, and her mind spun into action instantly. She'd spent enough time on her own that she'd made a point of being prepared for an attack at any time. It was an unfortunate reality that being vigilant against assaults had become a necessity for young women who lived alone. Living in San Francisco for years before law school and working in a bar in a questionable neighborhood in Oakland for a time had made her particularly aware of the dangers of carjacking, and she'd played out disaster scenarios—and her reactions to them—thousands of times before when she'd been alone in her car. Now, without hesitation or thought, she reacted as she'd rehearsed so many times before.

She reached down instinctively with her right hand, groping for the storage compartment just in front of the gearbox. Her hand brushed the knob of the stickshift, but she couldn't reach the small space in front of it—a place reserved for change and wallets and other sundries.

She tried to scream, but no sound escaped her throat, and she realized she was getting dizzy from lack of oxygen. Out of the corner of her eyes she could make out the face of the man who'd stopped to help her fix her tire, and the expression she saw terrified her.

She refocused and spun her eyes down and to the right. She was leaning too far back in her seat to reach the compartment, and she knew that she only had a matter of seconds. Bringing all her strength to bear, she threw her weight forward into the man's hand, her fingers clawing at the car's interior.

The pain and terror were overwhelming as the force of her own body weight added to the incredible strength of the man's hand around her throat, sealing her windpipe. For a moment, she thought it was over, as black spots began to hang in the center of her vision. But then her fingers closed around the object for which she'd been searching and she knew she had a chance.

It was pepper spray. Sydney kept a small canister in her car for her own protection. As she felt the man lean farther into the car, she brought the canister up, flicking off the safety with her thumb and aiming it directly into his face. Then she closed her own eyes and pressed the spray release.

His reaction was instantaneous; he bolted from the car in agony, releasing her at the same time. For a moment she thought she would vomit as her body convulsed, still trying unsuccessfully to take in air. She worried that her windpipe had been crushed when she realized that she wasn't breathing, but then she coughed once—a spasmodic, body-wrenching hack—and all at once her lungs filled, the rush of air burning through her, her body welcoming the pain as a sign of salvation.

She sputtered and gagged for a moment, allowing her breathing to return, and then pushed open the door and struggled out of the car. She knew that she wasn't yet safe; the pepper spray would incapacitate her attacker for a few moments, maybe more, but the damage she'd inflicted was far from permanent. She needed to make sure that he was in no position to harm her again.

He was rolling around in the dirt a few feet from the car, screaming in pain. His face was horribly contorted, and his hands clawed at his eyes like some overzealous thespian auditioning for the lead in *Oedipus Rex.* She stumbled around the car in a panic, looking for something with which to tie him up or further render him harmless. She could find nothing, and as she spun wildly around, keeping half her attention on the wounded man as he rolled on the ground, she was overpowered by the notion that he might regain his senses and renew his attack.

After a moment's search, she grabbed the tire iron out

of the trunk and hurried over to the man. He'd managed to raise himself up on his knees, and it looked as though he was getting his sight back. She worked her way behind him, holding the heavy metal rod out in front of her like a sword. Then, when she was directly behind his back, she raised it up like a baseball bat, taking aim at the back of his head.

She paused there for a moment, as a feeling of guilt and indecision grabbed hold of her. Left with even the briefest time to contemplate her actions, she balked at the notion of inflicting such serious harm on another person. After all, there must be another way. And yet she could think of nothing. When the man's hands dropped from his face—a motion Sydney took as a sign of recovery, however slight—she swung the iron around quickly without further thought or hesitation, connecting with a sickening crack to the back of the man's skull.

He dropped forward, his face sinking into the highway's shoulder. She bent forward to examine him and saw a thick smear of blood running from the back of his head, mixing with the dirt to form a thick, gritty mess. She knew at once that he must be dead, and for a minute she stood there over him, unable to move at all as she held firm to the tire iron that had saved her. Then as the realization that she'd killed a man settled into her, she began to shake.

It started in her knees as a minor weakness, and she thought she might simply steady herself as she straightened up. She couldn't, though. It spread too quickly from her knees up through her legs and into her hips. From there, it traveled along her spine and infected her entire body, sliding down her arms and into her fingers as it grew from a tremor to an earthquake. It racked her body until she dropped the tire iron and slumped to the ground. Without a word, and without even realizing it was happening, she rolled against the side of the car and drew herself tightly into a ball with her arms around her knees, closing her eyes against the reality of what had happened.

Chapter Thirty-four

WHEN SYDNEY OPENED her eyes, she had no idea for how long she'd been curled up by the side of the road. The sun was still hanging low on the horizon, and no one had driven by or stopped to examine the two people incapacitated next to their cars, so it couldn't have been too long—although she was beginning to wonder whether anyone ever passed by on this particular lonely stretch of highway. She felt woozy and tired, but the shaking had passed, and she was sure that she was in control of herself once again.

She looked over at the man's body, still facedown in the dirt near her car. *I killed him*, she thought again grimly. The knowledge that she'd acted in self-defense eased her guilt somewhat, but she still felt a gnawing at her conscience; a persistent illogical feeling that she was responsible for what had happened. She reached up and felt her throat, the bruise still fresh and raw where he'd tried to strangle her. Looking down at the tire iron, she felt sick again. She was lucky, she knew; but she was also angry. She picked up the iron and threw it in disgust toward the bushes at the edge of the forest that lined the highway. Maybe she'd feel better if she didn't have to look at it anymore. Besides, she had no intention of changing her tire now; someone would be by soon, and she'd get help.

She looked both ways down the highway, but there was still no one and nothing in sight. What horrible luck to have a breakdown out here, she thought. If she hadn't gotten a flat tire, she never would have been in this position. And what were the chances that the person who came along directly after her would take the opportunity to attack her?

As she considered the sequence of events, she began to wonder whether it was really all a coincidence. The man had mentioned D.C. as if he'd known she lived in Washington. How could he have known that unless he knew who she was?

Just then she heard a loud groan from over her shoulder. Her heart jolted as she spun on her knees and saw the man moving. His hand had reached around and was probing the back of his head, and his body rocked back and forth as if he were trying to roll over.

It can't be! She'd hit him so hard in the back of the head; she'd seen the blood, and she couldn't believe that he could have survived. She scrambled to her feet and raced toward him, searching for the tire iron so she could defend herself again. It took a moment for her to remember that she'd thrown it into the woods. She looked over in that direction, but knew instantly that the shrubbery was too thick for her to have any hope of finding it in time for it to be of any use.

She ran to her car and slammed the door, fumbling with the keys in her panic as she tried to get the motor started. She turned the ignition over once, and heard the familiar gurgling within the engine. Then it sputtered and died.

No! It can't be happening now!

She turned the key again and the same stunted sound bubbled up from under the hood, drawing a scream from deep within her chest as she slammed her fist against the steering wheel. She tried three or four more times before she knew for sure that the starter wouldn't cooperate.

Her mind raced as she glanced out the window and saw the man continuing to stir. She had to figure out a way to get out of there before he regained consciousness. It occurred to her to bludgeon him again, but the thought repulsed her. Besides, she had discarded the tire iron, and she had seen nothing else that presented itself as a suitable replacement.

She looked up in her rearview mirror and noticed the dark sedan the man had been driving, and she latched on to the notion of stealing his car. She opened her door, climbed out of her Accord, and raced back to the sedan. Throwing the door open, she climbed in, her right hand flying to the ignition in the desperate hope that the keys would be there.

They weren't, but she didn't let that dash her hopes. She quickly ran her hands through the car's interior to all those normal places people leave their keys. She flipped down the sun visor, reached under the seat, pulled up the swatch of carpeting covering the floor, and rifled through the glove box, but found nothing. He must have kept the keys with him, she realized.

The terror spread through her again as she realized she was trapped. She stepped out of the sedan breathing hard as she contemplated the idea of rifling through the man's jeans. He'd collapsed again, facedown in the dirt, and it occurred to her that perhaps he was dead now. It was difficult to believe that anyone could survive the blow she'd delivered to his head with the tire iron, and it seemed possible that the energy it had taken for the man to drag his broken body to its knees had been the last that he'd possessed.

She approached him quietly, her muscles taut, joints bent, ready to bolt if necessary. When she got near enough, she reached her foot out and nudged him in the leg, jumping back as she did in anticipation of any movement.

There was none. His leg rolled to the side and then settled back in exactly the same position. She reached out her foot again and kicked him, harder this time, every nerve in her body ready for an instant reaction from him. Again, though, there was no movement other than the rocking of the leg in reaction to the force of her kick.

Bending over the lifeless lump, she reached out her hand gingerly to feel around for the car keys. She started by patting the rear pockets of his pants, hoping against logic that he kept his keys there, rather than in a front pocket. Feeling a lump, she cautiously reached her hand into the pocket, drawing out the man's wallet. She opened it, and the sight of what was inside left her breathless. There, contained in a transparent plastic slip, was an identification card. It was white with a thick red and blue border and a picture of the man who'd identified himself as "Mike." He was staring at the camera with a serious expression—not even the hint of a smile. Next to the picture was a name: John Marine; and next to that was an official-looking seal. It was blue with a red and white shield surrounded by a laurel wreath and a circle of stars. Around the edges of the seal, she read the words three times, each time not believing what she was seeing: *Federal Bureau of Investigation.*

She closed the wallet and put it in her own pocket, unsure what else to do. She would think through what it all meant later. Then she bent down again, reaching around to the front of the man's pants, shaking them gently as she listened for any jingling that might indicate the location of his keys. She heard the telltale sound coming from the right side and reached across his body and slipped her fingers into his front pocket, straining to reach the keys and pull them free. The pocket was deep, though, and she found that she needed to lean over even farther, pulling her body off balance.

She had just felt the tip of one of the keys when it happened. She didn't even notice him move, but suddenly and without warning his hand was clamped around her wrist. She screamed and tried to pull her hand away from him, but his grip was like a vise. Off balance as she was, she pitched forward and her head hit the dirt hard. She flailed about, but was unable to break free. Then, as she struggled, she opened her eyes and turned her head to the side.

He was staring straight into her eyes. His cheek was still pressed against the ground, and his skin was swollen and red. The blood from his head wound had reached forward around his face, mixing with the dirt and clotting thickly in streams that looked like the legs of a giant spider.

She screamed again and wrenched her body with all her might, driving her left knee into the man's back with as much force as she could muster. She saw the expression on the face that hung before her change as the eyes widened in surprise and the cheeks exploded with a billowy, putrid expulsion of air. At that moment, she twisted her shoulders and pulled her arm back as hard as she could, and she felt the man's grip loosen, and then snap as her arm pulled itself free.

She scrambled to her feet, kicking out again at the man as she did, every muscle in her body seeming to contract in unison, fighting with each other in a desperate, spasmodic effort at escape. Then, once clear of the man's grasp, she struggled to her feet. Her mind was in complete disarray as her eyes darted in every direction, searching for a weapon, but finding nothing useful.

Finally, casting one last glance at the man still lying on the ground, she ran down the dirt shoulder to the road, throwing herself into the wall of vegetation at the bottom and disappearing into the woods.

Chapter Thirty-five

JACK CASSIAN LOOKED the menu over and pondered what he was in the mood for. Andolini's had only opened two weeks earlier, but it had gotten rave reviews from the food critics at both the *Washington Times* and the *Washington Post*. Given the infrequency with which those particular publications agreed on anything, Jack thought the place must be worth a try.

It was small and intimate—Jack counted only fifteen tables—tucked away on Twenty-first Street, just below Dupont Circle. Although the restaurant itself was cozy, Jack could see a lively bar section separated from the dining room by a frosted pane of glass. It was hopping. Young men and women moved easily through the place in crisp business suits, with thick, well-kept hair that advertised a self-importance they felt to their core. These, Jack knew, were the underlings of the power brokers who kept Washington greased enough to function: well-educated, highly competitive twenty-somethings who'd come from all corners of the country, seduced by the lure and false promise of power to work for senators and congressmen and agency heads. They'd forgone the riches of Wall Street and Madison Avenue and accepted the pitiable salaries offered by the government in the hope of becoming *relevant.* If they succeeded, the money would come later from lobbyists and law firms eager to capitalize on their connections. For now, though, they contented themselves with the pretense that they were making a difference.

Jack could feel the raw carnality of their desperation even through the thick glass. Facing disillusionment could be painful, and in a city as lonely as D.C., they reached for any façade of companionship, no matter how fleeting. Perhaps, Jack thought, he would adjourn to the bar after a good meal to see what might happen. After all, it wouldn't be the first time; he was unashamed to acknowledge that he'd played the game before, and played it well.

He wouldn't, though. The murder of Elizabeth Creay had gotten under his skin, and he couldn't get it out of his mind. He should have eaten at home for all the enjoyment he'd take from even an excellent meal. The thought of Amanda Creay coming home to find her mother was keeping his mind occupied, and making tangible so many of life's cold realities. The loneliness of a one-night stand would only make him feel worse.

It wasn't just his focus on the case that would keep him from seeking solace at the arm of some young woman at the bar. There was no getting around the fact that Sydney Chapin had become an infatuation for him. It was silly; they were so different in so many ways that nothing could ever come of it. And yet as long as his preoccupation with her survived, he'd have difficulty spending his affections elsewhere.

The waitress stopped by his table, hovering with an eager smile that Cassian recognized as a subtle invitation.

He passed on the opportunity to flirt with her, though, and ordered the veal piccata without any particular enthusiasm. She took his order with a slight pout, clearly disappointed at his lack of interest.

You're a fool, Jack told himself as he watched her walk away, the curves under her skirt swaying like a hypnotist's watch below her narrow waist.

Just then his cell phone rang, interrupting his thoughts. He fumbled through his jacket pocket, pulling out the phone on the fourth ring and flipping it open.

"Hello?"

He heard the nasal whine of an operator's voice on the other end of the line. "You have a collect call from Sydney Chapin, will you accept the charge?"

Cassian's heart quickened. "Yes, of course." He heard the line click over and the static increased. He could still hear her voice, though.

"Detective—Jack?" she said.

"Yes, Sydney, it's Jack. How'd you get my number?" He was excited at the notion that she had contacted him, and his mind toyed with various romantic possibilities.

"It was on the card you gave me."

"Oh, that's right, I forgot. What can I do for you?"

"I'm in trouble, Jack," she stammered. He wondered for a moment whether it was some sort of a joke, but he could feel her tension over the line. He could hear a man and a woman arguing loudly in the background, and the connection had a cold feel of danger he couldn't isolate. "I mean I'm in real trouble," she said, her voice almost a whisper.

His heart raced, and he forced himself to remember the basics of any emergency his training had taught him—get the most important information first. "Where are you?" he asked.

"I'm at a gas station—Mel's Mobil—somewhere in southwestern Virginia, just off Route 24."

"Southwestern Virginia? What are you doing—" Jack stopped and forced himself to stick to what was most important first. "Are you hurt?"

"I'm a little bruised, and scratched up, but no, I don't have any major injuries."

"What's happened?"

"I was attacked in my car. I broke down by the side of the highway and a man stopped and offered to help me, but then he attacked me."

Jack's mind raced. It would take him hours to get to her. "Did you call the local police?" They could get to her almost immediately to protect her, he knew.

There was a pause on the other end of the line. "I can't," she said finally.

"Why not?"

"I hit the man on the head. Hard. I think I hurt him pretty badly."

"Who cares?" He waved the waitress over to cancel his meal. "Sydney, if he attacked you first then you acted in self-defense. It's perfectly justifiable, and you won't get into any trouble."

"It's not that simple," Sydney said. The desperation in her voice made him go cold.

"Why not?"

"I took his wallet."

"You took his wallet?" None of this was making any sense. "Why would you take his wallet?"

"I was looking for his car keys so I could get away, and I pulled his wallet out of his pocket." She hesitated. "Jack, I opened the wallet, and there's ID in it. The guy's a cop."

"A cop?"

"FBI. Same thing. I think this has something to do with my sister's murder. Don't you see? If he's with the FBI and I call the police, he'll find me."

"Wait, wait, wait," Jack said. "I don't understand any of this. What makes you think this has anything to do with your sister? And how do you know this guy will find you if you call the police? This is crazy."

Her voice came back over the line. "Jack, I can't argue about this right now. I'm scared, and I'm stranded, and I don't know what to do. I'm asking you for help." She seemed on the verge of tears. "Will you help me? Please?"

He didn't hesitate. "Stay where you are. I'll be there as quickly as I can."

Mel's Mobil was a greasy little shack by the side of the road, a quarter of a mile off Route 24. It wasn't much to look at; two gas pumps and a mini convenience center that offered little more than out-of-date chips and soda. But it had a pay phone, and that was all Lee Salvage cared about.

It was dark outside—ten o'clock—nearly four hours since his misadventure with the Chapin girl by the side of the highway. He was still fuming over it on the inside, but on the outside he was nothing but business. It had taken him several more minutes before he had regained his feet sufficiently to drive, and he'd found another gas station with a bathroom, where he'd cleaned himself up. His head was still aching, and the rash on his face from the pepper spray was still evident, though fading, but he was moving again—and straightening out his mistake.

As he walked into Mel's Mobil, he could feel the man at the counter—Mel, presumably—staring at him warily as he asked if there was a pay phone at the place. He didn't care; he wasn't planning on ever being anywhere near this area again.

The phone was tucked away in the back of the shack, hidden from view by a row of shelving that offered wiper blades, engine oil, and an assortment of air fresheners and cleaning supplies.

As he rounded the corner, he saw that someone was using the phone. Her back was toward him, and she was hunched over into the wall, so that all he could make out was her blonde hair. He looked at his watch impatiently. Then he turned and leaned against the wall himself, looking up to see the man behind the counter watching him nervously.

It was probably only a minute or two before the woman got off the phone, but it seemed like hours to Salvage. Even after she had ended her conversation, the mere act of reaching over to hang up the phone seemed to take forever. As she started to turn around toward him, he realized that something about her seemed familiar. He started reaching into his jacket for his gun, dazed at the notion that luck might have brought him right to Sydney Chapin again.

"Linda, get off that damned phone and let this man make a call!"

The shouting came from the man behind the counter. Salvage turned toward the man and then looked back at the woman on the phone, realizing it wasn't her. She looked vaguely like the Chapin girl, he saw, but only in her most general outline. She was roughly the same height and weight, and the hair color was similar, but that was where the resemblance ended. She looked ten years older, at least, and there was nothing of the Chapin girl's attractiveness. She was a discount reproduction at best.

"I'm off the damned phone, Mel!" she hollered back at the man behind the counter in a backwoods screech that could peel paint. She looked at Salvage and rolled her eyes with an inappropriate familiarity that made him angry. "Asshole thinks he owns me," she said loud enough for Mel to hear.

"Ha!" he retorted from the front of the store. "I'd never admit makin' such a shitty buy."

Salvage pushed his way past the woman toward the phone, turning to shoot her a look that chased her away from view. Then he dialed a number and punched in a code from an untraceable calling card he kept for emergencies. The phone hummed and clicked as he waited, and then, after a moment, it began to ring.

"Hello?" came the voice from across the line.

"I'm on a pay phone," were Salvage's first words. "It's routed, so it should be safe, but we should be careful."

There was a pause. "Why?"

"We have a situation. The girl may have more information than we anticipated. I followed her into the mountains."

"The mountains? That's problematic. What did she find out?"

"I don't know." He hesitated. "I thought it best to fix the problem."

There was a grim silence from the other end of the line. "I trust your judgment. I'm sure you did what was best," the voice said at last, though there was no joy in its tone. "Will it look like an accident?"

Salvage stiffened. "There was a problem. I made contact, but the job was left unfinished."

"Unfinished?" Salvage could hear the anger and surprise over the phone. "How is that possible?"

"There was a mishap. She was better prepared than I anticipated. It's okay, though. I'll have the problem fixed before it spreads."

"Okay?" The voice was sharp with rage. "Don't tell me it's okay!"

"I'll have the problem fixed."

"You goddamned better! If this goes any further—"

"It won't."

"When did this happen?"

"Four hours ago."

"Four hours!" It was almost shouted. "She could be almost back to the city now for all you know! And this is the first that I'm hearing of this?"

"There is no cellular service here," Salvage explained. "This is the first pay phone I found. Besides, she was on foot, so it's doubtful that she's anywhere near the city yet."

"Still, it took you four hours to find a phone?"

Salvage hesitated, debating how much he should tell his client. "I had an errand to run," he said at last.

"An errand?"

"Yes, an errand," Salvage said. "There was a loose end that needed to be tied up back at the facility in the mountains."

Chapter Thirty-six

JACK CASSIAN PULLED his motorcycle into the parking lot to the side of Mel's Mobil at ten minutes before eleven. The trip, which at legal speeds would have taken nearly five hours, had taken him just over three. The roads were quiet, and armed with a badge and a purpose, he had no hesitation in exceeding one hundred miles per hour.

As he circled toward Mel's front door, he searched through the mud-spattered windows to catch a glimpse of Sydney, but could see only a balding, overweight cashier and a stringy blonde sitting on the counter. He was about to put the kickstand down and head inside when he sensed movement behind him and turned to see Sydney bolting out of the woods toward him.

"Sydney, I—" he started, but she cut him off.

"Let's get out of here," she pleaded as she swung her leg over the back of the bike, climbing on behind him.

"Wait, Sydney, we've got to talk," Cassian protested. "What's going on?"

"We'll talk once we're far away, but he was just here, and I don't want to be anywhere near this place if he comes back."

"Who was just here?"

"The man who tried to kill me." Seeing the confusion in his eyes, an exasperated look appeared on her face. "Just move!" she pleaded. "I'll explain later!"

Cassian considered arguing, but saw that it would be useless. He kicked his bike into gear. "Any particular direction? And you should know that I'm not ready to make the trip all the way back to D.C. riding double at the moment."

"Anyplace away from here, and closer to civilization."

He nodded. "I saw a sign for a motel ten or fifteen miles back." He reached around the side of the bike and unstrapped a helmet from the side of the seat. "Wear this," he said.

"I'm fine," she replied.

"Look, if there's really someone out there who's trying to kill you, I don't want him recognizing you on the back of my bike. Whenever a motorcycle tangles with a car, the bike loses. Always."

She took the helmet and put it on, tucking the strap under her chin and pulling it tight. Then she put her arms around his waist to hang on. "Now, please, let's just go." Her voice sounded tired and desperate, and he leaned on the throttle as he let the clutch out, pulling away from the parking lot and into the street.

The ride to the motel took ten minutes. Under other circumstances, Jack would have enjoyed the trip; Sydney was clinging to him from behind, her arms wrapped firmly around his torso and her hands clasped tightly at his chest. He could feel the insides of her thighs pressed against his legs as she molded herself to his shape for safety while the motorcycle hummed comfortably beneath them on the highway.

But Jack could take little pleasure from his predicament. Sydney's behavior, and what little she'd told him over the phone, raised too many questions, and he needed to start finding the answers.

The lodging sign by the side of the highway made few specific promises, notifying them only that there was a motel off the exit a mile ahead, and as they pulled off the exit ramp Jack could see why. The structure sagged by the edge of the road, its dingy paint peeling in great swaths from the long bunkhouse of separately accessed rooms. The motel sign out front, half lost in the night with burned-out bulbs, advertised nothing more exotic than color TVs and air-conditioning.

Jack stopped his bike in front of the office and waited for Sydney to dismount so he could pull his leg over the back of the seat. His legs felt rubbery after hours of riding without any break. "I'll get us a room," he said. "Then you need to start explaining this all to me."

She looked around the parking lot nervously. "I'm coming into the office with you."

"You'll really be safe waiting out here," Jack said. "I can see you through the window, and nothing's gonna happen while I'm in there."

"I'm coming with you," she repeated, and he could hear the fear in her voice.

Cassian shrugged. He walked over to the office door and opened it. "After you," he said.

The office was shrouded in darkness, the only light coming from a cracked lamp in one corner. The man behind the office counter looked like he weighed over three hundred pounds, and his dirty shirt hung over the counter in great folds of flesh as he stroked his thin goatee. Sydney hung back by the door, and he regarded her with a jealous leer.

"We need a room," Jack said.

The huge man's eyes traversed the silhouette of Sydney's figure twice before turning to Jack with a knowing wink. "You want it for the whole night?" he asked. "We rent by the hour, too."

"I'll pay for the whole night," Jack said, unwilling to allow the sleazy insinuation to stand.

"Suit yourself," the man said, clearly unconvinced. "But there's no refund if it takes less time than you're hopin' for." He smiled at his own joke. "That'll be twenty-five dollars."

Cassian slapped the money down on the table and shot him a glare.

"You want a receipt for that?" the man asked, unperturbed by Cassian's menacing look as he put a numbered key down on the counter where the money had been.

Cassian picked up the key and took Sydney by the elbow, steering her back out through the door. Over his shoulder, he could hear the obese young man still talking. "Come on back here, honey, if he leaves you with some time to kill and you're looking to pick up some extra cash on another trick."

Jack and Sydney walked down along the line of doors until they came to one with the number that matched the one on their key. Jack opened the door and stepped into the room, walking through it slowly, looking into corners and checking behind doors to put Sydney at ease. He opened the closet and walked into the bathroom, pulling the shower curtain back to reveal an empty tub. Then he walked back into the bedroom, where Sydney was standing in front of the bed, looking around the room with a combination of fear and disgust at her surroundings.

"All clear," he said.

She nodded, and her knees seemed to buckle slightly. She leaned to her side and sat at the edge of the bed, her head falling toward her chest and into her hands. It took a moment for Jack to realize she was crying.

He pulled a chair over, up close to where she sat, her shoulders shaking slightly as she rocked back and forth. "It's okay," he said. "It's going to be okay." He reached over and touched her chin, pulling her head up gently until he was able to see her. He was startled by what he saw. Her face had largely been hidden in darkness since she first ran to him outside the Mobil station.

Her cheeks and forehead were badly scratched and bleeding in a few places. On the sides of her throat there were dark purple bruises that were already turning black at the edges. Jack felt a rage growing within him.

"Tell me what happened," he said.

"I don't know," she began. "It's all such a blur. I came out here to visit the Virginia Juvenile Institute for Mental Health. Liz was out here two weeks before she died. I thought—" She paused and took a breath, trying to regain some of her composure. "I thought there might somehow be a connection with her murder."

"Why would you have thought that?"

Her tears were still flowing freely. "The last person she saw before she was killed was a professor at the law school where I work, Professor Barneton, and he said she asked him some questions about the Institute. A couple of hours later she was dead. When you and your partner told me there was a possibility that the drug dealer you've arrested didn't actually kill Liz, I started wondering if there was a connection, and I decided to check the place out."

"Why didn't you tell us?"

"Because it seemed so silly. I mean, what could it possibly have to do with anything, right?" Her voice was filled with irony. "I didn't want to waste your time; and I didn't want you to think I was crazy—like some deranged female Oliver Stone seeing conspiracies wherever I looked. So I decided to come out here myself, just to make myself feel better."

"Did you find anything?"

"I didn't think so." She frowned through her tears as she continued. "I've been over and over every conversation I had with the people out there in my mind, and none of it leads anywhere. It's all a bunch of ancient history. So when I left, I was satisfied that it had nothing to do with Liz's murder."

"But now you're not so sure," Cassian said. He couldn't take his eyes off her face.

"No, now I'm not so sure," she said. "When I was driving home, I got a flat tire. It didn't make any sense, because I didn't have a blowout, and the air in the tire wasn't low to begin with. Somehow, though, the air in the tire seemed to disappear. I didn't think that much about it at the time, and a minute later this guy pulled up behind me and offered to change the tire. I was sitting in the car after I popped the trunk for him, and the next thing I knew, he was on top of me—choking me through the car window." She pointed to the bruises on her neck.

"Let me see," Jack said, pulling her hands away and leaning in for a closer look. The bruises, he saw, were deep. "What happened next?"

"I managed to grab my pepper spray and squirted him right in the face."

"Pepper spray? You know that's illegal?" It was a reflex, but he regretted saying it as soon as it came out.

"You wanna arrest me?" she demanded in frustration.

He shook his head. "Sorry, I wasn't thinking. I'm glad you're okay." He tried to smile. "I bet it had an effect, at least."

She nodded. "It did. I can see why it's illegal. He was rolling around on the ground screaming, and I was so scared I got the tire iron out of my car and hit him in the head. I thought I'd killed him."

"You were wrong, I take it?"

"I was. He attacked me again a couple of minutes later, but I got away and ran into the woods." She pointed to the scratches on her face. "That's where I got these. I hiked through the darkness for a mile or so, until I got to a road that ran parallel to the highway and found that gas station."

"And you'd never seen this guy before? You have no idea who he was?"

"I'd never seen him before," she said. "And I wouldn't have any idea who he was if I hadn't taken this." She held up the wallet she'd taken out of the man's pocket.

He took it from her and flipped through it. The first thing he saw was an identification card in a plastic window that had an FBI seal on it, as well as a picture and the name John Marine. He continued flipping through the wallet and found several other pieces of identification, each bearing a picture of the same man, but each with a different name. One of the cards was a private investigator's license with the name Lee Salvage—a name that was also on the driver's license and several credit cards. He put the wallet on the bed next to Sydney.

"Is that it?"

"No," she replied. "After I called you from the gas station, I was waiting for you inside, but the guy at the counter was giving me the creeps, so I went outside and waited for you around back. After a little while—about twenty minutes before you got there—I saw the guy who attacked me go in and make a call. Then he came out and drove away."

Jack sat back in his chair, trying to absorb everything she'd told him. None of it made sense.

"What do you think?" she asked nervously.

"I think you need some antiseptic for those scratches," he said after a moment. "I also think I need to digest all of this for a little while. There's a convenience store at the gas station across the road; I'm going to go get something you can put on your cuts. When I get back, we can talk through this all again and try to come up with a plan." She looked crestfallen. "Don't worry," he said reassuringly, "we're going to get to the bottom of all of this."

"I'm not sure I want to be alone," Sydney admitted.

"I won't be gone for more than five or ten minutes," he assured her. "The door to this room will be in my sight the entire time, and I'll make sure no one comes near the place."

She seemed comforted by the thought. "Okay," she said. "I need to call my mother, anyway. I was supposed to be back in time for dinner." She looked at her watch. "I don't want her to worry." As she continued staring at her wrist, she noticed the grime with which she was covered and seemed to realize how she must appear. She gave Cassian an embarrassed smile. "I think I have to take a shower, too." A final tear traced a line through the dirt and grime on her cheek. "It's been a really crappy day."

Jack leaned forward and took her hands in his. "I don't know what's going on," he said, "but I promise I'm not going to let it drop until I do."

Chapter Thirty-seven

LYDIA CHAPIN SAT on the divan in the opulent living room of her palatial house in the nation's capital staring off into space. Water beaded on the side of the glass of chilled vodka that had remained untouched on the coffee table since she'd placed it carefully on the coaster in front of her nearly a half hour earlier. The house was silent and she absentmindedly fingered the pearls on the long strand that hung from her neck. Her eyes were glassy as she ran through the milestones of her life in her mind, scrutinizing them for the misstep that had led her here—to this moment of loneliness, fear, and despair.

The sharp cry of the telephone, electronic and cruel, shattered the silence, and she rose with efficiency and crossed the room to the receiver that hung from the wall near the bar. "Hello?" she said with strength and assuredness she didn't actually feel.

"Hello, Mother, it's Sydney."

"Good God, Sydney, do you know what time it is? I've been worried sick about you! Where are you? You were supposed to be home for dinner. It's as though you don't even care about Amanda. She was distraught, in case you care. I had to give her a sedative and tell her it was aspirin to even get her to sleep. I suppose I really shouldn't be surprised, though. After all, you've always—" The words came firing out of her like water out of a fire hose, pounding relentlessly until Sydney cut her off.

"Mother, please listen! I was attacked!" It sounded as though she'd shouted the words more in self-defense than in explanation.

"Attacked? What are you talking about? Don't be silly." Lydia tried to sound calm, but her pulse was racing.

"Mother, listen to me! I was attacked. I'm in Virginia now, and I'm not going to be home until tomorrow."

Lydia was silent, and it took her a moment to realize she wasn't breathing. She forced her lungs to expand. "Are you all right?" she asked finally. "Are you hurt? And what are you doing in Virginia?"

"I'm okay," Sydney replied. "I'll be fine. Detective Cassian is here now, so I'm safe. I don't have time to explain this all, but I wanted you to know I'm okay, and I'll call you tomorrow."

"Nonsense," Lydia said, regaining her composure. "I'll send someone to get you. Where in Virginia are you?"

Sydney hesitated. "I'm about two hundred miles southwest of D.C."

Lydia carefully considered what to say next. "Tell me where."

Sydney sighed heavily back into the phone. "I can't tell you, I'm not even sure myself. I have to go."

"I don't even know what to say, Sydney," Lydia responded in a voice tinged with anger.

"Then don't say anything, please."

"What are you doing so far away? Why didn't you tell me where you were going?"

"I don't know."

"What do you mean, you don't know?" Lydia demanded, the desperation in her voice growing more evident.

"I mean I don't know!" There was silence as they both tried to figure out what to say. "Like I said, I don't have time to try to explain this all. Maybe tomorrow I'll have a better idea of what's going on. Please tell Amanda I love her, and I'm sorry I missed dinner."

The line went dead and the silence engulfed Lydia again. She stood at the bar, cradling the receiver to her ear, reluctant to let it go. "Sydney?" She spoke quietly into the receiver, knowing already that the connection had been broken. A moment later there came a chime, and the dial tone returned. Lydia looked at the phone as if confused, holding it up and examining it before replacing it on its cradle on the wall.

How has it come to this? she wondered again. Then she returned to the divan and sat down, her legs crossed at the ankles, her back rigid as she reached for the drink on the table.

Sydney stood in front of the mirror in the bathroom examining her face. The shower had helped her appearance significantly, though there were still angry lines in the flesh covering her forehead and chin. The bruises on her throat, she suspected, would take weeks to fade.

She stepped back to examine the rest of her body. She was standing naked on the worn terrycloth bath mat, her hair still wet and hanging in clumps at her shoulders. She had several pronounced scratches on her forearms and hands, and there was a bruise and a cut on her shin where she'd collided with a low-hanging branch in the woods.

She reached over to the pile of clothes she had, slipping on her panties and bra. Then she picked up her pants and shirt. The pants were okay. They had a few mud stains on them, but a brief soaking in the sink and they'd be wearable again. The shirt, however, was a total loss. It was stained through with dirt and sweat, and had several lengthy tears that would be difficult to hide in the sunlight. She looked around for a robe to put on, but quickly realized that this was not the sort of place that would offer such amenities. She frowned as she considered putting on the same clothes once again without even giving them a rinse. Just then there was a knock at the bathroom door.

"Jack?" she called out hesitantly.

"Yeah, it's me," came Jack's voice. "I thought you might want these," he said. The door opened a crack, and Jack's arm reached into the bathroom. Clutched in his hand was what looked like a bundle of fabric.

Sydney took the material out of his hand and looked at it. There were two T-shirts that proudly proclaimed *I ♥ Jack Daniel's*, and a pair of nondescript sweatpants.

"The fashion section at the convenience mart was a little lacking," Jack called out, "but I did my best."

She smiled as she pulled on the sweatpants and one of the T-shirts. "No, I appreciate it," she said through the door. "I was just trying to figure out what the hell I was supposed to wear. These will be fine, at least for the moment."

"I also got you these," he said, his arm reaching into

the bathroom again, holding out a small spray can of antiseptic, a toothbrush, and a small tube of toothpaste. "I thought they might make you a little more comfortable."

"Thanks," she said. "I'll be out in a minute." She finished cleaning up and then looked at herself in the mirror quickly again before walking back out. The scratches were still evident, but the antiseptic seemed to have helped. And though her hair was still wet and matted, at least the dirt was gone from her face.

When she emerged from the bathroom, Jack was on the phone. The wallet she'd taken off her attacker was open on the bed in front of him. "Thanks, Deter," he was saying. "Yeah, the faster we can find out the better." He hung up.

"Who was that?"

"One of the forensics guys at the office," Jack replied. "I gave him a detailed description of the FBI identification card and asked him to run a search to see if the name John Marine checks out."

"You think it may be a fake?"

"It's possible. Looking through this wallet, there are a few identification cards with different names on them. If it is a fake, the quality is spectacular. On the other hand, usually ID cards like this are kept with the badge, not separately. There's enough that's odd here to check it out."

"Maybe he had his badge in a different pocket," Sydney speculated. "I didn't go through his pants very thoroughly."

Jack shrugged. "We'll know shortly. I've also got them running down any calls from the pay phone at the gas station. There are lots of ways to route calls to defeat a trace, so it's probably a dead end, but it's worth a try." He pulled a chair over near the bed and motioned for Sydney to sit. Then he perched on the corner of the mattress so they were facing each other. "I want you to tell me again everything you remember about today."

Sydney took a deep breath and told him the story again from the beginning, covering every detail she could recall. It took more than an hour, and he interrupted her often, asking follow-up questions, and forcing her to flesh out every possible detail. When she was done, he was left shaking his head, much as he'd been after the first time she'd told him the story. He frowned as he thought about the man who'd attacked her.

"And once the attack began, this guy didn't say anything to you? He didn't ask for anything, or make any threats, or anything like that?"

"No, nothing like that."

Just then the phone rang. He went over to the dresser and picked it up. "Cassian here," he said. He listened as the voice on the other end came over the line. Sydney could hear the voice, but couldn't make out any of the words. After a moment, Cassian said, "Okay, Deter, thanks for your help." He hung up the phone and looked at Sydney.

"What is it?" she asked.

"My guy at the office came through. He ran a check on the ID. There's no one named John Marine at the FBI. Also, the identification number's a fake."

"What does that mean?"

"It means that the man who attacked you isn't working for the feds. He probably has the IDs so he can intimidate people. Some private detectives use ploys like that to make getting answers easier. There was a PI's license in the wallet as well, with the name Lee Salvage on it. Mean anything to you?"

"No, should it?"

"I don't know. According to my guy, that's a name that checks out as real, so we'll have him run down back in D.C. If this was him, though, my guess is he won't be at his home or office anytime soon."

Sydney looked at Cassian, her eyes wide and searching. "So what do we do now?" she asked.

"The first thing we do," he replied, "is go back to the Institute and do some poking around."

Chapter Thirty-eight

THE RIDE FROM THE MOTEL to the Institute the next morning took a little over a half hour. With Sydney on the back of Jack's motorcycle, clinging to his midsection as the machine raced along the highway, conversation was nearly impossible. That was fine with Jack for the moment; after the awkwardness in the motel room that morning, he was afraid of what he might say—and terrified of how she might react. Silence between them was welcomed for the moment.

It wasn't his fault, he told himself. They'd spent another hour the night before going over everything Sydney had seen at the Institute, and everything that had been said in her conversations there, until both of them were exhausted and she was emotionally spent. Then he'd taken the bedspread and laid it on the floor, stealing one of the pillows off the bed and settling in for sleep on the stained carpeting, allowing Sydney sole occupancy of the queen-size mattress. He was just starting to nod off when she'd spoken to him.

"Jack?"

He fought off slumber as he opened his eyes. "Yes?"

He could sense her struggling with her emotions. "I

know this is going to sound pathetic, but I'm freaking out a little."

"It doesn't sound pathetic at all. After the day you've had—the week you've had, in fact—most people would have completely broken down by now."

"Yeah, well, I don't want you to get the wrong idea, but I'm pretty close to losing it at this point."

"Is there anything I can do?"

She didn't answer immediately, and Jack could hear her breathing. Finally she spoke again. "Would you mind sleeping on the bed with me?"

"You sure?"

"I am. Don't worry, I'm not going to take advantage of you or anything," she joked nervously. "I'll just feel better if I know there's someone here with me."

Cassian got up off the floor with his pillow and walked over to the bed. He pulled up a corner of the sheet and slipped under it, making sure to keep his body as close to the edge of the mattress—and as far away from any temptation he might have with her—as possible. He wedged his pillow behind his head and kept his eyes focused on the ceiling.

"Thank you," she said, her body turning away from him and her face toward the wall.

"No problem," he replied, the muscles of his throat tense with the warring impulses of his body.

He lay there for several minutes, listening to his heart pounding in his ears, afraid to move at all, lest the momentum of rolling over should break his will and carry him toward her. And then, as he lay there wondering whether his mind would ever clear sufficiently for him to function, it happened: she rolled onto her stomach and her leg slipped across the invisible boundary between them, her foot brushing against his calf with neither fear nor apology.

At first he thought she was asleep, and that she was unaware of the contact—that it was inadvertent and unfelt. But as he listened to her breathing, he sensed a change. What had been shallow gulps broadened into deep, relaxed waves rolling one into another with a rhythm that was at once natural and full. And as he felt her body collapse into comfort with the connection she'd made to him, he noticed his own body releasing the tension that had been building since he'd first received her call earlier that evening. One by one the muscles in his arms and legs unwound and the weight of his body settled into the mattress, his leg pushing ever so slightly into her ankle.

Finally his neck relaxed and his head fell fully into the pillow, lolling to the side toward the center of the bed. He looked at the silhouette of her back, only inches away, smooth in its definition as it rose and fell with her breathing underneath the thin cotton T-shirt. Then he closed his eyes and they both fell asleep.

When he woke in the morning, it took a moment to orient himself. He was no longer on his back, but had turned in his sleep onto his side toward the center of the bed. One arm was tucked under his pillow, and the other one, he noticed with some surprise, was draped over Sydney's torso, her own body folded neatly into his in unison with his shape. He had no recollection of the incremental shifts that had brought them together, and he wondered how she would react—whether she would think he'd taken advantage of the situation somehow. He lay still for a moment, enjoying the feeling of their bodies breathing together even as he wondered how to extricate himself, until he realized from her breathing pattern that Sydney was awake as well.

Neither of them moved for several moments, until Jack rolled toward his side of the bed, swinging his legs to the floor and heading toward the bathroom. He did it in one fluid motion to avoid any uncomfortable morning greeting, and by the time he'd reemerged, freshly showered, both of them seemed willing to behave as though nothing had happened.

Nothing *had* happened, Jack reminded himself as his motorcycle glided up the long driveway to the Institute's main building. It wasn't as though they'd shared a passionate night of lovemaking, after all. And yet, somehow, the connection they'd made seemed more intimate than sex, and it unnerved him.

He parked the bike and headed up the front steps with Sydney in tow. Rounding the corner into the main foyer, she pointed him around toward the hallway that led to Dr. Mayer's office. One of the orderlies behind the main desk rose to stop them. "Excuse me, ma'am, sir, you can't go back there!" He was hurrying around the desk as he spoke.

Jack pulled out his badge and flashed it at the man. "Yes we can," he said. "This is police business, and unless you want to personally get hit with an obstruction charge, you'll sit right back down."

The orderly hesitated, looming over the desk in indecision. "Don't you need a warrant or something?" he asked.

"Don't sweat it," Cassian replied, already guiding Sydney down the hallway. "We're just going to talk to the man in charge."

At the end of the hallway, they turned left into the

small waiting room outside Dr. Mayer's office where his secretary had her desk. The room was empty, and the two of them walked through it toward the door on the far wall that led to Mayer's office. The door was open, and Cassian could see a prim little man in his early fifties sitting behind the desk. There was an older woman sitting in the chair in the center of the room, across from him.

The man looked up as Jack and Sydney walked through the door. "Ms. Chapin!" he exclaimed in surprise. He looked at her for a moment longer, noting the scratches on her face and the bruises on her neck. "My Lord! What happened to you?"

"She was attacked after leaving here yesterday," Jack answered for her, taking control of the conversation.

Mayer looked up at Cassian. "Excuse me," he said in an offended tone. "Who are you?"

Jack took out his badge and flipped it open. "Detective Cassian," he said. "I've been investigating the murder of Ms. Chapin's sister, Elizabeth Creay. Now I'm also investigating Ms. Chapin's assault."

"I see," Dr. Mayer said slowly. "Well, I don't see how we can possibly help. This can't have anything to do with this facility, or anyone on this staff." He said the words, but there seemed to be little connection between them and the tone of his voice. He sounded instead to Cassian like a man clinging desperately to a lifeboat, afraid that if he let go he'd be dragged under.

"That's what I'm here to figure out," Cassian said. "Ms. Creay visited here a week before she was murdered. Then Ms. Chapin was attacked less than an hour after she left the premises. It would seem that this is one dangerous place to visit."

"You were attacked?" the woman in the chair asked,

speaking for the first time, with bewilderment in her voice. She looked lost to Cassian, and he thought perhaps she'd been crying.

"Yes," Sydney responded. "On the highway. Someone tried to kill me, Sandy."

The older woman looked back and forth between Jack and Sydney, an expression of total incomprehension and shock blanketing her face.

"I still don't see a connection," Mayer muttered. It sounded like he was losing his grip on the lifeboat, though.

"Then you're not looking hard enough," Cassian said. "Now, I want to talk to everyone Ms. Chapin spoke to yesterday." He looked down at the woman in the chair. "I assume you're Dr. Golden?" he asked. She confirmed his suspicion with a nod of her head. "So, I want to talk to you and Dr. Mayer, here, as well as Dr. Zorn. And then I want to spend some time talking to the handyman, Willie Murphy. If you all cooperate, this shouldn't take more than an hour or two."

"You can't talk to Willie Murphy," Mayer objected.

Cassian shook his head. "I don't think you understand what you're dealing with, Doctor. This is a murder investigation. One woman is dead, and another woman was almost killed. You don't have any options, and if you try to hide behind some sort of medical privilege, I'll have our prosecutors crawling so far up your ass, you'll smell their briefcases every time you pass gas." He looked at Dr. Golden and shrugged. "Pardon the language, ma'am."

"You're not listening, Detective," Mayer said with more conviction. "What you're asking for isn't possible."

"I'm willing to let a judge decide what's possible and what isn't, Doctor, if that's the way you want to go with this."

"No, no, you don't understand," Mayer stammered, losing his composure. He tried to continue, but the words seemed to get caught in his throat. His head fell into his hands, and he rubbed his forehead.

"What don't I understand?" Cassian demanded.

No one spoke for a moment as Cassian's glare penetrated Mayer. Finally, it was Sandra Golden who answered the question. "What you don't understand, Detective, is that Willie Murphy is dead."

Lydia lay on her bed, above the covers. She hadn't slept. At all.

The house was quiet now, in the morning, as it had been the night before. Amanda was still sleeping under the influence of the pharmaceutical aids Lydia had given her the night before. She'd been tempted to take some herself following the telephone call with Sydney, but thought better of it. After all, she needed a clear mind to determine what must be done.

The call with her daughter had bothered her in so many ways. Not least of which was the clarity with which it had demonstrated how fully she'd lost the ability to control her only remaining daughter. At one time, when Lydia was younger and stronger, she'd been able to hold final sway over both her children, indeed, over her entire family. Now her power over them was gone.

She was so lost in her own thoughts, and so used to the silence that blanketed her home, that she jumped when the phone rang. She rolled over toward her bedside table, sitting up as she grabbed the phone. "Hello?" she said, almost afraid of whomever she might find on the other end of the line.

"Good morning, dear Lydia. Consider this your wake-up call."

She paused, her anger growing as she recognized Leighton Creay's voice. "What are you talking about?"

"Tonight. I get my money tonight."

"Why are you calling me here, for God's sake? Are you really stupid enough to screw both of us?"

"Careful, old girl. I expect civility from you. I'm calling from a disposable phone—untraceable, so you need not worry. I just wanted to make sure you were still planning on showing. Otherwise, I have to start moving pieces around the board."

"I told you you'd have your money. No reminders are necessary."

"It's just a friendly phone call." Leighton chuckled.

"I'm not talking about the phone call, and you know it." She could barely control her anger. "The attack on Sydney was unwise."

"Sydney?" Lydia thought she heard a lilt of overconfidence. "I don't know what you're talking about."

"Oh, pardon my language, but bullshit!" She could be formidable when she needed to be, and she was perfectly willing to fight back. "You make a mistake like that again, and I'll end you, do you understand me, you sick bastard?"

When Creay's voice returned, it didn't sound nearly as confident. "That's right, Lydia, I am a sick bastard. And if you want to keep me away from your granddaughter, or your daughter, or anyone else in your family for that matter, you'll be there tonight, with the money."

Lydia straightened up on the edge of the bed. To the degree that she'd had any doubt about what she had to do, it was gone now. "I'll be there," she said after a moment. "You can count on it."

Chapter Thirty-nine

DARIUS TRAIN SAT at his desk in the precinct house, staring at the clock. He looked over at the empty desk where Jack Cassian should have been sitting. They'd agreed to get an early start on the investigation into Leighton Creay's life and finances, and Train was eager to talk strategy. He believed that he'd come up with a way to put some pressure on Elizabeth Creay's ex-husband, but he wanted to bounce some ideas off his partner.

That was difficult to do when your partner failed to show up at work.

Train looked at the clock again—the tenth time in as many minutes. Nine twenty-seven. They'd agreed to meet at eight, but as yet, Cassian was missing in action. Train had called the younger man's apartment and his cell phone, but without any luck, and he was beginning to cross the imaginary line where annoyance turned to concern. He was tempted to try Cassian's apartment again, but he'd already left two messages, and knew leaving a third would accomplish nothing.

Train was so edgy that he pounced on the phone when it rang. He scowled as he jerked the receiver to his ear. "Train here," he snapped into the phone.

"Sarge, it's Jack."

"Cassian, where the hell are you?"

"In the mountains—southwestern corner of Virginia."

It took a moment for Train to process that. "Southwestern Virginia? What in God's name are you doing in southwestern Virginia?" he demanded.

"I'm with Sydney Chapin. She was attacked yesterday. We're out at the Virginia Juvenile Institute for Mental Health."

"Wait! Slow down, for shitsakes! What the hell is going on?"

"I don't have time to explain, Sarge. I need you to do a couple of things."

Train took a deep breath. He felt like he needed more information, but then again, he knew that trust was what made a partnership work. And for all Cassian's youth and occasional immaturity, Train had never met a cop with better instincts than his. "Okay, fine," he said at last. "What do you need?"

"I need you to get on the phone to the Virginia State Police. There's been a death out here at the Institute, and I don't like the stink of it. The Institute's a state-run facility, so it's got to be on state land, and that means the states have jurisdiction if they want to take it. I want you to reach out to someone over there and get someone interested. If we let the local cops out here handle it, we'll probably never really know what happened."

"Not the most sophisticated group you've ever met?"

"They're not here yet, thank God, but judging from the surroundings, I have no doubt that Barney Fife would feel right at home. I want to make sure the state police take this over before the locals show up and start screwing up the crime scene."

Train rubbed his hand over his bald head. "You sure this is worth it?" he asked. "I'm gonna have to burn some favors in order to get the state police interested in a corpse that far out in the western part of the state."

"No, I'm not sure of anything," Cassian replied. "But Elizabeth Creay talked to the victim two weeks before she was killed, and then Sydney was attacked an hour or so after she had a conversation with him. Then we show up to talk to him this morning and he's dead. It feels pretty coincidental."

"No doubt." Train sat up in his chair and pulled out a directory of law enforcement personnel, flipping through to find the phone number for a captain in the Virginia State Police he was friends with. "I'll try to have someone from the state folks out there within the hour. What else?"

"I need you to check out a PI named Salvage. Lee Salvage. He may be the guy who attacked Sydney. We need to know who we may be dealing with."

"Lee Salvage." Train wrote the name down. "Okay. Is this more important than the Leighton Creay lead?"

"I think so."

"All right. I'll back-burner that and run this down. But the first time you get the chance, I want a phone call with some sort of kick-ass explanation for all this."

"Will do. And Sarge?"

"Yeah?"

"Thanks."

Cassian hung up the phone and turned to Mayer. "Take me to the body," he ordered.

Mayer looked for a moment as though he might object,

but then he stood and nodded and walked to the door. "He's in the basement," he said, leading the way.

Cassian fell into line behind him; Sydney and Golden followed as well. Cassian turned to Sydney. "You don't have to come down," he said.

"Yes I do."

"Have you ever seen a dead body before?" Jack asked, the concern evident in his voice. "It can get pretty nasty."

"I was with my mother when we identified Liz's body," Sydney said. She shivered at the memory, and her voice was hollow. "Think it can get any worse than that?"

Jack was unsure what to say. "Okay," he relented. "But don't touch anything, and let me know if you're going to be sick, or if you need to leave."

She nodded and Cassian turned back to address Mayer. "When was the body found?" he asked.

"Around ten minutes before you showed up," Mayer replied. "About eight-thirty, I'd guess. We were supposed to meet at eight to go over some of the things that he needed to do today. Willie was an excellent handyman, but he sometimes lost focus and needed some direction, so I generally met with him every day to make sure he had a clear schedule of chores."

"And he didn't show up today?"

"No, he didn't. I didn't think anything of it at first; Willie was often late. After twenty minutes or so, though, I began to get concerned. Dr. Golden and I had a meeting at eight-fifteen, and we both went down to find him together."

"Are you sure he's dead?"

Mayer cast a sharp glance in Cassian's direction. "Don't let the administrative title fool you, Detective. I'm a medical doctor first and foremost, as is Dr. Golden.

We've both had some training in this area. Trust me, he's dead."

They were in the basement, walking down the long corridor that led to Willie Murphy's dark office near the furnace and air-conditioning units. The building's various mechanical systems wheezed and groaned as the four of them approached, as if in a low dirge for the man who had cared for the physical plant for years.

As they rounded the corner into the office, Cassian could see instantly that Mayer was right; Willie Murphy was indeed dead.

He was seated at his desk, his body thrown back against the chair. His head was tipped backward at an awkward angle, his jaw locked open as if in some final, primal scream, his eyes open wide, staring blindly at the basement ceiling. One arm had fallen to his side, and his pale knuckles nearly scraped the floor. His other arm was propped up against the desk, the sleeve rolled up to the shoulder, just above the clear rubber strap that was wound tightly just above the bicep. Following the arm downward with his eyes, Cassian saw the instrument of Willie's death still clinging to its victim like some twisted, sated insect, lulled into a coma of satisfaction.

It was a syringe, and from the look of it, death had followed its use almost instantaneously.

"Such a tragedy," Mayer said. "He'd made such strides."

"He was an addict?" Cassian asked.

"Years ago," Golden replied emphatically, shooting a look of resentment and betrayal toward Mayer. "As far as I know, he hadn't taken any drugs since he'd come back to the Institute decades ago."

Mayer walked toward the body. "As far as you know," he emphasized.

“Please, Doctor,” Cassian said, putting his arm in front of Mayer, cutting him off from the body. “I’d appreciate it if you wouldn’t contaminate the crime scene.”

Mayer sniffed the air, but eased back from the body reluctantly. “ ‘Crime scene’ may be jumping to conclusions, Detective. It is well established that addicts often have lengthy periods of sobriety, only to go back to drugs again years later. It’s during these relapses that overdoses often occur. The addict begins using at the same dosage levels as when he was at the height of his addiction, and the body, which is no longer accustomed to having the drug in the system, is overwhelmed.”

Cassian walked carefully into the room, taking in the scene from its widest perspective. There were no windows, and it appeared that the only way in was back up the stairs and through the main lobby. “Is there any entrance or exit directly from the basement?” he asked.

“There’s a storm door on the other side of the basement,” Mayer replied hesitantly.

“Is it locked?”

“I don’t know,” Mayer said. “Probably not. Anyone who wants to enter the facility can simply walk in through the front door, so I’m not sure why we would lock any other doors. We’re a low-security facility in the middle of nowhere.”

Cassian leaned over and examined the body without touching it. “There are no needle marks in his arm, other than where the syringe is still sticking in,” he commented. “Probably rules out the notion that he’s been using regularly without your knowledge.”

“Yes,” Mayer admitted. “And if this was the first time he’d fallen off the wagon, it would be entirely consistent with an overdose, because he had no tolerance built up in his system, as I've already explained. There's also the issue of his having aged since his last drug experience."

Cassian stood up and shrugged. "You may be right," he said. "But tell me this: from what Sydney told me from her conversation with him yesterday, it appears that Willie was a recluse, correct? Did he go to town very often?"

Golden shook her head. "Never, as far as I know," she said before Mayer could answer the question. "He had us send out for anything he needed to do his job, and he ate all his meals in the cafeteria here."

"I wonder, then, how he got the drugs, and what kind they were." Cassian looked back and forth between Golden and Mayer, but neither of them seemed anxious to speculate. "I assume you keep a full store of pharmaceuticals here?" he pressed.

"We're a hospital, Detective. Of course we do."

"Good. And because you're a hospital, I assume that you keep very careful track of the amounts you have on hand of all the drugs you carry, correct?"

"Yes, of course."

"Good again. The first thing you need to do is check your stores to see if anything is missing. Then, if nothing's gone, I need you to put together a list of everyone who dispensed medication in the past forty-eight hours. An autopsy will tell us what the drug was, and that will help us narrow the field, but you need to start putting that information together now."

Mayer stood still for a moment, and Cassian could tell he was considering his options. As a bureaucrat, the doctor was used to taking orders. On the other hand, as an administrator, he was unwilling to admit the possibility that Willie's death was anything other than a suicide—and the notion that the drugs that had caused his death had come from the Institute itself was clearly too much to bear. "You can't really think—" he began, but Cassian cut him off.

"Doctor, I can think just about anything. That's my job—to consider every possibility. I follow the most likely leads in any investigation, but I'm not ruling anything out at this point. Right now, we have here a man who it appears hasn't taken any drugs in years, who as far as we know hasn't left the compound at any time recently, and who's sitting here dead with a needle sticking out of his arm. Whatever drug killed him either came from the hospital's pharmacy, or was brought in to him by someone else. You can sit here and try to protect your ass, or you can help me figure out what really happened here. But either way, I can tell you one thing for sure: I will find out the truth."

Mayer pulled himself up to his full height, and Cassian could sense that he was trying to appear indignant. "I resent the implication that I am hiding something, Detective. We will, of course, cooperate in any way we can. Nevertheless, I don't know where you find the gall to talk to me in that manner in my own hospital."

Cassian smiled. "Like I said, it's my job."

"No." A deep voice came from the door behind Mayer. "Actually, Detective, it's my job."

Cassian looked beyond Mayer, over toward the door, and saw a tall, barrel-chested man in a dark suit and striped tie standing next to Mayer's secretary. He looked like he was in his late fifties, and he had steel gray hair cropped in a military cut.

"Dr. Mayer, I'm assuming?" the man said, looking at the Institute's chief.

"Yes, I'm Dr. Mayer. What can I do for you?"

"The first thing you can do is clear out of this area," the man said. "I'm Lieutenant Casey with the state police, and I'm in charge of this investigation."

"I'm glad you're here, Lieutenant," Cassian said, trying to be polite while still keeping some semblance of control and authority in his tone. "I've made sure the area is secure and I was just telling the good doctor here to check the hospital's pharmacy to see if anything's missing."

Casey looked at Cassian and flashed him a broad smile. "You'd be Detective Cassian from the big city, I'd reckon," he said in his most polite southern drawl.

"That's right," Cassian replied, already sure that the relationship was going to start badly.

"Yes, sir, I was told you'd be here," Casey said, the smile never leaving his face. "Hotshot detective from Washington, *Dee See*, from what I understand, right?"

"Well—" Cassian began, but he never finished.

"I've been instructed to be polite to you, and to give you whatever information might be helpful to your investigation," Casey said. Cassian waited for the other shoe to drop. "But it was also made clear to me that I'm in charge of this investigation, and if you get in my way, I'll send you back to the big city with a pitchfork stickin' out of your ass. You got that?" The smile never left his face as Casey addressed Cassian.

"Of course," Jack said, trying to adopt a more conciliatory tone. It didn't seem natural to him. "This is your backyard, and I'm just a guest."

"I appreciate your recognizing that."

"But I'd like to offer whatever assistance I can," Cassian added.

"And I appreciate that, too. I understand that you have an interest in this matter—and your partner's the one who got my superiors in a snit about it. Like I said, I'll give you whatever information I think is appropriate. For now, though, I want everyone to clear outta here, and that includes you."

Cassian was reluctant to leave. "You sure? I might be able to help on crime scene."

Casey's smile widened even as his eyes seemed to go black. "That's mighty kind of you, but I've got a forensic crime scene unit from the barracks upstate on the way. I know we may not seem quite as sophisticated as y'all up in *Dee See*, but we'll get the job done." His eyes drilled into Cassian. "So, like I said, I want *everyone* to clear on outta here. Now."

There was no mistaking the message. Cassian had no jurisdiction, and he was not going to be allowed to be an active participant in the investigation. He might get some advance warning regarding information that was going to be released to the public, but that would likely be where the courtesy ended. It would be better treatment than he'd have gotten from the local police—but only slightly. Sometimes the turf wars endemic to law enforcement seemed a hindrance to the rational execution of justice.

Cassian nodded to Sydney. "Let's go," he said.

They began heading out the door and down the long corridor when he heard Casey's voice behind them. "By the way, Detective? Ms. Chapin?" Jack and Sydney turned around and looked at the chiseled trooper. "Please stay around here for a while. I'd like to ask both of you a few questions."

Chapter Forty

CASSIAN PACED BACK AND FORTH in the comfortably furnished waiting room off the main entryway to the Institute. It had the homey feel of a wealthy estate, with its high ceiling, comfortable leather chairs, and crown moldings. Ringing the space was a progression of portraits—all white men in business suits and lab coats—of past administrators, doctors, and important benefactors. But he didn't much care about the decor of the room. He was focused on figuring out a way to take back control over the investigation into Willie Murphy's death.

"I don't like this," Sydney said. She was sitting on one of the overstuffed chairs in the corner of the room, staring out of the window that overlooked the hills rolling away from the Institute at the rear of the building.

"Which part of it?" Cassian asked, continuing to pace.

"All of it." Sydney looked up at Jack and he could see that the upheavals of the past week had taken their toll. Her face had taken on the drawn look of a survivor. There was a hollowness to her eyes, and her cheeks looked like they were sinking slightly beneath her patrician cheekbones. "I hate every part of this. Nothing feels right anymore."

"I know," Cassian agreed, pausing in his stride. He walked over toward her and squatted down in front of her chair, his knees bent and his hand resting on her arm. "It will again," he said. "I promise."

She looked him in the eye. "You really believe that, don't you?"

"I do."

"How?"

"Comes with a lot of experience on the job."

The sound of footsteps approaching from down the marble corridor outside the room startled them both, and Cassian rose to his feet, feeling oddly as though he'd been caught in the midst of some indiscretion. The door opened and Dr. Sandra Golden walked into the room.

"I think we've determined where the drug came from, as well as what it was," she said. He looked at her expectantly, and she continued. "It appears that one of the medicine cabinets on the second floor—the minimum-security section—was broken into last night. Two vials of morphine are missing."

Jack frowned. "Does Casey know?"

Golden nodded. "He found the morphine in the bottom of Willie's desk. He's had his people dust them for fingerprints and he said he got a pretty clean pair. He suspects they're Willie's."

"How about prints on the medicine cabinet?" Jack asked.

"I don't know," she replied. "I'm a doctor, not a detective. I'm afraid we're a little outside my area of expertise. Besides, I only talked to Casey for a moment." Golden looked down at the carpet, as if studying the elaborate Persian design. "They're going to say that Willie stole the morphine, aren't they? They're going to say that he killed himself—either accidentally through an overdose, or on purpose."

Cassian nodded.

She frowned. "I thought so."

"You don't think it's likely?" Jack asked.

She shook her head, biting her bottom lip to choke back a wave of emotion. "It's possible, I suppose. Sometimes, as clinicians, we can get too close to those we treat, and maybe I just don't want to accept that I missed something this serious. But it just doesn't make sense."

"Why not?"

"Willie'd been off drugs for nearly two decades. Why would he feel the need to use now? If anything, I'd have said that he was more secure in who he was than he'd ever been in his life. Don't get me wrong, he still had a lot of issues, and we had a lot of work to do to get through those issues, but I thought he was finally making peace with his past. He'd had a rush of memories over the past month, and he seemed to be coming to grips with what had happened to him when he was a child here. Why would he throw all that away?"

"Maybe remembering and dealing with it all was too painful?" Sydney suggested, though her own tone sounded doubtful.

"Was that your impression when you met with him yesterday?" Golden asked.

Sydney shook her head. "He didn't seem to want to share too much of it, but he didn't seem tortured by it."

"That was my impression, too," Golden said.

"Maybe someone wanted to make sure that he never shared any of it," Cassian suggested. He was pacing again, circling the room like an agitated panther. "Of course, it probably doesn't matter. Dudley Do-Right and his band of mounted troopers will conclude that it was suicide, or an accidental overdose, and any clues we might have had will be swept away in whatever cursory investigation they conduct." He was angry and frustrated, and he was letting it show. He stalked his way around the room again and again, making himself light-headed as his mind flipped through what little he knew.

As he paced, the portraits that hung on the walls cycled by in an endless unbroken parade of old white men, each looking more smug than he had on the previous pass. Cassian was furious with them for playing God—deciding alone who would live and who would die, and who would be used in unthinkable ways to prove "scientific" fancy, draining away lives in the name of some false superiority without concern or compassion.

He walked around and around until his head hurt and he had to stop, and he found himself focusing on one of the portraits. It was one of the largest, and it held a position of prominence. It looked like it had probably been painted in the middle of the last century, and the subject stared down at Cassian over spectacles that were perched on a distinctively long, aquiline nose.

"Who is that?" he asked Golden after a moment.

She walked over and stood next to Jack, looking up at the painting with him. "That's Abraham B. Venable," she said. "He was in charge of the Institute from the 1930s through the end of the 1950s. He was the man most responsible for bringing this place to prominence."

Cassian was still staring at the portrait, almost hypnotized. "He looks familiar."

She nodded. "His son got the same distinctive looks."

"His son?"

"Yes, Abe Venable Jr."

Cassian was puzzled. He felt like something was still missing. "Should I know who Abe Venable Jr. is?"

"I would think so," Golden said, the surprise evident in her tone. "After all, he's running for president."

"That Abe Venable?" Cassian asked. "I had no idea he had a connection to . . ." As he spoke, the realization hit him squarely. He looked at Sydney, his eyes wide. "Abe Venable's father was in charge of this place!"

"Don't you see? It all makes sense," Cassian argued to Train.

He and Sydney had spent the rest of the morning on the drive back into Washington digesting what they'd learned. After a cursory talk with Detective Casey—an obligatory few questions that had hardly been worth the wait, and had clearly been intended by Casey to make the point that he was in control—they had headed out to the regional highway impound facility where Sydney's car had been towed early that morning. The engine had started on the first try and Cassian changed the tire. He arranged to have his motorcycle shipped back to the state central holding area in Alexandria on the next police transport of stolen vehicles so he could ride back with Sydney. Now they were bringing Train up to speed.

"Abe Venable's father was in charge of that place in the fifties," Cassian explained. "That means he was personally responsible for the inhumane treatment of the patients out there, and if that ever became public knowledge, it could prove fatal to Venable's presidential ambitions. Venable's a dyed-in-the-wool southern conservative, and his father's history would probably be enough to sink him with any moderate voters."

"So what are you saying?" Train demanded. "You think the country's leading conservative had Elizabeth Creay killed? You think she was going to do a story on all this, and he somehow found out about it?"

"That's exactly what I think," said Cassian. "The presidency's the greatest political prize on the planet, and the notion that someone like Venable might kill to win it hardly seems like a stretch. Think about it: he could have been tipped off by someone still up there. After all, his father ran the place for decades; you'd have to think he's still got some supporters working at the Institute."

"How is it that no one has found out about his father before?" Train challenged. "After all, it sounds like the Institute's pretty well-known, and lots of people must know about its history, as well as Venable's connection to it."

"Maybe no one has focused on it before," Cassian offered. "Who knows why, but what does it matter? If Liz Creay was about to splash it all over the papers, you can certainly see a motive to kill her."

Train gave an exasperated sigh. "Even if we assume that Sydney's sister was going to do a story—or even that Venable thought she was going to do a story—I'm not convinced that would provide a motive for murder. It all assumes that a big story on Venable's father would have doomed his chances at being elected. I'm not convinced that's the case. It's his father, right? It's not like he's the one who was experimenting on people himself. Besides, Venable is already known as such a conservative that some of his base might actually like the notion that his father was unapologetic in his approach to mental health. Any way you look at it, it's all still just speculation."

The three of them seemed to be at an impasse, and Cassian was feeling frustrated all over again. If he couldn't convince his own partner that Venable was a real suspect, how could he ever convince anyone else? And without Train's support, the idea of pursuing a major political figure like Venable in connection with a murder investigation was unthinkable. It was looking to Cassian like he'd have to let the Venable angle go, and he thought it was a mistake.

Jack was deep in his own thoughts, trying to figure out any way to convince Train to pursue the issue, when Sydney spoke up. "Sergeant Train, I don't know whether Venable had anything to do with my sister's murder or not, but I'd certainly like to find out. If someone who knows the political landscape well told you that these revelations about Venable's father would have ruined him politically, and that it could be a legitimate motive for murder, would you consider looking into it a little more?"

Train looked at her carefully. Finally, he sighed heavily. "Who did you have in mind?"

Chapter Forty-one

IT WAS A QUICK WALK from the police station on E Street to the Department of Health and Human Services. Up Washington Street and through the shadow of the Rayburn Office Building, which housed the offices of many of the nation's members of Congress, Train glanced to his right and shivered unexpectedly as he regarded the Capitol dome looming over them as if watching their every move.

They entered the building off Independence Avenue within a stone's throw of the Capitol, bordering the U.S. Botanic Garden in the heart of the District's pomp. As they walked down the corridor, Train listened to their footsteps echoing off the polished marble floors and through the narrow catacombed hallways. They reached the end of the passageway and turned to the left, headed down two doors, and through an archway that led into a large, well-appointed office suite. "Wait here," Sydney said as she walked over to a prim-looking woman in an out-of-season wool suit sitting behind a desk at the far end of the reception room. The woman took her name and directed the three of them to take a seat in the waiting area.

"Nice digs," Cassian commented. "For a bureaucrat."

Sydney laughed nervously. "He's hardly a bureaucrat; he's a cabinet member. The Secretary of Health and Human Services oversees most of the social programs run by the federal government. It's actually a very important position."

"Like I said," Cassian countered, "a bureaucrat."

"I'm surprised he could see us on such short notice," Train said to Sydney, ignoring his partner.

She smiled. "Irskin's always said he'd do anything for me or my family," she said. "I've never taken him up on it, but he's a man of conviction who keeps his word."

The buzzer on the prim-looking woman's desk rang. She picked up the phone, holding it to her ear for a moment, then setting it down without saying a word. "Mr. Elliot will see you now," she said, pointing to a door on the wall behind her.

The inner office was large, but hardly ostentatious. It felt, in fact, more like a glorified file room than the office of a powerful government leader. Metal cabinets lined one entire wall and papers were stacked in loose piles on top of, and all around, a broad-topped, functional desk. Behind the desk, looking like a cross between a kindly college professor and an ancient scribe, Irskin Elliot sat talking on the phone.

He held up his hand, indicating that he would be with them in a moment, then redirected his attention to the phone. "That's right," he was saying. "All fifty states. How can we expect children to learn if they're malnourished or hungry? The experts say that early nutrition is one of the keys to breaking the cycle, and I want every indigent child to have the opportunity to eat breakfast and lunch at school." There was a pause. "I don't care, just get it done!"

He hung up the phone and pinched his nose as though he had a headache. "I just can't understand the opposition in this country to feeding all our children properly. I swear, I'll never understand it." He sat quietly for a moment, until it appeared he had recovered. Then he stood, smiling as he stepped out from behind the desk. "Sydney!" he said, opening his arms. "How are you holding up?"

She walked forward, meeting his embrace. "I've been better, actually," she replied truthfully.

As she got closer to him his eyes narrowed and he noticed the scratches on her face and the bruises on her neck. "Oh! My child! What happened?" He looked accusingly at Cassian and Train.

"I was attacked last night," Sydney said. "Out in the sticks in Virginia. The detectives—Detective Cassian in particular—came out to help me."

Elliot looked at Cassian. "Your stock just went up in this office, young man. If there's ever anything I can do for you, please let me know. You've earned yourself a favor in my book."

"Good," Train interjected, sensing an opportunity. "Because we need a favor."

"Of course. All of you, sit down."

It was a pleasant enough invitation, Train thought, but a practical impossibility in the cluttered office, overflowing as it was with briefing books and binders and papers covering all of the sitting surfaces. Cassian moved some of the materials on the small couch aside and he and Sydney took a seat there. Train remained standing.

"I'm sorry about the office," Elliot said with an apologetic smile. "I need clutter to think properly. Now, tell me what I can do for you."

"We have a question about Abe Venable."

"The senator?"

"The senator." Train nodded, though he had no clear idea where to start. These were delicate questions that needed to be asked. "How well do you know him?" Train asked to start. Better, he thought, to feel his way into the conversation.

"Well, we're both products of Virginia politics, so I probably know him as well as a person can really know anyone else in this godforsaken city."

"You're on opposite sides of the aisle, right?"

"That's essentially correct, though that's a more complicated question than it might seem. As I explained the other day, I'm a Democrat working within a Republican administration, so I'm a bit of a man without a country right now. My presence in the cabinet allows the president to seem less partisan; in exchange, I get the opportunity to help direct policy to a certain extent." He sighed. "The compromise is that I often have to work alongside people like Venable."

"Not one of your favorites?" Train asked.

"We're too far apart politically to ever get along," Elliot admitted.

"Will he be the Republican nominee in the next election?"

Elliot folded his hands into a steeple as he leaned back in his chair and considered the question. "It's possible," he said at last. "The primaries are still six months away, and that's a lifetime in politics, so anything could happen. But I'd say he's probably the front-runner right now. Why do you ask? And what does this have to do with the fact that Sydney was attacked?"

"Sydney was attacked after she visited the Virginia Juvenile Institute for Mental Health."

"The Virginia Juvenile Institute for Mental Health?" Elliot raised his eyebrows.

"Yes," Train said. "It's a small mental institution out in the mountains in southwestern Virginia."

Elliot looked at Sydney with surprise. "What on earth were you doing out in southwestern Virginia?"

"I found out that Liz had been out at the Institute—that's what it's called—two weeks before she was killed. She was investigating some awful things that went on out there in the 1950s and '60s. Apparently, they used to conduct experiments on the patients out there—experiments that may have had to do with eugenics. I wanted to figure out if her visit had anything to do with her murder."

Elliot frowned and looked at Train. "But I thought the killer had been caught. I thought he was some local drug dealer."

"He's still a suspect," Train said. "But we're investigating every possibility, and we've found some things that don't fit."

"After I left the Institute," Sydney continued, "I was attacked by the side of the road after I got a flat tire. A man stopped and offered to help. Then he tried to kill me."

Elliot pulled on his ear unconsciously as he let out a long breath, digesting the information slowly. "And now you think your sister's murder has something to do with the Institute and the experiments that went on in the past?"

"I think it may," Sydney said.

"It's a possibility at least," Cassian agreed.

"But I don't see how Venable plays into all of this."

"His father was in charge of the Institute for decades," Train explained. "If Sydney's sister found out something incriminating about him . . ." He shrugged. "Who knows?"

"Really?" Elliot remarked. He turned his chair away from them and stared out the window, nodding quietly as he stroked his chin. "I had no idea. It's certainly a problem for Venable." He looked at them. "Is there anything else that makes you suspect that Liz's death is connected to the Institute?"

"Yes, actually," Cassian said. He looked at Sydney, nodding an encouragement for her to continue.

"Yesterday I talked to a man who had been a patient there before the place was reformed. He didn't tell me much, but Liz talked to him, too. This morning he was found dead. The police think it was suicide, or perhaps an accidental overdose."

"You think otherwise?" Elliot guessed.

"The man's doctor thinks otherwise," Sydney said.

"And once we found out about Venable's father, we began to wonder whether there was a connection," Cassian said.

"Whether it makes sense to look into," Train interjected, making sure to get control of the discussion before things had gone too far down a particular path. "Whether it makes sense to even start looking into it depends largely on whether a story with some sort of revelation about Venable's father could actually have a significant enough impact on Venable's political fortunes to provide him with a motive for murder. Sydney suggested that you might be someone who could give us a read on that."

Elliot leaned back in his chair, pulling on his ear again as he gave the issue serious consideration. "It's quite possible," he said finally. "If it were to come out that Venable's father was somehow responsible for illegal experiments—something like that might very well grab the public's imagination. There's no question that it could potentially have a devastating impact on Venable's political aspirations. It could even knock him out of politics altogether if the revelations were specific or grotesque enough."

There was silence in the room as everyone contemplated what acts of depravity could be sinister enough to ruin a son's political life. Finally Train asked the most important question.

"If Venable believed that there was a danger that someone was going to reveal something that would have that kind of impact, would that be enough to supply him with a motive for murder?"

Elliot raised his eyebrows and blew out a long breath as he sank into his chair. It suddenly looked to Train as if the dark leather had swallowed his tiny frame. "In pursuit of the presidency," he said ominously, "there's nothing that some men won't do."

Chapter Forty-two

"So what now?" Sydney asked. She, Jack, and Train were sitting on a bench in the Botanic Garden, looking up at the Capitol building. The day had turned gray, and as the light filtered through the clouds to the west, directly behind the Capitol dome, the building took on a sinister appearance with its marble façade towering over the Mall. "It has to be Venable. Who else would have a motive to kill Willie—and try to do the same to me?"

Jack rubbed his neck and Sydney could see the stress in his face. It was the first sign of weakness he'd shown since she'd met him. "Okay," he began, "let's break this down logically. Let's assume that Willie Murphy was murdered."

"That seems obvious," Sydney interjected, the irritation in her voice surprising even herself.

"Maybe, but if we're going to be rational about this, we need to remember the difference between fact and assumption." He continued. "If we assume that Willie Murphy was murdered, then it's likely that Liz was killed because of something he told her when she was out there. Or, if not something he told her, then because of something someone worried he'd told her. It follows that you were attacked for the same reason. The key to all this is to figure out what Willie knew and what he told Liz."

"The only thing that makes sense is that he knew something about whatever it was Venable's father did when he was in charge at the Institute. I mean, what else could it be?" Sydney's exasperation was showing.

"We still need to know the specifics if we're ever going to get to the bottom of this," Train said. "We can speculate all we want, but until we can prove something, it's just screamin' into the wind. We need to figure out what Willie knew."

Sydney's hands went to her face, rubbing her eyes as she bent over. "That's going to be difficult now that Willie's dead and we can't talk to him anymore."

"True. For the moment, we're going to have to rely solely on your recollection of your conversation with him." Train looked at her. "Tell us everything you remember."

Sydney threw up her hands. "I don't know! It was a short conversation, and I've already told Jack everything I could remember."

"Walk through it again. The more you talk about it, the more you're likely to remember, and this could be the key to your sister's murder."

"Great," Sydney said sarcastically. "No pressure there, huh, Detective?" She shook her head. "We only talked for fifteen minutes or so, and he really didn't want to talk about the past. He specifically told me that sometimes the past should stay in the past."

"Can you remember anything in particular that he did tell you?" Train pushed.

Sydney racked her brain, trying to piece together the entirety of her conversation with Willie. "He told me he was sterile," she said, choking out a bitter, ironic laugh at the uselessness of the information.

Train and Cassian both raised their eyebrows. "Sterile?" Cassian exclaimed. "How did that come up in conversation?"

"I think I asked him if he was injured as a result of his treatment at the Institute, and he said that he couldn't have children." Sydney caught the look that flashed between the two police partners, and she explained further. "He said they had experimented on him when he was there, and that he couldn't have children as a result." She looked at them, but the silence persisted as they digested the information. "He didn't seem to mind that much. He seemed to think he was so screwed up that the notion of having a family wasn't a priority."

Cassian made a face. "What did they do? Run electric current through his groin or something like that?"

Sydney shook her head. "No, he said he was fed something that had been treated somehow. He even said he was better off when they were conducting the experiments because when they were going on he didn't get beaten."

"Did he say anything else about the experiments?"

Sydney sighed, parsing her memory for any scraps she had missed. "He got some money as a result," she said at last.

Train frowned. "How did he get money for being experimented on?"

"From a lawsuit," Sydney replied. "How else?"

"Ah yes, the American way."

Sydney ignored him. The conversation was jarring loose something she hadn't reported to them yet, and she was focused on retrieving as much of it as she could. "It was a class-action lawsuit, he said. He was the named plaintiff. He ended up getting twenty thousand dollars or something like that for the damage caused by the experiments."

"Who did he sue?"

"I'm not sure he really knew. From the way he told the story, it sounded like some class-action plaintiffs' lawyer just used him to get a huge settlement for himself."

Cassian shook his head. "I don't understand how that works. I thought a plaintiff's lawyer gets a third of whatever his client gets. In Willie's case, if he only got twenty thousand, his lawyer should only have taken home ten, right?"

"That's generally true, but in a class action the lawyer is representing an entire group of people by using one person as an example."

"What do you mean?" Train asked.

"Basically, in a class-action situation, the lawyer picks a plaintiff as the representative of a much larger group of plaintiffs. The idea is that sometimes it wouldn't make sense for each individual plaintiff to sue for a small amount of money, so the system lets a group of people with similar cases against the same companies sue together. The lawyer can estimate that there were, let's say, a thousand people who were subject to the same experiments as Willie. The lawyer uses Willie as his example—what's known as the 'class representative'—and sues on behalf of all those who suffered the same way he did. If Willie got twenty thousand, then every potential plaintiff got twenty thousand. As a result, the lawyer would have made ten million, not ten thousand. The only trick is that the lawyer often doesn't know who or where the other people are."

Train grunted. "Sounds like a scam."

"Sometimes," Sydney admitted. "On the other hand, they do serve an important purpose by keeping companies in line. If it wasn't for the fear of class-action lawsuits, many companies wouldn't think twice about ripping people off for small sums of money because they would know that no one would ever spend the time to sue them. The system can be abused, though."

"Do we have any way of finding out who the lawsuit was against or what was alleged specifically? There could be something in there about Venable or his father," Train posited.

Sydney thought for a moment. "There might be, particularly if the suit was filed in federal court. Most of the dockets are searchable online, and there should be a record of it. Willie said the settlement came around ten years ago, so the lawsuit was probably filed sometime in the mid-nineties. Most of the federal courts were keeping case files electronically by then."

"What if it was filed in state court?" Cassian asked.

"Then we'll probably have more trouble finding it. I would guess that if they filed it in a state jurisdiction it would have been in Virginia because it involved a Virginia state medical facility—jurisdiction and venue probably would have been improper in any other state. I'm guessing that Virginia's court files aren't kept electronically, so searching for it would be like looking for a needle in a haystack."

"Okay," said Train, "so we start with the federal courts and hope we get lucky. How do we run the search?"

"We don't," Sydney replied. "I do. That is, unless you have free access to the PACER system that searches federal dockets, and you know how to use it. It shouldn't take me more than a couple of hours."

Jack was hesitant. "I don't want you putting yourself at risk any more than you already have."

"Fine," she said. "So I'm guessing you have someone else in mind who can run this search today?" The detectives looked at each other, their expressions making clear that they didn't. "Well then, I guess we're back to plan A, aren't we?"

"I don't think you understand, Sydney—" Jack began, but she cut him off.

"No, I don't think you understand, Jack. My sister's been dead for a week, and I haven't been able to do a damned thing about it. Look at the scratches on my face. I'm not letting go of this until it's over, got it?"

Jack looked at her, and she didn't avert her eyes. "Got it," he said.

Train was still rubbing his head, but it was clear that he too understood. "Here's what I propose, then," he said. "You go see what you can dig up on the lawsuit. While you're doing that, Jack and I will pay Senator Venable a little visit—ask some questions and see how he reacts."

"I don't think Sydney should be left alone. Someone tried to kill her," Jack pointed out.

"It's okay," Sydney assured him. "I'm not out on a highway in Virginia anymore, and I find it hard to believe that anyone's going to attack me at the law school. I'll be fine."

"Are you sure?"

"Yes, Jack, I'm sure."

Chapter Forty-three

SYDNEY USED A COMPUTER in a corner of McDonough Hall at the law school to do her research. She could have used one of the terminals up in Professor Fuller's office, also located in the building, but she didn't want to answer the many inevitable questions about what she was doing or how she was coping with her sister's death. Things were just a little too unsettled for her to talk coherently to people at the moment. She'd have to stop up in the office if she found anything worth printing out—her password linked all her printouts to the printer in the professor's suite—but she figured she'd deal with that if the need arose.

McDonough Hall, one of the newer buildings at the law school, with its rose-colored stone façade broken by clean, tall reflective glass, provided a sharp contrast with the surrounding area. Located down near Union Station, miles away from the rarefied environs of the main Georgetown University Campus, the law school was tucked just off the interstate and next to one of the city's most dangerous homeless shelters. Upon matriculation, students were warned not to wander the area alone at night, and muggings and attacks were not unheard of near the campus.

Although classes had ended and exams were over, the building, which housed large lecture halls on the first floor and offices on the upper levels, was nearly as busy as it would have been during the full swing of the school year. Recent graduates were packed into the building studying furiously for the bar exam, which was given each July. In various corners, study groups of soon-to-be-lawyers huddled cross-legged on the floor or around round, low-set tables, debating arcane issues of the law of trusts and estates, torts, and securities. Sydney could taste the tension in the air as her peers worked to the point of breaking to ensure their futures. A month ago, finishing law school and passing the bar exam had been the major focus of Sydney's life, too. Now the notion of studying anything as mundane as the rules of civil procedure seemed pointless to her.

She deposited herself in a cubbied terminal on the second floor, putting her oversized bag under the table and turning on the computer. The outdated machine hummed and whirred and struggled to life as she sat impatiently in front of the screen. Finally the prompt asked her to put in her student identification number, which she did, and after another extended delay she was connected to the law school's network.

From there, she navigated her way around to the federal courts' PACER system, which allowed users access to court documents online. She typed in another password, one that she'd been given to do research as Professor Fuller's assistant, and in moments she was on the system.

The actual search would take some time, she knew. There was no way to search all the courts in the system at once; rather, she would have to go court by court, searching the records of each separately before moving on to the next. Given that there were over one hundred federal districts in the United States federal court system, it might take her hours to find anything.

She decided to start with the districts in and around Virginia, where the Institute was located, as the most likely jurisdictions where a suit would have been filed. She identified one of the districts, entered the site for it, and started putting in search terms. Then, as the computer bucked and churned, she sat back and waited.

Cassian and Train sat in the reception room in the office suite of Senator Abe Venable, the senior senator from Virginia. An attractive twenty-something woman in a smart dark blue business suit sat at a receptionist's table guarding the door to the inner offices. They'd called ahead, and while they'd originally been told that the senator's schedule was full, they'd indicated that the visit involved an investigation into the Institute, and had received a callback a few minutes later indicating that Venable had freed up five or ten minutes to talk to them. They'd been waiting for more than a half hour in the reception area.

The couch on which they'd been directed to wait was low and soft, and Train felt uncomfortable with his knees poking up into his chest, so he got up and walked over to examine some of the pictures at the far end of the room. The receptionist watched him suspiciously as she went about her business.

The pictures hardly surprised Train. They showed the senator posing with statesmen and celebrities of every variety—an ego wall to be envious of, to be sure.

"The privileges of power," a deep bass voice sounded from over Train's shoulder.

Train turned and saw Venable standing in the doorway to his inner offices. His face was narrow, with a long, protruding nose and overhanging brow, but his frame carried the heft of age and rich food that seems to come so easily to those who spend any significant time in the endless governmental reception that is D.C. life. It occurred to Train that he looked very much like a caricature of how liberals envisioned conservative politicians. "Pardon me?" Train said, not having registered the senator's comment.

"Meeting with other powerful people," Venable said, pointing to the pictures. "I may not make nearly as much money as those who chose to work for investment houses or go into business for themselves, but it helps to remind people that power still has its privileges, and those privileges include having the ear of other powerful people."

"Effective," Train commented.

Venable tilted his head. "Detectives, come with me." He beckoned them through the doorway, and Train and Cassian followed him. They walked down a hallway, past several small offices, until they came to a set of large double doors that led into a huge, ornately decorated office of dark wood and leather. The surroundings seemed suited to their inhabitant; overbearing and clearly designed to intimidate any visitor. To the left, a large window looked out onto the Mall, running down from the Capitol out toward the Washington Monument and the Lincoln Memorial. As one of the most senior members of the Senate, Venable clearly had his pick of offices, and he'd chosen well.

Venable walked around behind his desk and sat down,

inviting Train and Cassian to take a seat in the two chairs that faced it. "Now, gentlemen," he drawled in a smooth country accent, "what can I do for you today?"

"First," Train began, following standard Washington protocol, "we'd like to thank you for agreeing to see us today. We understand how busy you are, and we appreciate your time."

Venable waved Train off. "Please, Detective, you can skip the standard ritual of blowing sunshine up my ass. I got a message from you people indicating that you were investigating my father's work at the Institute." He looked carefully back and forth between the two detectives. "That's a message that's calculated to bring a response."

Train drew his eyebrows up noncommittally, and Venable's gaze settled on him like a heavy burden. He held the stare, returning its intensity without aggression as they sat in silence for a long moment, neither one of them backing down. Finally Venable spoke again. "Well, congratulations, gentlemen, y'all have my attention. Now I think it's only reasonable for me to ask you what the fuck y'all are doing here in my office."

Chapter Forty-four

THE SEARCH TOOK Sydney less time than she'd anticipated. Within two hours she had located the electronic files on a case captioned *William L. Murphy et al. v. Virginia Medical Association et al.* She started looking through them, but quickly realized it was useless to navigate through everything on the computer—the files were just too large. It would be far more efficient to download the documents to the printer down the hall in Professor Fuller's office, so that she could flip through the materials at a reasonable pace. She was only supposed to use her school password and printer for official law school business, but she decided to break the rules this one time. Besides, anyone seeing the legal printouts would simply assume that she was conducting research for some article Professor Fuller was writing, so there was little risk.

Once the files had been downloaded, she saved the link on her computer and left her shoulder bag in the computer cubby so that no one would commandeer the terminal. This would save her time if there was a problem with the printer upstairs and she had to download the materials again.

She headed down the hallway and around the corner to retrieve her documents from the printer, keeping her head down the entire way, acutely aware that the scratches on her face, while less pronounced, hadn't fully faded. She'd tried to cover them with a scarf so they might escape the attention of a casual observer, but she was still eager to avoid anyone she knew at the school who might stop her to ask how she was doing.

How was she doing? The thought was ludicrous enough to draw a bitter, ironic laugh. How could she ever explain to anyone what had been happening to her life in the past week? There was no point to trying, and so she resolved to duck anyone who might try to engage her in conversation.

It was quiet up in the suite of offices Professor Fuller shared with two other professors and their assistants. Sydney wasn't surprised. With classes over, the professors' lair was most often deserted. Only on occasion would one of them venture in to get some work done on an article or a case.

She went quickly to the printer, and was dismayed to see that there was no stack of documents waiting for her where they should have been. She examined the machine and saw the blinking yellow light indicating that it was out of paper, and she grumbled to herself as she found a fresh ream and loaded it into the paper port.

It started printing at once, and Sydney pulled the first few sheets off the top of the printer to examine them. The first page contained the entire caption of the case, including the names of all of the defendants—there were more than twenty in all, comprised of various individuals, government agencies, and companies. She scanned them quickly to see if Venable's name was among them, but it was not.

After the case caption, there was a docket sheet listing all of the pleadings and motions and briefs that had been filed. While the documents were long, there were relatively few of them. There was the complaint and summons filed by the plaintiffs, and a motion to dismiss the lawsuit that had been filed in reply. These were followed by a series of complicated motions dealing with the appropriateness of treating all of the alleged plaintiffs as a class, and then there was a notice of voluntary dismissal based on a settlement reached between the parties. Any specific mention of Venable's father would most likely be found in the substantive pleadings, but Sydney had no interest in staying in the office to review them.

She checked the docket sheet against the documents that had printed out to make sure she had everything. Once she was sure, she looked around for an empty folder she could use to keep the papers together. Suddenly, she felt a hand on her shoulder.

"Sydney? What are you doing in here?"

She jumped at the sound of the voice, and at the feeling of the hand on her shoulder. "Oh my God, you startled me!" she exclaimed. "I didn't think anyone was here, Professor."

"I didn't either," Professor Barneton replied. "I'm sorry that I scared you. I thought Professor Fuller told me that you were still at home dealing with . . ." He paused. ". . . Taking care of your family," he offered finally.

"I was," Sydney lied. "I just had to get a little bit of work done."

He looked at her quizzically. "You shouldn't worry about anything with respect to your work," he said. "You should just focus on your family and yourself at this point." His eyes narrowed and he looked more closely at her face. "Oh my," he said. "What happened?"

She realized that he'd seen the scratches on her face, and her mind spun. She hadn't even thought to come up with a plausible story. "Oh, these," she said with a flip of her head, trying to give the impression that they were inconsequential. "My cat," she offered, hoping that would end the inquiry.

After a moment he said, "Your cat what?"

"Scratched me."

"Oh." He didn't seem convinced, and the way he was looking at her made her uneasy. She changed the subject.

"Thank you for all your understanding," she said. "I was just leaving anyway, but I'll be back in sometime next week to start getting back to work fully. I don't want to let anyone down." There was some truth in that.

"Well, as I said, there's no hurry." He waved her off, his gaze still focused on the scratches on her face. "I'm sure Professor Fuller will feel the same way."

The two of them stood there, and it seemed to Sydney as though Barneton had something else to say. After enduring a long, pregnant moment, she gathered her papers. "Thank you again," she said. "I'll see you when I get back to work." She started to walk past him, but his hand shot out and grabbed her arm.

"Sydney," he began.

She looked at him, and something in his eyes alarmed her. He had an intense, almost wild look. "Yes, Professor?" she asked nervously.

"We all need people," he said, the grip on her arm staying firm.

She looked down at his hand on her arm. His grip was strong enough to be uncomfortable. "Please, Professor," she said, her voice adamant. "You're hurting me."

He let go of her. "I'm sorry," he said. "It's just that the world can be a cold, dangerous place. I could help you. I could—"

"Thank you, Professor," she cut him off. "I'll see you when I get back to work, I'm sure." She spun on her heels and walked quickly out of the office suite. Over her shoulder she could hear him calling to her.

"I hope so, Sydney! I certainly hope so!"

Venable was angry; Cassian could see that. He made it plain in his every aspect, from his posture to his facial expressions. And there was no question that there was something intimidating about a man of his power and position willing to display such open hostility. Jack was sure that kind of intimidation was useful to the senator in his rough-and-tumble world of politics. It wouldn't help him now, though, Jack thought, when confronted by two police officers who would not be cowed by the man; in fact, it was clear that Train was trying to provoke him—to see what would reveal itself when he was under pressure.

"And so," Train was finishing his explanation of why they were there, "given your father's connection to the Institute, we were hoping that you might be able to shed a little light on what might be going on there."

Venable fumed, his chest expanding as he sucked in air aggressively. "Let me get this straight, Detective," he said, his southern accent dripping with disdain. "Some lifetime mental patient with a history of drug abuse takes an overdose, and because my father—who passed away over a decade ago—worked at the same mental facility fifty years ago, you think it's appropriate to interrupt the schedule of one of the most senior members of Congress. Is that about it?"

"As I said," Train explained calmly, "we're not convinced this was a simple overdose. Mr. Murphy hadn't used drugs in years. Add to that the vicious attack on Ms. Chapin after she visited with him, and her sister's murder a couple of weeks earlier, and it starts to look like this could be some sort of a conspiracy to conceal something."

"You still haven't explained to me what this has to do with my father—or with me, for that matter," Venable growled.

Train looked at Cassian, and Jack could see that his partner was deciding how far to push the issue. "Well," Train started, "it's true that your father was in charge of the Institute for many years, correct?"

"A half century ago, yes, you're correct."

"And, tell me if I've got this wrong, but when your father was in charge, he instituted a number of policies that would probably raise some eyebrows in these more enlightened times."

"I'm sure I have no idea what you're talking about, Detective."

Cassian interrupted. "Perhaps we have our information wrong, Senator, but it was our understanding that your father was one of the leading proponents of eugenics in his day. It seems that thousands of his patients were sterilized over the years, and it also appears that numerous experiments were carried out on the people he was supposed to be caring for."

Venable's face went scarlet with rage. "My father was a scientist. Science, by definition, sometimes leads even the best men down the wrong path. By the time my father passed on, he had renounced all elements of eugenics."

"Still," Train pressed, "by that time a significant amount of harm had already been inflicted. It seems to me that if the full truth about what went on at the Institute ever came to light, a lot of people's reputations would suffer."

"Your point, Detective?"

"Are you aware of anyone who might have an interest in keeping the past buried?" Train asked the question pointedly, and it hung in the air, increasing the tension in the room.

Venable stared at Train, his shoulders hunched forward over his desk as though he might leap across the mahogany surface at any moment and attack, his eyes burning his hatred into the other man. "No, Detective," he said at last. "I am not."

There was a long pause as the two men faced each other down, neither of them flinching, neither of them willing to give any ground.

It was Jack who finally broke the spell. "How about you, Senator?"

Venable's eyes remained on Train for a moment before he turned to face Cassian, like a jackal shifting its attention from one zebra to another. "How about me, what?" he asked.

"Wouldn't you be hurt by a full disclosure about what went on at the Institute while your father was in charge?"

"I don't follow you," the senator said in a low, challenging voice.

"Well, Senator—and I'm just spitballing here—but you're a prominent conservative politician making a run at the White House, right? Isn't it possible that you could be hurt by public revelations about what your father did to his patients at the Institute? I mean, isn't it at least conceivable that the fact that you're the son of a famous eugenicist would probably scare away a lot of moderate voters; and that if someone had real concrete information about what your father did while he was there, it could pretty much end your chances of being elected?"

Venable rose and leaned over the desk. For a brief moment, Cassian actually thought there might be a physical altercation in the offing. Then, after a pause, the senator hit the intercom button on his telephone. He stared at Cassian as he spoke into the phone. "Beverly?" he said. "You can come in and escort these gentlemen out of the office. This meeting is over."

Chapter Forty-five

SYDNEY HURRIED BACK to the computer terminal where she'd left her belongings, stuffing the papers she'd printed out into her bag and throwing it over her shoulder. Her encounter with Barneton had left her unsettled; what had he meant when he'd pointed out that the world was a dangerous place?

Her mind wandered over her experiences with the well-known professor, and she began to wonder about him. As far as she knew, he was the last person to see her sister alive, and he'd admitted that she'd asked him about the Institute. Was it possible that there was some connection she wasn't aware of? The notion seemed crazy, but then the look in his eyes had been just that—crazy.

She shook loose her suspicions as she walked toward the main stairway that led down to the main level of McDonough Hall. Better, she thought, to concentrate on whatever hard evidence she might find in the materials she'd printed out. Once she was back with Jack and Sergeant Train, they'd be able to sort all this out from whatever they found in the lawsuit. She had to hurry back to meet them at the police station.

First, though, she had to pee.

She ducked into the ladies' room and went into a stall, hanging her bag on a hook by the sink. After relieving herself, she stood in front of the mirror, running cold water over her hands. The stress was wearing her down, and the icy flow seemed to relax her. She cupped her hands and bent down, closing her eyes as she splashed water on her face and rubbed her hand around to the back of her neck. This was all insane, she knew, and she resolved to fight her growing paranoia.

She threw her bag back over her shoulder and headed out of the ladies' room, but as she opened the door out into the hallway, she froze.

He was standing there, not more than twenty feet away, his back to her as he scanned the area near the stairway. She recognized him instantly, his thinning blond hair unmistakable even from behind, and she thought for a moment that she might actually vomit right then and there. It took all the control she had to keep from screaming, or collapsing, or both.

She drew back into the bathroom, careful to keep the door from slamming, her chest heaving as she began to hyperventilate.

She stumbled back into the stall and closed the door as she tried to calm herself. Sitting down on the toilet, she forced herself to slow her breathing as she tried to think rationally, spinning out scenario after scenario as she tried to come up with a way out. She took out her phone and started to dial Cassian's number, but an annoying electrical chime let her know that her battery was too low for service. As she put it back in her purse she cursed herself for not having charged it.

Then she heard the door open and she quickly pulled her feet off the floor, hugging her bag to her chest, listening for footsteps. She heard nothing, and a moment later the door closed again.

She held her breath for what seemed an eternity, afraid to move. Finally, she put her feet down, leaned forward, and pressed the stall door open a crack. The bathroom seemed deserted, so she stood and walked out of the stall.

She regarded the door out into the hallway with dread, though she knew she had no choice. She couldn't stay in the ladies' room forever.

She approached the door with trepidation, sneaking up on it slowly. She was about to open it when she heard a loud explosion and the door of one of the other stalls behind her swung open. She screamed as her knees buckled and the nerves leading to her muscles fired indecisively. She whirled toward the stall, throwing her hands to her face defensively.

"I'm sorry," a woman's voice gasped. "I didn't mean to startle you."

She was a student, just a little younger than Sydney. The noise she'd heard, Sydney realized, was the toilet flushing, and the other woman was now regarding Sydney like an escaped mental patient.

"That's okay," Sydney choked out. "I was just . . ." She didn't bother to finish her sentence; there was really no rational way to explain her situation.

She took a deep breath and walked back to the door and pushed it open slowly. There was no one in the hallway, and after a moment's internal debate, she exited and hurried toward the stairs.

Salvage walked around the floor, poking his head into empty offices and taking the time to carefully evaluate anyone he encountered. Barneton had said he was sure the Chapin girl was working on this floor—he'd just seen her near his office—and yet she was nowhere to be found. It seemed hopeless, and if he had any better leads, he'd follow them, but he was running out of options.

He was turning the corner, heading back toward the main staircase, when he heard Barneton's voice up ahead, calling out.

"Wait! Sydney! Someone's looking for you!"

Salvage broke immediately for the stairs, his hand already inside his coat, reaching for his gun.

Sydney had made it halfway to the staircase, keeping her head down and moving with determination, before she heard Barneton's voice behind her. She turned and looked up at him.

"Wait! Sydney!" he called, moving toward her.

"I have to go," she said tersely as she turned and headed down the stairs.

He grabbed her, though, and pulled her back. "Someone's looking for you," he said, peering over his shoulder and down the hallway. "I think it's important."

"Let go of me!" Sydney demanded, trying to pull away, but Barneton held tight. Then she looked over his shoulder and saw the blond man hurrying down the hallway toward them. Her eyes darted back and forth between Barneton and the man from the highway, until they came to rest on Barneton's face and she had an awful thought. She stared at him for a second, searching his eyes for an answer; and then he seemed to nod, as if to suggest everything was all right.

She acted without hesitation or thought, bringing her

foot up and stomping on his instep with her heel, driving it down with all her weight. He crumpled, his face twisting in agony, but his hand still clinging to her arm. She took one last look at him and then swung her heavy backpack at his head, connecting with his nose, which cracked loudly as he crumpled to the ground.

She hesitated for a moment; just long enough to see the blond man still running toward her. To Sydney's horror, she saw a gun in his hand.

She turned and flew down the stairs, leaving Barneton heaped in pain. As she hit the main floor, the doors to three of the main lecture halls burst open and a flood of students poured into the main hallway, enveloping her. It was a lucky break for her. Although the law school year was over, most of the recent graduates took the bar preparation classes that were offered at the school. There must have been a couple hundred of them filing out into a crowded mash of bodies.

Sydney pushed her way past them, through them, in some cases over them, as she tried for an escape. She looked over her shoulder twice, and both times it seemed as though the blond man was gaining on her, though he was still twenty yards behind her. The gun was no longer visible, and Sydney hoped he wouldn't be brazen enough to shoot her in a crowded hallway. There were no guarantees, though, so she pressed on.

As she turned her head over her shoulder again, she felt someone grab her from the front, and she spun, leading with her fists, thrashing to get away from the person's grasp.

"Sydney! What the fuck? It's me, Mark."

"Mark!" she exclaimed, still moving forward as she recognized a fellow research assistant. He was huge—a former football player at Harvard who must have stood six-six and weighed well over two-fifty. She'd met him only two or three times, but she'd gotten the clear impression that he was attracted to her.

"Everything okay?" he asked, moving with her. "You look freaked."

"Fine," she said, still hurrying in the same direction. Then she had a thought. "Actually, no, I'm not fine. There's a guy who's been stalking me, and I'm trying to get away."

"Is there anything I can do?" He leered down at her, and she noticed that he was focusing a foot or so below her eyes.

"Yes," she replied quickly. "The guy's right behind me." She paused only long enough to point toward the man. "He's the blond guy, in his forties, heading this way. Could you just, maybe, slow him down a little? I'd be so grateful I wouldn't know how to thank you."

Mark's chest puffed out. "I'm sure we'll think of something," he said.

"Thank you so much," she said. "We can talk about it later. I'm going to run." She turned and headed toward a doorway that led to the stairs down into the basement.

Salvage fought his way through the swirling mass of students, keeping his head up as he watched Sydney head through a doorway and down another set of stairs. God, how he was tempted to pull out his gun and start clearing a path through the privileged, pampered, self-important crush of legal wannabes. It was a sign of his impatience, he recognized, though, and impatience could be deadly in his position. It was becoming more clear that he really needed to get out of the business as soon as possible. Just one more job to complete.

As he swam through the crowd over toward the stairwell where the Chapin girl had gone, a huge hand reached out in front of him and grabbed his chest.

"Where you goin', dude?" the owner of the hand asked in a deep, menacing tone. Salvage looked up at a behemoth as he knocked the arm out of his way.

"Excuse me," he said simply. "I'm in a hurry." He stepped around the man.

The giant stuck his hand out again. "Let her go," he growled, his face scrunching into a scowl that, had he not been in such a hurry, might have made Salvage laugh. He had no time to waste on this guy, though, so he decided to deal with him directly.

His arm shot out straight and lightning-quick from his side, his fist connecting squarely with the huge man's solar plexus. The man's face turned instantly from a scowl to a silent scream, his mouth forming a perfect circle as his eyes bulged. Salvage then took a step forward and brought his knee up between the wounded man's legs, and the man doubled over instantly.

He looked up at Salvage, his eyes shocked and pleading. If they hadn't been in a crowded hallway, Salvage probably would have put a bullet through one of those eyes just to punctuate his point. At the moment, though, he couldn't afford the disruption. "You're lucky," he said quietly as he pushed past him and headed down the stairs after his prey.

Chapter Forty-six

SYDNEY WISHED she was back at Stanford—her own school. There, she would have known the best route to take to safety, the best places to hide, and the easiest ways to escape. As it was, she'd only been working at Georgetown for a few weeks, and she had only a general idea of the school's layout.

She ran down a long hallway out toward the back of the building. She was fairly sure that it led to an exit out of the basement, from which she could get out onto the street.

The man was still behind her, she knew, but she had enough of a lead on him that if she could just find her way out of the maze of concrete hallways, she would be fine. She followed the passage down to the left—to where she thought the exit was—but it dead-ended into a set of offices. Above the door was a sign that read "Domestic Violence Legal Aid Clinic."

Shit! She wanted to scream. She turned around and considered briefly heading back out in the direction from which she'd come, but in all likelihood that would only lead her directly back into her pursuer. She was breathing hard now, and the sweat was running down her forehead. Perhaps she could hide, or even escape through a window in the clinic's offices. In any case, she decided, her chances were better than confronting him alone in the hallway back behind her.

She opened the door and stepped inside.

Antonia Vargas sat alone at her desk in the clinic's offices, filling out paperwork for her clients. They were primarily indigent women who lacked the resources to wrest themselves from what were generally horrific circumstances. Beaten by their spouses or significant others, and often without any means of independent support, they found their way to the clinic most often after some catastrophic—sometimes near-fatal—bout of violence. Antonia and the students she supervised provided legal advice and support free of charge, and helped the women find shelter and opportunity. It was a responsibility she took very seriously.

It was only a decade earlier that she herself had found her way into the clinic's offices. She'd been a dancer at one of the downtown strip clubs, and her "manager" had become increasingly dissatisfied with her efforts, culminating in a broken arm after one particularly vicious scolding. Those at the clinic had helped her. She'd gone back to school to get her degree, and then, inspired by what the clinic had done for her, she'd gone on to law school. Now she devoted herself to helping others the way she'd been helped back then. In the process, she'd earned a reputation around the city as one of its fiercest women's advocates, and a lawyer to be feared and respected in spite of her petite five-foot-two-inch frame and her shock of purple-and-pink hair that gave her the look of a refugee from a 1980s punk rock band.

She looked up when the attractive young woman burst into the offices, out of breath and clearly desperate. Antonia had worked with battered women for long enough to recognize the fear that accompanied the bruises and scratches on the woman's face, and she was out of her chair even before the woman could speak.

"Come in, come in," she said, leaning in to get a better look at the abrasions. "You're in the right place, honey, I can help you." She hadn't seen anyone this badly beaten in months, but nothing shocked her anymore. She took the woman by the elbow and led her into one of the cubicles that the students used when school was in session. "Is he your husband, or just your boyfriend?"

The woman was out of breath, gulping air as she shook her head. "No, you don't understand," she gasped.

Antonia patted her hand as she shook her neon locks back and forth. "Yes, I do, honey. Believe me, I do. We can help you here. He's not going to hurt you ever again; you have my word on that. Now, what's your name?"

"Sydney," she choked out, "but it's not what you think—"

"Girl, we all make excuses for them. It's never what anyone else thinks—except that it is. My name's Antonia, and you gotta believe me, Sydney, he'll never change."

"No, no, he's chasing me! He's right behind me!"

In the instant that it took for the woman's words to register, Antonia's demeanor altered radically, transforming from that of concerned mother figure to battlefield general. "Right here?" she demanded. "Right behind you?"

"Yes," Sydney replied.

Antonia nodded and led Sydney to another cubicle

where she was concealed from the front door of the offices. "You stay here," she ordered. She picked up the phone and dialed 911. "This is Toni Vargas at the Georgetown Domestic Violence Clinic," she said when the operator came on. "We have a potential situation here, and we're gonna need some help quickly." She hung up the phone. "They know me over at the station house, and they take me seriously," she reassured Sydney. "Someone'll be here in a few minutes." She got up and headed toward the door.

"Antonia?" the young woman said in a dazed voice.

"Yes, honey?"

"I think he has a gun."

She tilted her head. "Good to know." Then she smiled. "Relax, girl, we get this sort of thing here every now and then."

Salvage slammed through the door into the clinic's offices. He'd reholstered his gun, but his hand was inside his jacket, ready to pull it out as soon as he saw the Chapin girl again. He looked around the room and saw that it was dominated by cubicles set apart by gray industrial dividers. There weren't too many places for her to hide in here, clearly.

"Excuse me, can I help you?"

The voice came from in front of him, and he looked down to see a tiny woman in her thirties. He might have found her attractive were it not for the spray paint on her unevenly chopped hair; in any case, he knew, he had a job to do, and no time for diversions. "No," he said, dismissing her as he moved forward into the room. "I'm looking for someone."

The tiny woman stepped in front of him. "Sydney?" she asked, bringing him up short. "You're looking for Sydney, right?"

His eyes narrowed, evaluating her with new interest. "She's here, I take it?"

"Yes, she is. But she doesn't want to see you."

"I'm sure she doesn't." He sidestepped the Technicolor dwarf and started in toward the cubicles again, but she stepped in front of him once more, cutting him off. She was nimble, he had to give her that.

"You need to leave—now."

He shook his head; enough was enough. He started to pull his hand out of his jacket—perhaps a bullet to the brain would change the midget's attitude. He never got the gun out of the holster, though. Before he'd even moved his hand, she pulled a .357 Magnum revolver from behind her back and jammed it up under his chin hard, forcing his head back. The goddamned gun was bigger than the girl holding it. "What the fuck!" Salvage yelled.

"I'll tell you what the fuck," the girl spat at him. "You need to listen better. We have a little saying here at the domestic violence clinic. You should commit it to memory. It goes like this: *No means no, and go means go!* I'm telling you to go—you understand what that means?"

"You fucking bitch!"

"Been called worse by scarier men than you. Funny thing is, though, cops take me seriously. See, we have a deal. They show up quickly when I call, and I don't try to arrest anyone. I leave that to them. On the other hand, they know that if I have to shoot someone in self-defense, then that's just the way it goes sometimes, y'know? So the question right now is this: do I have to shoot you?"

"Fuck you!"

She cocked the gun. "You really want those to be your last words?"

He tried to pull away, but she had the gun thrust so far into his chin that there was little he could do. He had to distract her. "No reason to get touchy," he said, backing away.

She kept the gun pressed deep into the soft flesh at the back of his chin. "Yes, there is. There most certainly is a reason to get touchy. Y'see, women don't like it when you beat them. You may think it's sexy, but it's not. You may think it makes you a man, but it doesn't." She was pushing him back hard now, and he stumbled as he hit the door. "All it makes you is pathetic and weak." She grabbed him by the collar and pulled his face down toward hers, so that their noses were almost touching. "Consider this your official notice that this clinic will be representing Sydney in any domestic violence matter she cares to bring against you. If you have anything to say to her, please don't contact her directly. You can call me here—I'm Antonia—and I'll relay the message. You got that?"

This was getting humiliating. On the other hand, arguing with a .357 seemed to make little sense to Salvage. "Got it," he agreed.

"Good. One more thing," she said. She pulled him down by his collar again and leaned into his ear. "Now that she's my client, you ever touch her again, and I'll fucking kill you." She let go of him. "Now go."

Salvage thought briefly about reaching for his gun. There was always a chance that he could knock the woman's tiny arm away and buy enough time to free his weapon and get off a couple of shots. It was a slim chance at best, though, and if the police really were on the way already he probably wouldn't have enough time to find the Chapin girl, kill her, and get away cleanly. As humiliating as it felt, he quickly realized that a hasty retreat was his best option.

He backed through the door slowly, and then turned and headed back down the hallway. He'd live to fight another day, and he swore to himself that the Chapin girl would pay in the end.

Sydney had watched the entire exchange through a crack in the cubicle where she'd been hiding. Once she was sure that the man was gone, she stuck her head up. The petite woman was still pointing her gun down the hallway, ensuring that the man wouldn't return.

"You saved my life," Sydney stammered.

"For the moment," Antonia agreed. "But if you don't put some good distance between you and your boyfriend there, he will end up killing you."

"He's not my boyfriend."

"Heard that before."

"Can I ask you a question?" Sydney asked hesitantly.

"Sure."

"Where'd you get the gun?"

Antonia looked over her shoulder at Sydney. "Honey," she said with a tired sigh, "I handle over one hundred domestic violence cases each year. You don't separate that many women from that many violent men without making sure that you can protect yourself at all times."

Chapter Forty-seven

LYDIA CHAPIN SAT at the vanity in the alcove of the walk-in closet that served as her dressing room. She looked around the bedroom and it surprised her how little was left of her husband. The heavy mahogany dresser and matching valet that had dominated his side of the room when he was alive had been removed within a month of his death, replaced by an antique side table less at odds with the rest of the decor. The nautical oil painting that had hung on the wall over the dresser had been similarly removed without ceremony, replaced by colorful botanical prints she found more cheerful.

It was ironic, now, that she could find no joy in the decor, and would have paid dearly for any reminder of the man she had loved. She had loved him, hadn't she? Sometimes it seemed she had lost herself so completely in the social mechanics of their lives that she'd forgotten what real love was, but it had always been there, hadn't it? Lurking in the background like a mist, unnoticed and often unacknowledged, but there nonetheless? She thought so, and it was from that feeling that she gained the strength, waning though it was, to do what must be done.

She reached into her dressing table and retrieved the silver box from the back of the drawer. The top of it was adorned with an ornate monogram reading "L.H.C."—Lydia Handscome Chapin. She smiled as she remembered how excited her husband had been when he'd given it to her, and how proud she'd been the first time, during their engagement, when she'd first received a gift bearing those initials; how she felt she'd earned her place in the world.

She opened the box slowly, almost reluctantly, and then sat back, staring at the contents for a moment, steeling herself for the task ahead. Then she reached into the box, pushing aside the silk lining, and pulled out the guns.

She held them up in the light, admiring their craftsmanship. They were matching silver revolvers, smaller than most capable of handling the .38-caliber cartridges that fit into the cylinder. They'd been commissioned decades ago by her husband when, spurred by a number of old-line business associates and their wives, he and Lydia had shared a brief passion for the art of shooting. They'd started with trap and skeet, pastimes that went hand in hand with the polo and sailing and riding in which most of their circle engaged. At first they viewed it as more a social obligation than an enjoyment, but they both found themselves drawn in by the pageantry and upper-class civility of it. From trap and skeet, they'd moved to field shooting, and then, on a whim, to pistols and rifles. It had been so much fun at the time—the intoxicating combination of privilege and power surging through them with each pull of the trigger.

The thrill had worn off in time, and they'd stopped shooting altogether in the late 1970s, largely in a nod to the political correctness that was settling into many quarters in the business world. She'd kept the pistols, though, thinking of them almost more as pieces of jewelry than weapons. The craftsmanship was spectacular, and they were worth a small fortune, she knew. But would they set her free?

She picked one up and released the cylinder, breaching the gun, looking through the open chambers where the cartridges were loaded. Then she spun the cylinder once before setting the gun back down carefully in its case.

Reaching into her purse, she pulled out a box of ammunition she'd bought earlier in the day at a gun shop in Arlington. She'd been amused at the look on the face of the man behind the counter, which showed disbelief at the specific and knowledgeable request by the well-dressed, aging matron before him.

Carefully, so as not to chip a nail, she pulled out six rounds and lined them up on the vanity next to the gun. She picked them up one by one, holding each up to the light as though inspecting it for any imperfection before sliding it into one of the open chambers of the cylinder.

Once the gun was fully loaded, she closed the cylinder and latched the safety—"Safety first," her husband had been fond of saying—before she slipped it into her purse. Then she put the second gun back in its case and slid it, together with the box of ammunition, into the top drawer of her vanity, pushing them to the back and closing it tight.

She turned and looked out into her bedroom. The furnishings and paintings she'd chosen—light and airy, with subtle hints of green and magenta on cream backgrounds—seemed depressing to her now. Lifeless. Loveless. She really did wish that she'd kept some of her husband's things in the room after his death. Useless though they might have been, they would have at least reminded her of a life once full. And while she'd rationalized the redecoration with the notion that keeping reminders would only prolong her grief at a time when her family needed her to be strong, she was no longer certain of her decision. Now she thought that perhaps, just perhaps, having some mementos of the life she'd shared with her husband would have provided her comfort, not pain.

She sighed in a silent apology to a man dead for more than half a decade, then stood and straightened her skirt. In a voice so matter-of-fact and emotionless that it startled even her, she said out loud to herself, "Clearly, if you want something done right, you've got to do it yourself."

Then she picked up her purse and walked out of her room and downstairs.

Dr. Aldus Mayer sat at his desk in his plush office at the Institute going over work schedules, pay records, and administrative reports. He hated this type of work. There was a time when he'd actually considered himself a doctor, and that was something of which he'd been very proud. What was he now? A bureaucrat, that's what. It made him sick. He remembered the look on his mother's face the day he'd graduated from medical school; it combined awe, pride, and relief, and it made him feel so good. He wondered what emotions her expression would betray were she alive today.

The phone rang, and he turned toward it with a feeling of dread. This phone never carried good news.

"Aldus Mayer," he said, picking up the phone.

"Burn the program down," the voice said.

"Pardon me?" He knew who it was, but he couldn't believe the message.

"You heard me, kill it."

"All of it?"

"All of it. Records, notes, samples, everything."

"Do you know what you're saying?" Mayer still couldn't believe it, and he felt like his world was collapsing. "Do you know what will be lost?"

"I know what I'm saying; we have no choice. Do it." The line went dead.

Mayer sat there for a long time, the phone still pressed up against his ear. He'd heard his instructions, but he wasn't sure if he had the strength to carry them out.

Chapter Forty-eight

CHIEF TORBERT WAS PACING rapidly behind Captain Reynolds's desk. He hadn't said a word yet, which Train took as a bad sign.

"So, you've given up on the Jerome Washington angle?" Reynolds asked calmly.

"For the moment, yes," Train answered. "So far, his alibi continues to hold up. And with everything we've discovered and everything that's transpired in the last few days, there are other angles we have to work. We've still got Washington in custody on a slew of other charges, but for the moment he looks like a bad fit for the Chapin woman's murder."

"When were you planning on informing us of these developments, Sergeant?" The chief's high-pitched staccato whine broke in finally. "After you'd arrested the Senate majority leader, or before?"

Reynolds held his hand up to the chief to cut him off, and in spite of their relative rank, Torbert stifled his anger. There was no question as to who had more credibility between them. "Tell me about the Venable play," the captain ordered.

Train took a deep breath. "As we explained, with the

attack on Sydney Chapin and the suspicious death of Willie Murphy, we began to look for some sort of a connection. Venable's father was in charge of the Institute for years, and we felt he needed to be looked at."

"So you barge into his office and accuse him of murder?" Torbert was shouting now.

"We made an appointment," Train said, his voice devoid of emotion. "And we accused him of nothing."

"You might as well have!" Torbert continued to pace as the pores on his face seemed to open up and the sheen on his forehead became more pronounced. "Christ, he must've been on the phone to my office the minute you left, and believe me, it was not a pleasant call to take! Do you even know who he is? Do you know how much power he has?"

"That's part of our reasoning," Train pointed out. "It's a part of his motive."

"Motive! You're talking about motive?!" Torbert's head looked like it might burst.

"Captain," Train said, deliberately ignoring the chief, "we've got to go where the evidence takes us."

"No argument," Reynolds agreed. "But there are always two ways to do things." He looked up at the chief with an expression that seemed to convey the notion that he was dealing with the problem. "From now on, all contacts with Venable go through my office."

Train frowned. "You want us to run every hunch by you."

Reynolds shook his head. "Not every hunch. Just every hunch that implicates any of the most powerful people in the government. Like it or not, politics is a part of this job."

"Damned right it is!" Torbert chipped in. The captain's glare silenced him.

"What other leads do you have?"

Train rubbed his head for a moment. "The ex," he said at last.

"Who you also spoke to, against my direct orders," Torbert reminded him.

The captain ignored the comment. "What are your thoughts on him?"

"He's a prince," Train said sarcastically.

"Could he be our guy?"

"Could be. Hard to tell, but he's definitely high on our list."

"Anyone else?"

Train shook his head. "That's all we've got right now."

"What about this professor—what's his name? Barneton? I gather he was seen with this nut Salvage?"

Cassian nodded. "And he was the last person to see Elizabeth Creay, too."

"We questioned him," Train said. "He says he'd never seen Salvage before. He thought he was a friend of Sydney's and says he was just trying to help the guy out. We haven't been able to find any other connection with this whole mess, and it doesn't look like he'd even know how to find his way to someone as crooked as Salvage. We'll keep an eye on him, but we had to cut him loose. Besides, I still think Venable's a much more likely suspect. He's hiding something, I just don't know what it is."

Reynolds nodded. "Okay. It sounds like you've got a bunch of possibilities to check out. We've got someone watching Salvage's office, but I think it's safe to say that he's not going anywhere near his regular spots. Just keep me informed of everything that happens."

Torbert stamped his foot. "But—" he began, but Reynolds cut him off.

"No buts. These men are doing their jobs, and doing them well. Like I said, we'll run all official government contacts through this office from now on, but I'm not going to cripple this investigation."

The chief looked as though he might cry as he stormed out of the office.

"What an asshole," Cassian commented as the door closed.

"Stow it, Cassian. That asshole's still your boss," Reynolds said. "More to the point, he's still my boss. And he had some valid concerns. You boys are swimming in some deep waters here, and you'd better understand that there are some big fucking sharks swimming with you." His face turned grim. "How sure are you about Venable's involvement in this?"

Train shrugged. "We won't know until we've had a chance to dig through the documents Sydney Chapin pulled from the lawsuit this Willie Murphy character was involved with."

"Then get to it, and fast. You think this was any kind of a real shitstorm, you're wrong. This was a passing shower. The longer you keep Venable's name alive in this without finding something concrete, the harder it's gonna come down, and the umbrella I'm holding over your heads is already gettin' pretty fuckin' heavy."

Sydney pushed her chair back from the table in the interrogation room at the precinct house, rubbing her eyes as she stretched her neck against fatigue. They'd been through every piece of paper she'd printed out from the PACER system—every pleading, every motion, and every court filing.

"Nothing," she said, the frustration sounding in her voice.

"Nothing," Cassian repeated, trying to keep his own disappointment at bay.

"There's got to be something," Train said, more open with his annoyance. "We must've missed it."

"Well, if there's anything that ties something specific back to Venable's father, I can't find it," Sydney grumbled. "Look, it's sometimes difficult to figure out any specifics in a class action like this. Willie Murphy was the named plaintiff in the case, but he's meant to represent the entire class of plaintiffs—everyone who was mistreated at the Institute. His lawyer was careful to keep the allegations limited and general. All the complaint says is that Willie was kept against his will unlawfully, and that he was mistreated while in custody. There are no specific allegations about any of the individuals responsible for the abuse."

"How about in the papers that followed the complaint?" Train asked.

"There are a couple of other papers and motions, but they're mainly procedural. Then there's a motion to dismiss and some briefing on both sides of the issue, but that, again, is a legal debate."

"So what happened to the case in the end?" Jack asked. "It had to go somewhere, didn't it?"

"From the notice of dismissal, it looks like the parties reached a settlement that was approved by the court, but the terms were kept confidential, and there was no admission of wrongdoing by anyone."

"So we're left with nothing to connect Willie Murphy to Venable's father," Train noted. "As your friend Mr. Elliot pointed out, we'd have to uncover something specific involving the senior Venable to provide a real, tangible motive. What I'm hearing is that there's nothing in this lawsuit that does that. Am I right?"

Sydney nodded. "Like I said, if there's anything here, I can't find it. It looks like only Willie Murphy could have filled in the blanks." Sydney shifted again and looked at her watch. It was nearing seven-thirty. "I've got to get to my mother's house," she said wearily.

Train and Cassian shared a look, and Sydney could tell they were both thinking the same thing. "What?" she demanded after a moment.

"Sydney," Train said gently, "you can't go home."

"What do you mean I can't go home?"

"It's not safe," Cassian said.

"Don't be stupid, I have to go home."

Train, who'd been pacing through most of the conversation, sat down next to her. "I hate to be the one to point this out to you, Sydney, but someone's trying to kill you."

She stared at him as the concept sank in for the first time and the truth hit her hard.

"I'm sorry," Train said.

She looked up at Cassian. "I have to get to my family," she said urgently.

"They're fine," Cassian said.

Train nodded. "We've had patrols passing your mom's house every half hour to make sure everything's okay, and the place has been quiet."

"I've got to see them."

Cassian shook his head. "It's too dangerous. Whoever is trying to kill you knows where you live and work. How hard would it be for them to locate your mother's house?"

"I'll take that chance," she said defiantly.

Cassian sat next to Sydney so that he and Train were

bookending her supportively. “Even if you’re willing to take that chance for yourself, are you willing to put your mother and your niece in danger?”

She looked at him, not comprehending.

“Whoever is trying to kill you isn’t going to be deterred by the fact that you’re with a sixty-five-year-old woman and a fourteen-year-old girl. They’ll just kill your mother and your niece as well, if necessary. Not only that, but if they think you’ve passed on any information to your family, they may feel the need to make sure your family can’t pass that information on to anyone else.”

“But I don’t know anything to pass on.”

“Someone out there thinks you do. And whoever is behind this, it’s clear they’re willing to take out anyone they feel is a risk.”

“So what do I do?”

Train and Cassian shared a look again. “First, you should call your mother.”

Amanda Creay sat in the library of the Chapin mansion, flipping through a schoolbook, but she was unable to concentrate. She closed the book and rubbed her temples. She couldn’t handle it anymore; she was convinced that she’d lose her mind at any moment. It wasn’t the grief; she’d learned to handle grief long ago. She’d learned early that grief came in waves, and that if she clenched her fists hard enough—sometimes so hard that the tips of her fingernails dug painfully into her palm—she could ride her way through the waves and come out the other side.

No, it wasn’t the grief; it was the boredom. The boredom was endless, stretching out in front of her like a flat, calm ocean, offering only solitude and emptiness. It was the boredom that terrified her, and she hoped that she'd be able to return to school shortly, if only to give her something to do.

The phone rang, and she rose and crossed the room. "Hello?" she said.

"Amanda? It's Sydney."

"Sydney? Where are you?" Hearing her aunt's voice made things bearable at least.

"I'm down at the police station."

"Why?"

"It's hard to explain. Is my mother there?"

"No. She went out, and she said she'd be back later tonight."

Amanda could hear the sigh from Sydney through the phone line. "I need you to give her a message. I'm not going to be back there tonight. I'll stop by to explain everything tomorrow when I get a chance, okay?"

Amanda's spirits crashed. "You're not coming back?" She felt more alone than ever.

"I'm coming back, Amanda. You need to know that I'm coming back. Just not tonight. There are a lot of things that I'm dealing with right now, but I promise I won't leave you. Can you hang on?"

Amanda steeled herself. "I think so." Something in Sydney's voice gave her strength, and the knowledge that she wouldn't be alone forever was comforting. "Sydney?"

"Yes?"

"Does this have something to do with my mother's murder?" She held her breath as she waited for the reply.

"Yes," Sydney said after a brief pause. "Yes, it does."

She considered that for a moment. "Promise me two things?"

"Anything."

"Promise me you'll find out why all this happened. And promise me you'll come back safe."

Chapter Forty-nine

SYDNEY FELT NUMB as she hung up the phone. Amanda's courage made her feel helpless. With nothing to go on, how could she possibly keep her promise to sort all this out? As for her promise to stay safe—well, she didn't even want to think about that.

"Everything okay at home?" Jack asked.

"Fine," she said. She looked back and forth between Cassian and Train. "Really, it's fine. Obviously with all my family's been through, particularly my niece, it would be better if I was there, that's all."

"We'll make sure to have someone drive by the house every so often throughout the night, just to make sure everything's quiet there," Train reassured her.

"Thank you, I'd appreciate that."

"No problem," Train said. "Let me go talk to the desk sergeant and set that up." He left the room, closing the door behind him.

Sydney sat down and put her head in her hands. She looked up at Cassian. "So, what now?" she asked.

"Now we'll set you up with protection for the evening. Make sure that you're safe."

"How does that work?"

"You can probably stay with Detective Train. That may be the easiest thing to do. We could also assign a uniformed officer, if that'd make you feel more comfortable."

"Jack," she said biting her lip, "I have a favor to ask."

"What's that?"

"Can I stay with you?"

"Again?" Salvage's client's voice crackled with rage and disbelief. "She got away from you again?"

"It was unavoidable," he replied, though it sounded weak even to him.

"I'd hope so." Salvage said nothing in response to the wicked sarcasm; better to get through the conversation with as little acrimony as possible. "I'm beginning to wonder whether your reputation isn't overplayed."

"I understand," Salvage seethed. "If you have someone else in mind who's willing to perform the services I provide, I'll be happy to turn the matter over to them."

"You are the beneficiary of a striking lack of competition in this area," the client conceded. "But that's no excuse for sloppy and incompetent work. She's a twenty-seven-year-old student, for goodness' sakes. How hard can it be?"

"Does that mean I still have a job?"

Salvage could hear the anger in the short breaths coming through the line. "Yes, I intend to retain you. Do you intend on finishing the job?"

"There was never any question of that."

"Good." There was a pause on the line. "You understand what's at stake, I trust?"

"I do."

"I'm glad to hear it. But just in case there's any doubt, you should know that if this issue goes any further, you're finished."

Salvage thought that over. "You've already paid half. That's not refundable."

There was a laugh on the other end of the line. "I'm not talking about your money, Mr. Salvage. I have friends who are powerful enough to find you wherever you go. If this gets any worse, you'll never live to enjoy a penny that you've been paid. Do you understand? You'll spend your money in hell."

Salvage's blood turned cold and he took the flask he'd been saving for a celebratory drink once his mission was complete out of his pocket. He looked at it warily for a moment, and then gave in at last, swigging it quickly to put some warmth back into his body. He cleared his throat. "Yes," he said. "I understand perfectly."

Chapter Fifty

CASSIAN OPENED THE DOOR to his apartment, reaching in and turning on the lights before stepping back and holding the door open for Sydney.

She walked in slowly, absorbing the place as she panned around the entry hallway and living room. The apartment was located just off Dupont Circle, northwest of the White House, bordering on the fashionable Foggy Bottom area near the George Washington University campus. There was a time when the neighborhood was predominantly gay, and as such had been considered beyond the pale of the best areas of the city. Some once thought it dangerous, even. But as homosexuality lost its taboo among the cultured elite, the brownstone neighborhood had been invaded by young urban professionals and upper-government transients on temporary assignment to Washington, looking for convenient, hip places to call home.

The floors were hardwood, broken only in a few places by small area rugs, and the furniture was simple but clean and tasteful. A few pictures of those who had permanence in Jack's life—parents, brother, a few friends—peeked out from built-in cabinetry, and artistic black-and-white photographs dotted the walls.

"Nice place," Sydney commented as she walked into the living room.

"Works for me," Jack replied. "There are two bedrooms. I use one as an office, but there's a pullout couch. I can stay in there." He needed to get straight on the sleeping arrangements. He waited for her acknowledgment, but she said nothing. "I'm sorry about all this," he continued. "I know it's a huge inconvenience." "Inconvenience" struck him as an unfortunate choice of words, and he wanted to kick himself for it.

"How long have you lived here?"

"Three years."

"Do you like it?"

"Like I said, it works for me."

"It's nicer than I would have expected." Now it was her turn to look embarrassed at her choice of words. "I mean . . . I didn't mean . . . it seems expensive to me for a . . ." She paused, clearly realizing that she was only digging the hole deeper.

"Cop?" He rescued her with an understanding smile. "My parents passed away a little while back. I got a little bit of money. Nothing like . . ."

"Like me?" She returned his smile, and the tension in the air seemed to disperse somewhat, like white smoke in a breeze, leaving only its scent. After completing another three-sixty around the living room, she looked at him and nodded. "It suits you." She let her shoulder bag drop to the floor.

"Shitty day?" Jack commented.

She nodded again. "Shitty day. Shitty couple of weeks."

He was unsure what to say. He finally decided to keep it functional. "I'm gonna make some dinner. You want some? Or I can order something for you to be delivered?"

"What are you having?"

He shook his head. "I don't know. Depends on what I can find here that's edible."

"Edible, huh? Sounds delicious."

"Like I said, I can order something in for you."

She shook her head. "That's all right. I'll take my chances on edible."

"A little food will probably make you feel better."

"Food and a shower," she agreed.

He was already bending down in front of the open refrigerator, looking for anything that might be worth putting over heat. "Bathroom's down the hall," he said. "It's all yours if you want it."

He could feel her looking at him as he rummaged through the kitchen, and he wondered what she was thinking. The silence dragged on forever and there was a part of him that wanted to turn around; to see her looking at him; to catch a glimpse of her expression in the hope that it might betray a hint of the attraction he felt for her. It wasn't an option, though, he told himself.

Eventually he heard her pick up her bag. "I'll be out in a few minutes," she said.

"Okay," he replied. "Take your time."

There was another brief pause; another moment of temptation; and then he heard her pad on down the hallway toward the bathroom.

"Where'd you learn to cook?" She was sitting at the kitchen table, glass of wine in front of her.

She'd stood in the shower for over ten minutes, letting the streams of warm water pelt her neck and shoulders as she leaned against the wall; feeling them run down over her as they split off into different directions, running down her arms and back and chest; dripping off her elbows and fingers, and washing over every part of her. For a while she thought that maybe, if she stayed in long enough, the water might wash away the past, and all of the pain, and leave her new. It wasn't to be, though, and eventually she turned off the shower and stepped out of the tub, drying herself off.

When she walked out of the bathroom, the aroma from the kitchen swept through her, and she realized suddenly how hungry she was. Nothing had ever smelled as good to her as whatever Jack was cheffing up in his comfortable little apartment. She'd gone to the refrigerator and pulled out a bottle of white wine that was on one of the shelves. Catching a look from him, she felt defensive. "If any day deserves a drink, I think today is the one."

"Did I say anything?" he said, holding his hands high. "You can sit there and do tequila shots as far as I'm concerned."

"Wine will do fine, thank you. You want some?"

He shook his head. "I'm okay for the moment."

Now she was comfortably deposited in the wooden armchair at his kitchen table. "My parents were older than most," Jack explained in answer to her question about his culinary prowess. "My mom was nearly forty when I came along, and my dad was into his fifties."

"Bet you were a surprise, huh?"

"You could say that." He was working a pan with a spatula, a plume of thin smoke rising with each flip of his wrist. "It wasn't bad. My brother was seven years older than me, and he helped raise me. We had a lot of independence, so we learned to fend for ourselves pretty early."

"That's the brother who's a cop also?" She noticed him flinch as he turned quickly. "You told me that being a cop was a family thing and mentioned your brother," she explained quickly. He turned back to the stove.

"He was a cop first," Jack said, concentrating on the cooking. "I followed him into it."

She picked up a picture on the shelf in the kitchen; a man who looked remarkably like Jack, only older, stared out at her from a typical suburban setting. He was laughing, the kind of full, open, consuming laugh that had an infectious feel to it, even through the picture. "Your brother, I presume?"

Jack looked up and moved behind her, looking at the picture. "Yes," he said, taking the picture from her and holding it up in his hands for a long moment before replacing it on the shelf.

"I think I'd like to meet him," she commented. "Get the truth on what you were really like growing up."

"Maybe someday," he replied. His voice didn't invite further inquiry, though, so she decided not to pry.

She turned her attention to the pan on the stove. "What are we having, exactly?"

"I'm not sure it's anything 'exactly,' but it approximates fried rice."

"Fried rice?" Sydney was skeptical. "That doesn't smell like any fried rice I've ever had."

"Like I said, it approximates fried rice. There wasn't a whole lot in the fridge that would have made a meal on its own, but there were plenty of things that looked good enough to toss in a pan with some rice and some spices. You'll have to trust me on this."

"I do. It smells great."

"The secret is to fry up everything separately first, so

it retains its own flavor. Then combine it at the last minute so that each flavor seeps out just a little bit into the dish as a whole."

"Sounds . . . edible."

"Like I said, you're gonna have to trust me."

She didn't say anything for a moment. "I do," she said at last. She wondered if the broader meaning would be lost on him, but she didn't care. She wasn't sure she'd ever trusted anyone the way she trusted him at this moment. Maybe it was just the stress of the past few days, but he had somehow made it through her defenses, and it felt good to her.

He turned and looked at her, and for a moment she thought she saw some acknowledgment in his eyes. Then it was gone.

Chapter Fifty-one

SHE SEEMED TO LIKE the meal, he thought. Then again, he wasn't sure when she had last eaten anything of substance, and his cooking might have benefited in her estimation from borderline starvation.

The conversation had grown stunted between them, cut off at the knees by a growing tingle neither of them chose to acknowledge openly. He felt so sure there was something between them—something on which they both knew they couldn't act, but which neither of them could ignore.

Train had made it painfully clear to him that he wouldn't tolerate anything unprofessional between them when he reluctantly agreed to allow Cassian to act as her bodyguard. "No fuckups," Train had warned him. "Everyone's gonna be watching this closely." Jack had reassured him and promised to avoid any hint of impropriety. More than that, he was unwilling to risk the trust that Sydney had in him. If he ever tried anything and he was wrong about how she was feeling, he would shatter what little confidence she had left in the world. As a result, the tension continued to build.

"We talked to Leighton," he said at last, breaking an

extended silence, and hoping to stem the pace at which the wall between them seemed to be growing.

"Sorry?"

"Liz's ex. I wasn't sure I ever mentioned that we talked to him. After we spoke and you told us about what happened between them—what he did to her—Train and I went out to see him."

"And?"

"Didn't like him."

She stared at her fried rice. "Hope that's an understatement."

"I'm not sure he was exactly trying to impress us." He watched her as she looked down at her food. It seemed as though the full weight of her ordeal was finally settling onto her, and he wanted desperately to comfort her. He knew that he was walking close to a dangerous line, though, and so he decided instead to press forward with the conversation as the only means of keeping a connection.

"He made an interesting comment," he said, searching for something to say. She looked up at him expectantly. "He asked us whether your mother had sent us."

She frowned. "Why did he ask that?"

He shook his head. "I don't know. I was wondering if you had any thoughts."

She was no longer eating; just pushing the small portion that was left on her plate in a circle with her fork. She followed the path of the rice with her eyes, the furrows deepening in her brow. Then she looked at him again. "I don't know. My mother and Leighton were close to each other when he married my sister. I think he was exactly the kind of man my mother thought would be perfect for our family. They obviously haven't been close since . . .

since the divorce, and it would surprise me if they've even talked in the last few years. I can't think of any reason why he might think my mother would send someone to him." She sat back in her chair and sipped her wine.

"Nothing comes to mind?"

She sighed. "Nothing. Who knows how his mind works? He's the kind of man who marries for money. The kind of man who rapes his wife. That's someone I can't pretend to understand at all."

"Me neither."

She took another sip of her wine, a gulp really. "That was one of the best things about living on my own in California."

"What was?"

"The anonymity of it. No one knowing who I was or what I was worth. I never had to worry whether someone was interested in me because of my money or because of my family or because of what they thought I could do for them. I was just a normal person living off what I made myself."

"Do you worry about that still?"

"What?"

"The money. The way it affects the people around you?"

"Like I said, I haven't had to in a while." She brushed the hair out of her face. "But yes, I do. Wouldn't you?"

Jack shrugged. "Don't know. I've never had to think about it."

Sydney turned and looked out the window, her sights focusing on something on the street. Cassian followed her gaze and saw a young couple walking hand in hand on the sidewalk across the way. In the dark, their features were obscured, but they were leaning into each other slightly as they ambled along, in a posture of mutual dependence.

Sydney turned back to him. "Can I ask you something?"

"Sure."

She looked out the window again, and it seemed as if she was trying to formulate the question in her own mind. After a moment, she turned back to him and took a deep breath. "Is it . . ." she began, but then got stuck, letting the air out of her lungs in a long sigh. She started again. "I mean, do you . . ." She shook her head and laughed. Jack thought it was the saddest laugh he'd ever heard, and when she looked back up, there were tears in her eyes. "I'm sorry," she said.

"Don't be."

"I don't know what I'm doing anymore." She looked at him for a long minute. "I think I should go to bed." She got up quickly, grabbing her plate and glass to clear them.

Jack stood up as well. "Please, let me clean up."

"I'm just clearing."

Jack reached out and took hold of the plate. "I've got it," he said.

She turned and collided with him, sending her wineglass to the floor, shattering it as it hit the hardwood. The two of them were silent, looking at the shards spread out on the floor in front of them. "I'm sorry," he said. "I . . ."

He stopped short when he saw her eyes. She was inches from him, their fingers touching lightly along the edges of the plate they both still grasped. He could smell her hair, his own shampoo, which she must have borrowed, but mixed with her own scent, warm and comforting and powerful. He didn't want to move. He thought that if he could just stay still forever he might be satisfied.

Then it happened. She leaned forward slightly. Had they not been so close together, the movement might have gone unnoticed; it was barely a movement at all, just a slight shift in body weight that narrowed the gap between them. Her head was upturned, eyes closing.

He kept still, petrified. A screech of thoughts and emotions echoed confusingly in his head, snatches of phrases lost in the noise, warnings of consequences empty of meaning and drowned out by his heartbeat.

Her lips touched his, and the screaming in his head ceased. All he could focus on was her lips, soft and warm and inviting; perfect in every way. At last his body moved, drawing her to him, his hands caressing her with patient urgency. His thoughts lost all structure and language.

As their embrace crisscrossed the line between passion and tenderness, one word seemed to repeat itself over and over in his head, echoing endlessly until he surrendered to the lure of its simplicity. And even, hours later, when they both collapsed, exhausted and sated and happy, too tired for thought or worry or talk, the word remained in his head, a whisper now, soft and reassuring. *Home.*

Chapter Fifty-two

SYDNEY OPENED HER EYES SLOWLY. The tepid predawn light cast shadows in scarlet gray on the ceiling, and she let the shapes come into focus at a leisurely pace. She stretched her arms and legs, every muscle in her body recalling the prior evening in a dull, satisfying ache; every nerve resounding with an exquisitely raw, electrified feeling.

She smiled to herself as she replayed their time together over in her head, movements of smooth skin running wild in an endless flicker of desire that made her blush. She had been surprised at her own aggressiveness, and at the way in which her body had been so demanding in its needs—and eager in its natural inclinations to satisfy both her cravings and his. They together had been neither selfish nor subservient, giving of themselves without hesitation, and receiving each other in pleasure devoid of guilt. It had felt, she thought, the way she'd always thought sex should feel but did with disappointing infrequency.

She rolled over and draped her arm over Jack, looking up at his face. He was awake, propped on the pillows behind his head, staring off into space, a look of deep concern etched into his features.

"Hey there," she said tentatively.

He looked down at her, caught in the embarrassment of reflection. "Hey," he said. "Sorry. I didn't want to wake you, but I couldn't sleep."

"You didn't wake me. Who could expect more than a few hours of decent shut-eye with all that's going on." She took her fingers and rubbed them gently over his chest. He didn't move, and yet she felt him pull away from her. She sat up, pulling the sheets over her chest, self-conscious for the first time with him. "Anything you want to talk about, sailor?"

"I guess not," he said, unable to look at her.

"You'd be surprised. I'm a pretty good listener."

"Nothing about you would surprise me."

She looked at him, and he avoided her eyes. "Are you sorry about this?"

"No," he said, though she sensed some hesitation. "There's just a lot of shit in my past. Stuff you should probably know, to be fair. I was just lying here trying to figure out how to bring it up without convincing you I'm insane."

She put a hand to her forehead. "I've always thought the direct route's best. Throw it out there and see how it lands; it's better than hiding it."

He looked at her again, his eyes searching. "Her name was Kelly."

She blew out a heavy breath. "Go on."

"We went to high school together, and she was beautiful in a sad, lost kind of way. I thought I could save her."

"From?"

"Herself, I guess. She grew up in the same town as me; a nice upper-middle-class spot where everything was perfect. Except it wasn't. I think that was a huge disappointment to a lot of the people I grew up with—finding out that things could get so fucked up when there really wasn't anything to complain about. We dated back then, and then lost touch after high school until a few years ago, when she called me."

"Looking for a reconciliation?"

"Looking for a way out. She never really figured out what was wrong, and by the time she called, she was heavy into drugs. She was living with this guy who was a dealer, and he had her so screwed up she could barely get a sentence out. My brother, Jimmy, told me to leave it alone, that she was too far gone, but I didn't listen. There was still something in her eyes I thought I could reach."

"And?"

"Things went well for a while. She cleaned up, went back to school; for a few months I really thought we had a chance."

"You were wrong, I take it."

"One night she disappeared. I was out of my mind. And then I got a call, and all I could hear was her sobbing. I swear, I can still hear her sobbing in my sleep, and sometimes I can't tell whether she's crying or laughing."

"Did you find her?"

Jack nodded. "I knew she was with her old boyfriend. He'd been trying to get her back on the junk since she'd left him; even threatened to kill her. I didn't know what to do, so I called my brother. He was a cop, so I figured he'd have some idea how to handle it."

"Did he?"

He nodded again. "He and I went to the dealer's house. My brother pounded on the door, yelled 'Police,' the whole deal. We could hear them in there; he was screaming at her, and she was crying. After a couple of minutes of that, my brother kicked in the front door." Jack closed his eyes.

"What happened?"

"The guy had lost it. I mean totally lost it. He was ranting and raving—clearly high on something. He started shooting as soon as Jimmy was through the door; hit him in the forehead with the second shot."

Sydney held her breath. "Did he die?"

Jack shook his head. "Probably should've, but he was too damned strong. He probably would've been better off, for all that's left of him. He's in a hospital now. Sitting there, rotting away. There's nothing left of his mind."

"What happened to the dealer?"

"He kept firing away for what seemed like forever. I tried to get to my brother, but the door was shattering around me. Then the shooting stopped, and I heard the last two shots. One was for her; the last one he saved for himself."

They sat in silence. Sydney wanted to comfort him, but no words came, so she lay back again and stroked his arm.

"When it was over, I didn't know what to do. Everyone I'd ever cared about was gone, and I had nowhere to turn. I kept hoping Jimmy might recover, but there was too much damage. I didn't have anything left."

"That's when you joined the police."

"I felt so fucking helpless that night. I never wanted to be that helpless again. I don't know why, but I felt like becoming a cop might help—that way I'd be able to protect anyone I cared about again. Except that it hasn't really worked. If anything, all the time I've spent as a cop, all the shit I've seen, it's made me feel less able to protect anyone. There's so much ugliness out there, and it'll find the people it wants to, no matter who's protecting them."

She stopped her hand on his arm. "Is that it?"

He gave her a crooked smile. "Don't get me wrong, I've probably got lots of other issues fucking me up, too. I just thought you should know, it's gonna take some time for me. I have stronger feelings for you than I've had for anyone since Jimmy was shot—maybe more than anyone even before that. But that scares the shit out of me, and I'm just trying to deal with all that."

She lay there for a moment, letting her body settle into his as she started caressing his chest again as though massaging scar tissue. Then she sat up and took his face in her hands, pulling him close into a deep, soulful kiss. When it ended, she whispered to him, "Thanks for the warning, but I'll take my chances."

Chapter Fifty-three

CASSIAN MADE IT to the door on the second knock, opening it a crack; all he had on was his jeans.

"Rise and fuckin' shine," Train said, looking his partner over. He stood at the top of the stoop, his rumpled gray suit on, the tie already askew. He was holding three coffees and a bag of bagels, and he started to push his way through the door. "I hope you got a good night's sleep, because we've got a lot of work to do."

Cassian stepped in front of his partner, keeping him from entering the apartment. It was no easy task, given Train's size. "Gimme a minute, Sarge?"

"What do you mean, 'gimme a minute'? Take all the minutes you want. I'll be in the kitchen with the bagels." He started to push past his partner again.

"Seriously," Cassian said, refusing to budge.

"I bring coffee and bagels and you expect me to wait outside? Are you shitting me?" Suddenly Train's eyes narrowed, piercing Cassian. "What the fuck is going on?"

Just then, Sydney's voice sounded in the background. "Jack, where are the towels? If I don't take a shower, I'm not going to be fit for decent company, as my mother likes to say."

Train's glare intensified, and Cassian was immediately on the defensive. "Sarge, it's not what you think." Train pushed the door hard, knocking Jack back a step and giving him a full view into the room. Cassian turned and saw what his partner was looking at. Sydney stood at the edge of the hallway, wearing only one of his frayed T-shirts. Her figure—a fabulous figure, Jack noticed, not without a flash of pride—was clearly visible through the thin cotton, her nipples ever so slightly interrupting the otherwise smooth flow of the fabric. She saw Train and unconsciously pulled at the hem of the shirt, bringing it down over her upper thighs.

Cassian turned back to Train. He leaned against the door in defeat. "Okay, maybe it is what you think, but you don't have to worry."

"I don't?" Train asked slowly, his voice simmering.

"I'm sorry," Sydney said, clearly feeling self-conscious and recognizing the tension in the room. "I just need a towel."

"They're in the closet in my bedroom."

"It appears she knows where your bedroom is," Train grunted at Jack.

"I'm sorry," Sydney repeated.

Jack waved her off. "You have nothing to be sorry about."

She nodded and turned to head back down the hallway. Then she paused and turned around. "Good morning, Sergeant," she said tentatively.

Train's demeanor softened slightly. "Good morning, Sydney."

"It's not his fault, it's mine," she said. He looked at her noncommittally. Then she nodded and continued back toward the bathroom.

Once she was gone, the scowl returned to Train's face. "Good to know. It's her fault. That makes me feel so much fuckin' better. Maybe they'll mention that in our discharge papers."

"Sarge, wait. Before you—"

But Train wasn't waiting. He pushed his way past Cassian, carrying the coffee and bagels into the kitchen and slamming them down on the counter, the coffee slopping over and puddling on the countertop. "What the fuck were you thinking about, Jack? You know she's the sister of a murder victim, right?"

"I know."

"An unsolved murder, in case you've forgotten."

"I haven't."

"Technically still on our long list of potential suspects."

"That list would have to be very long for her to be on it, Sarge."

"Suspect or not, we put her in protective custody, for shitsakes. In your protective custody." He rubbed his forehead in disgust. "I should have my fucking head examined for letting that happen."

"Don't blame yourself, Sarge."

Train looked up, his face twisted in anger. "I don't blame myself! And regardless of what she says, I don't blame her either. I blame you!" He started to pace. "Didn't we talk about this?"

"We did."

"Didn't we specifically discuss this?"

"We did."

"I told you—no goddamned personal involvement. There're people watching this case. We may need this girl's testimony to convict whoever we find at the end of this twisted rope, and you put her in a position to have her credibility questioned. There's gonna be hell to pay when the defense lawyer finds out you've been fucking her!"

"Hey, back off!" Cassian erupted. "I'm not just fucking her!"

"Oh, sorry, Precious. What are we calling it? Love? Whatever you want to call it, it's still a major fuckup." He took a deep breath, calming himself a little. "It can't happen again," he said, his voice calmer now.

"I can't make that promise."

Train looked at him carefully, calculating his partner's resolve. "She's that important to you? You'd risk your career over her?"

Cassian shrugged.

Train shook his head in disbelief. "She better be worth it, because you're risking everything you got."

"Even you?"

There was a long silence between them. Then Train's anger broke like a storm clearing. He shook his head. "Been together for too long to let a little thing like gross misconduct shake us apart. I'm with you whatever happens. What the fuck, if I lose my pension, I guess we'll all just live off love, huh? I'm just pointing out that to put this much on the line, you better fuckin' marry this girl."

Sydney's voice came from behind him. "I leave the room for five minutes and you've got me married off already? Don't I get a say?"

Train turned. "Sorry, Sydney. I'm just pointing out that you two are playing a dangerous game. You might as well know it, too."

"That's his way of saying he's happy for us," Cassian said.

"Just sayin' is all," Train said.

She looked back and forth between them. "I take it we're all okay, then?"

Train shrugged. "Got no choice, do I?"

"Good," she said grabbing a cup of coffee. "So, what do we do now?"

"Now we figure out who killed your sister. If we bury that problem, people will have less of an issue with the two of you." Train sat down at the table and pulled one of the bagels out of the bag. He ripped off a piece, dipped it in the cream cheese container provided by the store, and popped it in his mouth. "Did either of you figure out how the lawsuit gives us a legitimate motive for Senator Venable?"

Cassian shook his head. "We've got nothing. The lawsuit doesn't even mention Venable's father."

"Besides," Sydney added, "the class of plaintiffs includes patients who were at the Institute both before Venable's father was there and after he left; so it's not like anyone can claim from what's in the pleadings that he did anything that wasn't already being done."

"And then there's the final kicker," Cassian pointed out. "Even if we could tie the lawsuit to Venable, we'd still have to prove that Sydney's sister was planning on writing an article about it, and that Venable somehow found out about her plans. At the moment, we don't have anything to suggest that she was even working on a story."

Train chewed on his bagel. "I had the computer forensics guys do another search on the hard drive of your sister's computer at work for Venable, the Institute, eugenics, and anything else I could think of that might be related to this, but they came up empty." He popped another piece of bagel into his mouth. "You told us a few days ago that you have her laptop, right, Sydney?"

"I do, but she generally didn't use it for work."

"Still, it's the only place we've got to start with, so we might as well begin there. Where's the computer now?"

"It's at my apartment."

Train stood up. "I guess that's where we're headed next."

Salvage sat in a coffee shop at the window across the street from Sydney's apartment. He'd spent the evening camped out in the shadows of the jagged entryways and walk-downs that carved their way along the streets of the funky Adams Morgan section of D.C. An area that was home to much of the city's artistic community, as well as many of the best bars in town, Adams Morgan was constantly moving, and he'd been able to shift from one location to another in the immediate vicinity on an irregular basis to avoid drawing attention to himself. He'd always stayed in sight of the apartment, though, and he was sure that she hadn't returned.

She'd have to come home eventually, he knew. Even if she was holed up someplace else—at a friend's place or a hotel—she'd inevitably need to come back for something. In his experience, people always did. Everybody grew overconfident with the passage of time, and everyone made mistakes. He would wait as long as it took for Sydney Chapin to make hers.

He was just bringing the large cup of coffee to his lips when he saw the Crown Victoria pull up and double-park in front of her apartment. The flashers came on and Sydney stepped out of the backseat. For a moment, he assumed that she was simply being dropped off, and that he might have his chance to finish his job and be done with this nightmare of a client. But then he saw the enormous black man emerge from the driver's seat. Clearly a cop, Salvage surmised. His movements were those of a cop, slow and deliberate, and he squinted and looked around almost unconsciously as he got out of the car. A second later another man emerged from the front passenger side; younger, white, better dressed. Still a cop, though, he concluded—just a newer, flashier model.

Salvage sipped his coffee as he watched all three of them enter the building. He was considering his next move. He wouldn't take her out while she was with the police unless it was absolutely necessary. He'd be able to do it, but it would most likely involve killing the police officers as well, and the cops never liked it when you killed one of theirs. It would stir up a hornet's nest, and that would be good for no one. He put his coffee down and pretended to look over the paper on the counter in front of him. He had to be patient; his time would come.

Sydney sat on a futon couch in front of the wooden coffee table in her walk-down one-bedroom apartment. The apartment was exactly what you might expect for your average twenty-seven-year-old law student. The place was dark and cramped, and the stink of coffee mixed with the odor of mildew that was a fixture in most sub-street-level flats in D.C. The moisture was unavoidable in this city built on swampland.

"Nice place," Jack commented as Sydney booted up the laptop.

"Suits my needs, and it's affordable," she replied.

"The whole independence thing, huh?"

She looked at him and he saw a flash of spirit. "That's right. Problem?"

"Not at all," he said, adopting a defensive posture.

The buzzing of the computer coming to life interrupted them, and they both turned their attention to the screen. After a moment the calendar function popped up and asked them if they would like to confirm Sydney's dead sister's schedule for the day. "That's how I learned that Liz had met with Professor Barneton the day she died."

"Skip over the Outlook program for now," Train directed her. He was seated on the couch to her right, his bulk making the wooden frame groan in agony as he leaned forward. "Go to the main screen and see if we can find any of her work files."

Sydney clicked on the *skip schedule* icon and the laptop buzzed and whirred until the home screen appeared. Various files were lined up on its left-hand side.

"Go to 'My Documents,'" Train ordered. Sydney clicked away and a list of folders appeared. "Anything on Venable?"

Sydney scrolled down. "Nothing obvious."

"How about the Institute?" Cassian asked.

"Nope. Nothing."

"Let me take a look." Jack slid in front of the computer. There were between twenty and thirty files in Elizabeth Creay's "My Documents" folder. None of them seemed particularly relevant from their titles. Most looked as if they were from long before her murder, and others were clearly outlines or notes from articles on unrelated topics. One file grabbed Cassian's attention, though. "Consolidated Pharmaceuticals," he said out loud, reading off the name of the file. He'd only looked briefly through the papers from Willie Murphy's lawsuit, but the name of the company rang a bell. "Does that sound familiar to anyone?" He turned to Sydney. "Did you bring the printouts from the lawsuit with you?" She reached into her bag and pulled out a sheaf of papers, handing them over to him.

Cassian scanned the case caption on the first page. "I thought so. Consolidated Pharmaceuticals is one of the companies that's named in the lawsuit," he pointed out. He turned back to the computer and clicked on the document bearing the company's name. It flashed on the screen and Cassian read through it.

"Well?" Train asked, unable to read the document from where he sat.

"This is what we're looking for, all right," Cassian said, hesitation in his voice.

"What does it say?" Sydney asked.

"You're not going to like it."

"I'm not going to like what?" she asked.

"It looks like your sister started her investigation looking into the eugenics program that was active at the Institute into the 1960s. As it turns out, Consolidated Pharmaceuticals is one of the companies that was involved back then. According to the notes here, though, the focus of her investigation changed when she realized that Consolidated was somehow connected with all this."

"Why?" Sydney asked.

Cassian took a deep breath and turned to look at her. "Because, according to this, Consolidated is a subsidiary of Chapin Industries."

Sydney gasped.

Cassian nodded. "That's not all. From the looks of

what your sister has written here, she was starting to suspect that a new set of experiments was started up again a few years ago. That's what she was really looking into. And according to your sister's notes, three years ago Leighton Creay was once the senior vice president in charge of medical sales at Consolidated."

Chapter Fifty-four

"IT DOESN'T MAKE ANY SENSE." Sydney sounded numb as she sat in the back of Train's car headed out to Old Colony. "What could Leighton possibly have hoped to gain?"

"It's not clear from your sister's notes," Jack said as he flipped through the sheets he'd printed out from Elizabeth Creay's computer. "It looks like your sister stumbled onto something. She thought Consolidated was involved in new experiments taking place up at the Institute. If that's true, we've got a whole new cast of suspects, including Dr. Mayer, who runs the place. Any way you slice it, we're going to have to have a long conversation with your sister's ex. New suspects or not, he just became our primary focus. The fact that your family's company is connected to the Institute raises all sorts of questions."

"I didn't know," Sydney protested. "My family's company owns so many different corporations, how could I?"

"Nobody's blaming you," Jack replied reassuringly.

"All those people who were tortured, experimented on, and my family's somehow responsible?" Her voice cracked. "How can I live with that?"

"There's plenty of blame to go around here," Train said as he leaned on the accelerator.

Cassian slammed his fist on the dashboard. "I knew we should have leaned harder on this asshole. I swear to God, if he pulls any of his smart-ass bullshit, I'm shoving his Weejuns so far down his throat, he'll be shitting Lilly Pulitzer for a month."

"Easy, Jack," Train cautioned. "We still don't know what exactly's going on here, and I don't want this guy to lawyer up too fast, or have what we do get out of him tossed out of court. If we want this to lead anywhere, we're gonna have to play this very cool."

"I'm cool," Cassian replied, assaulting the dashboard with his fist again.

"Right," Train agreed. "And I'm Caucasian."

"Just step on it."

Train shook his head. "This should be fun."

Salvage kept his car a discreet distance behind the unmarked police sedan, allowing other vehicles to thread in and out between them. The ascendancy of the SUV had made tailing people more of a challenge as the giant chunks of towering steel cut off his line of sight again and again, but he managed to follow the car carrying the Chapin girl. It didn't make it any easier that he stole swigs from his flask periodically.

He cursed his stupidity and carelessness as he followed them out in the direction of Old Colony. He had a feeling he knew where they were headed, and it occurred to him that if he had simply taken the girl out on the highway in Virginia, none of this would be happening. Now it was clear that she and her escorts were getting close to the truth, and the closer they got, the more likely it was that Salvage's client would make good on the threat to kill him. He recognized now that his own life was on the line, and he increased his own speed as the car he was following picked up its pace.

He wouldn't miss another opportunity.

Cassian was out of the car even before Train brought it to a full stop in the driveway of the house in Old Colony. He looked up at the porch that swept around the front of the structure, searching the windows for any movement. Although the place looked exactly as it had days before, Jack felt that something about it had changed. The overhanging windows looked down at them with sinister intent, and an anger seemed to inhabit every eave, post, and beam, seeping out through the clapboard siding.

"I want you to stay here," he said to Sydney, still looking up at the house as he drew his gun from under his sport coat.

"Not a chance," Sydney replied.

Cassian looked over at Train for support. "You have to, Sydney," the older man said.

"No way. I'm coming in with you."

Train's tone was understanding, but his voice firm. "This is police business, Sydney. We can't have you in there with us. We'll let you know what happens, and we'll be out as soon as it's safe. Until then, you have to stay in the car."

Sydney started to protest again, but caught her words as Train held up his hand, making clear that his word was final. "Fine," she spat. "But you tell that bastard that he's going to have to face me eventually." She opened the door to the car and got in, slamming it with all her might behind her.

Train and Cassian stood next to each other. "I think if I was Leighton Creay, I'd rather face us than her right now," Train said.

"No doubt."

"I like her."

"Good. Me too."

Train nodded. "You ready to do this?"

Cassian checked his gun and chambered a round. "As I'll ever be."

"Mr. Creay! It's Detectives Train and Cassian. We need to talk to you!" Train leaned in close to the door as he yelled through it, his voice clear and loud. "Open up, Mr. Creay!" His gun was in his hand, but his fingers were relaxed and his arm was at his side. He looked over at his partner and saw that he was already in a two-fisted stance, his arms directing the muzzle of his gun down toward the base of the entryway. Train lowered his voice. "You wanna do a walkaround? See what you can see?" They didn't have a warrant, and it would be difficult to argue that they had reason to believe a crime was in progress, so there was a real question in Train's mind whether they could legally enter the house without Creay present.

Cassian nodded and headed back around the side of the house. Train went in the other direction, so they could meet up in back. It was a quiet day in the neighborhood—the kind of a quiet day that was only found in the suburbs, Train thought. He was a city kid. While at college, he'd had trouble sleeping at night without the constant affirmation of life and death going on around him at all times. Car horns, sirens, angry voices—these were the sounds that somehow comforted Train. Birds just didn't cut it for him, and as he walked around the house, the quiet made him uneasy.

Near the back of the house, he passed a darkened window, the heavy shades pulled together inside, leaving only a crack through which to see. As he moved by, though, Train thought he saw some movement, a flicker of light and shadow he caught only out of the corner of his eye. He moved back to the window and put his face up to the glass, straining to see into the room.

The blinds afforded him only a limited view, but as his eyes adjusted, he saw the flicker again—a blue-white flash of light—and realized it was from a television off to the side of the room, out of sight from his vantage. He moved his head to get a different angle through the narrow opening, and from his new position he could see the side of a heavy wingbacked chair. A bottle was resting half empty on the floor next to a pair of feet flat on the ground, the legs running up into the chair. Train could only see the legs, though, as the rest of the person's body and head were hidden from view by the drapes.

Train knocked on the window with the muzzle of his gun. "Mr. Creay?" No movement. "Mr. Creay, it's the police! We really need to talk to you!" Still nothing.

Cassian came around the side of the house from the back, his gun still raised. Train beckoned him over. "He's in there," Train said. "From the look of the booze on the ground, he may be passed out. Either that or he's ignoring us. I'm going in through the front door, you make sure I know it if he moves out of the chair. I don't want to be surprised in there."

Cassian nodded. "Be careful. There's no guarantee he's alone."

Train moved back to the front of the house. "Mr. Creay, we know you're in there! If you don't open up, we're coming in!" He waited three beats and then tried the doorknob. To his surprise, it turned easily, and the door swung open. He hiked his gun up and stepped into the house.

The room where Creay was sitting was toward the back of the apartment, and Train made his way there carefully, down a long hallway and into the back den. He paused at each corner, swinging his gun around every blind turn, checking every corner to make sure there'd be no one sneaking up behind him.

When he got to the den, he took the same precautions, following his weapon through the door. He could see Creay sitting in the chair in front of the television. He was facing away from Train, and all Train could see was the top of his head over the chair from behind. With the curtains drawn, the room was dark, even as the hour approached noon. "Mr. Creay, we need to talk to you," Train said. "Put your hands where I can see them, please." Train's gun was aimed right at the back of Creay's head as he moved around to the side. He lowered it as soon as he saw the man's face.

The left side of his head was blown off, and it lay in splatters on the inside wing of the chair. He was still sitting up, supported by the curved contours of the seat, his head cradled in the wing, an expression approximating surprise on the side of his face left intact. Lying in his lap, near where his hand had fallen, was a revolver.

Chapter Fifty-five

"SUICIDE?"

Deter lifted his shoulders noncommittally in response to Cassian's question. Train and Cassian had notified the local Virginia authorities, and although the Virginia cops were technically in charge, given the connection to the Elizabeth Creay murder, they had given permission for Deter and his team to consult on the crime scene; it had taken them less than a half hour to appear at the apartment. "Looks that way right now. Why? Something not fit to you?"

"He just didn't seem the type. Too wrapped up in himself."

"Sometimes those are the people who do this—the selfish ones. He has powder on the side of his head, and the wound is certainly consistent with self-inflicted. We won't know for sure for a while, but I don't see any signs of a struggle or anything else that might point us to anything other than suicide at this point."

"All right," Jack said. "That's probably just as well. Saves us the cost of putting him away. I have to go out and talk to his sister-in-law, tell her what's going on."

"The girl out by Train's car?"

"Yeah."

Deter gave a low grunt. "Nice piece of ass there, huh?" Cassian just stared at him, and after a moment Deter squirmed. "What? She's attractive, that's all I'm sayin'." Jack maintained his stare for a moment longer. Then he left the room without a word.

Outside, Sydney leaned on Train's car, trying to ignore the leers thrown her way by the cops milling about as they tried to look busy in their boredom. She'd asked repeatedly to be allowed inside to see what had happened, but had been refused. Now she was clearly fuming.

"What's going on, Jack?" she demanded.

"They're just finishing up in there."

"I want to see him. I want to see what the bastard looks like."

Jack shook his head. "Not a good idea."

"I don't really care what you think is a good idea or not! He killed my sister!"

"We don't know that for sure, Sydney. There are still a lot of unanswered questions here." She shot him a dangerous look, and he put his hands in his pockets and lowered his head as he considered his options. "Okay," he said at last. "I'll take you up. But don't expect it to make you feel any better."

The two of them walked to the house, up the stairs, and through the door. They passed Train in the living room, and he opened his mouth as if to speak, but Cassian shook his head, and Train remained silent.

When they got to the den, Jack stopped. "You sure you want to do this? It won't change anything."

"I have to. For Liz."

Jack extended his arm in a reluctant invitation for her to enter. The crime scene team was just finishing up the last of their photos, and most of the evidence from the room had been tagged and bagged. The only task remaining was to remove the gun and the corpse, and the coroner's team was waiting outside of the room impatiently. "Give us a minute, okay, guys?" Jack asked. They looked at each other, and one of them looked at his watch. Cassian ignored him.

Sydney walked into the room slowly, her footsteps shaky as she approached her former brother-in-law from behind. When she pulled even with him, so that she could see what was left of his face, she gasped, her hands flying to her eyes.

After a moment, she let her hands fall to her side again and took a good look at the body. Watching her, Cassian could see the hatred in her stare; the empty satisfaction at the violent end of the man who in all likelihood had killed her sister.

Then she looked down into Leighton Creay's lap and saw the gun, and her expression changed. She gasped, the tears gathering in her eyes, her fists clenched and angry. After a moment, she looked back up at Cassian.

"Jack?" she said.

"Yes?"

"We need to talk."

Chapter Fifty-six

JACK STOOD ON THE STEPS of the Chapin mansion. Evening was upon the city, and the sun was dipping just below the horizon to the west, but with summer having blossomed in earnest, the humidity had gathered force, and he knew that nightfall would bring scant relief from the heat.

Sydney shifted her stance nervously between him and Train, and Jack felt the desire to reach out to her, but he kept his hands to himself. He couldn't imagine what she was feeling.

"It's my mother's," she'd told the detectives back at the station house.

Jack and Train had exchanged confused looks. "What's your mother's?"

"The gun—the one at his apartment. It was a gift from my father."

"I don't understand," Train said slowly.

"What's not to understand?" Her voice was distant. "Oh my God . . . it all comes back to her. Who stood to lose the most if people found out about Chapin Industries' role in what happened at the Institute? Who had access to the information about the company? Who would my sister have confronted? It all comes back to my mother. And now the gun clinches it."

"So how was Leighton involved?" Train challenged.

"Who knows, exactly? Maybe he learned something when he was running Consolidated Pharmaceuticals. Maybe he was involved somehow in something going on at the Institute. I don't know, and now that he's dead, we'll probably never know. But one thing seems clear: my mother is at the center of all this."

"You're not suggesting she had your sister killed, are you?" Jack couldn't believe his ears.

"I don't know," Sydney said haltingly. "I don't want to believe it, but what if she did? You don't know what she's capable of. Even I don't know what she's capable of anymore."

"I have trouble believing that she'd have her own daughter killed," Jack had argued. And yet when they ran a check on the gun's registration, sure enough, the computer spat out Lydia Chapin's name. A review of Chapin Industries also confirmed that after the death of her husband Lydia Chapin had inherited all of his corporate holdings, and was now a majority owner of the Chapin Industries empire. She stood to lose billions if any kind of scandal caused the stock to tumble.

Now, standing at the threshold of Lydia Chapin's house, Jack reached out and rang the bell, falling back into line with Sydney and Train as he waited for the door to open. When it did, Lydia Chapin stood before them, perfectly coiffed and suited in Valentino. She looked only at Sydney, ignoring the detectives, and Jack felt a cold mixture of betrayal and disappointment in her stare. Then she stepped back and turned around, leaving the door open for them as she retreated into her living room without uttering a sound.

Salvage sat in his nondescript blue sedan parked on Wisconsin Avenue across the street from Lydia Chapin's house. He drummed his thumbs unevenly against the steering wheel as he considered his options. God, he needed a drink so badly. His flask had run dry an hour earlier, and he'd actually considered stopping to get a bottle to refill it. It might have made sense, given the way his head was pounding. Another drink would have to wait for now, but as soon as this job was over he'd be able to crawl into a bottle for a year.

He'd been following the Chapin girl for the entire day, keeping his distance and waiting for the opportunity to finish his assignment. He'd had a brief opening at Leighton Creay's apartment, and had even started to move in, but by the time he was in position to take a clear shot, the two cops were outside with her again. Too close to risk it, he'd thought.

But now there was no question; he was out of time, he knew. He'd waited too long and squandered every opportunity, and now that the police were at the Chapin mansion, he knew he had to act. To say they were getting close to putting this all together would be an understatement of monstrous proportions. In order to save his own existence, something drastic had to be done. Under normal circumstances, he might just cut his losses, but his client's threat to him, hanging over him like the sword of Damocles, couldn't be ignored.

After the Chapin girl and her two new appendages had entered the house, he opened his car door and stepped out. He walked up the street toward the mansion and, after making sure that no one was observing him, ducked through one of the front hedges.

The front lawn was open, and he felt dangerously exposed, but the sky was dimming, and a spotty row of shrubs along the north property line gave him enough cover to get to the back of the house. Once there, he'd wait a short while for darkness to fall so that it would be safe to approach the mansion. He'd been given a key to the French doors at the back of the house and had been told that the alarm system wasn't turned on until nine o'clock.

He chose a spot behind a large tree and settled in for the wait, watching the house for any unexpected trouble. He would demand double the agreed-upon price, he told himself, given the stakes. He deserved it, and when this was all over, the drink would taste all the better.

The way her mother moved into the living room, with the confidence of a queen, ignited Sydney's anger. Until that moment she'd felt only shock and resignation, but looking at Lydia's stiff, proper posture as she led them wordlessly into her lair, an explosion of conflicting emotions consumed Sydney, and she had to fight to stay in control.

"You know why we're here, Mother," she said as they entered the living room.

"I'm sorry, dear, but I really haven't the faintest idea," her mother replied, her back still to Sydney. Then she turned around and looked at the detectives. "Gentlemen, can I offer you anything? A drink, perhaps?" Her words were sharp and cold, and the storm within Sydney continued to build.

"Bullshit, Mother," Sydney said, chipping her words out in her mother's face.

"Such language. I raised you better than that; at least I thought I did." Lydia walked over to the bar and poured herself a drink. "I assure you, I have no idea what this is all about."

"We found Leighton Creay in his apartment this morning," Train told her. "He's dead."

"How unfortunate." Lydia sipped her scotch.

"You killed him, Mother," Sydney said, moving in closer as she leveled the accusation.

Lydia sat down on the couch, crossing her legs. "Don't be absurd."

"The gun, Mother. It's yours. Only two of them like it in the world; you told me that once."

"I don't know what you're talking about."

"The gun that Mr. Creay was killed with is registered to you, ma'am," Train explained.

"Oh my." Sydney's mother hardly seemed surprised. "You're not suggesting that he killed himself with my pistol, are you?"

"I didn't say anything about suicide, ma'am," Train corrected her.

"My apologies, I just assumed. You see, I loaned a gun to him a few years ago, when he and my daughter were still together. I suppose I should have asked for it back, but it slipped my mind." She looked directly at Train. "I don't get much of a chance to shoot anymore, Detective. You understand."

"Is that really the best story you can come up with, Mother?" Sydney's anger was boiling over.

Lydia regarded her daughter with a look of triumph in her eyes that cut into Sydney's chest and ripped her heart out. "Yes, dear, it is," she said. Then she smiled. "I'm sure it will be sufficient."

Amanda was upstairs when the doorbell rang. She'd been spending much of her time in her room, primarily to avoid her grandmother. Lydia had always been a little difficult to deal with—Amanda was well aware of the tension between her mother and grandmother before her mother was murdered—but since her mother's death, Lydia's behavior had become even more erratic. It was as though she'd fallen into a severe manic depression, sometimes focusing on the most trivial details with frenetic precision—a flower arrangement, or the clothes Amanda was wearing—other times locking herself into her room for hours at a time, or disappearing from the house altogether.

The doorbell drew Amanda out of hiding, and she crept down the stairs to see who had arrived. When she recognized Sydney's voice, she was tempted to run to her, but something in the tone of the conversation in the living room made her hold back. She and Lydia were arguing, and Amanda knew well enough not to get into the middle of one of her grandmother's fights. Then, a moment later, she heard another voice, and realized that the detectives investigating her mother's murder were in the room as well.

Desperate to know what was happening, Amanda snuck down the stairs and stood just outside the living room, listening.

"We know about the Institute, Mother," Sydney said.

"What are you talking about?" Lydia's demeanor was calm, but there was an edge of panic to her voice now.

"You know what I'm talking about."

"Tell me!"

Sydney raised an eyebrow and tossed a look in Cassian's direction at the vehemence of her mother's reaction. "Liz was conducting an investigation into the Virginia Juvenile Institute for Mental Health," she said. "It started out as a story on the eugenics experiments that went on there ages ago, but it looks like she discovered something else. Something that led her to you."

"No. It's a lie." But the look of confidence was gone from Lydia's face completely.

"It's not a lie. Consolidated Pharmaceuticals. It's a company you own, Mother. It was involved in the experiments back in the 1960s, and according to Liz's notes, it's involved in new experiments out there now. She was trying to figure out what was going on. Now she's dead, and Willie Murphy is dead, and Leighton's dead."

"Their deaths had nothing to do with the Institute," Lydia insisted.

"No?" Sydney was pacing, though her eyes never left her mother's face. "Leighton was in charge of Consolidated Pharmaceuticals until two years ago, wasn't he?"

Lydia stared at her daughter. "You don't know what you're saying."

The hatred and rage was clear in Sydney's voice, though. "I know exactly what I'm saying, Mother. I'm saying that you killed your own daughter, just to save your company."

Lydia stood up and slapped her daughter. She moved so quickly it startled everyone in the room. "Don't you ever say that again!" She stared in horror at Sydney. "I loved Elizabeth! I would never have done anything to hurt her!"

"I don't believe you, Mother!"

"I don't care what you believe, Sydney. I gave up on you right around the same time you gave up on me. Amanda is my only real family now."

"You killed her mother!"

Lydia steadied herself and then sat back down on the sofa, having regained some of her composure. "You can believe what you want, dear. I suspect that your police friends here will agree that you'll never convince a jury beyond a reasonable doubt."

Sydney stared at her mother. If she'd had the means at that moment, she might very well have killed her. She tried to think of something to say, but no words would form in her mouth. As she stood there, lost in a nightmare beyond her comprehension, she heard a voice from behind her. Quiet but steady, it shook her to the core, and rocked everyone in the room.

"It's true, though, isn't it?"

Sydney turned to see Amanda standing in the doorway to the foyer, staring at Lydia with tears in her eyes, her hands clenched at her side.

"You killed my mother, didn't you?"

"No! Amanda, no!" The protest leaked from Lydia's throat, quietly at first, but gaining momentum as she shook her head, until it bordered on a scream. "You can't believe that! I would never have hurt your mother." Suddenly her hands started shaking and her knees buckled as she collapsed into the couch. The breakdown was horrific; like a mountain of granite crumbling in on itself, as her shoulders shook and sobs poured out of her.

"Oh God! What have I done?" she wailed.

Sydney bent down in front of her mother, pulling the older woman's hands from her face. "Tell me, Mother! Tell me what happened!"

"I thought he killed her," she moaned. "It was the only thing that made any sense."

"You thought who killed who?"

"Leighton. I thought he killed Elizabeth." She took a few deep breaths, and the hysteria abated somewhat. "He called me, the night she was murdered. He told me now that she was dead, he was going to take Amanda away. He threatened to hurt her."

"I don't understand." Sydney shook her head. "Why?"

"It was blackmail. He wanted more money."

"More money?"

Lydia nodded. "That was how Elizabeth got sole custody two years ago in the divorce. I paid him two million dollars to relinquish all of his parental rights to Elizabeth."

"How could you?" Amanda croaked from the doorway.

"It was the only way, don't you see?" Lydia pleaded with her granddaughter. "You remember what he was like, don't you? And your mother was destroyed by what he did to her. I couldn't let him near you, so I paid him. I had to get you free from him—from what he would do to you."

"So what happened?" Sydney asked.

"Elizabeth was murdered, that's what happened. Her death nullified the custody order. Leighton called me that night, saying he wanted money, otherwise he'd try to get custody of Amanda back." She looked at Amanda again. "He threatened to do such awful things to you . . . I couldn't let that happen. You understand, don't you?"

Amanda nodded slowly. "I understand."

"So, yes, I did it!" Lydia started crying again. "I thought he killed Elizabeth. And then, when you were attacked out on the highway, I thought he was coming after you. I couldn't let that happen, so I killed him. Don't you see, I didn't know you and Elizabeth were poking around the Institute; I thought Leighton was responsible. I thought he killed my daughter!"

"But not anymore?" Train asked. "Now you think it has something to do with the Institute?"

She nodded and hung her head in anguish. "Why didn't she come to me? Why didn't she ask me? I would have explained . . . I would have protected her . . ."

"From who, Mother?" Sydney demanded. "Protected her from who?"

She shook her head as she stood and walked away from her daughter. "You don't understand. It's not what you think. I can't."

"It's over, Mother," Sydney said, grabbing her by the shoulder. "It's over, and if you ever really loved Liz, you have to stand up for her now. It's Venable, isn't it? He's behind this. We know about his father, and now Venable's using the Institute to carry on his father's work, isn't he?"

Lydia began to speak, but just then a movement over Sydney's shoulder seemed to grab her attention. "No! Sydney, look out!"

Sydney spun and saw the blond man from the highway standing in the doorway. A gun in his hand was pointed directly at her, and he was holding Amanda from behind.

The room tumbled into motion around her, as Train and Cassian both moved for their guns and Lydia reached out to grab her. Sydney, though, remained transfixed, staring at the man with the gun. She saw the look in his eyes, and saw his arm pull up ever so slightly as the muscles in his hand contracted, pulling the trigger. And then, just as she heard the shot, she felt her mother push her, and she was falling.

Chapter Fifty-seven

SYDNEY HIT THE FLOOR hard. She lay motionless for a moment as she got her bearings, wondering in a strangely detached way whether she'd been hit. She felt no sharp pain, but she'd heard that people who are shot often go into shock and don't realize it.

She rolled over onto her back and looked down, half expecting to see a wash of blood covering her shirt, or perhaps even internal organs hanging loosely from a hole in her abdomen. Nothing was out of place, though, and she concluded, with little real relief, that she was unhurt.

That was when she saw her mother.

She was still standing in the spot from where she'd shoved Sydney, and she was staring down at her daughter, her mouth hanging open, her eyes blinking in terror and regret.

Sydney stared at her mother, wondering what she was trying to say. It took a moment before she noticed the deep red stain on the front of her mother's expensive silk blouse. At first she thought it was part of the fabric's design, but then she noticed that it seemed to be growing, slowly at first, but gathering speed as it swallowed her mother's torso.

Time was lost to Sydney. She watched as her mother sank to her knees, her mouth still moving, and her eyes trying to convey emotions too deep for words. Sydney thought she might be mouthing "I'm sorry," but couldn't be sure. Then, finally, her mother collapsed, facedown, nearly touching Sydney's feet.

Time caught gear again with a jolt, and Sydney realized the room was in chaos. More frighteningly, as her mind cleared, she realized that gunshots were still ringing out. Suddenly she thought of Amanda.

Cassian spun as soon as he heard Lydia Chapin scream. A man was standing at the doorway to the foyer, pointing a gun at Sydney. Cassian knew who he was in spite of the fact that he'd never seen him before; Sydney had described him well. Jack went for his gun immediately, but Amanda Creay was blocking him from getting off a clean shot.

Cassian felt his heart seize as he saw Sydney drop to the floor. He wanted to run to her, but he forced himself to stay focused; he needed to take care of the man with the gun first.

He leveled his pistol at the man. "Police!" he yelled, even as he pulled the trigger.

The man grabbed Amanda by the arm and dove to the side, behind the wall separating the front hall from the living room. Cassian held his fire, stealing a glance over toward Sydney. She wasn't moving, and it took all his self-control to keep from rushing to her.

The man's gun poked out from behind the wall and fired blindly in Cassian's direction, forcing him to duck behind a table.

"Jack! You hit?" Train yelled from behind him.

"Not yet!" Jack took a deep swallow of air. "Sydney, you all right?" he called.

"I think so. My mother's been shot, though. Where's Amanda?"

Jack didn't answer. Instead, he grabbed his radio. "Dispatch, this is Cassian. We've got shots fired and a potential hostage situation at 3507 Wisconsin Avenue. Request immediate backup."

"Where is she?" Sydney screamed again. "Jack! Where's Amanda?"

Jack crawled over to her and looked down at Lydia Chapin's chest. Train was by his side almost instantly and gave Jack a questioning look. Jack shook his head in return. "She's dead." Just then, they heard the front door slam.

"Sydney," Jack said. "He took Amanda. There'll be people here in a matter of minutes, but we have to go after him. Will you be okay?"

She looked dazed, but after a moment she nodded. "Get her back, Jack," she said in a voice so hollow Jack could hear the echo in her heart. "Please get her back."

He held her eyes in his for another moment, squeezing her arm gently, unsure what to say. Then he looked at Train. "Let's go."

By the time they hit the front steps, Train could see the blue sedan peeling away from the curb. The man in the driver's seat reached over Amanda, who was strapped into the passenger seat, and fired off two rounds in their direction, forcing them to take cover behind the large columns on the front steps, and then he hit the gas and sped off. Train and Cassian ran to their car.

Train jumped behind the wheel, turned the ignition, and threw the car into gear in one motion. They could still see the sedan ahead of them as it raced south on Wisconsin Avenue, picking up speed as it turned onto Massachusetts Avenue and headed down toward the city. Train took the police light off the seat beside him and reached out to put it on top of the car as he blared the sirens.

Cassian picked up the radio. "Dispatch, this is car 141, and we're in a high-speed pursuit heading south on the 3200 block of Mass Ave, request backup!" He waited for the response to come back over the speaker. "Come on, goddammit!" he yelled at the radio.

"Calm down," Train ordered. "We're gonna get her back."

"Unit 141, backup is on the way. Intercept at Dupont Circle."

Train picked up the handheld. "Dispatch, make sure everyone knows we're in a hostage situation here. I don't want anyone to go in shooting."

"Ten-four," came the response.

Train looked over at his partner. Cassian's gun was still in his hand, and he was leaning forward in his seat. "Calm down," Train said again.

"You're losing them."

Train shook his head. "Are you hearing me?" He shot a look at his partner.

"We have to get her back," Jack said, his jaw clenched. "I don't care what it takes."

Train turned his attention back to the road. "Okay, partner, I'm with you. Whatever it takes."

Salvage sped down Massachusetts Avenue, pushing his vehicle to the limit. As they approached the city, the houses gave way to townhouses, and the streets, which had been nearly deserted farther up near the Chapin mansion, became crowded and more difficult to navigate. Twice he had to bump cars as he passed them, weaving in and out of congestion, nearly losing control of the car.

He glanced in his rearview mirror and saw the flashing blue lights still behind him. "Shit!" he said out loud. The pounding in his head had grown steadily through the night as his blood alcohol level plateaued and then dropped steadily. He should have picked up that extra bottle of booze, he realized now.

He looked to his right, at the girl in the passenger seat. She seemed so small, drawn in on herself, like a hermit crab without a shell. He took his gun and put it under her chin, lifting her head up so that she was looking at him.

"I have nothing left to lose," he said to her. "Do you understand?"

She looked at him, and he was surprised to notice how calm her eyes seemed. He'd expected abject terror, but instead what he saw more resembled determination. Then she lowered her eyes and nodded.

"Good," he said, focusing again on the road. "Don't forget it."

Amanda was amazed at the clarity of her thought. She would have guessed that she would simply shut down in the face of the mayhem and tragedy that had swallowed her life, but that was not the case. Instead her mind seemed to quicken, and her focus seemed to sharpen, and a burning seemed to grow in her stomach as her anger spread.

She looked at the man with the gun as he spoke to her; the man who she'd watched kill her grandmother; the man who was, in all likelihood, responsible for her mother's murder. He was talking to her, but she wasn't listening. Her mind was focused on one thing only: killing the man. She determined at that moment that she would make sure the man beside her would not live through the night, even if it cost her her own life.

Salvage was flying as they approached Dupont Circle, one of the hubs of the city, with several main thoroughfares radiating out from it, an area that was constantly crawling with people. Up ahead he could see the flashing lights of the police cruisers converging on the circle, blocking off the sedan's path. He stepped on the gas and increased his speed.

The cruisers had pulled into the circle at an angle, leaving no room for the sedan to go around. They had failed, however, to cut off the circle itself, and he decided quickly that that was where he was headed. A gap roughly the width of a car separated the front two police vehicles, and he made for that opening, increasing his speed. If he could just make it through, he might be able to cut through the circle and escape cleanly on the other side.

He gripped the wheel and held his breath as he braced for impact. The sedan clipped both police cruisers, sending them spinning in opposite directions like pinwheels as its momentum carried the blue car through the gap and into the small park at the center of Dupont Circle. He was through, and that meant he still had a chance.

The park erupted in panic. The appearance of so many police cars had already sent those hanging out there—primarily an unruly assortment of bicycle messengers, small-time drug dealers, and New Age hippies—scurrying in fear of a drug bust. But the entry of the sedan at high speed into the middle of the park sent people screaming in terror. Salvage spun the steering wheel wildly, and for a moment he thought he had lost control, but the wheels grabbed on the cement, and he smiled at the notion that he still had some luck on his side. He even allowed himself a brief moment of optimism, and as he steered his way through fleeing pedestrians he didn't notice the small arm reach across and grab the steering wheel until it was too late.

The steering wheel spun to the right, ripped from his hands. He looked, bewildered, at the young girl next to him as she clung to the wheel, guiding the car toward the fountain. He let go with one hand and slapped her away, then turned back to try to regain control.

It was hopeless, though. The car, already the worse for wear for its collision with the two police cruisers and its climb over the high curb at the side of the park, careened off the solid park benches that ringed the fountain, and the body rode up the face of the stonework, separating from the chassis like a toy. The momentum was too much to allow any recovery, and the car gave in to the centrifugal force of the collision, flipping up and over, and landing top down in the fountain.

Train and Cassian followed the sedan as far as the curb at the edge of the park. There they screeched to a stop and leapt from their car, looking on in awe at the destruction. Cassian started running toward the wreck.

"Jack!" Train yelled, following him. "Take it easy, we don't know whether he's still armed."

Cassian ignored his partner, picking up speed as he raced toward the fountain.

"Jack! Be careful!"

Train was ten yards behind Cassian when his partner reached the car. The windows were submerged beneath the knee-deep water in the fountain, and Cassian hurdled the fountain wall, diving under the water next to the passenger door, and disappearing for what seemed an eternity. Train was wading in the fountain by the time Cassian came up, coughing and spitting as he tried to gain his feet.

"She's not there!" Cassian yelled. "I reached in, but she's not there!"

"What do you mean?"

"I mean she's not there." Cassian was doubled over, trying to catch his breath.

Train looked closely at the wreckage, which was pinned up against the statue at the center of the fountain. Water cascaded down from the giant bowl that topped the statue, roaring against the chassis. He grabbed his partner by the shoulder and leaned in toward him.

"What about Salvage?" he yelled over the din.

Cassian looked up at him, his eyes full of despair. "He's not there either."

Chapter Fifty-eight

SALVAGE ROLLED OUT of the broken window of his car. The water was only knee deep, but he'd been trapped briefly upside down in the car's interior, and he was gasping for breath as he hit the surface. He was on the far side of the car from the police, where he couldn't be seen, which was a blessing at least.

His head ached, and he was fairly sure that he'd smashed it on the steering wheel when they'd hit the fountain. He put his hand up to his temple and drew it away, the wash of deep red on his palm confirming his assumption.

Other than the head injury, he seemed intact, and his legs moved freely at his command. The real problem, of course, was that there seemed to be no avenue of escape. He could make a break for the far end of the park, but there was little likelihood that in his condition he'd manage to blend into the crowd and get very far.

He knelt down in the water behind the car to try to figure a way out. He had to come up with something quickly, he knew, because the cops would be on him any second. As he crouched there, considering his options, his left hand brushed against something soft and silky as it dangled in the water. He looked down and saw the girl's head, and suddenly he had hope.

He reached down and grabbed her hair, pulling her head up out of the water. She hacked out a mouthful of water, and he thanked God she was still alive. He put the gun to her temple and his finger to his lips, ordering her to be silent. Then he pulled her around to the other side of the fountain so they were concealed from the police.

He held her there for a few moments, listening as the two cops searched the submerged car. Then when it was clear that he was out of time, he stood, grabbing the girl around the throat, and stepped out from behind the statue.

The two cops saw him instantly and raised their guns. He pulled the girl up so that she provided a shield for as much of his body as possible. "Drop your guns," he ordered.

Neither of them moved, and he pressed his pistol harder into the girl's temple. "I said drop your guns," he repeated. "Otherwise the girl dies."

It was the white cop who spoke first. "It's not gonna happen. Where do you think you can go? Give it up, now!" he yelled.

Salvage moved around the statue at the center of the fountain, keeping the girl in front of him. "I said drop your guns!" he demanded again.

"Amanda, are you okay?" the black cop called to the girl.

She nodded, pulling against Salvage's arm. "I'm okay," she responded.

"She won't be for long, if you don't drop your guns," Salvage said. "As I've already explained to her, I've got nothing left to lose."

"Sure you do," the younger cop said. "You can cut a

deal, and put Venable in jail forever. That should be worth living for. For all we know, everyone back at the house is all right," he lied. "You might get out of this with a few years in a cushy minimum-security pen."

Salvage laughed. "You missed your calling, Detective. You should've been an actor. I'm not buying it; I'm walking out of here right now, and I'm taking the girl with me. Either that or we both die."

"It's gonna be okay, Amanda." The enormous older detective was trying to reassure her.

"No it's not," the girl responded. "I don't care anymore. Just make sure of one thing, okay?"

"What is it, sweetheart?" The younger cop tried to make his voice calm, but he was clearly scared. "Tell me."

She shifted her head against Salvage just slightly to the left as she stared at the white detective. "Don't miss him," she said.

And then, without warning, she was in motion.

"No!" Salvage heard both of the other men scream, but it was too late. She ducked as she swung her elbow in back of her, connecting with the soft spot at the bottom of Salvage's rib cage. The gun went off, and Salvage saw her head snap back as she dropped into the water, motionless at his feet.

Salvage hardly knew what was happening. He looked down and saw the dark red spreading out from the small figure in the water below him. Then he looked up and saw the two cops, their guns still pointed at him. He stumbled back toward the statue, raising his gun as his feet slipped from beneath him. He thought he might get off one good shot at least. He was wrong.

The hail of bullets took him instantly as the smoke

rose from the two detectives' guns. Salvage felt his body lifted off the ground and thrown back into the statue.

He lay there for a moment, looking up at the sky as the life drained out of him, mixing with the water as it swirled in the fountain. The two detectives appeared above him, hovering. They were shouting at him as they pulled the girl from the water, holding her to their chests, applying pressure to her wound as they worked furiously to keep the life in her. But he was beyond hearing. Sound went first, and then his sight began narrowing, until the only thing he could see was the white cop's face. He was yelling at him, and, stripped of distractions, Salvage could read his lips clearly. "Give us Venable!" he was shouting over and over.

If he'd had the strength, Salvage would have laughed, but as it was, all he could do was smile wanly as the blood belched up in his throat and out through his teeth. It was nice, he thought, at least to have the last laugh.

Chapter Fifty-nine

CASSIAN SAT ON THE COUCH next to Train in Amanda's hospital room. He kept a watchful eye on Sydney, who hadn't left her niece's side since they'd wheeled her out of surgery. Sydney's head was down, and her eyes had the glazed look of someone whose system was shutting down bit by bit, but she refused to budge.

Captain Reynolds walked in and motioned to both detectives. Train got up and left the room; Cassian walked over behind Sydney and put a hand on her shoulder.

"Go," she said. "You still have work to do. And you know where I'll be."

He walked out and found his partner in a conference room down the hall. Reynolds was there, too, sitting grim-faced as Chief Torbert stormed back and forth across the room. "Do you know how many calls my office has gotten about this mess?" he was shouting.

"How many?" Train asked dryly. Reynolds shook his head, clearly of the opinion that sarcasm wouldn't improve anyone's situation.

"A lot!"

Reynolds looked at Cassian. "How's the girl?" he asked.

Cassian shrugged. "In a way, she was lucky. The bullet missed her head and hit her in the neck. A little higher and there wouldn't have been any point. It severed an artery, though, and she lost a lot of blood. It's gonna be touch and go for a while."

Reynolds nodded. Then he turned back to Torbert. "I understand your frustration, Chief," he said. "But there's nothing else that could've been done, and any suggestion you have to the contrary is pure fantasy."

Torbert stopped pacing. He seemed to consider this, and then said, "Okay, I suppose you're right. But I want this thing wrapped up by the end of tomorrow."

"What?" Cassian moved toward Torbert menacingly. "You want it wrapped up by when?"

Torbert shrunk back, but held to his edict. "To—mor—row! That make it clear enough for you?"

"And how do you expect us to conclude our investigation by then, Chief?" Train asked.

"What's to investigate, Detective?" Torbert asked, ignoring Train's tone. "All your goddamned suspects are dead. From what you've told me, it looks like Elizabeth Creay's ex had her killed to blackmail Mrs. Chapin over custody of the granddaughter. Mrs. Chapin took it on herself to off the ex, and then this private detective killed her. Who's left?"

"We still need to figure out who Salvage was working for," Cassian seethed.

"Who the fuck cares?" Torbert yelled. "What does it matter whether he was working for Creay or for Chapin? They're both dead!"

"Beg your pardon, Chief," Train interrupted, "but if he was working for Creay, why would he hang around after he was killed? And if he was working for Chapin, why would he kill her?"

"Same answer: who—the—fuck—cares? Maybe he was working for Creay, and he was pissed that Mrs. Chapin had killed his meal ticket. Or maybe he was working for Mrs. Chapin and he killed her by accident when he was trying to kill the daughter. We'll never know now, will we?"

Cassian shook his head, unable to believe what he was hearing. "He might have been working for someone else. We need to at least check it out."

Torbert's sights lasered in on Cassian. "Who else could he possibly have been working for?"

"I'm thinking Venable," Train offered, taking the bullet for his partner.

Torbert turned on him. "And I'm thinking, Detectives, that if I hear anyone suggest that again, I'll have them up on charges."

"Charges of what?" Cassian demanded.

"Don't fuck with me. You're talking about one of the most powerful men in the country—quite likely our next president—and you want to tar him with this shit?"

"His father ran the Institute for years. Willie Murphy was killed up there, Elizabeth Creay visited there, and Sydney Chapin was attacked up there. He's the only person who connects the dots."

"There are no goddamned dots! All you've got is rank speculation and your own suspicions. Do you have anything that qualifies as evidence of Venable's involvement?" Train was silent. "I didn't think so." Torbert looked back and forth between Train and Reynolds. "Willie Murphy is not our problem; the Virginia State Police are handling that. And without any evidence, this department is not going to investigate Senator Venable. Am I making myself clear?" No one answered. "Twenty-four hours, gentlemen. After that, this case is closed." Torbert looked briefly at Reynolds and then walked out of the office.

"That went well, I think," Reynolds said.

"It's fun to watch his tail twitch, at least," Cassian said.

"As unfortunate as it may seem, if he aims that little rat tail at you, you will feel the sting," Reynolds said.

"You telling us to drop this, Cap?" Train asked directly.

Reynolds shook his head. "No, I'm saying that if you want to find something on Venable, find it quickly."

"Let's think this through," Train was saying.

Cassian had too much on his mind to think anything through effectively. First and foremost, he was concerned about Sydney. She was leaning her elbows on the chair by the side of Amanda's bed, barely able to keep her head up. The tear tracks seemed permanently etched into her cheeks, though she'd managed to stanch the grief over her mother's death and seemed to be devoting all her strength and focus to Amanda. She had said almost nothing since the violence at the Chapin mansion. Cassian had wanted to take her home, but she insisted on staying until they knew more about Amanda's condition.

"Your mother killed Leighton because he was blackmailing her and she thought he'd killed your sister; but once she found out that Liz was investigating the Institute, she seemed pretty sure that Liz's death was somehow connected to that investigation. This scumbag private detective—Salvage—he was clearly involved in all this, but probably just as a hired hand; that seems to be his reputation, anyway. He followed Sydney out to the Institute, though, so that ties him in to the Willie Murphy murder in all likelihood. But how do we prove Venable's involved?"

"I don't know what to think anymore," Sydney said, fresh tears running down her face. "All I want is for Amanda to be all right. She's the only family I have left in the world; I'd be willing to forget all this if only she'd wake up."

Jack touched her shoulder, saying nothing.

Train cleared his throat. "I understand how you feel. But we can't do anything to help her now. All we can do—all I can do—is to make sure the bastard pays for this."

Jack put a hand to his forehead. "His father ran the Institute for years, and he stood to lose the most if anyone went public with anything really bad about the place."

"That's motive, not proof," Train pointed out. "How do we nail him?"

"Follow the money," Sydney said quietly, her tears having subsided for the moment.

"What?" Train sounded startled.

"We're in Washington, after all," she said. "Might as well take Deep Throat's advice and follow the money. If Salvage was a hired hand, someone must've been paying him."

Train shook his head. "We issued subpoenas a few days ago for his bank records, after you found his wallet, but we've been getting the runaround from the lawyers. 'Right of privacy' . . . 'due process' . . . bullshit like that."

"He's dead now," Sydney said, her voice cracking. "I'm not sure the dead have any due process rights—or at least none that he's likely to assert. Call them again, and there's probably nothing they can do anymore."

Train rubbed his chin. "I hadn't had time to think about that, but you're probably right. Now that he's dead, we shouldn't have any problems getting the bastards to cooperate. Shouldn't take more than a few hours," he speculated.

"It's worth a shot," Cassian agreed. He was just happy to have Sydney pulling out of her despair. "If you concentrate on that, I'll go back to the Institute to take another look around."

"You have anything in particular you're looking for?"

"Not really. Liz's notes suggested that she thought there were new experiments going on up there. I think I'll just do some poking around. Maybe I'll talk to Mayer, too; if there's anything going on, I'd bet my paycheck he's involved. He seemed a little too eager to chalk Willie Murphy's death up to an overdose. There may be more that he's not telling us."

"Sounds good," Train said. "I'll probably have the financial records before you get down there, so call us from the Institute and I'll let you know what we've found."

Cassian looked at Sydney, who still had the glazed-over look of a Holocaust survivor as she hovered over her niece's bed. "Don't worry," he said. "We're going to find out who's responsible for all this."

Chapter Sixty

CASSIAN WALKED THROUGH the front door of the Institute with his badge already out. "I need to see Dr. Mayer," he said to the orderly working at the desk. The man looked at him suspiciously, but picked up the phone and dialed a two-digit extension. He turned his back when he spoke so that Cassian couldn't hear him. After a moment he hung up and turned back to the detective.

"He's with a patient, but he should be with you in fifteen minutes," he said.

"Fine," Cassian said. "I need to use the phone in the meantime. Is there someplace with some privacy?"

The orderly pointed down the hall opposite the one that led to Mayer's office. "Second door on the right. Is it local?"

"I'll make it collect." Cassian headed down the hall and ducked into a small room with a chair and telephone. He dialed the station house in D.C. and waited for the charges to clear. After a moment, Train's voice came over the line.

"We got him," Train said.

"Venable?"

"Looks that way. Several large payments were made over the last month to Salvage."

"And you can tie them to Venable?"

"Not yet, but they're from a government account. The account has some blinds on it, so it's gonna take a little time to unwind it all, but it's a safe bet that Senator Venable is holding the strings at the other end."

"Good. Looks like we're getting somewhere finally. Torbert'll be pissed."

"I know. Warms your heart, doesn't it? But that's not all, partner. We got more."

"I'm listening."

"We pulled a history on the account that was directing cash Salvage's way, and guess who's also been getting paid off?"

Cassian thought for a moment. "Gimme a hint."

"He's in your neck of the woods."

"Ah." Cassian smiled to himself. "Dr. Mayer, I presume."

"Give the man a prize. So you've actually got some work to do down there."

"Looks that way, doesn't it. I'll let you know what happens as soon as I talk to him. And if you get anything else, let me know, okay?"

"Will do. And Jack?"

"Yeah?"

"Say hello to this asshole for me, okay?"

"Will do."

Cassian hung up the phone and stepped out of the room. He turned back toward the reception desk, but there was no one standing duty. He was tempted to storm down to Mayer's office and begin demanding explanations, but there was no way of knowing whether he was there or whether he was off in a private room with a patient. For a moment Jack supposed he would simply have to wait, but then he had another idea.

He ducked down the hallway that led to the stairs he'd taken to the basement when they'd found Willie Murphy's body. The buzz of the generators and HVAC grew steadily louder as he descended into the dark cavern of the basement. He followed the concrete hallway around the maze until he came to the room that Murphy had used as a makeshift office.

The crime scene tape was still strung across the doorway, though now three days after the body had been removed there was no one standing guard. The place was a mess. Fingerprint dust covered every surface, and the furniture was askew, but the chair in which Murphy had spent his final painful moment was still pulled back from the desk. Jack went over and sat down.

From this vantage, he had a sense of the view of the world that Willie Murphy had experienced for much of the past three decades. It was dark and narrow, and yet somehow warm and safe. On the far wall, several pictures of mountains and landscapes inexpertly ripped from magazines over the years were hung carefully in order. In a corner, hidden from the view from the doorway, was an ancient rocking horse that looked as though it had been restored with love. Cassian looked over at the battered guitar case and remembered Sydney's description of the beautiful music the man had been able to produce without any formal training. It was all such a waste, he thought.

On the desk there were some sheets of paper and pencils, as well as a few tools, but nothing that gave Cassian any insight into what had happened to the man. He opened the drawers of the desk one by one; most of them were filled with more tools and nails and screws and all of the accoutrements necessary to a life as a handyman. He was about to close the last drawer when a slip of paper tucked deep in the back of it caught his attention. He gave a tug, and although it seemed caught in the joints at the back of the drawer, after a moment it came free.

He held it up and examined it. It was a large envelope, the kind one might use for business correspondence. There was nothing written on it, but at the bottom he could feel something rattling and shifting like pebbles. He opened the envelope and looked in.

At first he couldn't tell what he was looking at, so he reached his hand in and grabbed a handful of the contents, pulling them out and spreading them on the desk. They were pills. Most of them were large and green with the marking "X-286" on them, but there were others of different shapes, colors, and sizes. "What the fuck?" he muttered to himself.

"They're medications," came a voice from the door.

Cassian looked up and saw Mayer.

"I knew you were here, and when you weren't in the waiting room I figured you probably came down here to poke around. I hope you don't mind that I followed you." He looked tired, and there was an air of resignation about him.

"Medications for what?" Cassian asked, skipping the pleasantries.

"It depends on which ones you're asking about. The green ones are psychoactives to treat post-traumatic stress disorder. From the look of it, some of the other ones are earlier versions of the same medication, and others . . . I don't really know. I would have to go back through our records."

"What are they doing in Willie Murphy's desk?"

"He was taking them. Actually, the green ones seemed to be having a remarkably positive effect. He was much more comfortable in his skin over the last year, and he started to make real progress in gaining back much of the time he'd lost. Ironic, isn't it?"

"What?"

"That what's going on here—what was helping to make him better—also got him killed."

Cassian put the pills back into the envelope. "You wanna tell me about the money?"

Mayer scoffed. "That's what bothers me the most. When this all comes out, people are going to assume that this was all about the money. It wasn't, you know? The money was irrelevant; I suspect when you add it all up, the payments that went to me will seem remarkably paltry."

"What's it about, then?"

"It's about the future. It's about protecting this country, and the world. It's about healing people."

"I'm gonna need a little more of an explanation."

Mayer leaned against the doorjamb. "Perhaps I should call my lawyer."

Jack took out his gun and placed it on the desk next to the envelope. "If you think you can get out of here, be my guest." He glared at the older man. "I don't give a shit about you, Doc. And I don't care about my career anymore, so you should take that into consideration. Given what we've found so far, eventually we're gonna find out the who, where, when, whats. I want to know about the *why*."

"Put your gun away, Detective, I'm not calling my lawyer, I just thought that was what I was supposed to say. Isn't that what people in my position are supposed to say?"

"You watch too much TV."

"Probably, but there's not much to do all the way out here." The doctor sighed and walked into the room, taking a seat across the desk from Cassian. "Believe it or not, I'm glad you're here. It will be a relief to be done with this all."

"So tell me."

He shook his head. "I don't even know where to begin. Perhaps I should start by trying to explain to you that we never meant any harm . . ."

Chapter Sixty-one

THE STREETS OF GEORGETOWN were quiet, and the trees that lined the lanes sheltered the nineteenth-century colonial townhouses, shrouding them in privilege and secrecy. This was one of the nation's power centers, where the political elites held their private cocktail parties for friends and adversaries alike, and where gentlemen's agreements consummated over drinks in quiet parlors had ramifications throughout the world.

Train and Cassian stood on the brick walkway leading to the front door of one of the largest townhouses in the neighborhood, waiting. The door opened, and a butler peered at them through the crack. "May I help you?"

"Is he in?" Train asked, holding up his badge. "Tell him Detectives Train and Cassian are here. We've spoken before, and we need to see him again."

"Is he expecting you?"

"No, but he'll want to see us. Trust me."

The butler opened the door and ushered them into the entryway. "Please wait here while I see if he's receiving guests." He disappeared down a hallway, and neither Train nor Cassian spoke while he was gone. It took only a moment or two before the man returned. "He's in his study. This way." They followed him down the hall. "May I get you gentlemen anything?" He was clearly accustomed to helping his employer entertain.

"No thank you," Train said.

They came to a large dark beveled wood door. "Very well, then. He's in here," the butler said. "Please let me know if you need anything." He opened the door and extended his arm in invitation, then retreated back down the hallway.

"Come in, gentlemen, come in," came a voice from beyond the door.

Train felt numb as he walked through the door. It all fit, and yet none of it made any sense. In some ways, he dreaded whatever explanation he would find.

Irskin Elliot sat in a comfortable leather club chair at the far end of the room. A heavy book rested on his knee, illuminated by a small brass standing lamp next to his chair. "Come in, please," he repeated. He carefully folded a silk bookmark into his volume and set it onto the small end table next to his chair. "I enjoy reading philosophy these days. Perhaps it's so I can reconcile myself to my own impending demise. Speaking of which." He punched a button on an intercom unit on the table. "Matthew, will you please bring me two of my heart pills?"

"Two, sir?" came the reply.

"Thank you, Matthew." Elliot shrugged his shoulders at the detectives. "Without my medicine, I've no doubt I'd have been in the ground decades ago. As it is, the doctors won't guarantee any amount of time. Now, gentlemen, what can I do for you?"

Train heard his own voice. "We've fleshed out some of

the information in connection with the deaths of Elizabeth Creay and Lydia Chapin, as well as those of Willie Murphy and Leighton Creay. We wanted to run some theories by you, and get your take."

Elliot shook his head. "I just don't know what to make of any of this, but I'm happy to provide whatever help I can. The notion that Lydia was behind all this, that she might have had something to do with the murder of her own daughter . . . it's all so unbelievable."

"It is," Train agreed. "Although Mrs. Chapin claimed that she had nothing to do with Elizabeth's death. In fact, while she admitted killing her ex-son-in-law because she believed that he killed her daughter, and because he was blackmailing her over the custody of her granddaughter, she denied any involvement in her daughter's death."

"Interesting. Did you believe her?"

"We're starting to. We ran some checks on the finances of the corrupt private detective who killed Mrs. Chapin, and he was receiving payments from a blind government account. Interestingly, that account was also making payments to Dr. Aldus Mayer, the head of the Institute."

Elliot scratched his chin. "So you're thinking that Venable controls the account, and your theories about him are panning out?"

"That was the direction we were going in. But then we dug a little deeper, and found that there was no way that Venable could have controlled the account—it was attached to the executive branch, not to Congress."

"That would certainly make it difficult for him, though not impossible. He's a very powerful man."

"Yes, he is," Train admitted. He held his breath. "As are you."

Elliot looked long at Train before replying. "I'm a mere government functionary, I assure you."

"Oh, I think you're too modest, Mr. Elliot." Train walked over and sat in a chair across from Elliot. "I have to be honest, when we talked at Elizabeth Creay's funeral, I had very little idea what the Department of Health and Human Services was responsible for. It turns out that it's much larger than I thought. It controls almost the entire medical profession, including the Food and Drug Administration, the National Institutes of Health, Medicaid and Medicare, as well as research into bioterrorism, and the Centers for Disease Control."

"You've been doing your homework," Elliot said with a smile and a nod. "Very good for you."

"Thank you." Train was silent for a few moments, gauging Elliot's reaction before continuing. "You mentioned to me when we met that you worked for the Chapins' company when you were younger. Would you mind telling me in what division?"

Elliot smiled. "Oh, come now, Detective. I'm sure you've done enough digging to discover that already. Otherwise I find it hard to believe you'd be here."

"Consolidated Pharmaceuticals," Train replied, answering his own question. "According to the company's records, you were an executive vice president there in the late 1950s and '60s."

Elliot nodded. "Excellent," he said.

"You would have been involved in the experiments that were going on at the Institute, and when you were elected governor of Virginia, you had the power to clean the place up and destroy all the records."

Elliot shook his head. "Involved? No. I was aware of the experiments, but I opposed them. That's why I shut them down when I became governor." He gave Train an oddly amused smile. "So tell me, what's your theory now, Detective?"

"It looks to us like the government started a wide program of illegal medical testing on patients up at the Institute—at your direction, we think—once you became Secretary of Health and Human Services. You commented to us before on the amount of autonomy you have in your position. We traced the payments to Dr. Mayer a few years back, when you took your job. It also looks like Leighton Creay had nothing to do with his ex-wife's death. He was just trying to take advantage of her murder to blackmail Lydia Chapin. She killed him for it."

Elliot leaned his head back into his chair. "It's an interesting theory, but it will be very difficult to prove."

Train shook his head. "Dr. Mayer is cooperating. He'll do some time, but he's working with the prosecutors to get the full story."

Just then, there was a knock at the door, and the butler appeared with a tray containing a glass of water and two pills. "Thank you, Matthew," Elliot said politely. The butler perched the tray on the table next to him and retreated, closing the door behind him.

Once the butler was gone, Train continued. "You had the power to begin medical testing programs again. You had the ability to control the information; you had the ability to direct the resources and cover them up; you had the money. You also knew Lydia Creay, and had worked at Consolidated Pharmaceuticals, and had the connections to direct the production of experimental drugs. The only thing we can't figure out is your motivation. As near as we can tell, you never took any payoffs."

"It was never about money." Elliot sat in silence for several moments.

"What was it about?" Train asked at last.

Elliot sighed. "You're both too young to remember this," he began, "but in the early 1950s the country was in the throes of the worst polio epidemic in history. Sixty thousand people were diagnosed every year, and for many of them it was a death sentence. For others, it left them with varying degrees of paralysis. Then, in 1955, a team led by Dr. Jonas Salk at the University of Pittsburgh announced that a vaccine had been developed. Within a few months, polio was rendered a problem of the past." Elliot paused.

"That's interesting," Cassian said, "but what has that got to do—"

Elliot cut him off. "The prototype of the vaccine was first developed in 1952, and it was administered to the general population by 1955. Do you have any idea how fast that is? Under today's medical testing procedures, it would have taken between ten and fifteen years in all likelihood for the necessary testing to be conducted to generate enough data to pronounce the vaccine safe. Do you know how they managed to shortcut the system?"

Train and Cassian both shook their heads.

"The testing was conducted at mental institutions. The first testing in noninfected individuals took place at the Polk School for the Retarded and Feeble-Minded in Pittsburgh. More testing was then done at places like the Juvenile Institute for the Mentally Defective in Virginia and similar places around the country. As a result, the time it took to provide the vaccine to the public was cut by a factor of four. In terms of lives, that's over half a million people who were spared in the intervening years."

"How many of those healthy 'feeble-minded' children contracted the disease as a result of being used as human guinea pigs?" Train demanded.

"A few, no doubt. But the numbers were so small compared to those who were saved in the long run that the sacrifices were minimal. Besides, these were children, in many cases, without families or futures."

"Polio has been cured," Train pointed out. "What's your excuse today?"

"Ah, Detective, if only today's threats were as benign as polio." Elliot shifted in his chair. "The world today is a different place than it was a half century ago," he said. "Back in the 1950s and '60s, many, if not most, of the experiments were aimed at the pursuit of a policy of eugenics. I was always opposed to that. I disagreed with forced sterilization, and I thought the work done to 'purify' the gene pool was abhorrent. After the horrors of the Second World War, many of us saw the errors in that strain of Darwinist philosophy, and we fought to change the system. But now the need for preventative medical experimentation is paramount. It is the only way we can protect the country—and the world—from our enemies."

"Bioterrorism?" Train asked.

"Certainly. We live in a world today where hundreds of different factions hostile to the United States are spending enormous amounts of money to develop or distribute bioweapons to attack this country and its allies. Anthrax, smallpox, botulism, and a host of other infectious agents have been weaponized, and it's only a matter of time before they are deployed here. Two years ago, estimated mortality rates in major urban areas hit with a significant attack ranged from two percent of the population to twenty percent. In a city like New York, that translates to between one hundred and fifty thousand and one and a half million people dead. In order to be prepared for something like that, we have to have sufficient antidotes, not just for the well-known agents, but for all agents. You don't develop the antidotes and vaccines without human testing."

"That's bullshit," Cassian objected. "There are other ways to fight terrorism. There's no need to conduct illegal experiments."

"Perhaps," Elliot mused. "But it's not just terrorism we're fighting, Detective. Nature itself may be our greatest enemy."

"How so?" Train asked.

"Viruses," Elliot replied. "Did you know that in 1918 and 1919 the Spanish flu pandemic killed over forty million people? More than all of the people killed in World War I from all countries combined—more than the black plague killed in five years in the Middle Ages. It circled the globe in less than a year, with staggering mortality rates." He looked Train in the eye. "It's coming back."

"The Spanish flu?"

Elliot shook his head. "Avian flu, most likely. Most medical experts agree that a pandemic is a virtual certainty in the near future. It's no longer a question of if, but of when. Most estimates are that it will kill more than one hundred and fifty million people worldwide, perhaps more. This pandemic will likely be the most deadly event in human history. It will spread through the population like wildfire, and we will be powerless. Our best estimate is that it would take six months to a year to develop an effective vaccine, and longer to produce it in quantities sufficient for the population. That's even using the most expedited testing protocols possible. We must develop the vaccines now."

"You're crazy," Cassian commented. "If you really believe this, why did you shut down the illegal testing in the 1960s?"

"I was unaware of the dangers. Besides, as I told you, back then the experiments weren't being conducted for the primary purpose of saving lives. They were a front for eugenics programs. But now, those of us conducting these experiments are enlightened. We only test when necessary, and only for the good of mankind."

"That's an awfully subjective standard, don't you think?" Cassian noted angrily.

"You don't understand, Detective. Medicine has come so far. We are working to find cures for diseases that are wiping out generations—avian flu, AIDS, and cancer. But these cures take decades to be tested to the point of acceptance. What we're doing is shaving years off the approval process. It will ultimately save millions of lives. That's progress, no?"

"How many children at the Institute have been sacrificed in the name of that progress?" Train asked.

"Some, no doubt; but, as with the development of the polio vaccine, it's a tiny number in light of the overall benefits. And in the end, can you really say that, in light of what's at stake, we're doing something wrong?"

"It's illegal," Cassian stated outright. "And immoral."

"Illegal, I'll grant you," Elliot agreed. "But as to its morality, while we know that there are some risks to the test subjects, on a strictly utilitarian basis I'd say you're mistaken."

"What about Elizabeth Creay? What about her daughter?" Train challenged him.

At this, Elliot paused, and Train thought he saw a flicker of remorse, or perhaps doubt, flash on the old man's face.

Then it disappeared. "It was unfortunate, but necessary," he admitted coldly. "Elizabeth talked to Willie Murphy. He was very bright, as it turned out, and he began to link the testing that was done years ago on him with what he'd seen happening at the Institute in recent years. He hinted at this to her, and being the excellent reporter she was, she wouldn't let it drop. Given the benefits our program was providing, I had no choice."

"No choice? She was your goddaughter, and you had no choice? How can you possibly say that?"

"It may seem ruthless, Detective, but it is the truth. When you have the responsibility of protecting a nation, sometimes choice is a luxury not afforded to you."

"You're sick," Cassian concluded.

"One man's sickness is another man's salvation," Elliot retorted. "As to the relative morality of my actions . . ." He paused. "I suppose we'll have to agree to disagree, and let God be the ultimate arbiter of that point."

Train looked at the old man in front of him, thinking that he no longer seemed human. His gray head poked out of the folds of his oversized shirt and sweater; his frame seemed lost in the chair. This man whom Train had once admired now seemed petty and small. Train stood up. "I suppose that's right. But for now, I'll be satisfied putting you under arrest."

Elliot nodded. "Of course. I've been prepared for this moment since Elizabeth first came to see me to discuss this. I had hoped to avoid it, but . . ." He reached over to the tray left on the table. "If I might just take my heart medication?"

"Yeah," Train said. "Then we have to go."

Train watched as Elliot reached over and picked up his

pills, pausing as he touched them to his lips. Something about the man's movements struck Train, and an intuition of something gone wrong echoed in the back of his head, but he intentionally ignored it. Then Elliot pushed the pills into his mouth and grasped the water to wash them down. He set the water back on the table and looked at Train with contentment. Train even thought he saw the man wink.

Train knew it was happening even before the physical manifestations became obvious. It started in Elliot's fingers, as a trembling that escalated rapidly into a spasm. The man's eyes seemed to grow and then shrink back into his head; his lips turned from ashen to scarlet to blue; and finally his body convulsed.

For the rest of his life, Train would be left to wonder whether he could have saved him. If he'd acted to knock the pills from the man's hand before they were swallowed, or if he'd acted immediately once he realized what was happening, could he have stuffed the life back into the dying shell of the man? And yet the question was moot from the outset; Train's mind had been set as soon as the realization had taken hold. It was better this way.

Cassian rushed forward, pulling Elliot out of his chair. Elliot fought against him with all the strength in his eighty-year-old body. "Jesus Christ!" Jack yelled. "He's having a heart attack!"

Train moved forward, looking at the tray next to the old man. "Overdose," he said. "He knew we were coming. There's nothing we can do."

Cassian looked in shock at his partner. "We can't let him go!" he yelled.

Train shook his head. "It's too late. And what would happen if he did survive? Any trial would last longer than his health would hold out. During that time, his people'd throw enough lawyers at the charges to make a mockery of it all." He shook his head. "I won't let this turn into nothing more than a ratings bonanza for the twenty-four-hour news channels."

"So that's it?" Cassian asked. "That's the end of it?"

Train looked into Elliot's eyes. There was life there, still, waning though it was. Train spoke to him. "No, that's not it. We have Dr. Mayer, and he'll cooperate to make sure it's all shut down. Mr. Elliot's suicide will be enough to convict him in the minds of most reasonable people, and after he's gone, we'll clean up his mess. As for him, he'll face his judgment. Just not here."

Elliot gagged as he tried to speak, but there wasn't the strength left in him. And as he struggled with his last breath, a look of torment crept into his eyes; it was the look of a condemned man.

"Call it in, Jack," Train said. Then he walked out of the room without another word.

Epilogue

"GET HIM!"

Train's voice could be heard above the din, booming out directions through the crisp autumn air. "He's comin' around the corner! Don't let him get free!"

Out on the field, the protection from the front five was breaking down, and the left tackle for the Central High Cougars had slipped around the end of the line and was making for Leshaun Johnson in the pocket as the junior quarterback surveyed the situation downfield with a confidence and poise seldom seen from a high school athlete.

"Back side! Back side!" Train shouted out a warning as the 220-pound defensive lineman left his feet, launching himself at Leshaun from behind. Cassian couldn't bear to watch as the final seconds of the city championship ticked away with Anacostia High down by three. The collision was going to be brutal, he could tell.

But then, just as the outcome seemed inevitable, Johnson ducked to his right, raising his elbow to fend off the blow. The lineman sailed high and to the left, his fingers grasping at the quarterback's jersey as it slipped through his hand.

Johnson took two steps to the side, squared himself to

the line, and fired a bullet twenty yards downfield to a streaking wide receiver. Time paused as the ball hung in the air, the world narrowing to two boys racing down the sidelines. And then, as if released from indecision, it accelerated toward the ground and both boys leaped in perfect unison. The ball slipped through the defender's arms and into the hands of the wide receiver, who stumbled, tripped, and crashed gloriously to the ground in the end zone.

The pandemonium was complete. A roar went up from the crowd, half in anguish and half in jubilation, as the field was stampeded by the Anacostia High faithful, some rushing to pounce on the skinny wide receiver on the ground in the end zone, others heading straight for Leshaun Johnson, who knelt at the twenty-yard line, head down in joy and relief.

Jack looked over at the sideline, deserted now by all except a giant figure of a man—Darius Train, Anacostia High's volunteer head coach, at the end of his first season. His smile lit up the field brighter than any of the bulbs that rained light down on the cool Washington evening, and Cassian knew that he'd never seen his partner so unguarded and happy.

Later, when the celebration had died down and people were left standing around in small clusters marveling quietly at the impact of such a seemingly inconsequential event, Train made his way over to where Jack and Sydney were standing.

"Hell of a game," Jack said, smiling as he held out his hand.

Train accepted the compliment. "Hell of a game," he agreed, shaking his partner's hand. He swallowed Sydney in a hug. "Thanks for coming, it meant a lot to me."

"Wouldn't have missed it for the world." Sydney smiled back at him.

"Where's Amanda?" Train asked.

"She was with her friends in the stands. Now I think she's off boy-watching."

"Good sign," Train noted.

"Yeah, she's doing all right. It's still tough, but then, so's she."

"In your family? It's not a surprise."

"How does it feel to be back on the field?" Sydney asked.

Train looked down at the ground and poked a toe into the sod. Then he looked up and smiled. "Best damned thing I ever did," he said.

"Don't go gettin' all sentimental on me, Sarge; I don't have the patience to break in a new partner."

Train shook his head. "I'll always be a cop," he assured Cassian. "But this"—he pointed over his shoulder to the players still gathered in celebration on the field—"this is home for me. And it's great working with the kids. They're a good group; they just need role models."

"Good role models are hard to come by," Sydney said. "I should know. They're lucky to have you."

"You doin' okay with everything?" Train asked.

Sydney thought for a moment before answering. "With everything? No, not everything. Not yet. It's a lot to deal with. I suppose I should take comfort in the fact that my mother didn't have my sister killed, and wasn't trying to kill me."

"Always looking for the silver lining, huh?"

"It's good that you and Amanda have each other, at least," Train pointed out.

"Absolutely. I've transferred to George Washington,

and I'm finishing law school there. Then I'll figure out what's next."

"No interest in Georgetown?"

She shook her head. "Too many creepy memories."

"Barneton?"

She nodded.

Train laughed. "You know we checked him out. He had nothing to do with this. He was just unfortunate to have been the last person to see your sister; and then he was stupid enough to make a clumsy pass at you, which made him seem suspicious."

"I know," Sydney said. "It's still too creepy. Besides, I wouldn't want him hitting on me again. I seem to have that area covered." She slipped her hand into Cassian's.

"Me too," he said, looking down at her with a smile.

Train punched his partner lightly on the shoulder. "It's good to see," he said. "Jimmy'd be happy."

"You think?"

"Yeah, I think."

Cassian thought about it for a moment as he looked back and forth between Sydney and Train. "Yeah," he said at last. "Me too."

About the Author

David Hosp is the author of the bestselling thriller *Dark Harbor* and is a practicing Boston attorney. He lives with his wife and children south of the city.

September 1992

Madeline Steele looked out through the rain-spotted glass toward the bodega on Columbus Avenue in Roxbury, pressing the payphone handset hard against her ear so she could hear over the thunder of her own heartbeat. One ring. Two. Five. Where was he? Finally, on the seventh ring, a voice came over the line.

"What?"

"It's me."

"What's happening?"

"They're here. I think we've got them nailed." She looked out at the storefront, making sure that no one was going in and no one was coming out.

"Not to make a bust, but it's a start."

"It's more than a start, Koz," she said. "What else could they be doing here? Do you know how many people must be involved? How much money? If it's what it looks like, it's bigger than I ever thought, you know?" There was no answer on the other end of the line. "Koz?" Still nothing. "Koz, you still there?"

"Get out of there, Maddy," came the reply.

"Why?"

"You're undercover, and you haven't been properly trained for it. We'll deal with this in the morning, but right now I want you out of there."

"Are you kidding? I have to wait and see who else shows up. See who else comes out."

"Get out of there. That's an order."

"You're not my boss on this, Koz."

"No, but I'm your friend. Get out of there. Now."

She sucked in a breath, watching the raindrops splinter the colored lights from the broken sign on the liquor store across the street. "Fine. But this is still my case. I did the legwork; I deserve it."

"It's your case," he reassured her. "Let's just make sure we get it right. We'll talk in the morning, okay? Same place."

"You got it. And Koz?"

"Yeah?"

"Thanks."

She hung up, but stayed in the phone booth for a couple of minutes, looking out at the tiny storefront, desperate to know what was going on behind the neon signs hawking tobacco, lottery tickets, and beer. Then she slid the door open and walked out into the storm.

She crossed the street and walked up the block, slowing as she passed the storefront, looking in, trying to see through the cracks in the dirty cardboard advertisements. Anyone catching sight of her would think she was merely window shopping. She'd been too careful to attract any attention.

Once she cleared the window, she picked up speed. She was sure she hadn't been followed, but she kept her attention focused behind her nonetheless, making sure no one was coming out of the store to find out why she was there.

She smiled to herself. There was no one back there, and that meant she'd done her job well. Her father and her brothers had always questioned whether she could handle it. Tonight, if nothing else, she'd proved that she belonged to the job, and the job belonged to her.

She was still smiling, her head inclined just slightly behind her, when she passed the alley off Columbus. She never saw the dark figure behind the stack of boxes at the alley's entrance; never saw the man move toward her; never saw his hand raised as he swung quickly, the handle of a long blade coming down on her head.

Vincent Salazar climbed the stairs to the fourth floor apartment on the edge of Dorchester near the Roxbury line. The place smelled like home to him; the aromas of *platanos rellenos* and *nuegados en mile* mixing with the ubiquitous *pupusas* from different apartments, swirling in the hallways.

He opened the door and walked into the apartment, pulling off his jacket and hanging it on the back of the door.

"*Hola*," his mother greeted him from the sink. She was elbow deep in pots, and the stove was covered with sweet-smelling pans full of stuffed peppers. "*Como era su dia*?"

"English, Mama," he reprimanded her gently. "We speak English in this house."

"Ahh," she grunted, waving her hand dismissively at him. "How was your day?" she repeated in heavily accented English.

"It was fine," he replied, nodding in appreciation of her linguistic surrender. "The store manager says I am to have more responsibility."

"Good. More pay, too?"

He shook his head. "It is good, though, to be trusted."

"Trust should pay more."

He made his way over to the battered crib by the window and picked up his daughter. "And how are you, little one?" he asked as he held her up above his face. She beamed down at him, and he brought her in toward his body, hugging her and kissing her cheek as she gurgled and drooled through her smile. "Did you hear that, Rosita? Your Papa is getting more respect now."

"Respect should pay more, too," his mother said from the stove, her back toward him still.

"We are better off here, Mama. Here, we can have a life."

"In El Salvador you were respected. There, you were important."

"In El Salvador I was hunted. It was only a matter of time. Besides, my daughter is an American. She will grow up in America."

"If we can stay."

"Don't worry, Mama, I said I would take care of it, didn't I?"

"*Si*. Yes."

"Is Miguel home from school yet?" he asked.

"No. He seems bad. I think he is worried about school. You should talk to him."

"I will. Has the baby eaten?"

His mother shook her head.

"Well, then," he said to his daughter, "you must eat." He smiled as he kissed her again before he wedged her into her high chair and snapped a bib around her neck. He was mixing her baby food when the knock came at the door.

"Vincent Salazar?" a voice yelled from the stairwell.

He went to the door and listened. "Yes?" He answered without opening it.

"It's the police! Open up!"

A wave of terror swept over him and all of a sudden the smell of the sweet peppers frying on the stove made him ill. "What do you want?"

This couldn't be happening. Not to her.

Panic ripped through Madeline Steele as her forehead was pushed into the cement, the stink of oil and dirt and asphalt from the Roxbury alley burning her nostrils; the pounding of the rain filling her ears.

"Please! No!"

"Callese, la ramoa!" *the voice behind her hissed.* "Ahora usted se sentira el pader de Trece!" *He had her by the hair, and he pulled her head up hard, bending her neck back to the point she was sure it would break.* "Abra sus ojos!"

She looked up and saw the quicksilver gleam before her eyes; raindrops dancing on a long, thick blade as it was drawn slowly in front of her face. Then it was pressed to her throat and she felt a sting that paralyzed her as the machete slid lightly over her skin.

An eternal moment passed, and then she was face-down on the pavement again as she felt her skirt pushed up from behind and her underwear ripped off. In the rain, she found it difficult to tell: Was she crying? And if she was, did it matter anymore?

She found the answer with her eyes closed in the faces of her family dancing before her. It mattered. It mattered because of who she was. It mattered because of who they'd made her.

She choked back a breath and forced herself to focus. Out of the corner of her eye she could see her purse lying a few feet away where it must have fallen when the first blow took her on the back of her head. If she could only reach it . . .

The animal behind her was distracted; lost in his determination to position himself to enter her. She wouldn't let that happen.

Without warning, she spun on him, her arm shooting out, fingers clawing at him, glancing off his face and digging fast into the flesh where his shoulder met his neck. He screamed, and she gripped him tighter, feeling her fingernails sliding into his skin.

He screamed again, louder this time, and pulled away. It might just be enough. She rolled to her side, grasping at her bag. She could feel her gun, and she pulled it out, spinning back on her attacker, trying to aim and get a shot off before he could react.

He was too fast, though. He brought the handle of his machete down on her wrist, knocking her arm wide. Then he grabbed her hand and the two of them struggled. It was hopeless, she knew. He was bigger and stronger; and, on top of her, he had all the leverage. Slowly the gun turned inward on her, toward her abdomen.

When the shot rang out, she wasn't even sure which of them had pulled the trigger. All she felt was the searing in her stomach and the numbness in her legs. She heard footsteps and felt the warmth spreading out underneath her as she caught an unmistakable whiff of iron swimming in the rainwater.

This was better, she thought. As the feeling ebbed from her extremities and the numbness spread to her torso, she was secretly relieved. She wouldn't have lived well with the shame, and her family wouldn't have lived with it at all. They were all prepared for death. But shame?

She closed her eyes and let herself drift off as she heard the sirens approaching. Yes, she thought, this was definitely better.

"We want to talk. Open the door!"

Vincent Salazar stood at his front door for a moment, running through his options until he concluded there were none. He unhooked the safety chain and opened the door a crack. "Show me your badge," he said.

They unleashed hell without warning. The door was kicked in hard, blowing him back into the rattrap apartment, knocking him into the highchair, spilling the baby onto the floor. He stumbled and fell, watching as his daughter's head collided with the linoleum. He looked up and saw the flood of armored policemen washing into the room, then turned again to find his Rosita, who was screaming in pain and fear. At that moment, he felt the first set of boots on his ribs, hurling him against the wall.

"Please! My daughter!" he pleaded, but it was no use. The boots came again.

"Police! Freeze, motherfucker!"

He heard his mother scream, "Rosita!" and saw her moving toward the baby, but one of the storm troopers cut her off, throwing her back into the heated stove. "Stay where you are!" the man commanded, pointing a gun into her face.

The baby continued to cry on the floor.

"Please, I don't understand!" Salazar begged, but he was kicked again, this time in the face.

"I said freeze, asshole!"

In his pain, Vincent reached out toward the sound of his daughter's wails, his fingers groping for her in desperation until a heel connected with his forearm and he heard a bone snap. All around him there was screaming. He could hear his mother, but he couldn't make out what she was saying.

One of the policemen knelt next to him as he lay curled on his knees in agony. "You're in a shitload of trouble, cocksucker," he hissed, grabbing a fistful of Vincent's hair and yanking his head back.

"Please! Let me help my daughter! There's been a mistake!"

"Oh yeah, there's been a mistake, all right. And you made it." The man laughed derisively to his colleagues. "He doesn't look so tough now, does he, boys?"

Vincent tried to turn his head to see if Rosita was okay, but the man held fast to his hair.

"You know the woman you attacked last night?" the man asked, leaning in close and breathing in his ear.

"No, please . . ."

"The woman you shot and left to die in an alley?"

"No . . ."

"She was a cop!" The man slammed Vincent's face down into the kitchen floor, grinding his hand into the back of his head.

Vincent struggled back to his knees, but the policeman was behind him now, riding him as he grabbed onto his hair again. He pulled Vincent's head all the way back. "You like that, motherfucker?" he screamed as he pushed Vincent's face down to the ground again.